CLASSIFIED INFORMATION

USER: Liz Pennington
COMPANY: Millennium Software
PASSWORD: *******

SUBJECT: Tim O'Shaughnessy...

I've been working with him for years. We're business partners, best of friends--anything so long as it's utterly and totally platonic. So what's with this chemistry that's suddenly coursing between us? And does he feel it, too?

It has to be our situation-- living together. Sharing an office is one thing, but sharing a house, well, that can get a little intimate. And the fact that somebody's after our top secret research and seems to have targeted me, well, that's got me feeling pretty darn vulnerable...and in desperate need of some strong, loving arms....

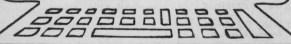

MEN at WORK

✈️—MILLIONAIRE'S CLUB   🍎—BOARDROOM BOYS   💥—MAGNIFICENT MEN

💼—TALL, DARK & SMART   💥—DOCTOR, DOCTOR   🔫—MEN OF THE WEST

🗡️🗡️—MEN OF STEEL   ⚓—MEN IN UNIFORM

MEN at WORK
RACHEL LEE
DEFYING GRAVITY

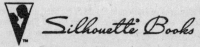

Published by Silhouette Books
America's Publisher of Contemporary Romance

SILHOUETTE BOOKS
300 East 42nd St.,
New York, N.Y. 10017

ISBN 0-373-81021-0

DEFYING GRAVITY

Printed in U.S.A.

Dear Reader,

This book was started to save my sanity! I was pursuing a degree in computer science and working full-time for a defense contractor. Between job and school, I felt I hardly had a moment to draw a deep breath.

One Saturday morning I awoke and realized that before I settled down to do my calculus homework and write a computer program, I needed to do something just for *me*. Something fun. Something that made me smile.

Writing has always been my first love, so I sat down and in an hour or so I wrote the opening scene of *Defying Gravity*. Then feeling a whole lot better, I went back to work.

Tim and Liz and their delightful relationship stayed in my drawer for a couple of years, until after I had sold my first two books to Silhouette. Then I took them out, dusted them off and did a major rewrite. They were an absolute pleasure, just as wonderful and slightly wacky as most of the people I knew in the computer business.

By then I had decided to pursue writing full-time, and I left college just a few credit hours shy of a degree. I have never regretted it. Writing is still my first love...although Tim and Liz come very close.

I hope you enjoy them and laugh as much as I did.

Rachel Lee

Please address questions and book requests to:
Silhouette Reader Service
U.S.: 3010 Walden Ave., P.O. Box 1325, Buffalo, NY 14269
Canadian: P.O. Box 609, Fort Erie, Ont. L2A 5X3

For Mary Osorio,
who noticed me in the slush—
Sometimes words just aren't enough.
Thanks!

Chapter 1

"Liz! Liz, what the devil did you do with my diskettes?"

The muted roar rattled the panes of the windows in the small steel building. Elizabeth Pennington looked up from the mail she was sorting at their secretary's desk in time to see Tim O'Shaughnessy's bearlike silhouette burst into the front office. Sighing, she brushed back her yards of auburn hair and regarded him impatiently from hazel eyes that were framed by dark, luxuriant lashes.

"I didn't touch your blankety-blank disks," she snapped. Even at thirty, Liz Pennington had never uttered a single expletive.

"Somebody did, damn it!" This time Tim didn't bother to temper his roar and Liz closed her eyes and winced painfully.

"Lower your voice, O'Shaughnessy," she said with feigned patience. "Whisper. My ears aren't acclimated to your volume this early in the morning."

The bear had the decency to look embarrassed. Running his strong, blunt fingers through hair the color of a ginger tomcat, he shifted from one outsize foot to the other. Timothy F. X. O'Shaughnessy was a huge man, scraping six-five if he reached an inch, and built like Mr. America to boot. Having worked with Tim for four years now, Liz was convinced that his entire existence consisted of computers, weight lifting and eating, with the occasional stunningly beautiful woman to brighten his evenings. That last thought always gave her a pang, and she always ruthlessly squashed it. She did so now, glaring at him.

Tim's rueful expression was giving way to suspicion, and he fixed his gray eyes on her. "Liz, my disks are missing." He hadn't whispered, but his roar was down to a tolerable level.

"I gathered as much," she said tartly. "Look, I'm busy. Ask Donna."

"She hasn't come in yet."

"I know. Learn the art of patience. She's bound to arrive at any minute." Liz glanced at her watch, verifying that it was only a couple of minutes past eight. "She's never late."

"She's late this morning." Tim glowered at her. "I've been queued up since yesterday afternoon for time on the Cray, and now there's only one person ahead of me. I need my data *now*, Liz." Since the Cray was a supercomputer that was only available to them on a time-rental basis through a modem, there were usually twenty or thirty other time-share users ahead of them whenever they needed to get on-line. "Help me look," he wheedled.

"No." She tossed another bill onto the growing stack and ignored him. The man had to learn to look after his own things, she thought irritably. It was, after all, part of being an adult.

Tim studied her from beneath a lowered brow and then played his trump card. He knew Liz Pennington's weaknesses as well as he knew his own. "I'll buy you seafood for dinner if you'll help me find my disks."

"I'll do no such thing! If you didn't keep an office that looks like the inside of a tornado, you wouldn't always be looking for things. I'm not your mother, O'Shaughnessy. Find it yourself."

"Lobster," he said coaxingly. "Shrimp. Clams. Oysters?"

Liz groaned and rolled her eyes. "Quit it."

"Help me find my disks. I'll stuff you with seafood."

"You accused me of stealing your disks."

"I did not! I asked what you did with them."

She regarded him coldly. "Six of one, half dozen of another."

"Don't be obtuse. There's a world of difference between an accusation and a mere question."

"You didn't ask."

"I did."

"You *demanded* to know what the devil I did with your disks. That's an accusation."

There was a sparkle in his smoky eyes now. "Drawn butter," he said wickedly.

"Cut it out, Tim." Sending him a glare calculated to turn him into smoldering ash, she reached for the phone. "Maybe something's wrong with Donna. She's *never* late."

Tim remained motionless while she reached for the telephone. One corner of his mouth twitched when she lifted the receiver and realized there was no dial tone. Liz's morning temper was legendary, and he could tell it was stretched to the limit. "My computer's on that line, Liz," he warned her unsympathetically.

"Darn!" she said, and then, in a mood of utter frustration, she moved her fingers toward the phone's touch-tone pad. Tim, initially certain that she was going to switch lines, suddenly realized with horror that she wasn't. And what she was about to do would disconnect him from the linkup to the Cray!

He let out a bellow like a wounded bull's and charged across the room, grabbing her hand when it was only inches from the pad. "Don't!" he roared. "Damn it, Liz, I told you, I'm almost at the top of the queue! How could you even think of—"

It was then that he saw the wicked sparkle in her eyes. Holding her hand in an iron grip, he drew his lips into a feral smile. "Why you little—"

"Apologize for accusing me of stealing your disks, O'Shaughnessy."

"I will not, because I didn't. Pennington, I've got the upper hand." He waggled her hand to make his point.

"Only temporarily," she said coolly.

True. He regarded her from beneath lowered ginger brows.

"All right," he growled. "I apologize. Now, Liz, will you *please* hang up gently and *please* help me find my disks? I'll buy you all the lobster and shrimp you can eat. Crab. King crab."

Gently Liz replaced the receiver. "Okay," she said, turning to scowl up at him across the foot difference in their heights. "But I will *not* help you find your disks. I'm busy."

"You're only sorting the mail. That's not busy. And you can have a truckload of seafood if you just help me find my disks."

Her chin thrust out. "This is blackmail."

"Bribery," he corrected. "This is bribery. You'd make a lousy lawyer, Liz. Come on," he cajoled. "Help me, and you can eat seafood until it comes out of your ears."

"Let go of my hand, O'Shaughnessy."

"If you'll help me."

Her chin thrust out angrily. "That's a threat."

He smiled. "Now you're catching on. I knew you weren't dumb."

Liz looked up at her business partner of four years and realized that she wasn't going to win this one. She never won any battle with Tim O'Shaughnessy, whether it was about the best way to tackle a problem or on the question of their latest client's level of intelligence. She supposed she ought to be grateful that ninety-five percent of the time they saw eye-to-eye. Because when they argued, Tim always won, not by mental power or physical strength, but by sheer, stone-wearing perseverance.

"All right," she agreed finally with a sigh. Rubbing her wrist with exaggerated movements, she stalked down the short corridor to O'Shaughnessy's lair.

As he followed her, Tim suddenly found himself remembering the first time he'd seen Liz Pennington. It had been at the computer fair in Denver five years ago. There she'd been, dressed in a gray iron-maiden business suit and black pumps, and yet the whole corporate power image had been destroyed by the glorious fall of rich auburn hair that reached all the way to her generous hips. O'Shaughnessy, halfway across the cavernous hall, and dressed in a corporate image of conservative blue himself, had looked down at the toes of his grungy joggers and yielded a heartfelt sigh. He had spied a kindred spirit.

Computer programmers were an odd lot. Corporate America did quite a bit of bending and stretching to accommodate them. In any other environment, Tim would never have noticed the contrast of Liz's suit and hair, just as he would never have noticed anybody like himself in suit and joggers. But at a business conference, overloaded with salespeople, Liz Pennington had stood out like a welcome beacon. A fellow programmer. Someone he could communicate with. Meeting the lady of the long auburn tresses had become an obsession—especially since hip-length hair turned him on.

He had stalked her all day, and managed, finally, to maneuver himself into a discussion she had been having with some salespeople about a program. The salesmen had been intimidated. They were used to dealing with purchasing agents, not actual programmers who asked detailed questions. O'Shaughnessy had leapt into the fray. Pennington had looked down at his joggers and smiled. Before long the salesmen had been forgotten. He and Liz had spent the entire night in a diner talking shop, exchanging ideas and bemoaning their restricted work environments.

Out of that night had come Millennium Software, Inc. and their partnership. Four years after its founding, MSI was making a tidy profit in scientific and defense applications, one-of-a-kind single-use programs that bigger companies couldn't be bothered with.

None of which was helping to find his missing disks, Tim thought as he stepped into his office behind Liz. From the stacks of printouts on the floor to the crumpled papers in the corners and teetering piles of books on the file cabinets, the office was a disaster area. For a moment Liz simply stood, shaking her head the way she had countless times in the past four years.

"Tim, you've got to get organized."

"I *am* organized. I know where everything is."

"Except your disks."

He looked wounded. "Somebody moved them. They were on my desk yesterday afternoon."

"I'm surprised you even know where your desk is. You *do* know where your desk is?"

He growled. "Just search, Pennington. Skip the sarcasm."

"That wasn't part of the deal," she reminded him pleasantly.

"It is now. No sarcasm or I'll refuse to stuff you. I'll make you settle for one little bitty shrimp cocktail."

"You said—"

"Forget what I said," he roared. "Just find the damn disks so I can dump my data and then dump *you* in the first lobster tank I can find!"

"Have you even looked?" she asked. "Or did you just start bellowing for reinforcements?"

"Of course I looked!"

"Hah!" she said, lifting a mountain of computer paper from the floor in the corner to reveal the missing items—two flat, putty-colored plastic cases. "You didn't search at all! I knew you didn't. Grow up, O'Shaughnessy."

"You're amazing, Liz," he said with exaggerated awe and admiration, ignoring her remarks. "You must be psychic. I've never seen anybody find things as fast as you do."

"Quit buttering me up. If you applied a little of your intelligence and a little effort you wouldn't have to be bothering *me* to find things for *you* all the time." She dumped the reams of printouts back on the cases. "Now you know where they are." Turning, she headed for her own office at the other end of the corridor. "I expect my seafood tonight."

He considered telling her he couldn't make it, just to watch her go off like a rocket again, but then he smiled to himself and rescued his disks from under the stack of paper. Working with Liz Pennington was comparable to strolling through a mine field, but by damn, it was never boring. A glance at his monitor told him that he was still the second person on the queue, so he had some time yet.

"Timothy Francis Xavier O'Shaughnessy, I'm going to kill you!"

The woman sounded just like his mother, Tim thought with a quirking lip. He paused long enough to slip the correct floppy into the disk drive, and then headed down the hall to Liz's office.

"I'm innocent, I swear," he said, placing a hand over his heart. "What did I do now?"

Liz glared at him over the top of her monitor. "This is truly juvenile, Tim. This is the most childish thing you have ever done!"

"What?"

She rolled her eyes. "Writing in crayon on my antiglare screen, you overgrown two-year-old. This is an expensive filter! It's polarized, coated and all the rest of it. I spent sixty dollars on it. And it's harder than heck to clean an antireflection coating!"

Tim's faintly amused expression vanished and he moved around behind Liz to see what she was talking about. Printed across the smoky glass filter on her monitor in red crayon was the single word STOP.

"It'll take forever to get that off without scratching the coatings, Tim," Liz grumbled. "Really, I would've thought you were more mature than this."

"I am."

Turning her head, she scowled up at him.

"I kid you not," Tim said flatly. "I didn't do it." Which left the question of who did, and he was getting an uneasy prickling sensation on the back of his neck, the way he had sometimes on patrol in Nam. It never paid to ignore that feeling. He snagged a folding chair from the corner and pulled it around so he could sit beside Liz and stare at her monitor. "I also know," he said after a moment, "that I didn't put those disks on the floor, Liz."

"Come on..." Her voice trailed off as she watched him shake his head.

"Honestly, Liz, I may have a messy office, but not even in my wildest, most insane moments would I put my disks on the floor. No way. Those disks are our bread and butter."

Her hazel eyes grew a little wider. "This *is* a joke, right?"

"Wrong. Somebody's been messing around in here."

Liz turned to look at her screen again. "But why? Why would anybody break in here to write a note like that and hide your disks? There's no sense to it." Disturbed, she found herself rubbing her arms. "It's got to be a joke, Tim."

"Maybe, but I don't like it." He stared at the crayoned word as if it would answer his questions, which of course it wouldn't. "I guess we ought to look around and see if anything has been stolen. And we'd better get a locksmith up here to change the locks. I didn't see any sign of forced entry. Did you?"

"No, but I wasn't looking all that closely, either." Liz rubbed her arms again and studied his profile. "Tim? Maybe we should call the police."

"What for? Unless we can find evidence of breaking and entering, or evidence that something's been taken, this'll get about as much attention as jaywalking. On a scale of one to ten, this will be a minus five. I ought to know. My father and brother are both cops."

Her gaze strayed to the thin, white scar that ran from behind his ear, down the side of his neck and into his green Millennium Software T-shirt. Quickly she dragged her eyes away, not wanting him to catch her staring.

She had often wondered about that thin scar, and just as often speculated that he had gotten it in Vietnam. He never talked about the war. She only knew that he was a veteran because, as the facility security officer for their tiny company, she had handled all the paperwork for their security clearances.

In fact, there was a lot she wondered about Tim O'Shaugh-

Defying Gravity

nessy, but their buddy-buddy relationship, which seldom extended outside business hours, and then only for business reasons, had never encouraged those kinds of questions. Tim, for all that he was a friendly bear and behaved like a brother toward her, kept a very firm distance between them. As much time as they spent together, she really knew next to nothing about him.

Just then a computer tone sounded from his end of the hall. He jumped up immediately. "I'm next. We'll talk about this some more after I get the data uploaded."

She watched him dash down the hall and then looked again at the word on her screen. Stop what? And why? She glanced at her watch. And where was Donna? She always called in when something delayed her.

The bell hanging on the front door jingled gaily, alerting her to the fact that someone had entered the front office. She left her desk and went out, expecting to find Donna. Instead, it was the NPS delivery man, his arms full of yellow carnations and a box.

"Morning," he said cheerfully. "One package and some flowers for Donna. Is she sick this morning?"

"I don't know, Chuck. Flowers? Do you have something going with my secretary?"

Chuck grinned. "Naw. The florist up the street throws them away when they get to this point. Donna says she gets a week or more off of them."

Liz accepted the clipboard and signed her name. "I'll put the flowers in water for her."

"Thanks, Ms. Pennington. Say, don't you guys ever worry about spending all your time with computers?"

Liz looked up and found a teasing twinkle in his eye. "Should I worry?"

"Sure. All them X-ray beams and things. Don't you read the paper?" He grabbed a disposable cup from the dispenser at the coffee bar in the corner and poured himself a cup, as he had been doing nearly every workday for four years.

"The last I heard, coffee was bad for you, too."

Chuck laughed as he opened the door. "Worrying is probably the worst thing of all for your health!" he said as he left the office.

"I'm sure he's got that right," rumbled Tim behind her.

"What's with the flowers? He brings them to Donna at least once a week."

"He says the florist up the street dumps them. It wouldn't surprise me if Chuck brings bouquets to all the ladies on his route. Did you finish your upload?"

"Yeah." The Cray would signal Tim with another beep when it was ready to transmit the results back to him. He watched Liz get a yellow vase out of the supply closet and fill it with water. She set the vase and flowers on Donna's desk, a bright spot in an otherwise humdrum office.

Without any warning, he was suddenly aware of the femininity of the activity. Well, hell, he told himself, his partner was a woman, wasn't she? Yep, and he'd been forcing himself to ignore that very fact since they'd begun working together, so he would just have to keep right on ignoring it. Sometimes it was a little difficult to forget, but so far he'd kept the lid on it simply because Liz wasn't his type. Definitely not his type. She was strings, ties, chains and a wedding ring. He'd sworn off that a long, long time ago.

"I didn't find anything missing from my office," he remarked.

Liz made a small, very ladylike snort. "As if there was any way humanly possible to know in that mess."

"Give a guy a break. I can tell."

"Just like you know where everything is." She looked at him suddenly, coming back to the missing disks. "That's so weird, Tim, to think of someone tucking those cases beneath the stack of printouts."

"Maybe it's James's idea of a joke. I'll ask him when he comes in this afternoon." James was Donna's son, a college student who worked as a part-time janitor for them.

"James wouldn't do anything like that, Tim. He's not a prank-ster."

Tim sighed and leaned against the door frame. "I guess not," he said after a moment. If anything, James Proctor was too quiet, too serious and too well behaved. He was exactly the kind of kid every parent would love to have. "Well, I guess there's nothing to do except get the locks changed. In fact, I'll see about having a better lock put on. It must have been somebody looking for money, Liz. What else could it be?"

"Nothing, I guess." Satisfied with the carnations, she stepped back and looked at the arrangement. "It feels a little creepy knowing that someone got in here overnight." She bit her lip and looked up at Tim. "I still think we should call the police."

"I told you—"

"I know you're right, Tim. I know they'll just dismiss it, but we keep classified information in our safes. If something happens later and it turns up that this happened and we didn't phone the police, we might find ourselves in a lot of trouble."

"Hell, I didn't even think of the safes." He'd been so busy looking for signs of something missing that he hadn't thought of checking the obvious. Straightening, he walked over to the row of three heavily armored file cabinets with built-in combination locks. Signs on each announced that they were CLOSED but that didn't mean a thing. One by one he tested levers and found that the drawers were all tightly locked. No one could have broken into them without damaging them, which was one of the requirements for safes storing classified information.

In that moment, he knew a vast sense of relief. "No problem there," he told Liz. "But if it'll make you feel any better, I'll call the cops."

Liz hesitated, unsure. She didn't have a whole lot of experience with the police, but she felt Tim was probably right about how little they could do in these circumstances. At best, they'd probably advise getting the locks changed.

Donna arrived just then, complaining about her car. "I never would have gotten here if some nice man hadn't stopped and fixed it for me," she told Tim and Liz as she hung her fall coat on the hook in the supply closet and smoothed her gray hair back. "He said the choke was stuck and he opened it with a screwdriver. I'm supposed to take it to my mechanic and get it cleaned or lubricated or something. Have I missed anything?"

Liz and Tim exchanged looks and in unspoken agreement said nothing about the misplaced disks and the word on Liz's glare filter.

"Not a thing," Tim said. "We were just beginning to worry about you."

"I'd have called, but I wasn't anywhere near a pay phone." She looked at her two employers. "Did I interrupt something?"

For some reason, Liz felt a faint blush steal into her cheeks. She sometimes wondered if Donna had ever guessed about her attraction to Tim, an attraction she kept firmly hidden, and now the look in Donna's eye was speculative.

"We were just talking about the security of this building," Tim said, saving Liz from the necessity of thinking up a reply to Donna's question.

Donna settled into the chair behind her desk and looked attentively up at him. "Security? For the classified documents? But they're in safes."

"I'm thinking more about our computer equipment," Tim said. "Maybe I've been getting paranoid lately, but I've been thinking it might make sense to have a better lock on the outer door. If anyone broke in here and stole the equipment, it would take a month or more to get back up to speed."

Donna nodded. "I should think so, what with all the special equipment you have. Oh, did Chuck leave these carnations? They're beautiful! Do you want me to call a locksmith today, Tim?"

"As soon as you can get around to it, Donna. Thanks."

Back in her own office, Liz removed the glare filter, which was attached by Velcro strips, from her monitor and stuck it into her briefcase. Tonight, at home, she would soak it and try to get the crayon off without damaging the delicate antireflection coating.

Her first impression had been correct, she told herself. It had been an act of pure childishness. Mischievousness that hadn't been intended to be harmful. Whoever had done it probably didn't have any idea how delicate the coating on the glass really was. After all, if this person had intended any real damage, it would certainly have been easy enough to do.

With that thought, she pushed the matter from her mind and booted her computer. There was a lot of code she hoped to write before lunchtime.

At quitting time, Tim poked his head into Liz's office and reminded her they had a dinner date.

"It's not a date," she told him sharply, and kept her attention on the glowing lines of code she was studying. The last thing on earth she wanted him to guess was how her heart had leapt to hear him call it a date, so she refused to look at him.

"I'm wounded."

"And I'm a fool if I believe that."

He sighed. "Five minutes, Liz."

"Ten."

He left without another word, but just a couple of minutes later he reappeared, standing in her doorway and shifting restlessly.

"What is it now?" she asked irritably, typing in the exit command.

"Ah, Liz?"

"Yeah?"

"I don't have my wallet."

Groaning, Liz looked up at him. "You lie, O'Shaughnessy."

"I do not. I haven't told a lie since I was eight years old and my dad wanted to know who dumped paint on the cat. I forgot my wallet. I think it's still on my dresser. We can stop by there if you really want—"

"You need a wife," she told him flatly.

"You volunteering?"

"I *work* with you, O'Shaughnessy. I *know* better. I'll buy dinner, but you pay me back tomorrow."

"I promise," he said meekly.

She eyed him distrustfully, knowing better than to believe Tim had a meek bone in his body. She saw the amused sparkle in his smoky eyes and realized she was being unnecessarily touchy. Well, so what? she asked herself as she stalked down the hall. Everyone was entitled to be irritable some times.

Tim followed her, battling down a smile that kept wanting to show up on his lips. Liz got this way occasionally. There were spells where you couldn't even breathe right around her. Not that he minded. Whenever she got like this, she always reminded him of a cat with sadly ruffled fur. Or a spitting kitten.

She had, he noticed for the umpteenth time as he followed her denim-clad rump to the front, generous hips. And generous breasts. And generous lips. And that gorgeous waterfall of auburn hair down to her hips. He missed a step and caught himself.

"You need a haircut, Pennington," he said gruffly.

"What?" She looked at him almost blankly as she reached for her jacket, which hung on the hook just inside the supply closet. Her breasts strained at the green fabric of her MSI T-shirt. Tim closed his eyes briefly, wondering what the hell had gotten into him all of a sudden. Yes, he was aware of her feminine attractions, but never before had he been quite so unable to control that awareness.

"Your ends are split," he said shortly.

"They are?" Immediately she yanked a handful of hair around and held the ends up in front of her eyes. "You're right," she said. "Guess I better take an inch off."

She dropped the hair and started to pull on her coat. Like a man possessed, his mind wondering wildly why he was doing this, his body doing it anyway, Tim O'Shaughnessy stepped up behind her and scooped her hair up out of the way while she pulled on her coat. How many times had he watched her pull it out of her collar?

It was heavy, he realized. Heavy and soft as silk and fragrant with baby shampoo. X-rated images of that hair trailing over his skin, his thighs, curtaining him as— He blinked and dropped the hair as if it were hot. Damn, he thought. What a surefire way to ruin a business partnership.

"Thanks," she said.

He was relieved to see that she hadn't noticed anything. The coat covered her voluptuous curves, but didn't hide her generous mouth. She was looking vague, worrying her full lower lip with her teeth.

"We'd better take my car, Tim," she said as they stepped into the crisp Catskill autumn night. "If you don't have your wallet, you probably don't have your license."

Tim looked at her Toyota. "There's no way I can fit into that tin can. We'll take my truck."

Liz looked from her Toyota to Tim's ancient, battered pickup. "Why don't you get yourself a new truck, or a Bronco or something? You can afford it now."

"This one still isn't worn-out."

She sniffed. "There's no way I'm going to drive that."

"So I'll drive."

"You don't have your license."

"The worst they can do is give me a summons to show up with my license in court. I haven't been stopped by a cop since I was eighteen. It'll be okay."

"Knock on wood, O'Shaughnessy. You tempt fate."

He looked down at her. "Superstitious? *You*, Pennington?"

"There's a lot you don't know about me," she said tartly, and stalked toward his truck. "I'll drive."

There was suddenly a lot he wanted to know about her, he thought, a shiver trickling down inside him. But what he really wanted was to kiss her, to mold those soft lips with his, to taste her tongue, to crush her curves to his angles. "You're awfully crabby tonight, Liz. What's got into you?" A better question was what the hell had gotten into him!

"You," she said shortly, heading for the truck. "You drive me crazy. You can't get through a day without somebody to look after you. I signed on as a business partner, not a den mother. If you're going to forget your wallet, you could at least be courteous enough to fit into my Toyota."

"Liz, Liz, be realistic. I can't help my size!"

"You might not be able to help being six foot four—"

"Five," he said. "Six foot five."

She glared at him. "—But you don't have to spend so much time trying to look like Arnold Schwarzenegger."

"You don't like my body?" Lord, the devil was in him!

She spluttered. She actually spluttered.

"Liz," he said, enjoying himself hugely. "Liz, I *don't* spend much time at it." He raised a hand to his heart. "I swear. A couple of hours a week. Can I help it if I have so much testosterone that muscle just grows practically by itself?"

A strangled sound escaped her. Her face contorted strangely. He wondered if she was having a stroke or a seizure.

"Liz?"

"Shut up," she said, her voice strangled. "Just shut up, O'Shaughnessy."

For once he complied, even holding his peace when she ground the unfamiliar gears of his truck. It wouldn't be wise to rile her while she was driving.

"Where do you want to eat?" she asked a few moments later.

"Colby's. It's the only place we can go to in jeans and T-shirts."

"He better have seafood."

"He does. By the bucketload. Haven't you been there?"

"No."

"Not fancy enough for you, Liz?" Without looking, he could tell she was glaring again.

"I just haven't been there before," she said succinctly.

Tim decided it might be a good idea to change the subject. "We're going to have to put in a dedicated line soon. I shudder every time I make a data transfer."

"Yeah."

"I'm thinking about a secured line so we don't have to make as many trips to Washington."

"You're talking big bucks, Tim. Things like that might eat up our profits for the year."

"But it'll open up a whole range of potential contracts for us. It's like getting that Tempest equipment three years ago. It hurt, but we wouldn't be doing any classified work without secure computers."

"I guess."

Wrong subject, he thought, and tried to think of something else. Ordinarily Liz was ready to discuss business at the drop of a hat. What was eating her tonight? "There's Colby's," he said, pointing out the restaurant.

"I see it, O'Shaughnessy."

Colby's wasn't at all fancy. Wood floors, wood walls, low-beamed ceilings and country music wailing softly in the background. The tables didn't even have cloths, and the napkins were paper, held in a dispenser on the table. They selected a crescent-shaped booth in an isolated corner so Tim would be able to stretch out his legs. The seafood menu made up for the lack of atmosphere, though, and Liz decided she could forgive Tim a few of his sins, after all. She'd never tried Colby's before because it had a reputation for getting a little wild as the evening wore on. It wasn't the kind of place a lady went to by herself, and when she had a dinner date it was always at some place far fancier. At the moment the restaurant was quiet. By the time the waitress brought frosty mugs of draft beer, Liz was feeling pretty relaxed.

Then Tim asked a question he had no business asking. "Do you ever get lonely, Liz?" Yep, the devil was in him tonight. As soon as he asked the question, he thought of all the reasons he didn't want to get involved with this woman in any way aside from that of business. Why, then, was he poking his nose into nonbusiness places?

"Do you?" she countered, her eyes flashing.

"Yes." He said the word flatly, truthfully, and watched as

something in her face eased, changed, softened. Softened? An image came out of nowhere, making his pulse pound.

"Are you okay?" she asked.

"Fine," he lied. This was bad. This was unthinkable. For five years he'd known this woman, and for four years he'd worked daily with her, managing, all this time, to see her as just a slightly touchy software wizard. Now, without warning, his self-control seemed to have gone up in smoke, and all he could see was that she was a woman. A tempting, voluptuous, generously built woman. A woman with a cornucopia of curves to explore. He ground his teeth.

"Tim, what is the matter with you?" she asked, impatience and worry both in her voice.

He liked her voice, he suddenly realized. He'd listened to her insults for four years because he liked her voice. He'd even provoked her more than once just because he enjoyed lighting her fuse.

"Tim?" She leaned toward him and put her hand on his arm. Lightning streaked through him.

"Relax, Liz," he said between his teeth. "It'll pass." And it damn well would, even if it killed him. There was no way a sane man would play fast and loose with the affections of his business partner. And despite momentary evidence to the contrary, he was a sane man.

She regarded him doubtfully. "What's wrong?"

Well, he'd go to hell and dance barefoot on glowing coals before he would tell her the truth. There was no way a man could tell a woman that her innocent touch had streaked through him like wildfire and made him ache as he hadn't ached since he was sixteen. "Not a thing," he said evenly. "Everything's fine." And it was going to stay fine, because they were business partners and he couldn't think of a better, swifter way to ruin everything than to tell her the truth.

But Liz, who had been born with a bulldog's natural temperament, wasn't the kind to let a puzzle pass by that easily. Curious, a little worried, she peered intently at him, but could read nothing from his expression except an unusual stiffness.

Uneasy and not sure why, she finally gave her attention to the crab legs and broiled shrimp. Something had changed. She had felt it, as if something inside her had responded to a change in atmospheric pressure. And somewhere deep inside, not knowing why, she mourned.

She insisted on dropping him off at his place and picking him up in the morning so that he wouldn't get stopped without his license. He grumbled about it, but gave in simply because it was so unlike Liz to go so far out of her way for him without grousing loudly about it. But she didn't grouse. In fact, she was too quiet. He began to wonder if he had somehow blown their easy camaraderie after all.

"Liz," he said as she pulled up in the street in front of his apartment house, "you're mad at me."

"No."

"You are. You're not talking. You're not complaining. You're not giving me a hard time. This isn't like you."

"It'll pass," she said. "Lay off, Tim. I'm in no mood for your pestering. I'm tired."

He hesitated, trying to read her expression in the dim light given off by the dash, with a little help from the streetlights. The hesitation was one of the biggest mistakes he had ever made, because his treasonous senses took the opportunity to swamp him in awareness. In the confines of the truck cab, he smelled the faint, enticing fragrance of woman, a beckoning perfume that promised delight and release. The shadows highlighted her just so, drawing attention to the soft line of her cheek, the delicate shell of her ear, the swelling curve of her breast.

All his good resolutions flew out the window before the simple, soft impact of her femininity. Like a man possessed, for the second time in one evening, he watched his hands reach out and do something his mind was still trying to object to. Taking Liz gently by the shoulders, he drew her across the seat toward him. Nothing mattered except finding out how she tasted.

Her foot left the clutch and the truck choked into silence. Neither of them noticed. Liz drew a sharp breath in the instant before Tim's mouth closed over hers. In a moment he'd gone from civilized man to conquering male. Finesse escaped him. With one thirsty thrust, he pushed his tongue past the barrier of her lips and teeth and found the heat and promise within.

Her response was shy and uncertain, which only maddened him more. Some corner of his mind babbled wild warnings, but he ignored them. Instead he coaxed and teased, sucked and nipped, until that shy tongue darted back at him, taking everything he had to give and giving it right back.

He lifted both hands from her shoulders and plunged them into her hair, holding her face to his, preventing her escape, though he could tell she wasn't thinking of escape. No, she was making this provocative little whimper deep in her throat, a sound almost like an ecstatic plea, and she was leaning closer and closer.

And then, like a shocking bucket of cold water, reason erupted into his mind, reminding him of who he was, who she was and where they were. Shuddering with reluctance, he tore his mouth from hers and lifted his head. For a while he was incapable of movement or speech, could only gasp for air.

Her eyes were hazy, he thought, full of the tangled needs and wants he was feeling himself. Even through the fog of desire, though, he remembered that this woman was his business partner, not someone he had picked up for the night. He owed her honesty. He owed her a warning.

"Liz?"

"Hmm?" The corners of her swollen lips lifted a little.

"I'm not a forever kind of guy." He tensed inwardly, awaiting her anger, anger she had every right to feel, considering the way he had just come on to her. She blinked, and he could see her shift mental gears. He was relieved that when his statement registered she looked neither shocked nor dismayed.

"No," she agreed, pulling back a little. "I know you're not a forever kind of guy."

"You do?" Hell, was he wearing a sign?

"Of course I do, O'Shaughnessy!" Her tone grew sharp. Surely the man couldn't think she had been utterly blind to the parade of short-term, long-stemmed lovelies who occasionally passed through his evenings. Certainly not when they had a distressing tendency to drop by the office or keep calling after he had dumped them. "I wasn't born yesterday. Besides, you're exactly the kind of man my mother warned me against."

He wasn't sure he liked the sound of that. "What's that supposed to mean?"

"That you're not a forever kind of guy," she said tartly, and slid back behind the steering wheel. "That you don't make commitments."

Now he *knew* he didn't like the sound of that. "What do you call our business partnership? An ongoing accident? A long-term one-night stand?"

She sighed. "That isn't what I meant, Tim."

"No? Maybe you'd better explain."

"Just that you're not the marrying kind!"

For a long time the only sound in the cab was the occasional one of an unsteady breath. Finally, Tim spoke.

"I was married once, a long, long time ago." He reached for the latch and pushed the door open. "I won't make that mistake again."

Liz watched him slide out, and she suddenly, unexpectedly, ached for him. "Was it that bad?" she asked with unwonted gentleness.

"No." He faced her. "It was just that *good.* Good night, Pennington."

The slam of the door effectively silenced her thousand and one questions. How dare he drop a bomb and then walk away without allowing her to ask questions! Eventually, unable to do anything else without creating a public spectacle, she started the truck and headed toward her house.

Well, that explained a great deal, she found herself thinking. A very great deal. In fact, it was a relief. It meant they could continue to be friends, because neither one of them wanted to get tangled up in anything else.

Men, she thought, made great buddies, but only a foolish woman gave a man either her heart or her body. Look at her own mother, pregnant at fourteen and abandoned by her young husband just a couple of years later. No, Liz had long ago discovered a basic truth that most of the human race apparently kept forgetting: there was no such thing as a forever kind of man. The creature didn't simply exist.

Chapter 2

In the morning Tim regarded Liz warily as he climbed into the truck beside her. After a moment, he realized she was just her usual early morning grumpy self, and he relaxed. There was a box of doughnuts on the seat between them, and he reached for it.

"You might ask, O'Shaughnessy," she said acidly.

"Please, Pennington."

"Help yourself."

"I knew you were going to say that, so why should I ask?"

"Common courtesy."

"Have a doughnut," he said, holding the open box out to her.

"No thanks. Did you remember your wallet today?"

He patted his hip pocket. "Got it right here."

"So pay up."

"As soon as we get to the office. By the way, Liz, you're a cheap date."

She glowered at him briefly. "It wasn't a date."

If it wasn't a date, he found himself thinking, why had he lain awake half the night imagining the myriad ways he'd like to make love to her? He'd awakened this morning feeling bruised from his restless night, and aching with unsatisfied needs. Well, he was glad Liz so obviously hadn't felt the same. Things would get back to normal faster this way. For both of them.

When they reached the office Donna was already there, standing just inside the door with a fresh mug of coffee for each. It was a standing joke that had turned into a tradition that O'Shaughnessy and Pennington weren't fit to talk to each other or anybody else until they'd had that first cup of coffee. With mumbled thanks, they took their mugs and headed to their individual offices.

Before booting her computer Liz went over her office with a fine-tooth comb, looking for any sign of the vandal's return. All she found were a couple of dust balls that indicated James kept forgetting to dust behind the stack of file baskets she kept on top of her filing cabinet.

Relieved that yesterday's discoveries apparently weren't going to become an ongoing nightmare, she settled down at her desk and turned on her computer.

"Anything?" Tim stood in her doorway.

"Not a thing," she replied. "You?"

"Nope." Satisfied, he returned to his own office.

Staring at the blinking cursor on her screen, Liz spared a moment to ponder the fact that Tim, too, had checked things out this morning. Evidently she wasn't the only one who still felt a little uneasy. Reassured somehow by that knowledge, she called up the text editor and loaded her program code. Before noon she was going to find out why she was getting occasional negative values where she should be getting only positive numbers.

Tim O'Shaughnessy made a lot of noise in his office that morning. For a man who supposedly made his living by thinking, writing and using a computer keyboard, he made surprising quantities of noise. Things banged against walls. Others scraped gratingly on the linoleum floor. Crashes and thuds resounded, intermixed with Tim's colorful curses.

At about ten-thirty, utterly frustrated, Liz stormed to the door of her office. "Cut it out, O'Shaughnessy! I can't think!"

"It's your fault, Pennington. Live with it," he roared back.

"How can it be my fault that you're throwing things all over the office?"

He stuck his head out his door and glared. "You'll see," he

said darkly. "Now go back into your tidy mouse hole and hide before I get a mind to throw things around *your* office."

"Don't threaten me!"

"Don't push me!" He stepped into the hall, hands on his narrow hips, and scowled. "I am pushed, Liz. I am pushed to the bitter edge."

"You look like a chimney sweep," she said frostily. "There's dirt on your nose. Don't you ever dust?"

He roared and charged down the hall, hands extended as if they wanted to grab her by the throat. Liz stood her ground, arms folded across her breasts.

"Go ahead and kill me," she challenged. "At least then I won't have to put up with any more of your childishness."

"Childishness!" He shouted the word and came to a dead halt not six inches from her nose. For a moment she stared at his broad, cotton-covered chest and then he stooped, bringing his hot gray eyes level with hers.

"What's eating you, Tim?" she asked, unwisely.

"You," he growled. "Just you. You're driving me to the edge of madness, damn you. Just for once in your life, Liz, zip your lip and lie low until the storm passes."

"I think I'd rather let you kill me."

"I will," he promised.

Dramatically she flung her arms wide. "Do your worst, O'Shaughnessy!"

The corner of his eye twitched. Then the corner of his mouth twitched. The next thing Liz knew, Tim O'Shaughnessy had thrown back his head and was roaring with laughter.

Infuriated beyond speech, Liz shot a glare up at him and then stormed into her own office, slamming the door pointedly. Moments later she was further enraged to hear Tim laughing and telling Donna about it.

"Did you see her?" she heard him crow. "Standing there with her arms flung out as if she were a sacrificial victim. 'Do your worst, O'Shaughnessy,' she says, like in a fourth-rate movie. Donna, I swear, I could have kissed her to death!"

Donna's unintelligible murmur answered him. Liz realized her hands were clenched into tight fists. With great effort, she returned to her desk and tried to concentrate on the program she was writing for a nearby research-and-development firm. Darn

O'Shaughnessy, she thought. He'd finally gone and slipped over the edge into madness.

The phone started ringing insistently and she scowled at it, wishing it to the devil. She could still hear Donna talking to Tim, however, so she reached for the receiver and snapped a greeting, prepared to give short shrift to anyone but a customer. A short silence ensued after she answered, and just as she was about to hang up, sure there was no one on the line, a voice said, "Stop disturbing the gravity." Then a soft click indicated that the caller had hung up.

Well, heck, Liz thought, glaring at the receiver. She was in absolutely no mood for jokes. Some kid home sick from school, no doubt, and he'd call again in ten or fifteen minutes wanting to know if she had Prince Albert in the can. Just exactly the kind of nuisance she needed today with Tim acting crazed.

O'Shaughnessy continued to thump and bang throughout the morning, but at a more restrained level of volume. Liz lost herself once more in her work, looking up only briefly when Donna announced that she was going to lunch and asked if Liz wanted her to bring back anything.

"A sandwich would be nice," Liz admitted. "Chicken. Thanks, Donna."

Tim had grown silent, Liz realized abruptly, and then she shrugged. He'd probably gone out to lunch.

Suddenly money fluttered down on the keyboard in front of her.

"I pay my debts," Tim said over her head.

"Great. Wonderful. Thank you. Clear out, I'm busy."

"You're always busy. Take a break. I want you to see something."

"Later."

"Now."

"It can wait, O'Shaughnessy."

"It can't wait, Pennington. It might not last until quitting time." Leaning over, he surrounded her with his massive arms and typed in a save command.

"Tim—" She tried to turn her chair but his arms prevented her. And then, like the serpent in Eden, the memory of last night's kiss undulated into her mind. No, she thought almost frantically. No! She didn't want to remember, refused to remember that once in her life, just once, she had come close to succumbing. She didn't want to remember that one man in her life could have made her feel things she had believed were a fiction existing only in the minds of maudlin writers of romance. The power of those feelings scared her when she thought about them. And right now she was terrified because she practically had to sit on her hands to keep from touching those powerful arms, to keep from leaning back against Tim's strength. Lord, she'd lost her mind!

"Come on," he said coaxingly. "Don't you want to know what all the uproar was about? Don't you want to see what I did just for you?"

"Don't be ridiculous." Fright added more than the normal acidity to her tone.

"Just for you," he repeated. "Come on, Liz. It won't take two minutes."

Sighing, she agreed, realizing he'd just keep dripping on her like water on stone until she gave in. "Okay. I'll come. But just two minutes."

"That's all I ask." He freed her and stood back.

Annoyed as much with herself as Tim, Liz followed him to his office.

"*Entrez vous,*" he said with a grandiose wave of his arm. Frowning at him, Liz stepped into his office and froze. She gaped. She looked around. Tim had cleaned. The place was unrecognizable. And on his desk, where once there had been mountains of computer paper threatening to avalanche on some unsuspecting victim, there was now only his disk file cases and computer...and a red checkered tablecloth, a bottle of wine and some cheese and crackers.

"Cups," he said suddenly, snapping his fingers. "I forgot the cups." He disappeared, returning a minute later with two paper cups. Liz still stood frozen, as if she couldn't believe what she saw.

"Your two minutes are up," he said, pouring wine into the cups. He offered her one. "Care to extend it to twenty minutes?"

She nodded slowly, dazed. When he held a chair for her, she sank into it gratefully.

"Tim—"

"I know," he said smugly. "It looks great, doesn't it? It occurred to me last night that you're right. I could find things better if I'm organized, so I got organized. Besides, it's like my old boss used to say to me. 'O'Shaughnessy,' he'd say, 'you've got to keep your office organized. If you ever get hit by lightning, somebody else is going to have to come in here and find things. You owe it to the company and to that poor slob to make the job easy.'"

Her hazel eyes settled on him doubtfully. "Are you planning to quit, Tim? Is that what this is all about?"

"No." He put his hand over his heart. "I'm trying to impress you, actually."

"What do you want?" Now her look was suspicious.

"A date, Liz. A real live date, with candlelight dinner, fancy clothes—the works."

For a long moment astonishment kept her silent. "I think that would be a dead certain way to ruin a great partnership." Especially given the sparks he had stirred up between them last night. Lord, she'd spent half the night trying to convince herself that she could live without another experience of that kind—and she hadn't quite succeeded, judging by her reaction to his proximity a couple of minutes ago.

"We're adults, Liz. We can handle these things." He waved his hand airily. "A date is an easy thing to deal with. It'd hardly stir up the kind of tempest you'd expect with marriage, divorce and a custody battle. We can handle a date, and that's all it would be, because we both would know from the outset that we didn't want any more than that."

Her look grew even more suspicious. "Are you losing your mind?"

"Actually, at this moment, no. I'm perfectly sane and rational. Nor are my hormones involved in this. I'm asking you because I'd like to know you better."

"How much better?"

He smiled. "Is that any question to ask before even the first date?"

Much to his wonder and amazement, Liz flushed faintly. "There won't be a first date," she said sharply. "Dates make things messy."

He shook his head. "I just explained, Liz. We're both adults. We can handle these things. We can have a nice, adult, uninvolved relationship that won't mess up either one of us." He'd thrown down the gauntlet, and sat back now to await her reaction. During the course of this endless morning, it had occurred to him that he didn't know Liz Pennington well enough to know if she was or wasn't his type. It was entirely conceivable that she might be amenable to an, uh, adult relationship. An uncomplicated, friendly, go-nowhere kind of thing. His kind of thing. And if she was, he could work out this sexual attraction before it drove him insane trying to repress it. That's all it was, of course, and he knew the moment she understood him by the sudden flare in her hazel eyes.

After the first blast of shock passed, Liz found there was something seductive in his reasoning, but with a flash of insight she knew that a light, uninvolved adult relationship was not in her programming. She had remained uninvolved only because she had never let anyone that close. Not for all the pleasures of Eden would she risk ending up like her mother. That didn't keep her from feeling a pang, though, when she realized that was all he wanted.

"Look, Tim. We're business partners. Maybe we ought to just leave it that way." In fact, there was no "maybe" about it. It was the only wise, safe course of action.

"Maybe we ought to, but I don't think I'm going to be able to. I spent all morning trying to talk myself out of this. Have some cheese and crackers."

Instead, she sipped her wine. She was nervous, and it wasn't like her to be nervous. She didn't like the feeling. She was also painfully aware that men generally wanted one thing from a woman, and it very definitely involved their hormones. "Look, Tim, if you think you're going to get between my sheets with this sham, you've got another think coming. I have no intention of sleeping with you or anybody else."

He looked at her narrowly, and suddenly there was an expression of dawning wonder on his face. "My God," he said. "You are."

"What? What am I?"

"I'm impressed," he said, and sounded like he really was. "How did you manage it, Liz? You must have more willpower than a monastery full of monks."

"What are you talking about?" Now she was getting annoyed. This foolhardy, obtuse, typically untrustworthy male was upsetting all the comfortable dynamics of their relationship by dragging in all kinds of complicating factors. After five years, why should he suddenly keep noticing she was a woman? And if he had to notice, couldn't he have had the decency to keep the awareness to himself so it didn't make her uncomfortable?

He leaned forward, and there was an expression of such gentleness on his face that Liz caught her breath in spite of herself.

"Tim? Quit riddling. What are you talking about?"

"You're a virgin," he said softly, and saw the answer in her full, glorious blush.

Liz carefully set her cup down onto the desk. "You've gone too far this time," she said coldly, and stormed back to her office. What she really would have liked was to slap his face. How could he—*how could he?* Her heart galloped like a stampeding horse, and for a moment she was absolutely certain that somehow all the air had been siphoned from the building.

"Liz?" He followed her. "Liz, what did I do?"

"What did you do?" she asked incredulously, gasping the words out, unable to believe that he could even ask. She kept marching and he kept following.

"All I did was make an observation—"

"Observation! Hah!" Grabbing her door, she tried to slam it in his face, but he barreled right through.

"Liz, be reasonable! All I did was ask you for a date. You were the one who brought up other things."

"Get out, O'Shaughnessy! I don't want to see your ugly mug for at least a week." Chin thrust out, she glared up at him.

"Why? Because I figured out that you're a virgin?"

She gasped in fury and raised her arm to swing at him. He caught her wrist easily, and suddenly he was grinning. "Why, Liz, don't tell me you're ashamed of your virtue."

"O'Shaughnessy, I swear—"

"You can't be ashamed of it, Liz," he said reasonably. "You must have gone to an awful lot of trouble to keep it."

"I can't—I can't believe you're talking about this!" She was gasping, chest heaving, but whether from horror or fury he really couldn't tell.

And suddenly, very suddenly, Tim saw past her anger to the truth behind it. The understanding ripped a hole in his heart, and filled him with remorse. She had reasons for avoiding involve-

ment just as he did, and her reasons were every bit as powerful
as his own. He was embarrassing her with his frankness, and he
was a cad to be pressuring her this way. Hell, only the lowest life
form would suggest an "adult relationship" to a virgin. Of
course, he hadn't realized at that point she was, but still…!

"Oh, Liz," he said gruffly, and hauled her against his hard
chest, closing her in his powerful arms. "I'm sorry. You're right,
I'm behaving like an uncivilized slob. I only meant to ask you
out to dinner, not to get into all this other stuff." Rapidly he tried
to think up a cover story for his offer of an adult relationship.
Maybe this euphemism would prove his saving. "Really, Liz, I
just thought that it's been a long time since we got together like
we used to to hash out a game plan for the business." Yeah, that
was reasonable. "We've been too busy working, and I thought
we could just combine a little business and pleasure."

She wiggled, trying to escape his hold, but his massive arms
simply moved with her, making escape impossible. "Forget it,
Tim," she said desperately, embarrassed beyond belief and wanting only to abandon this entire discussion. Oh, God, had she mis-
understood what he meant by an adult relationship? *She* had been
the one who mentioned other things, and realizing it, she wanted
to die. Well, almost. "Just forget the whole thing. All of it, including dinner. And please let me go."

But her wiggling was having a seriously debilitating effect on
him. At that instant he couldn't have let go to save his life. Instead, he warned her, "Liz, if you don't stop wiggling, you'll
incite a riot."

She grew instantly still. "Just…let…go…of me," she said with
exaggerated patience, ignoring the sudden, incredible awareness
his words had awakened in her.

"In a minute," he said. "In a minute." There was something
so exquisitely warm about holding her close like this, about feeling Liz Pennington in his arms, that he just couldn't let her
go. It was something he had never felt before, something…
frightening. He didn't want to feel things he had never felt before.
Feelings like that were dangerous.

But still he continued to hold her, closing his mind to the
knowledge of the exquisite curves she kept hidden beneath her
baggy T-shirt. Holding her, he shut his eyes and absorbed the
knowledge that this woman was innocent and pure, and that he

had no business sullying her with his baser needs, certainly not when he could offer her nothing else. He was, by nature, a damn-the-torpedoes kind of guy, but this time it would be utterly irresponsible to charge ahead.

Somehow, for both their sakes, he had to get matters back on an even keel.

"Hell, Pennington," he said as he let go of her, "I must be losing my last few marbles. Of course we'll forget about this. You're absolutely right. It would kill our partnership. I can see it already."

Wary at this quick about-face in his attitude, she peered up at him. "See *what* already?"

"How rough it would be if we spent any more time together than we already do. I mean, we already spend half our time quarreling, and over such stupid things. What do you think it would be like if we had anything *important* to argue about? World War III?"

She felt the corners of her mouth tugging upward, and the tension inside her dissipated. This was the Tim O'Shaughnessy who was her good buddy, the one whom she had known these past five years. He was going to let everything return to normal.

"Armageddon at the very least," she agreed, unable to hide her smile of relief. "You've always said I have an impossible temper."

"Mine is hardly any better. So forget all this, Liz. It's nothing but a temporary insanity. I'll recover."

She watched him head back to his office, and thought she would feel a whole lot better if he didn't look quite so much as though he were fleeing from a narrow escape.

But of course, that's probably how he felt about it. And why shouldn't he? She was not, after all, a suave sophisticate who would give him the "adult relationship" he wanted—assuming that was what he meant at all, and now she wasn't even sure about that. But what else could anyone mean by "adult relationship"?

Sighing, she sat at her desk and tried to concentrate on her program. She didn't want to think about the sinking sensation in her stomach, or about the feeling that she had just lost something. Their relationship was too important to her to jeopardize over fleeting desire.

* * *

"Hi, Liz."

Liz looked up from her monitor to smile at James Proctor, Donna's son. He was a moderately good-looking young man with a football player's build, who was making his mother proud of his academic achievement at a local college. Three afternoons a week, he janitored in the offices of MSI, mopping, sweeping, dusting and taking out the trash.

"Hi, James. How's it going?"

"Pretty good." Stepping into her office, he reached for her wastebasket. "If you have time, you really ought to try to come to the club meeting this month."

Behind him, Tim's bulky form materialized. "Club?" he asked. "What club?" He saw the faint tinge of pink come to Liz's cheeks and began to grin. This promised to be interesting.

Liz discovered right then that real life could be exactly like a nightmare. She knew what was coming, dreaded it and yet couldn't do a thing to prevent it. Anything she said to silence James would only make Tim more determined to find out what was going on. Clenching her hands into fists, she waited for the ax to fall. This was like putting a loaded weapon into the man's hands, she thought desperately. Now he would tease her to death.

"The club is called SCUFO," James answered with all the eager honesty of an innocent who had no concept of what he was unleashing. "Student Committee on UFOs."

"UFOs," Tim repeated levelly.

It was interesting, Liz thought with a strange kind of detachment. She had never seen a man's face turn wooden before. Never had she imagined it possible for anyone to become so completely and utterly expressionless. If Tim was thinking or feeling anything, no one would ever guess it.

"I see," he said in that same level tone. "Fascinating."

The look, the remark, the jokes that Liz expected didn't materialize. In fact, Tim didn't even glance at her.

"Just what does this club do?" he asked James.

"Oh, we trade books and swap stories, and do some research into UFOs. Sometimes we have guest speakers who tell us about their own UFO experiences, or about investigations that are going on. It's really a lot of fun." James grinned. "Kind of crazy sometimes, too."

"I imagine," Tim agreed pleasantly enough. "Liz is a member, too?"

Wouldn't you know he would ask *that* question? Liz thought miserably. Why couldn't he be satisfied to know that she was associated with the club? Why did he have to know how?

"Oh, no, she's not a student. She can't be a member."

"Oh." Little by little, in jerky fits and starts, Tim's eyes were shifting toward Liz.

"No, she was a speaker for us last month," James continued, cheerfully oblivious to tension. "She told us about the UFO she saw."

Tim's gaze snapped back to James. When he spoke, his voice was curiously toneless. "She...saw...a UFO."

"Yeah, you ought to ask her to tell you about it. It was neat!" James returned his attention to Liz. "You said you'd bring in those books that Ryvek wrote back in the fifties, and that you wouldn't mind lending them to me."

"Sure," Liz managed to say despite the fact that she felt as if she were choking. No way was O'Shaughnessy going to let something like this pass. No way. She'd be lucky if he didn't drive her to the funny farm. "They're right over here."

She wished, as she pushed back her chair and turned toward her bookcase, that she hadn't brought these books in. She wished that she had never *seen* these books. She wished an innocent remark to James last summer hadn't led to her speaking before the club. And it wasn't going to do her a damn bit of good to wish her heart out, because Tim O'Shaughnessy was standing right there with that wooden expression on his face, and even the Rock of Gibraltar couldn't look any more immovable.

Stifling an urge to run or hysterically deny all knowledge of James and his club, Liz pulled the stack of books from the bottom of the shelf and set them on the corner of her desk.

"They're in pretty good condition, James, so you don't have to worry about them falling apart when you handle them. The paper's starting to get a little brittle, though."

Tim snatched one of the hardcover volumes from her hands and read the title. One by one, he scanned the rest of the book covers and then, without comment, he passed the volumes to James.

He was bound to say something, Liz thought tensely as she

checked the shelves to make sure she didn't overlook a volume that James would enjoy. She just couldn't imagine Tim letting a golden opportunity like this pass. He'd practically teased her to death over her choice of car two years ago. If he could give her such a hard time over something so mundane, how could he possibly overlook a UFO?

"You really ought to come to the meeting this month," James said to her. "We're having another speaker—Wilfred White."

Liz shook her head, determined to never again come within hailing distance of SCUFO, but unwilling to hurt James by saying so. Heck, if she hadn't been so unwilling to hurt the young man's feelings, she never would have gone even that once! "I don't recognize the name."

"Even *I* know who he is," Tim said. "White is the guy who's been kidnapped a dozen times by aliens." Tim glanced back at James. "Do you really buy that kind of stuff, James? I mean, do you honestly believe that aliens are kidnapping people and using them for medical guinea pigs?"

To Liz's vast relief, the question was in no way challenging or mocking. Tim sounded honestly interested, nothing more, nothing less.

"Well, no, I don't exactly *believe* it," James said. "But it's fun to listen to the stories and speculate. And it kind of makes my spine tingle the way people all over the world have described the aliens in exactly the same way."

"Lots of people claim to have seen aliens, huh?" Tim remarked.

"Hundreds, from all over the world. I guess it could be mass hysteria." Then, picking up the volumes, he turned to Liz. "Thanks for the books, Liz. I'll take good care of them."

While James carried the stack of books out to his car, Tim remained where he was, studying her surprising bookshelf as if it were a work of art. Funny, he thought. Four years of working cheek by jowl with Liz, and he had never noticed that not all of the titles on her wall-to-wall bookshelves were technical in nature. Until this very moment, he'd have said this woman didn't have an impractical, whimsical, mystical or otherwise off-center bone in her body.

Liz shifted impatiently, waiting. She knew O'Shaughnessy. There was no way on earth he would walk out of here without

saying something. Much to her dismay, he didn't say anything at
all, just kept studying her bookshelves. Finally she couldn't stand
it.

"Well?" she demanded.

"Hmm?" He sounded distant, absorbed in thought.

"Come on, O'Shaughnessy. I can take it."

He turned his head to regard her from gray eyes that betrayed
only a faint amusement. "Is this another one of those do-your-
worst-O'Shaughnessy scenes? You're really magnificent when
you throw your arms wide and bare your, ah, chest to my daggers."

Liz felt color creep into her cheeks, but at this point she
couldn't tell whether she was embarrassed or angry. "I know
you've got something to say about my UFO, darn it, so just say
it!"

"*Your* UFO? I wasn't aware you had one, Liz."

"You know perfectly well what I mean, Tim. You heard what
James said about me having seen a UFO. So ask me about it."

His expression grew gentle. "A great many people have seen
UFOs, Liz," he said kindly. "Most sightings are rather ordinary
and unspectacular—bright lights in the sky, that kind of thing. I
presume that if you had seen something more spectacular, you'd
have told me about it years ago."

"Of all the nerve!" The man's ego was incredible! "What
makes you so sure I'd have told you?"

"Well, I guess there's only one instance where you wouldn't
have told me about seeing something more spectacular than lights
in the sky." His expression grew even kinder. Liz thought a candy
striper in a mental hospital couldn't have looked any kinder.

"What instance is that?" she asked acidly. She really had to
know what circumstances he believed would make her keep a
sighting from him. She could hardly wait to learn the limits of
his superlative ego.

"Liz," he said gently, "do you think you saw an alien?"

Liz's mouth opened. Then closed. Then opened again. Did she
think she had seen an alien? She didn't know what made her
madder, the question or the implication inherent in his choice of
words. Not had she *seen* an alien, but did she *think* she had seen
an alien. Slow roasting over hot coals for a century or two was
too good for this man. Someone, somewhere, surely must have

devised a worse torture for people like O'Shaughnessy. Maybe
she should research the Spanish Inquisition....

"Liz? Are you okay?"

She'd have loved to take his concern and shove it back down
his throat. "I'm fine," she said shortly. "And I'll be a whole lot
better when you get the hell out of my office."

"Liz!" He pretended shock. "You don't swear."

"You're right, I don't. It must be something in this office. Out,
O'Shaughnessy. Out!"

The corners of his mouth started twitching, but he manfully
repressed the grin. "I'm gone," he said over his shoulder, and
burst out laughing when she slammed the door behind him.

"What are you doing to that poor girl now, Tim?" Donna
demanded from the front office.

"Not a thing, I swear. I only wanted to know if she saw an
alien when she saw her UFO. That wasn't an unreasonable question, was it?" Still laughing, he ducked into his own office. Will
wonders never cease? he asked himself. Imagine. Practical, no-
nonsense Liz Pennington had seen a UFO!

"Are you ready to leave, Liz?"

She looked up dazedly from her monitor and saw Tim in her
doorway, zipping up his jacket. "Uh, no," she responded
vaguely. "I want to finish this." As always when she found a
problem in a program, she turned into a bulldog. She hated to let
it go, even to get some sleep.

"Want me to hang around?"

She shook her head, her attention already drifting back to the
glowing lines of program code in front of her. "I'll be a while.
Don't bother."

He hesitated. "Are you sure?" He knew all about sexual equal-
ity, and how women could do anything just as well or better, but
that didn't do much to alleviate his protective instincts, particularly when autumn nights were darkening so early.

Liz looked up, and this time her attention focused on him. "I'm
sure. Tim, when I leave here, I'm going to be at home *alone.*
What's the difference?"

He looked sheepish. "Yeah. Guess I just get all macho sometimes."

Her gaze softened. "It's okay."

"Yeah. Your car is locked, right? I don't want you climbing into a dark car that hasn't been locked."

"It's locked." Her tone sharpened slightly.

"Okay. G'night." Turning, he marched away, unable to shake the feeling that he was abandoning her. Dumb. This wasn't the first time she had worked late alone. Still, he double-checked when he locked the front door behind himself. It wasn't dark yet, but it would be before long.

Liz lost track of the time. For security reasons there were no windows in the building other than the one in the front office that was covered with a vertical blind. Consequently, she received no subtle cues as to the lateness of the hour or the darkening of the evening outside. When she emerged from her preoccupation enough to glance at her watch, she was astonished to realize that it was past nine.

Time to quit, she thought, and yawned. Definitely time to quit. A couple of times a week she made extra copies of the disks that she and Tim were using, in addition to their regular backups, and took these home with her for safekeeping. That way, if the building burned down, they wouldn't lose more than a day or two's worth of work. Tonight seemed like a good time to make those extra copies, so she puttered for a while in Tim's office and hers, doing so.

At some point, she started to feel uneasy. She was suddenly, inexplicably and acutely aware that it was night, that she was all by herself in the building, that the businesses on either side of her were closed. That, in fact, she was utterly alone on this street.

Unease settled over her and clung like wet leaves to her back. She tried to shame herself out of the feeling, tried to laugh it away, and failed. The building was too silent for her to forget that it was night and that she was alone.

Suddenly she wished she hadn't been so quick to send Tim on his way. He would have hung around without a second thought and labored contentedly away in his own office. He would have made noise, and paced up and down the hall while he worked. He'd have made at least two pots of coffee, and he would have irritated her with his restlessness, and she would have snapped at him and...

And she wouldn't be alone right now. They'd be chatting casually while they closed up. Eventually he would make one of those outrageous remarks that she always rose to like a fish taking bait, and they would have passed through the front door together, squabbling cheerfully. He would have walked her to her car—funny, she only just now realized that he always did that after dark—and would have seen her safely on her way. Once home, she would have felt safe.

That's how it would have been, and thinking about it relaxed her a little. Nevertheless, she hurried more than she would have if she hadn't grown uneasy. She stuffed the duplicate disks into her briefcase, pulled on her jacket with impatient hands and checked the safes in the front office to make sure everything was properly locked up.

Satisfied, she braced herself to step out into the dark. The night was quiet and calm, disturbed only by the whine of traffic on distant Route 9W. She locked the door and turned to walk to her car and bumped straight into a man.

She screamed.

He jumped back. "Lady, I'm sorry! I thought you saw me!"

Gasping, she leaned back against the door and stared. Saw him? If she had seen him, she never would have come out the door. He was a tall man with long, shaggy, dark hair, and he was dressed in black leather and chains. Chains! God, he looked like a biker from hell.

He held up a hand and backed up farther. "Really, I didn't mean to scare you. Honest. I'm just looking for Tim. He's not at home and I thought he might still be working."

"You...you know Tim?" Her voice was a thin thread over the hammering of her heart.

"Yeah. You're Liz, right? His partner? Look, honest, I'll just move away. That your car? Great. I'll just stand way over here while you get in your car and drive off. I'll make sure you're safe, okay?"

The biker had one arm in a sling, and was backing up swiftly and making such placating gestures that Liz relaxed a bit and started edging toward her car.

"Don't forget your briefcase," the biker reminded her. "Say, you wouldn't have any idea where Tim is hiding out, would you?"

Liz shook her head and grabbed her briefcase up from the

ground, reluctant to take her eyes from the biker for so much as a second. "No. I don't know."

"Hell." The biker sighed, and put his good hand on his hip. "Guess I'll have to wait." He backed up yet again when he saw Liz's continued uncertainty. "Really, lady, I'm not going to hurt you. I wouldn't hurt a fly, honest." He flashed a surprisingly white grin, showing off perfect teeth. "I only *look* bad. I really wouldn't do anything to shame my mama. Really."

Liz felt the corners of her mouth twitching upward. He looked somewhat edgy himself, as if this whole situation had upset him as much as it had her. And he was certainly standing far enough across the parking lot to reassure her that he meant no harm. Nevertheless, as she unlocked her car, she hardly dared take her eyes from him.

"Hey, Liz," he called as she slipped into the driver's seat, "don't work alone so late at night. It's not safe."

She slammed the car door behind her and locked it, thinking that she had certainly met the strangest biker on the face of the earth. After she got the car started, she tossed one last look his way and found he was already gone, vanished as if he had never been.

It was only then that she realized she had never seen a motorcycle. Maybe he wasn't a biker at all.

Chapter 3

Liz argued with herself until she fell asleep about whether she should try to call Tim and tell him about the biker or whatever he'd been. But the biker had said Tim wasn't home. Besides, not once in the time they'd been partners had Liz found it necessary to call Tim at home during off hours, and she didn't want to start the very night he had offered her an "adult relationship." Lord, that rankled!

In the morning, when she stumbled down the stairs to let her cat out, she was still arguing with herself about whether the biker meant anything at all—and whether she had been a fool to turn down Tim's proposition. And whether it really *had* been a proposition.

"Out, Mephisto," she said to the black cat, nudging him with a toe. He glared at her over his shoulder and then stepped outside with princely disdain.

"Am I really letting a cat treat me like this?" Liz asked herself as she closed the door. Yes, she was. And not only a cat. There was the matter of her business partner, who seemed to have lost all his marbles.

The sad fact was that a thirty-year-old woman, whatever her principles and convictions on the matter of sex, eventually began to wonder what she was missing. She began to think that maybe, just once, she ought to nibble on the apple. Just a little nibble, to find out what it was all about. Sometimes she even had the wild feeling that she absolutely, positively didn't want to die a virgin.

And she thought about kids, but that was the dangerous thing. That was in fact the very thing that kept her from succumbing. She wanted children. Oh yes, she was very normal in that respect. The problem was that she didn't want to raise a child without a father. Having been a child without a father, a child who had been abandoned by her father, she very definitely didn't want to do that to her own child. Nor would a visiting father be enough. No, if Liz Pennington had a baby, it was by golly going to have a full-time, live-in father, and nothing less. Unfortunately, she had never met a man who even appeared to be a good prospect for sticking it out. Except Tim. She had, at one time, believed he might be a stayer, but he'd corrected that erroneous assumption, and damned himself, with his very own mouth.

Lord, she found herself thinking an hour later as she backed out of her driveway, the whole world seems to have slipped off center in the past couple of days. There was that weird vandalism, Tim's strange behavior and that biker—who had, she admitted, only *looked* threatening. He sure hadn't done anything threatening. And he hadn't even ridden a bike, as far as she could tell. How could he have anyway, with only one arm?

She wondered where Tim had met anyone like that. Of course, what did she really know about Tim? Then she found herself spending a ridiculous amount of time wondering about his marriage. When had he been married? And to whom? What had she been like? What had happened to her? But mostly it was thoughts of what had happened to his ex-wife that kept her puzzling. Damn, she could kill Tim for throwing out a morsel like that and then walking away before she could ask for an explanation. Of course, she could always ask him at work, but that would be the same as advertising that she was worrying about it, and then his incredible ego would start imagining she was interested in him as a man....

Nope, she couldn't ask him.

Braking at a stoplight, she drew a deep breath to try to relax, but her grip on the steering wheel remained tight enough to whiten her knuckles.

Part of what was disturbing her, she admitted finally, was that she had always been attracted to Tim. From the very first she had felt uncomfortable yearnings and fleeting longings. Over time the feelings ebbed and surged like a slow tide, for months almost vanishing, only to become acute once again. To make things worse, like all women, she occasionally drifted into romantic fantasy, and when she did, Tim always seemed to play a starring role.

Well, fantasies were harmless, and her yearnings were private, and she'd never worried about either one because Tim didn't know. Couldn't know. After all, as long as he was unaware of her as a woman, he would hardly consider that she might be seeing him as a man.

Now the big lummox had changed all that. He had let her know that he was aware, that he was feeling similar urges toward her. It followed that he was bound to be interested in what she might feel toward him. If he noticed—if he suspected—God, she would be so vulnerable!

The thought absolutely petrified her. She could hear her mother's voice, a constant drone from her childhood, spouting ceaselessly about the faithlessness of men, the hardship of womanhood, the exhausting, fatiguing, thankless labors of single parenthood. The realities in store for an imprudent woman were enough to terrify anyone.

Had anyone asked, Liz would have said that she already had quite enough on her plate, thank you, but life didn't bother to ask. She arrived at the office to find both Donna and Tim in the middle of havoc. Both stood ankle-deep in torn and crumpled documents, Donna with her fingers over her mouth in a pose of profound shock, Tim livid with barely leashed fury.

"What happened?" Liz asked, completely unable to believe the mayhem surrounding them.

"We've been robbed," Tim said grimly.

"Of what? We don't even keep any cash!"

"How the hell should I know what they took!" he roared. "Donna, call the FBI."

"Why not the police?" Donna asked weakly.

"Because they got into the security containers," Tim bellowed. "Because I'm standing knee-deep in classified documents. Because we don't know what they took, and because the safes are damaged and we can't protect this stuff. Because the cops don't have clearance to see classified information." Suddenly he lowered his voice. "Will that do, Donna?"

He turned to Liz. "Go ahead and cry, Liz. God knows I want to. Cry for us both."

But she didn't cry—not then. Instead she raised huge, frightened eyes to him.

"We're out of business for a while, Liz."

"I know."

"Don't let it scare you. I've got enough to carry us through."

"That's not what scares me, Tim."

"What then?"

She waved her arm at the mess. "This was wanton. This was deliberate. This was pure, unadulterated violence."

He nodded slowly, his gaze never wavering from her face. He was waiting for the emotional reaction to hit her. It was also hard for him to believe that anyone would be so destructive merely to cover a theft. It didn't seem right, somehow. "I was trying not to think about that."

"Sorry." Shivering suddenly, she looked around again at the destruction. "Our offices?"

"Just as bad. The equipment's smashed, the disks are soaked with water...." He caught her as she started toward the hall. "No. Don't. Liz, honey, believe me, there's no need to go back there. This—" he waved at the front office "—says it all."

She wrapped her arms around herself. "It must have been that biker," she whispered, shivering again. He had been so close. Why had she—why hadn't she *done* something? Called the police? Called Tim? All of this might have been avoided.

"Biker?" Tim roared. "What biker?"

"Tim, please, my *ears!*" Blinking rapidly, Liz fought back her tears.

"What biker?" Tim demanded again, moderating his roar.

"The one who was looking for you when I left last night. He was waiting in the parking lot."

Tim closed his eyes and whispered, "My God." It sounded like a prayer. And then his eyes snapped open and he shouted, "Damn it, Liz, don't you ever, *ever* work late alone again!"

"Who are you to tell me what to do!" she yelled back, glad

for an excuse to be angry rather than scared, even if the feeling wouldn't last. "Come off it! He didn't hurt me!"

"He could have...he could have...you *know* what he could have done to you!"

Anger drove her past caution. "Yes, but he didn't, and I don't see why it matters to you anyway. Only yesterday you were...were...!" She bit the ill-advised words off at the last second.

For a timeless instant it looked as if Tim would really explode. Liz had an uneasy, queasy feeling that she had never really seen Tim angry, not in a way that mattered, and that now she was going to see something that would have been far better left dormant. For at least a full minute the office was so quiet that Liz could hear the rush of her own blood. And in that silence she was seized with regret for her rash and utterly unfair comparison. There was no similarity, and she knew it. The suggestion of an adult relationship hardly compared to rape.

"I'm sorry, Tim," she croaked, hoping to forestall the eruption. "Really, I didn't mean that. I didn't!"

His fists clenched as if he wanted to strangle her, and for another endless moment he didn't respond. When he at last spoke, his voice sounded like grinding gravel. "Watch your step, Pennington. My temper's on a short tether this morning."

Before Liz could utter a word, he turned his back on her. "I thought I told you to call the FBI, Donna."

"I'll call from the back office," Donna said. From the way she held a handkerchief to her mouth, it was clear she needed a few moments to herself. Tim let her go with a quick, gruff pat to her shoulder.

Behind him, Liz wrung her hands. She'd done it this time, she realized miserably. After all these years of saying just about anything that popped into her head, she had almost said something unpardonable.

Tim stooped suddenly, reaching for something concealed around the side of the filing cabinet. When he straightened, he turned to Liz and thrust a cone of green florist's paper at her. "I nearly forgot. These are for you," he said gruffly. "Sorry the circumstances aren't more auspicious." He felt stupid handing them to her now, but damn it, he had bought them last night, and if they didn't get into water soon, fifty dollars' worth of flowers would be so much blackened waste.

Wrapped in the paper were at least a dozen long-stemmed yellow roses. Crazily, Liz felt her throat tighten. Never had anyone given her a bouquet, and certainly not roses. "They're... beautiful," she said huskily around the sudden tightness in her throat. "Uh...why?"

Tim shrugged. "Just an apology for acting like a crud yesterday. My timing's lousy, as usual." Double lousy, because for an instant she had looked ready to weep over the destruction, and now she looked ready to cry over the flowers. The thought of Liz crying did uncomfortable things to his insides. He didn't like the feeling at all. "Just forget it, huh? It's no big deal."

No big deal? Liz, her arms full of beautiful yellow roses and her eyes burning with unshed tears, watched Tim turn away as if he wanted to prevent her from saying another word. No big deal? The big palooka had just made her feel cared for in a way no one had ever made her feel before. He had made her feel cherished someplace deep inside that had never felt cherished. He had made her feel warm and...

Donna's voice, from the hallway, interrupted her dazed reverie. "The FBI is on the way," she said shakily. "Should...should I make coffee?" A sob escaped her. Turning, she fled for the bathroom.

At that exact instant, the tears slipped past the dam of Liz's rapidly blinking eyelids. She managed to swallow a sob, and then another one, but Tim saw the tears spill anyway.

"Oh, hell," said Tim almost desperately, watching the silent trail of one silvery tear, and then another. For lack of anything else to do for her, he wrapped Liz in his huge arms and hauled her up snug against his chest. "It's okay, Liz," he said roughly. "Nothing's broken that can't be fixed."

Except me, he thought, as he held her close and felt every one of her lush curves. Except me. I can't be fixed, I can't be the man you deserve. Every cell in his body screamed for this woman's touch, but he couldn't have her. No way.

Gritting his teeth, he held her and rocked her and tried to concentrate on the destruction around them. That was something he could deal with. The destruction inside him was another matter altogether.

* * *

Liz expected a couple of FBI agents. Maybe even three agents. She didn't expect an invading mob of government agents from three fully different organizations. Recalling, after the first embarrassing inquiry from an agent, that she was the facility security officer, she remembered her duties enough to demand identification at the door from each successive wave of neatly dressed invaders.

The first arrivals were two FBI agents, a pair of gentlemen named Woodrow and Carter. Woodrow looked lanky, tired, but likable enough. Carter was short and balding, and his eyes were too close together. Those eyes bothered Liz somehow. Woodrow and Carter, Carter told her, would be handling this case. They were, he assured her, the only agents she would have to deal with after today.

Hard on their heels arrived the three members of an FBI crime-scene team, who began dusting for fingerprints, taking photographs, and checking the doors, the single window and the safes for signs of forced entry.

Behind them came five agents of the Defense Investigative Service. As soon as the crime-scene team gave permission, they began gathering all the damaged and scattered documents into steel-lock boxes for transport to a safer place. There they would be sorted and cataloged to determined if any classified information was missing. The DIS people were gone by one o'clock.

Midafternoon, two agents of the Naval Investigative Service showed up. Because two of Millennium Software's current defense contracts were navy procurements, the DIS had notified them of the possible compromise of naval classified information. Liz looked glumly at the two uniformed officers, who waved their credentials under her nose. "I suppose," she said stiffly, "you're going to yank our contracts."

The taller of the two, Commander Norton, looked surprised. "Certainly not, unless there's proof of deliberate negligence. These things happen, Ms. Pennington, unfortunately. We just want to assess the damage. And while we're on the subject, I suggest you consider requesting time extensions on your DOD contracts. It appears it'll take you a while to get back up to speed."

Request extensions? She hadn't gotten over her shock enough to begin thinking that far ahead. Propping her chin on her hand, she sat at Donna's desk and watched all the neatly suited men mill around and talk in quiet voices. When questioned, she answered automatically. She was still too shaken up to even get angry when the questions began to repeat themselves. It was as if the investigators hoped to trip her up.

Donna had gotten hysterical at some point during the afternoon, and Tim got permission from Special Agent Woodrow to take her home. For a while Liz was utterly alone with all the multitudinous agents, and that was when they asked her if she suspected anyone.

It was also when she told them about the bikeless biker. For the second time that day you could have heard a pin drop in the office.

"Last night?" Woodrow repeated.

Liz nodded. "He didn't hurt me or anything. In fact, he seemed really concerned about letting me know that he wouldn't hurt me. I guess," she added, her eyes narrowing as she thought over the encounter, "he was as uneasy about encountering a solitary female in a dark parking lot as the solitary female was about encountering him."

"Did he say what he wanted?"

"He was looking for Tim."

"He *said* that?" Carter sounded disbelieving.

"Yes," said Liz sharply, feeling a brief surge of her usual spirit. "He *said* that. He said that he had looked for Tim at home, and when he found him gone he assumed Tim was still working. And," she added in sudden recollection, "he knew who *I* was. But Tim told me this morning that he doesn't know any bikers."

There were suddenly six conversations in the room at once, and Liz stared at her yellow roses, ignoring the cacophony. She really needed to get those blooms into some water. And she really needed to get out of here. If only she could get hysterical as Donna had. Surely then they would let her leave.

But the grilling had just begun.

"Exactly how was he dressed?"

"How tall was he?"

"Could you make out his coloring?"

"What was he driving?"

"Did he have any kind of accent...?"

The questions went around and around like a bad dream, first directed at Liz, and later, upon his return, at Tim. But finally,

finally, there was nothing more that any of them could do except tell Liz and Tim to keep themselves available for further questioning.

Alone at last in the offices of Millennium Software, Tim and Liz looked at one another without expression.

"I'm going home," Liz said, and picked up her purse and the flowers. At the door, she hesitated. "Tim?"

"Hmm?"

"Do I come here in the morning?"

He saw the quiver of her lower lip, the frightened tightness around her eyes, and he ached, but there wasn't a damn thing he could do to lessen this blow. Damned if he knew himself what he was going to do in the morning.

"Just go home and rest, Liz. I'll call you. We'll think of something, but we can think of it later."

She nodded slowly. "Yeah. I feel kind of dazed...." Her voice trailed off and she left.

He knew what she meant. Turning slowly, he surveyed the front office and thought that things didn't look a whole lot better with the floor cleared of documents. No, they didn't look much better at all.

Somehow much later—much, much later, as the autumn twilight was darkening into early night, Tim gravitated to Liz's house. He parked his truck, then stood on the sidewalk and stared at her neat, two-story clapboard home, which boasted a front porch that harkened to a more gracious age before the advent of TV. It reminded him, in a way, of the home he had lived in during his early childhood, just a few miles down the Hudson River from here, before his dad had taken a better paying job in Dallas. Of course, the O'Shaughnessys had lived in a somewhat bigger house; with four kids, that had been a necessity. It hadn't been as nicely kept, but then money had been tight.

Standing there in the deepening night, he watched golden light pour from Liz's downstairs windows, and thought what an inviting picture it made. All of it—the clapboard, the trees just beginning to hint at autumn's blazing colors, the cracked cement walk and the detached, slightly sagging garage to the left. Damn it, it looked like *home,* and he had forgotten what home felt like.

Too many years and too many dusty, gritty miles lay between

him and home. Too many painful, terrible events. Too much innocence had been lost, too much experience had been gained. At
times it shocked him to realize he was barely forty. Most of the
time he felt older and more worn than the Catskills that cradled
this town in their elderly arms.

So, before he went up that walk and barreled into Liz's tidy
little life, he had to lecture himself sternly. He had to patch up a
self-control that had nearly shredded where she was concerned.
He couldn't believe he had all but propositioned her so bluntly.
Hell, he might not be a tactful man by nature, but he sure had
more finesse than that! Or so he would have claimed before yesterday.

She thought of him as a sort of brother. He knew that. He'd
been treating her like a sister since day one, largely because some
of her touchiness reminded him just a little of his older sister,
Colleen. But also because it seemed a safe way to treat a business
partner, as a buddy. It had worked really well for four years, too.

And it was going to keep on working. Squaring his shoulders,
he took a step toward the house. A decent man didn't corrupt
virgins. No. A decent man married them, and there was no way
on earth Tim O'Shaughnessy was going to set himself up for that
kind of pain again. Besides, he was too old, too soiled, too experienced, too disillusioned and too damn graceless for the likes
of Liz Pennington.

When she opened the front door to his knock, Liz didn't look
at all surprised to see him. Without a word, and only the merest
inviting gesture, she stepped back and asked him in. For a moment he allowed himself to survey his surroundings. He had never
entered Liz's house before, but he was somehow unsurprised to
feel it wrap around him like a warm blanket. The foyer was large
and square, the staircase rising along the right wall just beyond
the arched doorway to the living room. To the left he saw a dining
room, and presumed the kitchen was to the rear of the house
behind it.

Nor was the foyer empty. Liz had filled it with charm—a pad-
ded deacon's bench, a coat tree, a table and a vase spilling over
with his yellow roses. The polished wood-plank flooring was covered in an earth-toned braid rug. He had no doubt that the rest of
the house would be just as welcoming.

Liz waved him toward the living room. "Make yourself com-

fortable, Tim,'' she said tonelessly. "I'll get us some coffee."
She hesitated, then said, "But maybe you'd rather have a beer?''

"Coffee will be great, if you have it.''

God! he thought as he stepped into the living room. The place
was a jungle! Half the floor area was taken over by plants of
every shape and size, several of them threatening to erupt through
the ceiling. If she let this go on much longer, a man would need
a machete to get to the sofa. From behind one of the plants a
black cat glowered at him, and Tim returned the look in kind
before turning abruptly. This was not a room he could be comfortable in. Not this one. Grim-faced, he went looking for the
kitchen.

As long as he lived, Tim would never be able to explain why
his awareness of Liz Pennington as an attractive woman had suddenly gone out of control, but he knew the exact moment he
realized that he wasn't going to be able to ignore it. When he
walked into the kitchen, he found her leaning over the counter
and gripping its edge as if her life depended on it. The freshly
poured coffee sat in steaming mugs on a tray, forgotten. Liz's
head was bowed, hidden behind the thick, shiny veil of her hair,
and she suddenly looked small, defenseless. She was a woman
and she needed protecting. The problem would be getting her to
accept his protection without setting her off like a nuclear bomb.

Tim cleared his throat, warning her of his presence. "That's
quite a conservatory in your living room. Did you actually buy
all those plants?''

She whirled and scowled, but remembered her manners just
before she demanded to know what he was doing in her kitchen.
She was horrified that he had found her clinging to the counter
like a Victorian heroine who fainted on every other page, but he
had, and she just hoped he didn't ask for an explanation. She had
cried on his shoulder once today, and she'd be darned if she
would do it again. It was just that, for an instant, she'd had to
struggle to hold on to her emotions.

Before she could speak, he pulled out a chair at her table and
sat, making it perfectly clear that they were going to have coffee
in her nice, sunny, yellow-and-white kitchen—not the living
room.

"Did you buy them all?'' he repeated, ignoring her scowl.

"Uh...'' She blinked and then realized he was asking about

the plants. "Yes, I did, but when I bought them they weren't so big." She gave him a faint, rueful smile. "I seem to have a green thumb."

He leaned over and snagged one of the forgotten cups of coffee. "You could get rid of some of them," he suggested.

Liz was horrified. "How can you even suggest it? They're alive! I can't just...just..."

"No, I guess not," he agreed soothingly. It wasn't his problem, after all. "Sit down, Liz. You look exhausted."

"I am," she admitted, and took a seat on the other side of the table.

"We're ruined," Tim said after a moment. "All our software was on disk. Damn it, he even found the backups we hid in the supply closet."

"No."

"What *no?*" He didn't even have the heart to look up.

"I have copies of most of it in the basement."

"What?" He looked up then, hope springing to life.

She shrugged, too upset for the moment to take pleasure in the surprise she was about to give him. "I never believed in keeping all of my eggs in one basket. I copied everything that wasn't classified and stored an archival copy here. The classified stuff we can get back from Uncle Sam, if we need it for something. The really irreplaceable stuff is in my basement."

"Liz, I'm going to kiss you." Oh, hell. The minute the words were out of his mouth, he wanted to snatch them back. It was the kind of brotherly remark he'd often made to her, but after the past couple of days, it didn't sound brotherly. Hell, it didn't *feel* that way. Not to him. No, for him it made him notice what he was trying *not* to notice. He wondered if she had any idea just how sexy that long hair was when it fell across her breasts, as it was doing now, outlining, accentuating.... Damn it, man, quit it!

"Skip it, Tim. I'm really not in the mood."

At least she didn't seem to have taken his remark wrong. She looked beat, he thought sympathetically. Her shoulders slumped and the corners of her mouth drooped. She needed somebody to light her fuse, but he wasn't in the right frame of mind to do that at the moment.

"We're not ruined," he said, still trying to adjust to the new idea. Constantly, at the back of his mind all day, he'd been trying to plan a comeback from this, had been trying to figure out how they were going to recover from the loss of the software base they had created over four years. They could have recreated it, but it would have been costly in so many ways. Now she was telling him that it wouldn't be necessary.

"No, just temporarily set back." She tried to smile but didn't quite make it. For the moment, it was all she could do to cope. Forget trying to put a bright face on it. "It's going to cost a lot to replace all that equipment."

"That's what we have insurance for."

"Yeah. I wonder how much of a hassle that's going to be." She'd heard, off and on over the years, that it could be a huge hassle. And at the moment she didn't feel as if she had energy or endurance enough for even a small hassle. Today's blow seemed to have left her an empty husk.

"We'll find out."

She nodded grimly, then voiced the thought that had been worrying her sick. "Tim? It wasn't just a random burglary and vandalism. It looked intentional."

"I know." He figured no one could mistake that degree of destruction for a momentary rage. Not only had documents been torn and scattered, but their very expensive Tempest-shielded computers had been smashed beyond repair.

"It felt as if—as if it was meant to be vicious."

"Yeah." He swigged some coffee. He didn't want to add to her worries by letting her see *his* worry. For now, he figured the biggest favor he could do her would be to act as if he were confident everything could be handled and resolved. "Well, we can work at my place until we get things sorted out. I have a couple of computer systems and a modem. We can do basic stuff while we wait."

"I have a computer, too." It disturbed her to think of working in his apartment. Which it wouldn't have, just a few days ago, before he had made a pass at her. She could kill him for that, but she couldn't seem to find the energy.

"That's not the point. The point is we're going to be together every single minute from now on, until somebody gets to the bottom of this."

"Tim—" *Every single minute?*

"Liz." He reached across the table and covered one of her

knotted hands with one of his. "Damn it, Liz, *think*. It was deliberate. It was vicious and malicious. You said so yourself, so I know I'm not imagining it. What if they come back? Do you think I want you to come between these bastards and whatever it is they want when you're all alone in the middle of some dark night? If somebody's really out to destroy us, what do you think will happen when they realize we're working at home?"

She paled. She really hadn't thought along those lines. Trying to absorb the fact that someone had set out to destroy their offices and equipment was quite enough to deal with, and it had never occurred to her that the perpetrator might actually return. That he might try to physically harm them.

Tim was sorry to scare her like this, but for her own safety she had to be scared enough to be cautious. The thought disgusted him.

"We'll work at my place, Liz. We'll work over there and keep copies of everything over here. That way all our eggs won't be in one basket, like you said. And I'll sleep over here. I'm not letting you out of my sight for an instant."

The thought of him sleeping in her home was like a file rasp to her nerves. Fatigue vanished as irritation ignited. "And just where are you planning to sleep, Tim?" Her tone conveyed her displeasure.

"On your couch," he said gently. "I think I neglected to tell you how beautiful your eyes are, Liz."

"That's a non sequitur," she observed drily, some of the color returning to her cheeks.

"Not at all. There is a definite relationship in my mind between volunteering to get stiff on your couch night after night and the beauty of your eyes. I'm convinced Helen of Troy had your eyes, Liz, and very likely your figure, too," he admitted ruefully. "I've never been crazy enough to offer to sleep on a couch before."

Her color deepened. No one had ever said such outrageously extravagant things to her, and automatically she would have dismissed them as poppycock except that there was a light in his eye and a set to his jaw that warned her such a dismissal could be dangerous.

"Thank you, but no thank you," she said firmly. "And let's not waste any energy arguing about it, Tim. We've got more serious things to worry about, such as who might be trying to wipe us out.''

Tim settled back in his chair, and thought fleetingly that he should have accepted her offer of the beer. If Liz thought he was going to drop the subject of her physical safety so quickly, she had another think coming. For the moment, however, he let it go.

"I have a hard time believing this could have been done by one of our competitors," Tim said after a moment. "It's not as if we have all that much competition. In fact, I've been hard-pressed all afternoon to try to think of who among them would stand to gain a damn thing. We're all small two-and three-man firms, and the stuff we bid on is so obscure that the big guys aren't even remotely interested. What's more, I think it's been at least a year since anybody at all bid against us."

"I'm not even thinking about competitors," Liz said. "I'm thinking about that biker."

Tim looked suddenly rueful. "God, yes. The biker. Damn, did I get grilled about *him.* Carter was convinced I was lying when I said I don't know any bikers."

"Why should he think you were lying?" Liz was indignant.

"Well, I suppose because Carter needs a motive for what happened, and somebody being mad at one of us is a good one. And then, of course, the biker was asking for me and he knew I wasn't at home—I was taking in a movie—so that would seem to indicate that the biker and I are acquainted."

"But you really don't know anyone like that."

Tim half shrugged and shook his head. "Not that I'm aware of. I'm not going to say it's entirely out of the realm of possibility that someone I know might have dressed that way, but I'm not *aware* that anyone I know owns black leather and chains." His shaggy brows drew together. "Is there anything else you remember about this guy that you haven't mentioned?"

After a moment's thought, Liz shook her head. "Sorry. But I'll bet he was the one who did it, Tim. The fact that he knows both of us when we don't know him is awfully suspicious."

Tim leaned back in his chair and rubbed his chin thoughtfully. "I guess," he said slowly. "I keep trying to tie up the mess we found this morning with the sign on your glare filter two days ago. If this guy got in on Monday night, I don't understand why he waited two more nights to do his thing."

Liz looked up suddenly. "Maybe...maybe he was planning to toy with us. You know, a little scare here and there. And maybe my seeing him in the parking lot scared *him*. Maybe he decided to do it all at once because I would recognize him if I saw him again."

Tim nodded. "That's good. In fact, it's brilliant. I can buy that without any trouble at all. So now all we need to know is *why*." His frown deepened.

Liz poured some more coffee and then took her seat once again. "And maybe we could think up some way to set a trap for him. I mean, if he came back a second time, and is interested enough to learn who we are, surely he won't just vanish. There's something he wants. If we can figure that out..."

"We haven't got a whole lot to go on," he reminded her. "To set a trap, you've got to know what kind of bait to use, and I don't have the foggiest idea what this creep wants. Do you?"

Miserably, Liz shook her head. "But if we think about it, Tim..."

"Sure. I'll think about it. In fact, I'll be surprised if I think about anything else." Except for the lovely lady sitting across from him, who was looking lovelier with each passing day. Damn it, boy. Down! he told himself sharply. In silence, they both sipped coffee.

"I can't believe those FBI agents!" Liz burst out suddenly. "Did you hear how they were talking to me? 'Are *you* the facility security officer?'" she mimicked in disbelieving tones. "Honestly, you'd have thought that anyone looking at me would have had the common sense to see instantly that I'm a Russian spy!"

"They didn't seem to believe a whole lot," he said sympathetically. "It *did* look kind of weird, though. I mean, all that destruction and all those documents ripped and thrown all over. Damn it, Liz, it gives me chills to even think about it."

The idea of Tim having chills struck Liz as a chilling thought in itself. He was so big, so solid, so secure. How could *he* be frightened of anything? But if he was frightened, then *she* certainly had cause to be.

"Donna was sure upset," she said in lieu of confessing the depths of her own fright.

"Of course she was! We're all scared sh—I mean, well, you know."

"I know." Her green eyes met his uncertainly. "I wish you weren't scared, too," she confessed.

In the past forty-eight hours, Tim O'Shaughnessy had come to realize that he didn't know a damn thing about Liz Pennington. Nothing that really mattered, anyway. He'd never imagined her as being vulnerable, or soft, or frightened, but in the past two days he had seen all of these things in her. Used to thinking of her as a partner and a wizard, both sexless roles, he was suddenly faced with her incredibly appealing femininity. Pennington could be soft, frightened and vulnerable, and liberated male though he was, there was still enough of his primitive ancestors in him to make him respond to those qualities.

Yet, even as his protective instincts came racing to the fore, making him want to flex a few massive muscles and make some rash but bold promises, he remained an honest man.

"I'm not exactly scared," he said over the top of the coffee mug. "I'm just...uneasy, I guess, for lack of a better word. I wouldn't be nervous at all if this had been a common break-in."

That was the one fact that caused Liz to rub her arms to warm them, and then to cup her hands around her coffee mug. "Well, since it obviously wasn't some kind of industrial sabotage..."

Tim's head snapped up. "What makes you so sure of that?"

She blinked. "We agreed..."

"We don't know anything for certain, Liz. Let's not make any broad, sweeping assumptions here."

"Well excuse me!"

He almost smiled. Damn, but he enjoyed lighting her fuse. And this time it had served a dual purpose, for now her color was high where it had been pale, and her eyes were snapping with green venom. He waited a moment and then offered an apology he knew would be even more infuriating.

"No, excuse *me*," he said. "I *did* say we could eliminate our business competitors, didn't I? I apologize, Pennington."

"Well, thank you, Mr. O'Shaughnessy," she said sarcastically.

"I knew you'd be gracious about it. I guess it's safest not to eliminate any possibilities until we have more information."

Jaw set, Liz nodded her agreement. How, she wondered, had she managed to remain sane all these years when she'd had to deal daily with this man?

And *man* was the operative word. The realization slammed into her suddenly. He was always so boyish, so unaffected, so energetic and exuberant, that she had never really noticed it before. Not even when he had held her and made her feel fragile. Not even when he had kissed her into the early storm of passion. He had seemed *safe*. He had seemed like a brother, a pal, a...friend.

He was the guy who lost his disks and forgot his wallet and pumped iron like some high school jock. The guy who preferred a knotty programming problem to the best spy thriller in the world. He was, in short, her partner.

But her heart skipped a beat or two and slipped into high gear with her new understanding. He was busy staring into his coffee and was unaware of her scrutiny as she studied him with new eyes.

He was a man and he was older than she, somewhere in his late thirties. In the corners of his eyes, she saw fine laugh lines. Just below his left ear was the pale beginning of that scar she had never had the nerve to ask him about because it looked as if someone had slashed him with a knife. It was then she realized that they both lived in citadels of their own making and that she didn't know him at all.

But he was very much a man, a flesh-and-blood man, who was sitting across the kitchen table from her and exuding some kind of male pheromone that was doing wacky things to her insides and making her notice that his hands were powerful, large, sprinkled with gingery hair. Making her notice too, that a tuft of that same hair showed in the V of his shirt.

"Well," he said, looking up from his coffee and interrupting her rather astonishing line of thought, "I guess I'd better go get my stuff if I'm going to be staying here for a while."

"Forget it." The words were out, flat and forbidding, before her mind even formed them. She just plain panicked at the thought of sharing a roof with this man. With any man.

"Forget it?" he repeated. Now his own eyes were sparking warningly.

"Sure. That FBI agent was probably right. It was most likely some drug addict who was infuriated because there was no money in the safes."

"You really think so?" His voice betrayed nothing, and his usually open face was suddenly inscrutable.

Liz shivered suddenly, aware that some part of her *didn't* think

so. "Of course," she said. "I can't see any point in being paranoid about this."

"You lie," said O'Shaughnessy bluntly. "You're as paranoid
about this as I am."

"Oh, just shut up!"

"Temper, temper." He leaned across the table and seized her
hand in a painless but unbreakable grip. "Liz, I'm not going to
let you bury your head in the sand—even if it would put you in
a delightfully interesting position—"

"Tim!" His name emerged as little more than a shocked croak.

"Never mind. You're not an ostrich and I'm not going to let
you behave like one. As long as there is the remotest possibility
that these people intend any further violence, you're going to have
to prepare for the worst."

"I don't need a watchdog!"

"I was thinking of myself as a bodyguard," he said drily.

"Men! A few muscles and you develop these crazed notions
about being invincible! What makes you think you can protect
me any better than I can protect myself?"

His face suddenly grew grim and remote. A long moment
passed before he replied, and Liz had time to regret her remarks.
She was old enough to know better than to tell a man he was no
stronger, braver, swifter or smarter than she was. At least, not
unless she was prepared to suffer the consequences. Men were
touchy about such things.

"Tim, I didn't mean—"

"Of course you did," he interrupted. He had a bad habit of
interrupting her. "I guess you have a right to know the credentials
of someone who's offering to protect you."

"Tim, really, I—"

"Let's just say that I have some training in this area and leave
it at that, shall we?"

Ten million questions immediately occurred to her, but she
swallowed them all. The answers, she felt, lay beyond a door
labeled Vietnam, and pushing her way in there would be trespassing unforgivably. That was a place no one had the right to
enter without invitation.

"Okay," she said. "Fine. You have some training. That
doesn't mean I'm going to let you move in here. In fact," she

said, rising with determination, "I am telling you in plain and simple terms, O'Shaughnessy—there is no way on God's earth that you're going to move in here!"

Chapter 4

"Tim O'Shaughnessy, you are *not* moving into my house!"

"Don't screech, Pennington. It doesn't become you." He moved forward, his arms laden with a heavy box, and Liz had no choice but to back up.

"I'll call the cops," she warned him. Her heart was thudding so loudly she was sure he could hear it. Tim in her house, all the time. How was she ever going to survive that without turning into a babbling idiot?

"Go ahead. I'll leave before they get here and come back as soon as they're gone."

"I'll tell them that's what you're planning to do."

He smiled at her over the top of the box. "Ah, but will they believe you? Or will they think you're just a frustrated spinster who's gone over the edge?"

That almost—but not quite—silenced her. Trust O'Shaughnessy to throw her virginity up to her as if it were a failing she should be ashamed of. The devil of it was, around *him* it *was* embarrassing! "I'll show them your things!"

"How will you prove they're not yours?"

Frustrated almost beyond bearing, Liz clamped her teeth together. "I'll get even for this, O'Shaughnessy."

"I can hardly wait." Still smiling, he strode past her. "This is your last chance to tell me where to roost. Otherwise I'll set up housekeeping in your jungle. Damn it, Pennington, don't these plants give you claustrophobia?" It was, somehow, easier to remember that she was his business partner when he called her by her last name, and it was doubly imperative that he keep that in mind while he was under her roof.

"I like my plants, thank you."

"I can imagine. If I fall asleep in here, I'll wake up in the morning the prisoner of a crawling vine of some kind. You'll find my naked body being absorbed by some hungry—"

"Just shut up, damn it!" More disturbed than she wanted to admit by the notion of O'Shaughnessy naked, she felt something inside her snap like a stretched rubber band. Turning, she began to stalk away, wishing him to the devil.

"It's rude to abandon a guest," he remarked from behind her. She heard the sound of his box hitting the floor.

"I don't recall inviting you!"

He caught up with her before she made it to the second stair. Turning her into his arms, he hauled her up against a broad chest that seemed unexpectedly comforting. All the fight drained out of her.

"I'm sorry, Liz," he said gently. "You've had enough to contend with today. I shouldn't be lighting your fuse."

"No, you shouldn't." Darn, she was hovering right on the edge of tears and his gentleness wasn't helping one bit. His powerful arms surrounded her and cradled her as carefully as if she were a delicate blossom. She was astonished by how comforting that embrace was, how satisfying. She could easily become addicted.

But she didn't want to become addicted, not to O'Shaughnessy at any rate. The man was infuriating. Egotistical. Muscle-bound. Crazy.

Warm. Strong. Hard.

Hard?

With a twist, Liz wrenched free. She climbed backward up an additional two steps to place a safe distance between them.

"O'Shaughnessy." Her voice cracked. She wasn't prepared to deal with this. Not even when they had kissed had he allowed her to become aware of his arousal. It was…frightening. And they had done nothing but embrace!

"Yes, Pennington?" The devil couldn't have smiled any more charmingly.

"If you're going to stay here, we need to lay down some ground rules."

"Sure." His smile faded. "What's the first one?"

"No touching."

He nodded. "Okay. No touching what? No touching your plants? Your cat? Your furniture?"

Liz ground her teeth and then snapped, "You *know* what I mean, O'Shaughnessy!"

"Right," he said quietly, and all devilment was gone from his expression. "No touching Elizabeth Pennington. Got it. You're safe with *me*, lady. I got enough holes in my hide already."

Without another word, and giving the best performance Liz had ever witnessed of an offended male, he turned and stalked toward the door. She bit her lip, worrying it. He reached the door.

"O'Shaughnessy?"

He halted, keeping his back to her, and angled his head a little, just enough to indicate that he was listening.

"You know what I meant," she said pleadingly.

"Do I?" He turned and faced her. "I was comforting you, Liz. I can't help how my body reacts to you, but you didn't have to act as if I were going to rape you. You don't have to lay down rules so I don't take advantage of you. If you don't realize that without my telling you, then you haven't been paying very good attention these past years."

She had hurt him. That jarred her as much as anything, and shook her crumbling control. So much for his impenetrable ego. "I'm sorry." She really was, and she hung her head contritely. "I just...I guess I..." She looked up, her whole expression pleading for understanding. "I know it's ridiculous at my age, but I don't know how to handle these things! I never...I mean nobody ever...Tim, I don't want to be a *tease!*"

He stepped toward her, hardly able to believe what he was hearing, even less able to believe that prickly, proud Liz was actually admitting such things to him.

"And I've heard that men can't stop..."

"Shh," he said, and once again folded her into his arms, feeling the tension in every rigid line of her body. He'd heard enough, and he wanted to spare her the agony of admitting any more.

"What do you do when your program goes into an endless loop?"

Her voice was muffled against his chest. "Pull the plug."

"I have a plug, too, Pennington. All you have to do is say, 'No, O'Shaughnessy,' and I stop. I can *always* stop. And I promise, I'll never think you're being a tease. Just relax, Liz."

And amazingly, she did exactly that. She leaned against him, and let him hug her, feeling again the aching urge to weep, this time because it felt so good to be held. Because it felt so good to be held by Tim. In an instant of bleak honesty, she admitted just how much and for how long she had wanted to be held by him. And with equally bleak honesty, she faced the fact that he would never be the kind of man she could give herself to. That, beyond sex, he would never want what she had to give him. He had told her so himself.

But that didn't prevent her from soaking up the unprecedented warmth and goodness of being in his arms. Nor did it prevent her from taking this little bit from him, this one little hug that was surely safe because he was only trying to comfort her.

Abruptly he let her go, unwilling, any longer, to endure holding what he could not have. "Now, you never did tell me where you want me to roost."

Liz watched him heft his box once again as she tried to adapt to the unsettling realization that Tim was a much more complex man than she had ever imagined. The brotherly bear was proving to be an enigma. A mystery. And, unfortunately, she loved mysteries.

"Liz?" He startled her back to reality.

"I'll give you the guest room," she said.

Watching her bottom sway up the stairs ahead of him, he had time to regret his tactlessness about her innocence. How the hell was he supposed to have guessed that she was *this* innocent? Short of being cloistered in a convent her entire life, there seemed no conceivable way that she could have attained her present age in such an uneducated state. Hell, until this moment, he never would have believed a woman even half as attractive as Liz could have reached the age of thirty without at least some heavy petting. The virginity bit, rare as it was, was not incredible. The innocence was what was incredible. Utterly, totally, stunningly inconceivable.

It was another warning. He might be hotter than Hades for her, but inexperience and innocence were not to be taken lightly.

The guest room reminded him of an arbor. The furniture was white wicker, the walls a pristine white, and plants grew on every flat surface except for the bed. Vines twined up the wall over the wicker headboard and spilled out of baskets on the window ledges.

"Have you seen a psychiatrist about this obsession?" he asked mildly.

"Have you seen a psychiatrist about your aversion to plants?" Liz retorted, returning to their more quarrelsome mode with relief.

Tim set his box down on the colorful quilted bedspread and flashed her a roguish grin. "I'm not averse to plants, m'dear. Just jungles." Looking down, he saw the malevolent green gaze of her black cat. "That critter hates me, Liz. If it goes for my jugular, I won't be responsible."

Liz glanced down at her cat. "Mephisto is a sweet creature and he'd never do anything so gruesome, Tim. You have a horrifying turn of imagination! First carnivorous vines and now this."

"Mephisto, huh?" Squatting, he held out his hand and made a soft clucking sound. After a perceptible hesitation, Mephisto deigned to approach. Tim scratched behind the animal's ears, and the traitorous cat was won over forever.

She should have expected this, she thought later that evening. Tim O'Shaughnessy was not a man to do things by halves. Anybody else would have arrived with a toothbrush and a change of clothes. Not O'Shaughnessy. Oh, no. By ten o'clock that evening he even had his weight-lifting equipment set up in her basement.

The basement had been finished by the previous owner and made into a pleasant family room. When she'd bought the house, Liz had envisioned it as a place where children might someday play, if she ever chanced to meet that mythical beast, the Forever Man. But never, not once, had she envisioned it as a Muscle Beach gym.

With the amount of tonnage he was carting in from his truck and down those stairs, Tim broke into a heavy sweat. Before long, his shirt clung damply to every bulging muscle. For an instant, Liz thought he was going to strip it off, but then he dropped his hands and sat on the tiled floor in order to assemble a weight bench. She felt absurdly disappointed. Considering how hard he worked on that body, it must be a sight to behold.

"Liz? Hand me that three-quarter wrench, will you?"

She pulled it out of his large red toolbox and passed it to him. "When did you start lifting weights?" That seemed like a safe enough avenue of conversation.

Tim wiped his forehead with the back of his hand and glanced at her from the corner of his eye. "Would you believe that when I was in high school I was the proverbial ninety-seven-pound weakling?"

Liz felt the corners of her mouth tipping upward. "No."

"Well, it was more like one hundred and forty-five pounds," he admitted. "I grew straight up without filling out. More than anything else I wanted to be a tough he-man." He shook his head. "Take it from me, Liz. There's nothing stupider on the face of the earth than an eighteen-year-old boy."

The admission had a curious effect on her. Suddenly she felt less wary of him than she had in the past two days. She sat cross-legged beside him and watched him tighten nuts and turn screws. "So you sent away for your amazing Charles Atlas bodybuilding stuff?"

"I should have been so smart." Picking up a rag beside him on the floor, he scoured his face with it. "Excuse me. I'll cool off in a minute or two." He twisted another screw into place. "No, Liz, bulging biceps weren't enough for me."

"What did you do?"

"Enlisted in the army and volunteered for the Special Forces. You could say Uncle Sam made me into a man."

Something in his voice warned her that this was a topic she should skate over lightly, so she did, despite an incredibly urgent desire to know everything about him. "And that's when you started lifting weights?"

"Not exactly. That came *after* the army. It's a great way to burn off steam."

Liz nearly succumbed to an urge to touch his arm in sympathy. This bold, brash bear of a man had secret depths and secret scars, and she suspected that in a roundabout way he had just tried to tell her something he didn't tell very many people. Tim O'Shaughnessy held his nightmares at bay with an iron bar and iron plates. But even though he'd just hinted at the truth, she suspected he didn't want her to acknowledge that she had understood. He certainly didn't want to talk about it.

She cleared her throat. "I thought you burned off steam by insulting me."

He flashed a grin. "Yeah. That, too. I like the way you get mad, Liz. Your eyes flash fire, your, ah, chest heaves, your cheeks get these bright red spots and you squeak."

"I do *not* squeak!"

"Yes, you do. Your voice soars right up the register and you get this little crack in it."

He was doing it again, she realized as her temper flared. He was lighting her fuse, but this time she understood why. He was distracting her from uncomfortably personal ground. Her anger trickled away.

"Okay," she said mildly. "I squeak."

"Damn it, don't take all the fun out of it! Where's your grit? Your steel? Your magnificent fury?"

Liz's mouth dropped open and then a laugh spilled out of her. "My 'magnificent fury'?"

"A little poetic license," he admitted, returning his attention to the partially assembled bench. What the hell had possessed him to bring up the army? he wondered irritably. The last thing on earth he wanted to do was to try to explain Vietnam and its aftermath to somebody who had never been there. He had the veterans' center if he needed to talk.

Yeah, said a voice in his head, but sometimes it's not enough to talk to someone who was there. Sometimes you need absolution from someone who *wasn't* there. Someone untouched. That was something he'd never found.

"I thought you lifted weights at a health club," Liz said after a moment.

"Nothing so trendy. I work out at a gym—a sweaty, smelly, male-oriented, macho dive. The last woman who darkened the threshold had hair on *her* chest."

Another peal of laughter escaped Liz. "Then why are you setting up all this stuff here? Won't you miss your B.O. fix?"

"Sure, but you're more important, Liz. I'm not going to leave you unprotected for so much as a minute."

"Tim…"

"No. If anything happened to you, I wouldn't be able to handle the bookkeeping. Besides, you're our graphics expert. Bite your tongue. Accept the inevitable.''

From experience, Liz knew just how "inevitable" Tim could be. It would have been easy to get angry. She wasn't used to other people running her life. She couldn't conceive of how she was going to handle having Tim breathing down her neck all the time. On the other hand, she was touched that he cared enough to inconvenience himself in this way. And when she thought of the insane destruction she had witnessed at their office, she was grateful to him, as well.

"Just don't expect me to do all the cooking," she said finally, by way of surrender.

He winked at her. "Just tell me how you want to divvy up the chores.''

She couldn't sleep. Having Tim under her roof was proving to be a horrendous distraction and temptation. She had left him in the basement setting up his equipment, and she had come up to bed long before she finally heard his step on the stairs. She should have been asleep by then.

Instead, she lay awake, staring at the patterns made by light creeping around the edges of her curtains from the streetlight and tried not to feel sorry for herself. Liz hated self-pity with a passion that kept her chin up and her eyes dry in very trying circumstances, and she had known her share of difficulties.

Twelve years ago, virtually the instant Liz had begun her freshman year in college, her mother had remarried. Liz had been happy for her. Her mother was a young woman in her early thirties, and it had seemed natural and right that she start another family, this time with a man who cherished her. Liz had even managed to believe that she wasn't at all jealous of her mother's attentions to her new family even though they excluded Liz entirely. She convinced herself that she was quite content her mother had only come to visit her twice, and had asked Liz to visit only once. They spoke on the phone, after all. Two or three times a year.

But on rare occasions, Liz felt lonely, and was aware of her solitude in life. Friends—and she had quite a few—didn't fill some of the gaps in her heart. They weren't the same as fathers, brothers, mothers, lovers. All the things she didn't have. All the things she had never had and apparently would never have.

Now, in her weakened lonely state, she thought of Tim, just down the hall, just a couple of steps away. If she walked into that room, he would take her into his bed. No man would pass up such an opportunity—or so her mother had warned her, among her many warnings. But she wanted more. She wanted everything that nobody in the world seemed to want to give her.

She wanted love. And the absolutely ridiculous thing about that was that she had no idea whatsoever how it felt to love or be loved. The thought tightened her throat and made her eyes burn as she lay alone in the silence of a deep, dark night.

Early the next morning, Liz was roused from a restless sleep by a strange, intermittent clanking noise. Darn, she thought as she staggered to the bathroom, the heater must be dying. Naturally it would happen just as fall was setting in and repairs couldn't be postponed. Just as their business had been…had been…

What the hell had happened to the bathroom?

Hideous, revolting, eye-jarring orange towels hung beside her dusty rose ones. Her creams and lotions had been shoved to one side of the counter to accommodate a mess—literally—of shaving gear. In the dish beside her pink bar of skin soap sat a bar of pumice soap that bore dark, greasy-looking stains. O'Shaughnessy didn't use shaving cream, she discovered. Beside the pink-flowered can of her own cream was a shaving mug and brush. An *old* shaving mug. It must have had at least ten years' accumulation of soap drips on its sides. The shower curtain, which she always kept drawn to prevent mildew, was crushed up against one end of the enclosure. A wet towel hung over the tub edge. Her tube of toothpaste had been used, squeezed from the top and left with the cap off.

And not until she sat down did she realize that the toilet seat had been left up.

Somehow, she managed not to screech. She even managed not to lose her temper. She was a terror in the morning, but this morning she managed to hang on to her cool. The heater was more important, and O'Shaughnessy couldn't be changed no matter how mad she got, anyway. She ought to know that by now.

If she blew up at him, he'd just grin back at her. Why did he have to get so darn amused when she was mad?

She put down the toilet seat, drew the shower curtain across the enclosure so it could dry evenly, screwed the top back onto the toothpaste and headed downstairs in her robe and scuffs. The man's presence in her house was discomfiting enough. She refused to let it force her to dress before breakfast.

Tim had already made the coffee. The kitchen was full of its rich aroma, and Liz poured herself a mugful before following the clanking noise down into the basement. How much would a new heater cost? she wondered.

And then she forgot completely what she was supposed to be doing. Transfixed, she halted halfway down the stairs and stared.

Clad only in the skimpiest, tightest, thinnest royal blue nylon shorts she had ever seen and a pair of jogging shoes, Tim lay on his weight bench like a pagan sacrifice and bench pressed what even her inexperienced eye recognized as about two hundred and fifty pounds. His arm and chest muscles bulged, his face strained into a reddened grimace and at the last instant he gave a muffled shout before dropping the bar into the rack over his head. The familiar clank it made told her the noises she'd heard hadn't been her heater after all.

It would have been a great time to let her morning temper fly. She could have blasted him for waking her at such an ungodly hour, she could have raked him over the coals for the mess in her bathroom. Instead, quietly, not even letting him know that she was there, she settled onto a step and watched him.

He breathed deeply and raggedly for a minute, and then sat up, shaking his arms to loosen them. Then he started in on another exercise.

She supposed she had never really appreciated the amount of effort involved in pumping iron. She hadn't really thought about the amount of solitary dedication, the amount of determination, or even the amount of pain. There *was* pain. She saw it on his face, heard it in his grunts and muffled shouts.

She had also never realized just how well-constructed Tim was. Color crept into her cheeks as she admired narrow flanks and powerful thighs. Her breath quickened as she studied that broad, hard, furry chest. He was really a splendid specimen.

Except, she realized suddenly, for the scars on his legs. There were dozens of them—pale, slashing lines, so old that they had almost faded completely.

"Shrapnel."

He spoke the word and her eyes snapped upward to find he had caught her staring. He had draped a towel around his neck while she had stared at him, and he mopped his face with it.

"Shrapnel?" she repeated.

"It's a pretty generic word now," he remarked easily as he lifted the weight bar from the rack and set it on the floor. "Originally it came from an English artillery officer, Henry Shrapnel, the inventor of something called spherical case shot, back in the early 1800s. It was a cannonball that exploded in the air over the heads of enemy troops and shot a hail of musket balls downward at them. Now we use it to cover any kind of flying debris from an explosive shell."

"Oh." She forced herself to keep her eyes on him. The last thing she wanted was for him to think she was staring at him as if he were a freak.

"Imagine having your name remembered like that." Turning, he smiled at her and changed the subject before she could ask the questions that were gathering in her hazel eyes. "Did you find the croissants?"

"Uh, no. I didn't even look." She stared up at him, unable to move or react normally. As if she were caught in some kind of honey or molasses.

"I went over to the bakery on Sunrise this morning and got them fresh out of the oven. The bag's on the counter." His smile widened a shade as he bent over her and took the still warm mug from her hands. "The smell of this coffee has been driving me crazy ever since you came down here." Without so much as a by-your-leave, he downed it.

"You knew I was here?" The realization made her heart pound. To think that he had known she was staring at him like a...like a...groupie! "Why didn't you say anything?"

"Because *you* didn't." His eyes twinkled. "I know your morning temperament, Liz. If you want to be quiet, I'm not going to start talking."

So he had known she was watching, gawking like any teenage girl. Her cheeks fired and she tried to stand up, but his hand settled on her shoulder. Her heart started a heavy, slow beating and her eyes followed the movements of his other hand as he set the mug on the step beside her. Then that hand, too, came to settle on her other shoulder, but not so heavily. No, this hand moved gently, and one of its fingers ran lightly, enticingly along her jaw and neck. Slowly, with gentle pressure, he tilted her face up to his. Only inches separated them as he bent over her.

"You're lovely, Liz," he said in a husky whisper. "Even first thing in the morning, and that's no small feat."

She felt hypnotized, drugged, as she looked into his gray eyes. Strange ribbons of sensation seemed to run from the touch of his fingertips to the rest of her body and she wanted more, so much more. Seeking it, she leaned into his touch as if she were a kitten.

"Good morning, sweetheart," he whispered, and covered her mouth with his. His last rational thought was that no healthy male could have resisted the way she had looked at him, the way she had leaned into his hand. He promised himself that he would keep it light, just a good-morning salute, but he broke the promise as soon as he made it, and then he quit thinking about anything but the feel of her, the taste of her, the way she made his blood race.

Sweetheart? Before she could wonder at his choice of endearment, she was lost in his kiss. He may have intended only a gentle salute, but her lips parted at once in yearning, and he took her invitation seriously. He kissed her as if it were the first time. His tongue sought gently, swept tenderly, heightening the sensitivity of every nerve ending in her mouth. He explored, learning every texture and every taste of her moist warmth.

But slowly something changed, bringing Liz to her feet so that she could lean into him, causing Tim's chest to heave with deepening breaths. She was standing two steps higher than he, and it brought her face level with his. Without hesitation, she threw her arms around his neck and returned his kiss with every bit of the passion he was awakening in her.

"Ah, Lizzie," he whispered roughly, when he broke from her to catch his breath. "Darlin' girl...."

He was wearing next to nothing, a realization that penetrated Liz's pleasurable haze in the most satisfying way. Her hands left his shoulders, moving downward, and then her inexperience caught her between one breath and the next, freezing her hands, beginning to clear her head.

"Touch me, Lizzie," he murmured against her lips. "Go on, touch me. I want you to."

His roughly whispered words were an aphrodisiac, banishing her hesitation in an instant and setting fire to her blood. She forgot her fears and her hands dived into the pelt on his chest, combing through the soft hair in kneading, hungry movements. Crazy half thoughts flitted through her mind, a swarm of impressions. *Soft hair. Smooth skin. Hard muscle.*

He drew a harsh, shuddering breath at her daring caresses, and then his tongue plunged into her mouth in a primitive mating rhythm. Deep inside her, a responsive throbbing began, weakening her knees until her legs tingled with a strange, numb fire.

Tim felt her surrender, felt how far he had taken her, and it shook him into awareness. This was *Liz*, for crying out loud! Of all the stupid, unforgivable things he could have done, this took the cake! He had no business arousing her like this, when he couldn't satisfy her without betraying her. She needed far more than he could ever give, and he knew that. He knew that.

Though it was nigh impossible to let go of so much tempting, willing womanhood, he gently broke the kiss and held her soothingly, waiting for her to recover.

Waiting for *her* to recover? Hell, who was he kidding? Waiting for *him* to recover. Him, Tim O'Shaughnessy, a man who was rapidly proving himself to be the world's greatest masochist. With all the easy pickings in the world, why did he have to want this one woman with a hunger bordering on desperation? Why was he standing here with a pounding in his body so fierce that it felt like the hammer of war drums? Why was he risking a perfectly good friendship, and a perfectly wonderful partnership, at the promptings of a base part of his anatomy—a part which had ceased to rule him years ago?

There were no answers, of course. Nothing but Liz's trembling warmth, which rested so trustingly in his embrace. That trust pierced him with sharp awareness. He wasn't worthy of it. Hell!

Suddenly Liz pulled away from him and turned so quickly that she nearly tripped on her bathrobe. "I need to get ready for work," she said huskily, and fled.

Oh my God, she thought, as she climbed the stairs swiftly, feeling his eyes on her back. How could she have let herself go like that? How could she have touched him like that? How could she have been so bold? What must he think of her? Hadn't she been the one to lay the ground rules about no touching? And hadn't he been the one to warn her he wasn't a forever kind of man? And knowing all that, she had practically invited him to help himself to her.

Oh, Liz, she thought as she reached her bedroom and closed the door behind her. Leaning back against the door, she tried to catch her breath and found that her heart didn't want to slow down, her breathing didn't want to ease up and her mind didn't want to let go of all the vivid sensual feelings that had branded her nerve endings like wildfire. The vague tinglings and yearnings she had felt in the past couldn't begin to hold a candle to what Tim had just evoked in her.

How would she ever be able to look him in the eye again? *He knew now.* He knew just how vulnerable she was to him. She could snap and grump and snipe at him as much as ever, but he would know now *why* she did it. Oh, God, why couldn't things just go back to normal?

But they couldn't, and she knew it. She was no longer the innocent she had been one short half hour ago. Trembling with her newfound knowledge, she crossed her arms over her breasts and tried to hold in the ache.

She felt as if she were standing, naked and alone, in a cutting cold wind, yearning for warmth and shelter. She had been standing in that wind for years, and had never thought much about it until now, because she'd never known anything else. It was a bitter realization that innocence, not conviction, had been her shield all these years.

How could she continue to live a cold and barren existence having this newfound knowledge?

Chapter 5

"I guess we should go to the office first," Tim suggested as he backed his truck out of her driveway later that morning. "The Feds made off with everything that remotely looked classified, but we can probably salvage notes and stuff that can be useful."

When she didn't immediately reply, he hit the brakes and looked at her. She looked lost somehow. Sad. He feared he was the cause of that, and cursed himself for the hundredth time. How could he have forgotten his control like that?

"Liz?"

She expelled a long breath and gave him a wan smile. "Sorry. I'm just trying to get myself mentally ready to face that mess. Every time I think about it, I get goose bumps."

This was not like Liz, he thought. His Liz was feisty, always sharp and ready for a scrap, especially first thing in the morning. She ought to be yelling at him about the way he had manhandled her, or berating him for waking her so early.

"Are you feeling okay?" he asked with genuine concern.

"I guess. Why?"

"You haven't snapped my head off once yet, and we've been together for the past hour. And first thing in the morning, too."

The corners of her mouth lifted a little higher. "Do you *like* me yelling at you?"

"That depends. When you're spitting mad over some little thing, you're cute, and I can enjoy it because I know it'll blow over. But having you mad about something important is something I wouldn't like at all."

Liz was touched by this left-handed indication that he cared, but she definitely didn't want him to know that. She managed a light retort. "Well, I almost got mad about your towels."

He blinked. "My towels? What the hell is wrong with my towels?"

"They're *orange,* O'Shaughnessy."

A martial gleam came to his gray eyes. "So? Orange is a nice, bright color. It reminds me of pumpkins, of autumn and Halloween. And Thanksgiving."

"Fine. It has its place. But in a room decorated in maroon and dusty rose, it's an act of visual violence."

"Ah!" Understanding dawned. "Well, it's only temporary, Pennington. If it looks like it may last a few weeks, I'll buy some white towels so I don't offend thine eyes."

"Right. That's why I didn't yell. It's only temporary. Besides, I have to admit I was impressed that you even thought to bring towels. Especially when you didn't bring toothpaste."

He lifted a shaggy brow. "You noticed?"

"How could I *not* notice? You left the cap off and you squeezed the tube at the top."

He winced dramatically. "Damn, I hoped you wouldn't notice that." Then he chuckled. "I'm sorry. Really. I have every intention of buying my own toothpaste today."

Liz threw up her hands. "Just how am I supposed to snap your head off if you're going to be so agreeable?"

He laughed, and after a moment she joined him. Somehow, he had managed to lighten her mood, and the improvement lasted right up until they pulled into their small parking lot. Then it dissipated, as if a cloud had passed over the sun. Without looking at her, Tim reached over and gave her hand a brief, reassuring squeeze.

Donna's car was already there, a small surprise to Tim since he had told her to take the day off. Knowing Donna, she probably felt embarrassed over her hysterics yesterday and wanted to make it clear that she was once again in firm control. And considering her distaste for the least bit of disorder, chances were she was already cleaning like a fiend.

"We'd better stop her," Tim said as he slid from the truck. "She might throw out something we can use."

Liz had more respect for Donna than that. At least that was her immediate reaction to Tim's remark—until she started thinking about the variety of things that only she or Tim would recognize as important.

"What are you doing here?" Tim demanded of Donna once they found her. "I thought I told you to take the day off."

"You did, but I couldn't stand being in the house with that kid one more minute."

Tim's lips quirked. "Which kid?" Donna had two sons.

How could Tim be amused? Liz wondered, her gaze wandering over the unbelievable destruction. How could he possibly carry on as if this were a *normal* day?

"James," Donna said tartly. "The oldest. The college student. The one everyone believes is mature and courteous."

Tim valiantly suppressed a full-fledged grin. "What did he do?"

"Nothing, really. He just didn't go to bed last night. He wandered through the house all night. I had to get up at least four times to tell him to turn down the TV, and I lost track of the number of times he banged or rattled something." She shrugged. "I don't think it was deliberate, but he was still buzzing when I got up this morning. I figured if I didn't get out of there I'd probably kill him."

"Is he all right?" Liz asked, forgetting the mess. "He's not sick or anything?"

"He's done this before. Sometimes he just can't sleep. I pity his wife."

Tim unleashed his grin. "Once he *has* a wife, the problem will probably stop."

Donna pursed her lips and Liz spoke his name in those roundly disapproving tones only she could achieve, disturbed that he might have embarrassed Donna.

"Sorry," he said, too meekly. He cast a devilish look at Liz.

"It's all right, Liz," Donna said soothingly. "Don't be mad at

Tim. He's just being a man, and there are few enough around anymore who know how to act like one.''

"You know why men aren't men anymore?" Tim asked Donna. "It's all this women's lib stuff. Now don't get me wrong, I think women are just as competent, capable and smart as men. Hell, I've got a woman for a business partner, right? I couldn't possibly be a male chauvinist."

"Absolutely not," Donna agreed. "Not a hint of it anywhere in your makeup, Tim."

"Certainly not. The problem with men today, Donna, is that women's lib has forbidden us to be men. Think about it. We get turned on by pretty women. Women *are* sex objects to men. That doesn't mean we can't admire their other qualities, but hell's bells, the last thing a man is allowed to do these days is admit that a woman *does* turn him on. We're born to be sexual aggressors, but the minute you make a pass some woman is calling you an M.C.P.''

"I never thought of that," Donna said.

"It's true. Men love to look at women. These days if you watch a woman's buns as she walks down the street, she's apt to call the cops. And forget taking in an eyeful in the workplace. That's sexual harassment. So men can't look, they can't talk, they can't make a pass, and before they can uh...get friendly, they have to prove they're sensitive and that they really admire her mind. So here we are, unable to be men. Is it any wonder that we've turned into such a bunch of wimps?''

"You'll never be a wimp," Donna assured him.

Liz was seething, but before she could marshal a suitably cutting comment, Tim plunged on.

"That's only because I refuse to believe that being male is a crime of some kind. You know, it's really awful when you think about it. Biologically the entire race has evolved to give women attributes that turn men on, and *make* men turn on when they see a woman. All this so the species can survive. Whether women want to admit it or not, survival of the human race depends on them being sexy and us being horny.''

Donna sounded suddenly stifled. "I never thought of it quite that way, Tim."

"Of course you didn't," he said kindly. "You're a woman. Women don't think in those terms. They prefer things being all gauzy and soft. They want romance all tied up in a great big bow of love. That's natural. After all, they bear the children and want to ensure that those children will be fed, sheltered and cared for. I'm not arguing that there's anything wrong with the way women think and feel about these things. I'm just saying that there's nothing really wrong with the way *men* feel about these things, either. Believe me, no guy was ever attracted to a woman's mind *first*, but that doesn't mean he can't come to admire it later.''

Liz suspected Tim might have gone on forever in this irritating vein, but Chuck, the NPS delivery man, chose that very moment to make his morning appearance, with a delivery of office supplies. He hardly stepped through the door before he looked around the office and gave a low whistle.

"This doesn't look like spring cleaning," he remarked.

"Nope," Tim agreed. "We were vandalized the night before last."

"Bad luck, Mr. O'Shaughnessy. You've got insurance, haven't you?"

"Yeah, we've got insurance."

"Well, then, it's not so bad."

Liz couldn't take any more. She quietly turned and went down the hall to her office. Everything was ruined, she thought, and felt her throat tighten. Everything. All that she had worked so hard for had vanished. Her business. Her business partner. Tim had turned into a stranger. She couldn't even rely on him.

Why was it that things couldn't just stay the same? Especially the good things. Why did they always have to go away?

"Liz?"

Liz had her back to the door, but she didn't even turn when she realized O'Shaughnessy stood behind her. She had no idea how many hours had passed, how long she had been sitting cross-legged among the ruins on the floor, but she had a feeling that she wouldn't be able to stand up to save her life. Nor did she care. She just wanted to be left alone.

"You interested in lunch?" Tim asked.

"No. Thank you."

There was a sound behind her, and the next thing she knew Tim was kneeling behind her. His knees were splayed, resting on either side of her hips, and he began to massage her neck with surprising gentleness. At once, she stiffened and tried to pull away, but his hands followed her and her legs betrayed her.

"Easy, babe," he murmured soothingly. "It's just a little neck rub. Liz, I know all of this is awful, but we'll put it back together again. Hell, it can't be anywhere near as hard as getting this business started was. I mean, at least now people know who we are and what kind of work we can do."

He was making her throat tighten again, but she absolutely refused to cry, so she took refuge in tartness. "O'Shaughnessy, the last thing I'm in the mood for right now is a pep talk."

"You mean you *want* to sit here and mope?"

"You got it."

"I don't believe it."

"Believe it. I don't lie."

His hands tightened a little on her shoulders, almost a squeeze, and then continued rubbing. "Of course you don't lie, Pennington. You're as honest as the day is long. However, from time to time you do delude yourself."

"Tim—"

Whatever epithets she was about to fling were silenced beneath the pressure of his fingers against her lips.

"Shh," he said quietly. "You don't have to holler at me, Liz. When are you going to realize that I'm your friend? If you're blue, you can tell me. I won't laugh, I won't think you're weak and I won't think less of you. Honest." He shook her gently, and then eased her back against his chest. "We've known each other for five years, Lizzie, and weak or helpless are two words I'd never apply to you, even if you took up crying twice a day."

"I don't want to cry," she said.

"You're yelling at me because you want to stop yourself from crying?" He sounded as if that were a possibility he hadn't considered before. He'd assumed she was doing it to hide her real feelings from him. "Well, that's okay then. Go ahead and yell."

But strangely, she didn't feel like yelling anymore. Instead, she shifted her legs out from beneath her, and leaned back against him while he rubbed her shoulders.

Tim suddenly realized that his hand was wandering dangerously near her breast as he kneaded her small shoulders. He wanted badly to touch her there, to discover if her nipples would harden quickly, or if they would need coaxing....

Damn! he had to stop thinking like this or he'd take the girl right here on the hard floor.

He didn't want to think about it, but the simple fact was that a gulf of experience separated them. He couldn't imagine how Liz had gotten to the age of thirty as sheltered as she was, but somehow she had. Somehow she had gotten through life wearing some kind of blinders, too, because there was a naïveté to her that went far beyond the sexual. No, not naïveté. Purity. Yeah, that was a better word.

Purity. And Timothy F. X. O'Shaughnessy was as far from pure as it was possible to get without breaking a law. You couldn't walk through mud without getting some of it on your shoes, and you couldn't go to war without losing purity and innocence. Tim figured his innocence had lasted just about seventy-six hours after he'd gotten off the troop plane. Oh, he might have carried a few shreds of it through the next eighteen months, but not much. The whole reason he had gotten into computer programming as soon as he got out of the VA hospital was because he never wanted to have to deal with people again. People sickened him. People revolted and disgusted him. People were a blight on the face of an otherwise pretty nice planet.

Some of that had worn off over the years, of course. He'd learned that he liked and even enjoyed some people. Liz, for one, delighted him. And he worked off a lot of his bitterness and his sense of degradation by helping out in a storefront counseling center for vets who, unlike himself, still hadn't found a way to cope with the past. Helping others, even if it was only listening when they needed to talk, eased his self-disgust a little. These days he could even admit he wasn't such a terrible guy.

But he *would* be a terrible guy if he abused Liz's trust and innocence, if he took her with disregard for her feelings. She was no lady for a casual affair. Hell, she deserved a lot better than that.

So he hugged her close and wondered if he was ever going to reach a point when he felt as if he had anything to offer her. And wondered why he should even care.

Liz heard Tim's heavy, heavy sigh and wondered what was troubling him. The concept of Tim O'Shaughnessy being troubled was a new and startling one, and she found herself wondering if she had been blind all these years or if he had just never been troubled before.

Giving a sigh of her own, she snuggled closer and allowed herself to enjoy the totally unprecedented sensation of being protected. Last night and this morning she had acknowledged only the sense of being invaded by his determination to move in and not let her out of his sight. Now, right now, she recognized that what he was doing was priceless, precious and uniquely Tim O'Shaughnessy. In her entire life she had never met another soul who would have placed himself between her and danger.

"Tim?"

"Hmm?" The sound was a deep rumble in his chest, a vibration against her ear.

"Tell me about the shrapnel."

She felt his sudden tension. Hard muscles that had somehow softened enough to cushion her suddenly became steel again. "Nothing to tell," he said finally. "An incoming round hit a little too close. How about lunch now?"

But this time she wasn't going to let it go. If this man wanted to drive her crazy by taking over her life, if he wanted to touch her and turn her into a puddle of hungry nerves any time the whim took him, he was going to have to let her past the facade to the man beneath.

"How badly were you hurt?"

He went utterly still, and for the longest time he didn't even breathe. "Why?" he said eventually, a harsh note in the word. "What difference does it make?"

Liz liked neither his question nor the tone of it. Her temper flared and she struggled free of his hold, at last managing to kneel facing him. "Why?" she demanded, her voice rising. "*Why?* Because you were hurt! Because I *care* that you were hurt, dumb as that may be. What difference does it make? Not one damn little bit! Not if you think I'm some kind of sick voyeur—"

She'd already gotten to her feet and was trying to hurry past him when he reached out and caught her. He could have let her go—there wasn't anywhere she *could* go unless she was prepared to walk a far piece—but there was no point in postponing what was apparently going to be inevitable.

"I guess I *do* make you swear," he said as he stood and seized her by the shoulders.

"You do more than that," she said in a low voice. "You make me violent. I have never in my life wanted to hit anybody, O'Shaughnessy, but I positively *long* to hit you!" Her clenched fists, held tensely at her sides, confirmed the urge.

"So hit me."

The calmly worded invitation startled the anger right out of her. With wide, doubtful eyes, she looked up at him. "What did I do, Tim? What did I say?"

He cursed. Liz was accustomed to his casual *damns* and *hells*, and scarcely heard them any longer, but this was different. This time his words were at once colorful and embarrassing. She blushed to the roots of her hair.

"You didn't do anything," he said gruffly. "You didn't say anything. I reacted like a jerk and I apologize." He squeezed her upper arms gently.

"Why did you react like a jerk?" she asked.

She was practically another generation, this woman. Ten years his junior. Could she even remember the bitterness that had accompanied that war? Probably not. And if not, then why should he tell her how thoroughly rotten people could be, even without provocation?

"It's a long story," he said after a moment, careful to keep his tone neutral. "A long, ugly story. You won't want to hear it, and I don't like to tell it. So let's skip it, Liz. Please."

She searched his face intently before she nodded, realizing that he was genuinely disturbed by this conversation. "All right. I didn't intend to upset you. I guess I had no business even asking."

"Sure you did," he managed to say casually, although he was feeling far from casual. "Natural curiosity."

She hunched her shoulders, stepping out of his hold. "It wasn't just curiosity."

Oops. He'd done it again. "That isn't what I meant, Liz. Look, could we just get away from this subject before one of us is wounded for life?"

Clearly it wasn't easy for her to agree to that, but after a moment she did, raising her head and smiling at him. "Sure, Tim. Now what about that lunch?"

* * *

Donna refused to join them, insisting that she preferred to go home and check on James.

"I wonder what's with that kid," Tim muttered to Liz as they watched Donna turn her car out of the parking lot. "Honestly, Liz, I've been that age, and I've been randier than hell, and I can tell you it doesn't keep you up all night like that." He looked at her and there was suddenly a devilish gleam in his gray eyes. "Not unless the lady of your fantasies is only a couple of yards down the hall...."

"Are you telling me you were up all night, O'Shaughnessy?"

"Absolutely not. Now if I'd met you twenty years ago, I might have been, but I'm too damn old these days."

"Right." She said the word doubtfully and allowed him to help her into the truck. "And twenty years ago I was ten and you never would have even glanced at me."

He evidently didn't have anything to say to that. Climbing into the truck beside her, he turned over the ignition and pointed them toward Fusco's, a nice Italian restaurant where he could satisfy a sudden, wild craving for anything swimming in tomato sauce.

When he finally did speak, the direction he took astonished her. "What were you doing twenty years ago, Liz?"

"Me? Just being ten years old. Mom had to work full-time, so I probably had a lot more freedom than most kids my age."

"I'll bet you didn't get into any trouble, though."

"Well, no. I didn't have much time between schoolwork and housework."

"You call that freedom?"

She looked at him. "I was born well behaved, Tim. Surely you've noticed. I never had any urge to do things I shouldn't."

"Is that how you grew up to be so..." He dropped that train of thought fast. There was no word he could use that wouldn't set her off like a skyrocket.

"So what?" she asked belligerently. "So boring? So dull and uninteresting? *What*, O'Shaughnessy?"

She was already set off. Sighing, he pulled into Fusco's parking lot. "So innocent, Liz," he said heavily. "So innocent and pure and sweet and a million other things that are driving me out of my ever-loving mind!"

He practically bellowed the last couple of words, and Liz

shrank into her corner of the cab. The truck slammed to a halt and for a minute or two neither of them spoke or moved.

"Tim?" Liz's voice was small, tentative.

"Yes?" He bit the word off as if it were a piece of licorice.

"I'm not any of those things, not really. Certainly not sweet. You've told me yourself that I have a personality similar to a cactus."

He made a muffled sound.

"And I'm certainly not pure or innocent," she said in a stronger voice. "I'll grant that I'm *inexperienced*, but that's a whole different thing...."

He turned suddenly, his expression so angry that she tensed once again. Not for an instant did she believe Tim O'Shaughnessy would harm a single hair on her head, but he was formidable and frightening nonetheless.

"Shut up, Liz. Just *shut up*. Take it from me, you don't know what innocence is until you've lost it. And you don't know what purity is until you don't have any. So just be quiet and take my word for it. As for being sweet, my God, woman, you taste like wildflowers smell!"

He was shouting and she really couldn't imagine why. It made her angry. "Don't you dare yell at me, O'Shaughnessy! You've no call to browbeat me just because I don't agree with you!"

"Browbeat?" He repeated the word on a roar. "Why shouldn't I browbeat you? You're driving me to an early grave, and every time I try to tell you why, you argue with me about it."

Liz's mouth opened and closed several times as she glared at him, but even as she was glaring, she thought how strangely the two of them were behaving. And she remembered how she'd felt when he held her and kissed her, and the sweet things he'd said to her and the way he was trying to protect her.

The next thing Tim knew, Liz had slid across the bench seat and thrown her arms around his neck. She hugged him tightly and he felt his throat constrict with a sudden burst of emotion. His own arms closed around her, and he hugged her back, taking care not to squeeze too hard. She was so small, so fine, so fragile and delicate, his Liz, for all she had a temper like an irritated polecat.

"Tim," she whispered. "Tim, let's not fight. Please. I'm scared, and I'm scared about more than what happened at the office. I don't even know what all I'm scared about! But it scares me even more when you're mad at me.''

His fingers found their way into that long, glorious fall of hair and stroked the silky strands. "I don't think I'm really mad at *you*," he said presently. "I think I keep getting mad at myself."

"Well, I guess I can handle that. As long as you're not really mad at me."

"Naw. Mostly it's just frustration anyhow. Now how about getting that lunch we keep talking about?"

"All right." Astonishing him, she tilted her head and brushed a kiss on his cheek. "I'm glad you picked Fusco's."

Another thing in common, O'Shaughnessy thought as he climbed down from the truck and walked around to help Liz out. A passion for Italian food.

As they crossed the lot, Tim put his arm around her shoulders, hauling her up against his side as if he'd been doing it for years. "Got your purse, Pennington?" he asked casually as he opened the restaurant door for her.

"Sure. Why?"

"Because," he said, grinning down at her, "I just remembered my wallet is—"

"On the dresser at home." She completed his sentence, rolling her eyes. "I'm driving, O'Shaughnessy. In fact, I am never again getting into a vehicle with you unless you prove first that you've got your license! How you have ever survived all these years..." She kept right on lecturing as she walked into the restaurant.

Still grinning, Tim followed, thinking what a cute tush she had. Damn, he loved to get her wound up! He enjoyed it so much that he seriously contemplated not telling her he had only been teasing, that he hadn't forgotten his wallet at all.

Fusco's was busy, but they got a quiet corner table, thanks to Mrs. Fusco's apparent infatuation with Tim. She blushed and giggled and tittered like a girl forty years younger as she led them to their table and gave them menus. Tim played right up to it with obvious enjoyment.

When Mrs. Fusco moved away, Tim smiled at Liz. "She's a doll, that lady. Take your time, and have a beer or something, Liz. We've got stuff to discuss and I'd rather do it here where we won't have any serious interruptions."

Stuff to discuss? That sounded ominous. Liz ordered a glass of red wine to go with her salad.

"A salad?" Tim said. "Just a salad? Nothing more? Liz, you're *not* dieting! It'll ruin your temper, and your temper is already bad enough!"

"I'm not dieting, Tim," she said tartly. "Not that it's any of your business—"

"Anything that affects your temper is my business," he interrupted.

"What I eat is *my* business!" When it looked as if he was going to object yet again, she reached out and touched his arm. "Tim, I can't eat as much as you do. I'm only half your weight."

She was right of course, and he was showing incredible stupidity by even bringing up the subject. He'd dined out with enough women over the years to know that most of them ate like birds, at least around him. Somehow he had placed Liz in a category so far removed from other women that this had surprised him. But, of course, she couldn't possibly eat as much as he did. Still, to have only a salad when faced with a menu like Fusco's seemed close to self-torture.

"You'll taste my spaghetti at least?" he said hopefully.

His concern touched her. Darn it, every time she turned around lately, he seemed to be touching her tenderest feelings. "Sure, I'd love to taste your spaghetti, Tim."

Satisfied, he let the subject go. "The insurance adjuster is supposed to come by this afternoon, and while you were moping in your office we had a call from the FBI. Those two agents want to ask some more questions about the first break-in."

"Great. I don't have one blessed thing to add to what I've already told them."

"Me neither, but we have to convince them of that." Tim leaned toward her. "Remember last night, how we were talking about setting a trap for this guy?"

"Yeah, except that we have no reason to think he'll come back, and we don't know what bait would draw him back. Tim, it'd be a waste—"

"Wait just a second, Liz." Reaching out, he covered one of her hands with his, swallowing it whole in a gentle grip. "Talking about traps got me thinking. I'll be double damned if I'm going to put forty thousand dollars' worth of advanced computer equipment into that office again with no more protection than a dead-bolt lock. It's not just the expense, it's the inconvenience. Look at us now! We can work on the unclassified stuff, but all our classified work is on hold until we can get Tempest-approved systems. The sales reps from two different suppliers told me today that they've got a two-month backlog. It's the same with the safes. Sure, we can get delivery extensions from the navy. That's not the problem, but—''

"No money on those contracts until the work is done. I know." And it seriously affected the profit picture. "What are you driving at?"

"Protection. Two years ago we talked to that security expert and agreed we couldn't afford the stuff he was offering. Maybe we can't afford it now, either. But maybe we'd better afford it anyway. I've got a double-E degree. I can sure as hell wire up some alarms and cameras and a few obvious deterrents like that. And under the circumstances," he finished rather glumly, "I sure as hell have the time."

Instinctively wanting to comfort him, though she didn't really have any comfort to offer, she turned her hand over and squeezed his fingers. "I guess you're right. It's really going to pinch, though, with our income halved for the next couple of months. And I'll be surprised if the insurance company pays replacement cost on all that stuff."

"They damn well better. We're paying for a replacement-cost policy." But suddenly he looked rueful. "You're right. We'll probably be arguing dollars and cents with them for months. Well, I'm a frugal person. I've got enough socked away to fill in the cracks, and I'm willing to make a capital investment in the company again." His gray eyes held hers warmly. "I think Millennium Software is worth saving."

That look caused a fluttery sensation in her stomach, and the feeling wasn't unpleasant. "Me, too. I'll match you dollar for dollar."

"One for all and all for one." He suddenly looked wistful and boyish. "You know, Liz, the saddest damn thing on earth is growing up."

Her heart ached for him in that instant, because she felt his growing up hadn't been very pleasant. But it was a foregone part of their relationship that she try to rally him. "And here I thought you were a classic case of arrested development."

"I am."

She was shocked because his reply was utterly serious, not at all teasing. "What do you mean?"

He half shrugged, moving his head as if to say that he didn't have the words to explain. "Nothing, really. Oh, hell." He sighed. "I mean that every now and then I just wish dreams and ideals didn't have to die."

He honestly expected that practical, no-nonsense Liz Pennington would say something bracing about how that was the price of adulthood, or that dreams were utterly wasted. But she astonished him. Instead her grip on his hand tightened and she looked at him with the kind of softness that made men long for women in their lives.

"That's not arrested development, Tim," she said tenderly. "Dreams and ideals are the most precious, priceless things in the world. And losing them is the worst pain in life."

Tim realized right then that Liz had lost a few of her own dreams and ideals. He looked at her, seeing her differently from the way he'd seen her before. She was no longer the touchy software wizard, the prickly business partner, the innocent, naive, inexperienced woman whom he had always figured to have led a sheltered life. Suddenly he saw Liz Pennington as a woman with the guts to keep going even when it hurt, with the strength to pick up the pieces of shattered dreams.

He looked down at their clasped hands, and then looked up with a smile. "I didn't forget my wallet, you know. It's right here in my hip pocket."

Liz gasped and tried to glare at him, but she couldn't manage it. Something had just happened between them, and she couldn't bring herself to scold him. Not right now. "You owe me lunch for that one, O'Shaughnessy."

"Certainly, Pennington." He withdrew his hand, placing the appropriate distance between them once more. It wouldn't do to let her get too close, he reminded himself. She needed a forever kind of guy.

She looked away for a moment and then turned back to him, completely composed. "What kind of alarms and cameras were you thinking of?"

He leaned forward, eager to share his ideas with her. Electronics had always fascinated him, and his enthusiasm was contagious. By the time they finished lunch, he was sketching plans and diagrams on paper napkins, and Liz was on her second glass of wine, watching him with a degree of affection that would have panicked her if she had thought about it.

At the back of her mind, though, scarcely acknowledged, was a niggling awareness that no amount of security measures could provide absolute protection against the surprises of life. Tim would secure their office with alarms, and she would build walls around her heart, but a thief could still get in through some unexpected way.

Smiling wryly, she lifted her wineglass in toast to Tim. ''Seize the day.''

He lifted his beer glass in acknowledgement. ''Absolutely,'' he replied. ''You don't always get a second chance.''

For a moment she seemed to lose her ability to breathe, as icy fingers closed around her heart. *You don't always get a second chance.* It was a trite sentiment, one she had heard often over the years, but this time she really heard it. She felt it. Like an earthquake. Like an awakening to painful reality.

You don't always get a second chance.

Chapter 6

Their entire afternoon was taken up by a team of insurance adjusters and the pair of FBI agents that Tim had immediately dubbed Laurel and Hardy. Liz, who had been raised to show a proper respect for American institutions such as the FBI, was a little shocked by his levity, especially since the agents in no way resembled the comedians. In fact, if anything, they both appeared to completely lack a sense of humor.

"Relax, Pennington," Tim said as they drove home. "You can't be arrested for laughing at the FBI."

"It just seems disrespectful, that's all. They're doing an important and difficult job."

He glanced at her. "Yeah. Right."

Liz looked at him. "Why are you so cynical about it?"

"Never mind. It doesn't matter."

"Yes it does. It obviously matters to you. I'd like to understand why."

"I doubt if you can. You're probably too young to remember."

She turned the truck into the driveway and switched off the ignition. "Let's get something straight here, Tim."

He turned on the seat and faced her. "I'm all ears."

"You want to get into my bed, right?"

To his own horror, he felt his cheeks heat. He'd been hoping she'd forgotten his terrible act of stupidity in offering her an adult relationship, hoping she had been taken in by his smoke screen of a fleeting curiosity. "I wouldn't quite put it that way, Liz."

"Why not? I thought it was a pretty accurate interpretation of what you're after."

He wanted to argue with her, but visions of where such a discussion would probably lead turned him into a coward. He was frank about his desires, and perfectly willing to admit that this woman turned him on, but he definitely didn't want to get into any kind of discussion about how or why or what he was feeling. "What's the point, Pennington?" he asked with uncharacteristic desperation.

"Simple, O'Shaughnessy. Stop treating me like a kid who's too young or stupid to understand anything, or I promise you you'll never even get to first base." As soon as the words were out, she could hardly believe she had spoken them, leaving open any possibility that he *would* get into her bed. Had she lost her mind?

She had a point, Tim thought, and if he had half a brain he'd climb out of this truck right now before he let this woman get any closer. Instead, he stayed put and tried to find the right words. The tough part was that he was totally and completely unaccustomed to revealing his genuine feelings on any serious subject. Sex, sure, he could admit to those needs. Anything funny, light and humorous, okay. Natural human sympathy and commiseration, fine. It was the deeper, darker feelings, the ones that exposed his soul, that he couldn't share. Had never shared. The ones that showed Timothy F. X. O'Shaughnessy could be hurt, could be betrayed. The ones that showed how he cared about things like his country and his duty and the Constitution. Embarrassing things like that.

"Damn it, Pennington, you don't want much."

"Neither do you."

He winced.

"Right," she said drily. "I guess that settles the matter."

"Wait." He caught her hand as she started to turn away. He didn't know if he was going to be able to do this, but by God he had to try. *Why* he felt compelled to bare himself was something he'd puzzle out later in private.

"Okay," he said. "I'm cynical about the FBI because Nixon and Hoover practically turned them into a secret police. And because while they were doing that, I was risking my neck to bring freedom to Southeast Asia. Because, when I came home, I found out the FBI was keeping files on people simply on the premise that they had different political opinions."

Liz stared at him as she pondered what he had said. On the surface there didn't seem to be anything in those words that would be difficult for him to say. And then she understood. O'Shaughnessy's ideals had been betrayed by his country.

"Oh, Tim," she said sadly. "Oh, Tim."

"Oh, Tim what?" he said irritably. "Everybody knows that stuff. It's no big national secret."

"No." She realized he'd probably die on the spot if she let him know how much she understood. He'd certainly die if he knew that she was suddenly having a vision of him as a tall, gangly eighteen-year-old who had marched off to fight for all the right reasons only to come home and find that half the battle had been nearly lost on his own doorstep.

Practicing a little of the psychology she'd studied back in college, she leaned over and, as a reward, kissed him.

"Thank you for explaining," she said, and climbed out of the truck.

Well, that wasn't so bad, he thought as he followed her. If he had known it would be that easy to satisfy her, he wouldn't have balked in the first place.

Tim cooked dinner. Liz wasn't at all certain she wanted him messing up her kitchen, but Tim was adamant. He would only accept an even-steven division of labor. And to him that didn't mean that she would cook every night and he would wash up every night.

"It's because I burned the eggs this morning," Liz grumbled. "You think I can't cook because I was upset and ruined one lousy meal."

"This has nothing to do with this morning's eggs—which weren't burned, by the way. A little dry and crisp, yes, but not burned. No, this has to do with my pride."

"Pride? How could this possibly have anything to do with pride?"

"The great chefs of the world are all *men*, Liz," he said as he began pulling various items from the refrigerator. "In spite of this well-known fact, you women persist in thinking that men are hopeless in the kitchen, that only *you* can cook. Well, I refuse to be relegated to the unskilled role of chief dishwasher. I *can* cook, and I *will* cook. Every other day. Accept it."

"You forgot Julia Child."

He waved a dismissing hand. "A mere anomaly. A singular exception. I *cook*, Liz. I cook well."

"It's not your *cooking* I'm worried about," she admitted.

"No?" He arched a brow at her. "What, then?"

"Well..." She hesitated, and then thought, what the heck? He never hesitated to speak *his* mind.

"Okay," she said. "I don't want my kitchen messed up."

"Cooking is messy."

"I know. But men tend to make it messier."

"How many men have you watched cook?" he wanted to know, a pleasant expression plastered to his face.

"A few." When he looked doubtful, she snapped, "I *do* have married friends, Tim. They have husbands who believe themselves to be great chefs. What is it? A common male delusion? They pull everything out of the cupboards, they buy all kinds of exotic and expensive ingredients that nobody in his right mind would ever use again, and throw together totally unheard-of concoctions in the name of culinary superstardom. Then they walk out of the kitchen, leaving strange splotches on the ceiling, floor, walls and counters, every dish filthy, every ingredient on the counter.... In short, O'Shaughnessy, they create a disaster and leave it for the little woman to clean up. I am not interested in cleaning up any disasters tonight!"

Tim listened to all this with apparent equanimity, and when she pulled to a nearly breathless halt, he nodded calmly. "I guess I deserve this after my remarks about women's lib to Donna this morning," he said.

"Women's... This has nothing to do with that!"

"Okay," he said agreeably. "Tell you what. I promise I'll clean up any mess I make. I promise you won't be able to tell anyone cooked in here. How's that?"

She was beaten. She knew it and didn't like it, but there wasn't a darn thing she could say about it. Left with nothing to do, she stomped off to the living room and tried to occupy herself with a book.

It was impossible to concentrate on the written word, however, as Tim turned out to be a noisy cook. In fact, the last time she'd heard him make this kind of noise was when he had cleaned his office two short days ago. She winced every time the crockery clattered, and then calmed herself by giving Mephisto another stroke. The black cat regarded her with sleepy, enigmatic green eyes.

"I know, I know," she told him. "It's utterly ridiculous. I've misplaced my backbone somewhere, and I'm letting this man walk all over me. It's not like me. I realize that. And in a day or so, I'm sure I'll recover from this malaise, whatever the heck it is. I certainly don't intend to let Tim O'Shaughnessy make a complete shambles out of my life."

Mephisto replied with a slow, lazy blink.

"All right, so I'm scared. Wouldn't *you* be scared if you were me?" Sphinxlike, the cat just stared back. "Probably not," Liz sighed. "But I'm just me, a poor human female who's never had any contact with any kind of violence in her entire life, and it scares me, 'Phisto. Every time I think of all that destruction, I shiver. I can't even imagine what kind of anger would make somebody do something like that. Or what kind of fear."

The cat kneaded Liz's thigh with his front paws.

"Tim knows about violence," Liz murmured. "He's a man who's had to fight. He's been to war. And as unliberated and wimpy as it sounds, I'm grateful as heck that he wants to protect me."

Disgusted, the cat put his head down on his paws.

In complete agreement, Liz let her head fall against the chair back and closed her eyes. She was weak and wimpy and an utter failure, and she didn't give a good goldarn. There was something to be said for brawn and all those warriorlike attributes women pretended to scorn. It was something you only realized when you needed it.

And the more she learned about Tim, the better she liked him. That was as scary as anything else. It was hard to believe how readily she had taken him at face value all these years. And he was right—there was no way they could go back. Nor did she really want to, even though it might destroy their partnership.

Certainly they were never going to be able to recover the easy camaraderie of the past. No, they'd become too intensely aware of one another in other ways for that to be possible.

And Tim. She felt the corners of her mouth tugging upward. In the everyday world you didn't often question other people about their ideals and things of that nature. You assumed a basic honesty, a basic commonality in beliefs about right and wrong, but you didn't ask people what they believed in. Yet over the past couple of days she had gotten some glimpses of what Tim believed in, and she was impressed.

Impressed? No, it was more than that. The guy was a veritable knight in white armor beneath all that gruff arrogance and boyish exuberance. And *he* thought he'd lost his purity and innocence? Ideals like his required a certain amount of innocence to survive. In fact, she was beginning to think the cynicism she'd always associated with him was a sham.

Furthermore, she was beginning to think that Tim O'Shaughnessy himself was one great big sham, and that underneath all of it there was quite some guy hiding. A sensitive, caring, idealistic, altruistic, wonderful, romantic guy.

A guy she would really like to know.

It really galled her, but Tim left the kitchen looking as if no one had used it since she'd straightened it after breakfast that morning. All the noises, all the banging and clattering, had yielded nothing but a truly tasty Chicken Kiev and a salad with a zingy homemade dressing. Who made salad dressing anymore? O'Shaughnessy, evidently. Galled or not, she complimented him sincerely on both his meal and the state of her kitchen. She even managed to ignore the smug I-told-you-so look he gave her.

And then the FBI called. Laurel and Hardy wanted to know if they could stop by.

"I guess they must have found out something," Liz said uneasily to Tim after she'd hung up the phone. Another thought struck her. "Did you tell them you were staying here?"

"Sure." Because he was. But the expression on Liz's face told him that that had been a tactical error. "Liz, I explained that I was worried about your safety. I didn't give them any reason to think..." He couldn't believe this. Not in this day and age. Women didn't worry about their reputations any longer. They had demanded and won the right to be as promiscuous as they chose, not that that was necessarily a good thing.

But Liz was looking at him with wide, wet eyes. Wet, for crying out loud. "Liz, I'm sure they don't think anything about it."

"Probably not," she said, turning her shoulder to him. "I'm sure they wouldn't care, regardless. They must see all sorts of...things."

"Yeah." Tentatively he touched his fingertips to her shoulder. She stepped away. Hell's bells! Now how the devil was he supposed to handle this? She hid it well, but he had glimpsed her vulnerability and her defenselessness. He had wounded her by not considering that she might care what other people thought of her living arrangements. And it was a mistake he never should have made, since he'd had plenty of warning that Liz didn't treat these matters lightly.

"Liz, I swear I'm sorry. I'll just tell them straight out—"

"No!" She whirled, facing him with evident horror. "Don't say anything at all about it. They're not going to believe anything you tell them if they've already decided something else is going on. You'll only make it worse. And I'll die. I swear I'll die if I have to listen to you try to explain...things."

"Okay. Okay." Helpless, thwarted in his desire to make it all better for her, he threw up his hands. "Maybe I should just go jump in front of a train."

"Tim!" His name came out on a shocked note and then was followed by a gurgle of laughter.

Laughter? Yes, she was laughing. Relief started to wash over him in a warm wave. "Look, I'm really sorry...."

But she cut him off. "You're right." She blushed to the roots of her hair. "I'm being melodramatic about this. The days of the scarlet letter are long past. I'm overreacting, and I'm sorry."

He stepped toward her and took her elbows in his hands. "Don't apologize, sweetheart. One of the most charming things about you is that you *do* take these things seriously. I was kicking myself for forgetting that."

"Well," she said, and another chuckle escaped her, "offering to throw yourself in front of a train was a little extreme for an apology."

"I guess it was." And then a huge sigh of complete relief

escaped him as she leaned trustingly against him and rested her cheek right over his heart. There was something...warming in the way she did that. Lord, how he wanted to kiss her, explore her! But mostly, mostly, he wanted to savor her trust, to enjoy the realization that she felt free to lean against him. He wanted her always to feel that way.

The doorbell rang. Liz sprang away from him like a startled deer, telling him they were a long way from her feeling perfectly comfortable in his embrace. Sighing, he went to get the door while Liz headed to the kitchen to get the coffee.

"You don't have to kill the fatted calf, Liz," he called after her. "They're a couple of Feds on a job, not guests."

"And they're not responsible for the actions of Hoover and Nixon," she called back tartly. "I'm going to treat them like human beings."

Special Agents Carter and Woodrow accepted the coffee gratefully, commenting on how chilly the evening had grown, and what a long day it had been. They were attempting to be pleasant and friendly, Tim noted sourly, but he wasn't ready to buy it. After only a couple of minutes, Woodrow turned to business.

"We've been combing through all the debris we took from your office yesterday," he said. "Trying to find anything that might give us a clue as to what happened. At this point we're not a hundred percent sure that none of the classified information was taken, but we're beginning to think we can gamble that none of it was."

"Why is that?" Tim asked. "What did you find?"

Woodrow opened a stiff file cover and pulled out a clear sheet protector that held a wrinkled piece of yellow legal paper. "We found this," he said. "It could be a brilliant red herring, or it could be real. And frankly, the latter possibility is more frightening than the former."

Tim took the vinyl sheet protector and held it so both he and Liz could read at the same time. The message had been crudely printed in crayon, and something about that alone was enough to make Liz's neck prickle.

THE ELECTROMAGNETIC RAYS FROM YOUR MA-
CHINES DESTROYED MY GRAVITY SO THE COM-

PUTERS COULD TAKE OVER MY MIND. I STOPPED
THEM. IF YOU START IT AGAIN, I WILL STOP YOU
FOREVER.

"My God," Liz breathed, and felt fear crawl across her skin.
"Tim...?"

He looked disturbed, too, and heedless of the agents, he placed
a protective arm around her shoulders. And suddenly Liz didn't
care what they thought. She edged closer to Tim.

He broke the silence. "What do you make of this?"

"Well," said Woodrow, "our experts have a couple of different ideas. First, like I said, it could be a red herring, meant to
divert us. Second, it could be the work of a sick mind. In this
case, a paranoid schizophrenic."

Tim stared blankly, while Liz gave a small nod.

"I'm no analyst," Woodrow said, "but our staff psychiatrist
thinks this guy is definitely paranoid, and that he demonstrates a
delusion common to schizophrenics—thought insertion. Which
means he thinks someone or something is putting thoughts into
his mind."

Carter spoke. "When he said schizophrenic the first time, I
thought he meant split personality, but that's evidently not schizophrenia at all."

"No," Liz agreed, relieved that her voice sounded steady despite how shaken she suddenly felt. "I studied abnormal psychology in college. Multiple Personality Disorder is a disease all
by itself. Schizophrenia is a thought disorder. A common symp-
tom is auditory hallucination. Schizophrenics hear voices."

"Well," said Woodrow, "our experts think this guy is hearing
voices, and that somehow he attributes them to you folks and
your computers. He evidently believes someone is trying to take
over his mind."

"Great," said Tim. "I was happier with the idea of a frustrated
drug addict who couldn't find money. If this guy has it in for us,
how can we possibly protect ourselves? You can't predict what
a mentally ill person will do."

"That's where you're wrong," Woodrow said. "Dr. Hanes—
he's our expert—says that within the context of his delusion, the
schizophrenic behaves in a perfectly rational manner. In other
words, folks, this guy will do exactly what you or I or anyone

else would do if we believed someone was actually taking over our minds.''

Liz nodded and looked at Tim. "Only the *delusion* is crazy, Tim. The rest of it is perfectly logical and sane.''

"Wonderful," Tim muttered. "If *I* thought someone was trying to take over my mind, I'd probably try to kill him.''

"*That's* the big problem," Woodrow said heavily. "It's what we're worrying about. Hanes said most schizophrenics aren't violent, that, in fact, they're more of a danger to themselves—since they can't care for themselves—than they are a danger to anyone else. But it's possible for them to get violent, particularly when paranoia is involved. Right now we don't know what this guy is capable of. We *do* think, though, that he's likely to come back at you if you start working with the computers again.''

Liz's mind was swinging into gear, and she reached once more for the note. Woodrow handed it to her readily. Disturbing my gravity? Electromagnetic rays? That was when she suddenly remembered two very different things. She drew a sharp breath, causing Tim to look swiftly down at her. "He called me," Liz said. "Or maybe it was a woman. I'm not real sure.''

"This guy *called* you?" Woodrow demanded. "When? What did he say?''

"A couple of days ago. I thought it was a kid playing a prank, and I really expected to get a series of calls, but that was the only one." She looked at Tim. "You remember, when you were cleaning your office. All he said was to stop disturbing the gravity. That's all." She leaned closer to Tim. "God, that's creepy.'' Chills raced up and down her spine.

"That's it? No other calls? Nothing else?''

"There was Chuck, too.''

"Chuck?" Tim repeated disbelievingly. "Not *our* Chuck, the NPS man.''

Liz stared at him, feeling the stiffness of her face. "The very same, Tim. The morning of the first break-in when he brought those carnations for Donna. Remember?''

Tim nodded grimly, and the two agents leaned forward intently.

"Chuck asked me why I wasn't afraid to work around computers all day. He asked me if I hadn't heard about all the X-ray beams and things. He sounded like he was joking, though. I sure thought he was.''

Woodrow pulled out a pad. "Tell me everything you can about this Chuck guy. He's with NPS, you said? Your regular route man?"

"He's been delivering to us every day for four years," Tim answered. "And he seems like a perfectly ordinary guy. A nice guy." God, it stuck in his craw to have to sic the FBI on anyone, but mostly on someone he felt friendly toward.

Woodrow and Carter had a few more questions, and tried to get Liz to come up with further impressions of the phone call, but as it was, she remembered its content and very little else. She really had dismissed it as a kid playing a prank.

After she walked the agents to the door, Liz turned to find Tim propped against one side of the living room archway. He looked so good, she found herself thinking irrelevantly. Broad shoulders, narrow hips, incredibly flat stomach. Muscled buns. She felt the corners of her mouth lifting as she wondered how many men in the world had buns as well muscled as O'Shaughnessy's. She knew just how well muscled they were because his should-be-illegal exercise shorts didn't hide a thing. And because his jeans didn't hide much more.

"What are you thinking about?" he asked. But he had a good idea. There was no mistaking the way her eyes had trailed over him, or the way they had darkened. And of course his body was responding, so he shoved his hands into his pockets and hoped that cutting off his own circulation would help.

The interest in Liz's gaze faded as her attention returned to his face. "You realize what they were telling us?" she asked. "Essentially, we go back to work at our own risk."

"Yeah, I heard." Damn, he was losing his marbles. He didn't want her to think about this right now. He wanted her to concentrate on him. He wanted her to give in to her wakening arousal and desires. And that was crazy because somewhere out there was a madman who might conceivably hurt them. Damn and double damn, he *had* to get his priorities straight.

Levering himself away from the door frame, he headed for the kitchen. "I need coffee," he said gruffly. And a dose of good sense.

Liz trailed after him, unaware that she had prodded the lion. "I guess we need to keep it really secret that we'll be working at your place."

"Secret from who? Whom? Who? Damn it all, Liz, I'll never get that straight!"

Liz was startled, thinking he was overreacting to a simple little problem of grammar. "Who cares?" she said. "I sure don't. What do you mean *'secret from whom'?"*

"Whom? See? I was right that I was wrong. I'm always wrong about that."

"Well, you're not wrong about much, Tim," Liz said soothingly.

He glanced up from the coffee he was pouring. "Did I hear you right? Did you actually say that?"

"Admitting you're not wrong about much is a far cry from saying you're never wrong," she said stiffly. "Don't let it go to your head."

"The only thing that goes to my head these days is you," he groused. "And that's not doing me a damn bit of good!"

It wasn't doing her a damn bit of good, either, Liz thought. She slumped into a chair at the kitchen table and nodded her thanks when Tim placed a streaming mug of coffee in front of her.

"I think," she said presently, "it would be best if we put our personal feelings on hold until we solve this problem."

"Sure it would be *best*," he said immediately, sarcasm dripping from every syllable. "All my life I've known what's best for me, but I can't say I've always done it."

She regarded him glumly. "Me, either."

That was when he laughed. It was a reluctant, rusty sound, but it defused the moment. "What a pair we make, Liz." Leaning forward, he covered one of her hands with his own. "Okay, let's talk about this mess. If Laurel and Hardy are right, we've got a psycho after us."

Liz shifted uncomfortably. "I don't like that word, Tim."

"Why not? They said the guy's crazy."

"That's not psycho. When people say psycho, they mean a sociopath, a pathological killer or rapist or something. Most mentally ill people aren't sociopaths."

With his hand over his mouth, Tim studied her, realizing that this distinction was somehow important to her, but utterly unable to understand why it should be. "Okay," he said after a moment.

"Suppose you give me *your* evaluation of what this guy is up to. Damn it, Liz, you were the one who described it as vicious!"

"I know. But that was before I realized that he's probably scared."

"Scared?" Damn, how was a man supposed to *think* when a pair of bright hazel eyes were imploring him the way hers were right now? Liz's gaze was begging him to hear her out. Well, he'd listen, but it wasn't going to be easy to convince him that a guy who wielded a sledgehammer was really peaceable in his intentions.

"Scared," she repeated. "How would *you* feel if you believed some external force was trying to control your mind? Admit it, you'd be scared to death."

"Damn straight, I'd be scared. And like I said before to the Feds, I'd also be looking to kill whoever I thought was doing it. Look, Liz," he said heavily, "you've obviously got this figured out somehow, so why don't you just tell me instead of playing Twenty Questions?"

At the moment he wasn't looking very boyish, Liz thought. In fact, he was looking frustrated and tired, and the lines fanning away from his eyes seemed to be suddenly pronounced. He'd been hiding it well, she thought, but he was every bit as upset and worried about what had happened as she was.

"I don't think he *wants* to hurt anyone, Tim," she heard herself say.

"Well, great!" His patience, never very strong, snapped. "I suppose he didn't want to destroy our office, either, but fear does funny things to people. My God, Liz, wake up! If this guy thinks it's a matter of his survival, he'll do whatever he feels necessary, whether he *wants* to or not."

"But if we can avoid frightening him—"

"Fine. How do you suggest we do that? And before you say anything, keep in mind that neither of us ever threatened anyone with mind control!"

He was disappointing her and upsetting her. He could see it in her eyes, on her face, yet he couldn't stop himself. He was scared to death that she would delude herself into believing that there was no danger. Maybe there really wasn't. Maybe this poor sick person would develop some new kind of delusion and turn his attention elsewhere. So what? They couldn't afford to take that chance.

"Look, Liz, I know mentally ill people get a raw deal. I know that most of us have all kinds of misconceptions about insanity, and that the sick people are the ones who pay for our ignorance. I readily confess that a shocking number of homeless people are really mentally ill persons who have been cast out of hospitals and other care facilities.... Am I hitting the high points?"

Liz nodded mutely, her face expressionless.

"I will even concede that this person may not wish to harm us personally. But, Liz, *you* have to concede that even a mentally ill person might—just might—be capable of a violent crime such as murder. Especially if he feels threatened."

When she offered no response, he sighed. "Liz, is it so hard to accept that a mentally ill person could also be a criminal, just as easily as the normal guy across the street? What is it with you?"

"Why is it so important to you that I agree with you?"

He wanted to shake her. Yes, he really wanted to shake her. "I want you to admit that there might be danger because I want you to be careful. I don't want anything to happen to you, Liz, but unless you accept the possibility of danger, you won't even protect yourself."

"All right. There might be danger." She gave a little shiver. "I didn't mean that I'm not frightened, Tim, because I *am* frightened. Really frightened. I just meant that if we consider that this guy might be scared and sick, not mean and vicious, we might think up ways to deal with him. Ways that might keep worse things from happening."

"Well, why didn't you just say so?"

"I was trying to!" Her chin thrust out.

"Okay. Okay. Pax." He held up a hand. He had gone off a little half-cocked, he guessed. "I'm sorry. I guess I'm more tired than I thought."

"I know I am." She pushed back from the table and stood. "I'm going to bed. Lock up, will you?"

"But we haven't discussed—"

She rounded on him, eyes flashing. "I have discussed all I am going to discuss with you tonight. You are in no mood to hear anyone but yourself, O'Shaughnessy."

She marched two steps toward the door and then looked back. "And by the way, *don't* clank those weights around in the morning or I'll kill you."

"Sorry," he said meekly. It behooved a man to know when he had overstepped with a woman, and Tim had the definite feeling that he had managed to push Liz to a snapping point of her own. At a time like this, the better part of valor was to be as inconspicuous as possible. "Not a peep or a clang, I promise."

As tired as she was, Liz should have slept straight through the night and still had trouble getting up in the morning. Instead, at three, she was wide-awake and anxious. After twenty minutes of tossing and turning and trying *not* to think about the events of the past couple of days, she conceded defeat, got up and went downstairs. She might not be able to sleep, but she didn't have to spend the time rolling restlessly around her bed.

She went into the kitchen and was pouring herself a glass of water, when a soft sound behind her startled her. With her heart in her throat, she whirled around and screamed.

There, barely more than a hulking shadow in the dim light from the sixty-watt bulb over the sink, was Tim O'Shaughnessy. Clad only in his scandalous shorts, he was crouched, feet apart for stability, arms spread wide. And in his right hand gleamed the long blade of the ugliest knife Liz had ever seen.

"Damn it, Liz," he growled hoarsely. "*Tell* me if you're going to wander around in the middle of the night. I thought..." He never finished. Muscle by muscle, he relaxed slowly and straightened up. "Damn it!" he said again, with even more emphasis.

Liz was utterly speechless. Her heart seemed to be stuck in her throat, but more than that she was stunned by what she had just seen. Was seeing.

A warrior ready to do battle. No other description seemed apt. For the first time in her life, Liz saw a man ready to fight, prepared to face danger, injury and possible death. Even as he made a visible effort to relax, she could still see the harshness in his face, the hardness in his eyes, the pounding pulse in his temple.

He spoke roughly. "When I found your bed empty, I thought... Never mind what I thought. Hell!" His hand tightened once more on the hilt of his hunting knife, and then he set it on the counter.

Hesitating, he peered at her. "Liz? Are you okay?"

She blinked and started breathing again. "Why did you check my bed?"

"Because I heard noises and I wanted to be sure you were okay. *Are* you okay?"

Her gaze strayed to the knife. "What were you going to do with that?"

A cold, hard mask settled over his face. "Whatever was necessary." Without another word, he picked up the knife and stalked from the room.

Trembling suddenly, Liz turned and grabbed the edge of the counter for support. Why had she questioned him like that? Why had she been so harsh? She *knew* why he had that knife ready in his hand, and why he had checked her bed. Why the devil had she implied something else? To make him furious? Why?

Because, by making him mad, she had made it impossible to do what she longed to do—throw herself into his arms. After that remark, he would probably pack up and go home. Why was it that lately Tim brought out the worst in her? The perverse. The nasty. The catty, bitchy, awful part of her.

With a sigh, she closed her eyes and let her chin droop to her chest as she leaned against the counter. Darn it, she was too old to be behaving like this, and too old to be running scared from her attraction to a man.

So what if she was attracted to a man. It was no big deal and she ought to be able to handle it. There was no reason in the world for her to be a rabbit about this.

Oh yes, there was. She was scared to death that his interest in her was only momentary. She was terrified that once he got what he wanted he would lose interest in her. Oh, not immediately. She honestly didn't think Tim was trying to use her. He wasn't that kind of person. But eventually he was bound to lose interest. After all, they'd been working cheek-by-jowl for four years now, and he'd never found her fascinating before. There was no reason on earth to believe that this was anything other than a passing aberration on his part.

And that's why she was scared. Deep down inside she knew that at some point or other she was going to give herself to him. At some point or other she wasn't going to be able to resist the need to touch him and hold him, the need to be touched and held by him. Sooner or later, simple aching need was going to overwhelm her. The problem was, Liz Pennington had realized at a very early age that she would never be able to give her body without giving her heart. And if she gave her heart, she wanted to give it to someone who would take good care of it. A forever man.

"Liz." Big, warm hands closed on her shoulders, and then Tim drew her back against his chest.

He had come back, she realized with amazement. She'd been monstrous to him, but he had come back, and he was holding her as gently and as sweetly as if they were lovers. His arms closed around her waist, his head bowed until his rough, stubbly chin rested on the top of her head.

"Are you okay?" he asked.

"Sure. I just couldn't sleep." She drew a deep breath. "I'm sorry I was so bitchy."

"It's three in the morning. Nobody's responsible for anything they say or do at this hour. Is something bothering you?"

"Only what you'd expect, considering what's been going on."

He turned her to face him and she discovered that he had donned a navy blue sweat suit. He smelled like laundry soap and man, she realized as she leaned into him. That enticing, musky male odor made her want to move even closer. With one hand he held her close, and with the other he stroked her hair.

"I haven't said anything nice to you today," he remarked.

"Sure you have." She liked being held this way, liked the calming, warming feeling he gave her.

"I don't remember. What did I say?"

"You told me I looked nice first thing in the morning."

"That's right. I forgot." He smiled into her hair.

She sighed and permitted herself to snuggle a little closer. Somehow she didn't feel anxious now, with his arms around her. She felt secure. Safe. "I guess I didn't say anything nice to you at all," she admitted.

"Yes, you did."

"I did? What?"

"You said that you cared that I had been hurt."

Liz drew a deep breath and looked up. Tim wasn't grinning; he didn't look even vaguely amused. Instead, he was searching her face as if it were important that he find something there.

"I *do* care," she admitted in a small voice. "I didn't say anything this morning when I saw the scars because I can tell you don't like to talk about any of that. I guess I can understand why you wouldn't.'' His gray eyes were intense, burning, but she refused to look away. Summoning her courage, she reached up and with one finger touched the pale scar that ran from just behind his ear down into the crew neck of his shirt. "Was this shrapnel, too?"

"Bayonet."

She flinched. She wanted to be strong and brave, but she flinched anyway, and knew the horror showed on her face. Against her, he began to stiffen, but the stiffness vanished as soon as she laid her palm against the scar. "So close," she murmured. "So very close. Tim, it makes my insides twist to think how you must have hurt. How frightened you must have been."

Her green eyes defied him to deny his hurt and his fear, and to just about anyone else he probably would have. Right now, though, he just wanted to tell the honest truth. "I thought I'd bought the farm," he admitted. "I was scared spitless."

"I bet." He wanted to get away from this subject, she realized. He was discussing it at all only to make up for the way he had reacted earlier when she had questioned him. "I'm glad you're here," she said, making a confession every bit as difficult as his had just been. "I'm glad I'm not alone with this fear."

He hugged her tight and dropped a kiss on the top of her head. "Do I get to remind you of that the next time you holler about my towels?"

She laughed. She couldn't help it. Bless the man, he was so like a kid in some ways. "Somehow I suspect you'll remind me more often than that." Reluctantly, she stepped out of his arms. "How about some hot chocolate?"

He was silent for a while, as she buzzed around mixing up the cocoa powder and water, measuring the sugar. She made cocoa the old-fashioned way, he noted. The good way. None of that preserved, artificially vanillaed stuff. And she looked so damn sad.

"We'll make it, Liz," he said gruffly.

"Sure."

"We *will*."

"I just agreed with you, Tim. You don't have to insist." Her tone was acerbic.

"Vacation," O'Shaughnessy said.

Liz looked up from the pot she was stirring slowly. "What?"

"We need a vacation. Both of us. We need to get away from all this crap for a while."

"We've got delivery deadlines to meet," she reminded him. "We need to get back to work."

"So we'll work a little harder when we get back."

"That defeats the purpose of a vacation."

"Don't be ridiculous! Nothing defeats the purpose of a vacation. It's a change of scene, a change of pace. You don't even need to get rested. The change of perspective is what's important."

"I've had my perspective changed enough lately," she said tartly. "I'd like to go back to my old perspective. Prevandalism."

Tim shook his head. "I expected better of you, Liz."

"Better?"

"What happened to the adventurous soul who quit her job to start a business with me?"

"I'm adventured out. I want peace. Security. Stability. The conviction that I'm not going to starve to death."

"I won't let you starve," he said gently.

Her throat tightened and she drew a deep breath, fighting down a strong, ridiculous urge to fling herself, sobbing, into his amazingly strong arms. "I can't afford a vacation," she said instead. "Neither can you. Half of our income is on hold until we can get going on those defense contracts again."

"Liz, you've got circles under your eyes. If you don't take a regular vacation, you're going to wind up taking one in the hospital."

"Cut the crap, Tim. Do I look fragile?"

"Actually," he said, "you do. Incredibly, terribly fragile. As fine as spun glass."

Her throat tightened again. Damn the man, he could look sincere spouting the worst blarney. "Hogwash."

"Shut up, Liz. You're as tough as boiled leather. I realize that. But you're still incredibly fragile."

She snorted. "That's a contradiction in terms."

"It's not. I've held you, Liz. I've looked into your eyes. I know just how vulnerable you are."

Her teeth snapped together audibly.

His laugh rumbled across the table. "I'm man enough to handle you."

She decided enough was enough. "No vacation," she said flatly. "You go ahead and go, but not me."

"Okay."

She scrutinized him suspiciously, but found him looking as innocent as a cherub.

"Okay," he repeated, spreading his hands. "We'll talk about a vacation a little later. I guess there's no point in taking one if you're just going to worry your way through it."

"That's right." She motioned to the hot chocolate. "Do you want a marshmallow in yours?"

"Always. Damn it, Liz, nobody's made me hot chocolate like this since I was knee-high to a toad."

That tickled her deep inside, and warmed a place in her heart. Not since he was a little kid. She made up her mind right then and there to make it again soon.

And then, maybe because it was the middle of the night and her brain wasn't functioning correctly, she asked the question that had plagued her for the past two days. As soon as the betraying words escaped her, she wanted to snatch them back, but it was already too late.

"Tim? What happened to your wife?"

Chapter 7

Moments passed and Tim didn't respond. He stared into his mug and didn't twitch so much as an eyelid. Just as Liz was about to say something dismissing and let them both off this particular hook, he spoke.

"She died," he said.

Liz's heart beat painfully, and she drew a slow breath, trying to calm it. "I'm sorry," she said softly. "I'm so sorry. I shouldn't have asked." Shouldn't have reminded him. But, oh, how she wanted to know!

He looked at her then, giving her the faintest of smiles, a sort of pro forma expression that had nothing to do with what he was feeling, but that was intended to put her concerns to rest. "It was a long time ago. It's okay."

He lifted his mug and drank, and for a while it seemed he would say nothing more. But then he looked at Liz again, and spoke in jerky bursts. "She was Vietnamese. Montagnard, actually. We were a couple of kids. I was nineteen, and she was sixteen. And there's nothing in the world like being in love for the first time in your life. Nothing."

He closed his eyes, and the set of his mouth grew grim. His words made her ache so badly, so deeply.

"What happened?" she asked softly.

"Plenty." His voice was harsh, ragged. "The army doesn't approve of soldiers marrying locals. That was a fight. Then I got wounded and was shipped to a hospital in Hawaii before I even regained consciousness. It took me a couple of months to find her, and a couple more to get her out of the country. We rented this little house with a big yard and Tranh planted a million kinds of flowers. She loved flowers. Then...then she got pregnant. An ectopic pregnancy. I guess the common term is tubal pregnancy. I came home one afternoon to find she had hemorrhaged to death."

"Oh, Tim!" In that moment she would have given five years of her life to spare him even the memory of that pain. All she could do, though, was grip his hand and ache for him.

He shrugged. "Like I said, it was a long time ago. I've recovered." But his expression gave lie to his words, and inwardly he knew he would never recover from the guilt. He felt Liz's fingers tighten around his, and the words started coming, words that gave shape and substance to the guilt he'd been carrying, words he had never, ever told anyone.

"I...sometimes wonder if she would have lived if I hadn't brought her here."

Liz was horrified. "Tim, oh, Tim, that's the kind of accident nobody can prevent! It could have happened to anyone!"

"You don't understand." He made himself look at her. "Tranh didn't speak any English, and she was painfully shy. She didn't know how to call for help. She didn't know how to call me to come home to her. She didn't know how to get a doctor. If she had been in Vietnam—"

Liz bit her lip, holding back protests. What did she know, after all, about conditions in Vietnam? Besides, nothing she could say would make Tim feel any better about it. Feelings weren't something that could be rationalized away. She couldn't, however, let this pass without saying something.

"Did she come from a big city?" Liz asked.

Tim shook his head, gray eyes hollow. "A village. Maybe three hundred people."

"And they had a hospital?"

"No."

"Oh." Uneasy at her own temerity in prodding this man's

grief, she hesitated before saying, "I thought—Tim? How could they have saved her then? I mean, wouldn't she have needed an operation? Right away?"

He sighed heavily and passed a hand over his eyes. "Yeah. But she could have told someone. They might have been able to get help for her."

"And you just as easily might have been home with her when it happened, and *you* could have gotten her help. But it didn't happen that way." Feeling she had said more than enough, afraid to stir up the ashes of his grief any more, she rose and rinsed her cup at the sink. Without looking at him, she headed for bed, struggling against an almost overwhelming impulse to throw her arms around him and commiserate.

In the doorway, she paused, keeping her back to him. "The what ifs are the hardest thing to live with, aren't they? Good night."

Liz was right, of course. She hadn't said one thing he hadn't told himself before, and intellectually he recognized that there was no blame in what had happened. Emotionally, though, was something else. He kept thinking of what a hard, brief life Tranh had known. He kept thinking of how much she had loved her family, and how much she had sacrificed to come to America with him. He kept thinking that he had carried her away from one kind of privation only to give her another.

She might have died had she stayed at home, but she sure as hell wouldn't have died alone. In the end, that's what hurt the worst. Tranh's life had slipped away in silence and solitude, without another soul nearby to comfort her. No human being could have been more alone than she had been in her last hours.

For that he couldn't forgive himself. And that was a pain he would never risk again.

Tim half expected to feel awkward with Liz in the morning. Confession might be good for the soul, but it was also downright embarrassing. Liz, however, arrived at the breakfast table in a waspish mood, complaining about lack of sleep and the seat having been left up on the toilet again. It was impossible to feel awkward around someone who was acting like a two-year-old who needed a nap.

Two cups of coffee later, she was mellowing enough to discuss the day's plan of action.

"I want to get that security equipment this morning and start installing it," Tim told her. "I figure we need a couple of surveillance cameras and an alarm system. But I was also thinking of something else. It struck me last night that we're in the perfect position to set a trap."

Liz groaned and propped her chin on her hand. "Tim, let the FBI handle this. This is what they get paid to do. It's even possible that they have some experience at this and might even be good at it."

"You're just overtired, Liz," he said kindly. "When you wake up you'll see I'm making sense. Besides, Laurel and Hardy made it plain that we go back to work at our own risk. That's as good as saying we're bait in a trap."

Liz knit her brows in confusion. "I don't exactly see how you arrive at that translation. There's no logical connection."

"Sure there is. They warned us that this gravity man might come after us again if we go back to work. If we go back to work, we'll be acting like bait to draw this creep out. Do you think those two Feds wouldn't take advantage of it? Besides, Liz, what's the alternative? Early retirement? Job hunting in Silicon Valley?"

Liz shuddered. "Not that. Anything but that."

Tim chuckled. "I knew you'd see reason. Look, I'm not planning anything outrageous. Just that we get some camera equipment in the place for surveillance, a couple of cheap, cheap clone computers that won't break the bank and pretend to go back to work. If the gravity man is really weirded out by the computers, he'll come to smash them. And we'll get a picture of him."

It didn't sound too off-the-wall, Liz thought. "Well, if it's okay with the FBI—"

"Quit worrying about the FBI. If it'll make you feel better, I'll tell them exactly what we're doing, but I honestly don't see what difference it makes. We're not doing anything we wouldn't be doing otherwise, except for buying garbage computers so we don't get bled a second time. You know, if this gravity guy hits us again, we'll probably lose our insurance policy—unless we catch him. There's a lot riding on this, Liz—too much—to stand around doing nothing."

There was no argument for that. "So we just pretend to work? For how long? Tim, we've got deadlines."

"We'll have to do our real stuff in the evenings for a while, Liz. It'll be two months before we get the Tempest-approved stuff, and until then we can use our personal equipment."

"My equipment's not that good," Liz admitted. "I never upgraded because we always had top-of-the-line at the office that I could use whenever I needed something better. It'll be like working with a dinosaur."

"Me, too," he admitted. Like Liz, whenever he had needed better equipment, he'd gone to the office. "I'm sure we can have a couple of new machines burned-in and delivered early next week."

"Have them delivered here. I don't see any point in working at your place the way you suggested the other night. I've got plenty of room in the basement to set up a couple of work stations. We can use that big old game table in the corner down there for a desk. It'll hold two systems easily."

His initial reaction was to flatly refuse. He was no less concerned now than when he had originally suggested they work at home that Liz might somehow come between this creep and whatever he wanted. His intent in working at his place had been to keep any and all bait as far away from Liz as he could. Still, if the gravity man decided to come after them personally, maybe it wouldn't matter whether or not there was a computer in the vicinity. Besides, if they were pretending to work as usual at the office, why would anybody suspect they were actually working at home?

"Okay," he said, wishing he didn't feel as if there were some angle he'd forgotten to consider. "We'll have the systems delivered here."

Indian summer had come to the valley. Brilliant crimson and gold leaves had begun to appear amidst the green and the sky had taken on the incredible blue of October, but the day was balmy. They drove Tim's truck into a larger nearby town, with the windows down and the fragrant breeze whipping through the cab.

Liz wrapped her hair around her hand to keep it from blowing into an impossible snarl and leaned her head back, enjoying the rush of wind on her face. Sometimes, just occasionally, a day came along that was just too beautiful. A day where it was impossible not to be glad to be alive. This was one of those days, and for now she let tension and worry seep away beneath the warmth of the sun and the caress of the breeze.

Turning her head a little, she could open her eyes just a fraction and watch Tim as he drove. His bronzed, muscular arms and large hands made the steering wheel look small, almost toylike. He was such a large, powerful man, she thought dreamily. Built on mythic proportions. When she looked at Tim O'Shaughnessy, it was easy to imagine being literally swept off her feet and carried away as easily as if she were featherdown.

It gave her strange, edgy, pleasurable feelings in the pit of her stomach to imagine those hands on her. Easy to imagine them nearly spanning her waist. Twice he had kissed her, but never had his hands strayed out-of-bounds. Nobody's hands had ever strayed out-of-bounds with Liz Pennington. Well, she had always discouraged men who tried to move past a chaste good-night peck. Now she wondered just how a woman encouraged a man to stray. How did she ask without asking for sensual touches and caresses? How did she let a man know she wanted something more?

And what was she doing wondering about it? Such musings never got her anything but a dissatisfied, hollow ache in places she preferred to pretend she didn't have. But surely her curiosity was natural? And surely, in this day and age of sexual frankness, she could satisfy her curiosity without getting pregnant. All she had to do was visit the doctor and she could be sure—well, almost sure—that she wouldn't wind up a single parent. And then she could find out just what it was those kisses of Tim's promised. She could find out if reality lived up to its billing.

And then she could face this man every day for the next thirty years, over their computers, and pretend nothing so intensely personal had happened between them. Right! *Grow up, Liz.* You'd never be able to look him in the eye again. And worse, you'd probably give him those last little bits of your heart that don't already belong to him. If there were any such fragments still left, and she wasn't at all sure about that.

She sighed, then hoped the sound had been covered by the growl of the engine. Tim seemed not to have noticed anything, just kept his attention on the road.

It sure hurt, she found herself thinking. She'd been calling it friendship for five years, and maybe that's all it was, but it was a little scary when she looked within herself. All this time she had been using Tim as a measuring stick by which all other men fell short. She hardly even dated anymore, because other men looked stupid, unattractive, or immature by comparison. When she looked at her future, it had ceased to hold any images that didn't revolve directly around Millennium Software and Timothy F. X. O'Shaughnessy.

And all *he* wanted was an adult relationship!

Maybe…maybe she could manage that. Maybe, if she was very careful not to let him know just how involved her feelings were, she could convince him, at least, that she was the kind of sophisticate he wanted. Maybe she could seize what he was offering and keep the hurt inside where no one could see it.

Because it already hurt. And as far as she could tell, it wasn't going to get any better. Maybe…maybe if she didn't try to bind him with any of those ties he didn't want, maybe he could settle into a relationship with her that would be as comfortable for him as their business relationship. Maybe he'd dumped all those other women because they had wanted more than he could give. If she didn't ask for any more—

She cut that thought off, coming abruptly to her senses. *Men only want one thing from a woman, and as soon as they get it they're gone.* That had been one of her mother's favorite warnings, and it sounded like an alarm in Liz's head right now.

On the other hand, though, she found herself thinking suddenly, that hadn't kept her mother from getting involved again and again. Maybe it shouldn't keep her from taking a chance, either. Deciding to give the matter more thought, she turned her attention away from Tim and watched the passing scenery.

They lucked out at the computer store. Not only did they manage to get a promise of a Monday delivery to Liz's house of the machines on which they could perform their unclassified work, but the shop had two outdated clone systems in the storeroom that they gladly sold for a song. Well, *almost* a song, Tim grumbled as he cosigned the check. Even old technology had a price tag.

"You know, I started programming nearly twenty years ago."

Liz turned to look at him, too interested to pretend otherwise. There was a whole lot she suddenly wanted to know about him, but there never seemed to be any good way to ask. Now that she was interested and alert, she had come to realize that large portions of Tim O'Shaughnessy's mind and past were off-limits.

"Back then, I worked on a System 360. Damn thing needed a whole huge room to itself, air-conditioning—the works. And we typed our programs on punch cards. Have you ever used a keypunch machine, Liz?"

"Yes, briefly. It was awful."

"Awful barely begins to describe it, especially if you had a program that was a few thousand lines long. As a student, I had to do my own keypunching. Then I'd turn in the stack of cards and wait days—*days,* Liz—to get back a note saying that the damn thing hadn't run at all. They didn't have debuggers and smart compilers back then."

He shook his head and smiled. "It still awes me that I can sit down to a machine every bit as powerful as that 360, a machine that fits on my desk and talks back to me instantly, and tells me whenever I screw up program syntax. Hell, it awes me that I can go out and buy a pocket calculator for a couple of bucks. Calculators used to be these huge machines that we had to sign up for time on. For that matter, when I was in school we were still using slide rules."

The salesman was looking at Tim as if he were an extinct species, and Liz felt laughter bubble up inside her. Tim remained blissfully oblivious.

"Damn," he said, distracted by his own train of thought. "I can't remember the last time I saw a slide rule. I wonder if you can still buy them?"

"Maybe they sell replicas at the Smithsonian," Liz suggested facetiously. She accepted the bill of sale and took Tim's arm, urging him toward the door. She knew this mood of Tim's. He could follow an intriguing idea to the exclusion of everything else, becoming totally absorbed in it.

"That's a thought," he said. "Maybe I'll call them and ask them. You know, they must still be making slide rules, Liz. Really. There are places in the world where they're probably still useful...although I have to admit I'd take a solar-powered scientific any day."

Their next stop, the store that sold electronic security equipment, provided a distraction that totally drove all thought of slide rules from Tim's mind. Liz, having only a minimal background in electronics, was almost instantly lost, but Tim and the salesman, both aficionados to judge by their instant rapport, were off and running.

On this subject, Liz was content to let Tim make the decisions, so she occupied her time by reading brochures. It wasn't long before she was utterly appalled by the kinds of surveillance equipment that were available to the general public. Cameras that looked like overhead water sprinklers. Eavesdropping devices that could hear conversations simply by picking up the vibrations in window glass. It boggled her mind.

Tim bought three of the water-sprinkler cameras. Well, nobody would ever notice them. He also bought an infrared detector, a motion detector and a tie-in silent alarm that would phone him automatically if anyone got into their offices.

She nearly strangled when she cosigned the check.

Back at the office, Tim shooed Donna on her way for the weekend, assuring her that he and Liz were merely going to set up their new computer equipment, and that they could handle the few phone calls they might get. Donna appeared reluctant, but Tim was adamant.

"Why did you make her go?" Liz wanted to know. "Donna wouldn't say anything about what we're doing."

"Probably not. Then again, why chance it? People *do* have slips of the tongue."

Tim bent to gather up his purchases and carry them to the back, but paused as the NPS man made an unexpected appearance.

"Not a delivery," he said hastily as he handed Liz a manila envelope and saw her reach automatically for a pen. "We were talking about this the other day, Ms. Pennington, and I just wanted to be sure you knew about this. See you." He left.

Liz looked at Tim, shrugged and opened the envelope. Inside was a photocopy of an article from a popular computer magazine, titled "VDTs and Radiation Hazards: Dangerous Devices?" She lifted her eyes to Tim's. "He warned me about X rays from the monitors. You don't suppose...?"

Tim hesitated. "It's not quite the same thing as disturbing the gravity, but maybe...maybe you'd better show that to Laurel and Hardy."

She tucked the envelope safely into her purse, and then forced the matter from her mind. It couldn't be Chuck, she assured herself. The concern about X rays was a genuine one, unlike the stuff about gravity. Right? Right.

Liz might not know a lot about electronics, but she knew how to put a computer system together, so she took over that task while Tim went to work on the alarm system and cameras.

He had just finished installing the second water-sprinkler camera, this one in his office, when he came down the hall and turned into Liz's office, ready to install the last one.

Liz was on her knees, head tucked under her desk, as she struggled with cords and plugs. Tim came to an abrupt and complete halt as the view hit him right between the eyes. Damn! she had a cute tush, he thought. He had the worst urge to touch her there, just a gentle little squeeze to see if that tempting little rump felt as sweet as it looked. She'd probably have a conniption fit over it, though, and would bang her head on the desk. He could see it already.

But for a moment he indulged himself with the view and felt the burning ache build. It had been a while, he found himself thinking, since he had ached so swiftly, and with so little provocation. Long gone were the days of his youth, when he'd felt like a kid in a candy store, every woman an erotic sight. These days it took more than just a sight of anything to turn him on.

Except with Liz. Suddenly just knowing she was in the next room was enough to turn him on. Great. He could just imagine her reaction to that. So he did the Tim O'Shaughnessy thing. The outrageous thing. The kind of thing that always made her take off like a rocket and was guaranteed to put a safe distance between them.

"You've got beautiful buns, Liz. I think I'll take a snapshot. Or better yet, maybe I'll sneak a squeeze while you're stuck under there."

He waited. She tensed. He saw her grow very still, all her struggles with the cords coming to an abrupt halt. She froze, but that sweet little tush stayed up in the air. She didn't jerk up in indignation and bang her head, and she didn't screech in fury.

No. She just froze. Almost as if she were caught in the same

molasses that suddenly swamped him. That made him uneasy. It
was one thing to admit he wanted her when she was trying to
keep a distance, another entirely to admit he wanted her if she
wanted him, too. Because if they both faced their desire at the
same time, there would be no one to protect Liz. And that was
suddenly of paramount importance to Tim. He had to protect Liz
from himself and from herself.

"Liz? Are you okay?"

She moved then, backing out from under the desk. "What do
you want, O'Shaughnessy?" she asked irritably. Turning, she sat
cross-legged and scowled up at him.

Perversely, he was irritated by her annoyance, even though that
was exactly what he'd hoped to provoke. "What's eating you?"
he grumbled. "I was only teasing, for Pete's sake."

"Were you?" Her tone was frosty. "That kind of teasing con-
stitutes sexual harassment, Tim."

"Sexual harassment! If that isn't just like a woman! You stick
your tush up in the air where any man who isn't dead and buried
is *bound* to notice it, and then you accuse him of sexual harassment when he does!"

Liz pushed herself to her feet. "I was *working,* not sticking my
tush in the air!"

He opened his mouth to say something maddening and then
forgot what it was. She looked so...so *lovable* standing there glaring at him that he wanted to swallow her up in a bear hug and
squeeze her until she squeaked. That yearning was so far from
the sexual that it unnerved him, and he began to wish he had
never opened his mouth. That he had never kissed her. That he
had never noticed her. That he had never...oh, hell, who was he
kidding? He wouldn't have missed knowing Liz Pennington for
the world.

And now that he did, he was just going to have to live with
the discomfort that went along with knowing her and wanting
her. He reminded himself of his promise to behave like a gentleman with her, at least for as long as he was sharing her roof.
Hell, only the worst kind of cad would put a woman in the position of sharing her home with a man who was trying to take
advantage of her.

Of course, he thought, drawing a deep breath in the hopes that it might quiet his rising sap, Liz would just tell him to get out if he *did* get out of line. She was no shrinking violet, his Liz.

And Tim O'Shaughnessy was no gentleman. No, he was the son of a hard-drinking, hard-swearing, hard-living Irish cop, a damn-the-torpedoes kind of guy, and Tim was more than a little like his dad. What he knew about gentlemanliness had been gleaned from Arthurian legend and an innate instinct for gentleness.

Right now, though, his instincts were more warriorlike, and they were telling him to sweep this woman up in his arms, to bear her down beneath him and claim her. To make her his with his lips and hands and body, and to bring her to submission by awakening her to her own womanhood. His palms itched with the need to feel her silky skin, and his loins ached with a hunger to be buried in her satin heat.

And he was going to be a *gentleman?*

Yes. He was.

"Sorry," he said. His voice was so rusty it cracked, and every inch of him rebelled at the decision he had just made. "Sorry," he said again, and turned away. The damn camera could wait.

What the heck had gotten into him? Liz wondered as she watched his broad back disappear down the hall toward his office. First he had come on like a rutting bull...

That was when she realized her own knees were weak, that she was trembling and her mouth was dry, and that right alongside her panic was a yearning so deep it was ripping her up. Oh, God!

Shaking, she sagged back against her desk and wrapped her arms around herself, unconsciously comforting herself as she had since childhood, because there had never been anyone there to comfort her. Oh, God, she thought, she wasn't going to be able to stand this! How could she stand wanting him so bad that she ached, so bad that she could nearly weep from the longing? How could she stand not giving in?

But how could she stand herself if she did?

Well, he'd done it again, Liz thought sourly several hours later as she rattled pots and slammed cupboard doors. After getting her all stirred up at the office, he'd retreated into monolithic silence. He wouldn't even give her the satisfaction of an argument to work off all the steam he had built up in her.

She hated to cook. She cooked only because she had to, and tonight was going to be worse than usual: bottled spaghetti sauce, pasta and lettuce wedges. The activity gave her an excuse to work off some of her frustration, though.

Darn it! For the first time in her life she wanted a man enough to say "be damned" to the consequences. She wanted him enough, and sometimes he seemed to want her enough, too. Enough to give her a few tender buds of confidence. And then, poof! he was all nobility again, backing away from her inexperience. Protecting her. Oh, she knew perfectly well why he kept pulling back. Galahad couldn't have been any more noble-minded!

If it *was* nobility. She paused in the middle of slicing the lettuce and stared blindly out the window that was over the sink. Maybe he was scared, too?

Of what? O'Shaughnessy *scared?* She couldn't begin to imagine it. But why ever not? He'd admitted to being scared when he was wounded, and he was only human after all.

So maybe they were both equally scared, she thought. They were certainly giving a wonderful imitation of two people stumbling by fits and starts into dangerous and uncharted territory.

And maybe she would be wise to let things cool down and blow away. Surely she didn't want to give in to simple lust at this late stage of her life. That kind of thing might be forgivable in a woman of thirty. She had always made her choices intelligently, not in a burst of—of hormones!

Oh, Lord, who was she trying to kid? This wasn't simply lust or hormones. She'd been dealing with *that* since the instant Tim O'Shaughnessy had first materialized beside her at the Denver trade show. Five years later she still remembered his initial physical impact and the way everything inside her had turned softly, warmly feminine. She'd never forget the way he had, O'Shaughnessy fashion, simply plunged in, taken over and carried her away with him. And in no time at all, she had discovered how much she liked him.

With a sigh, she closed her eyes a moment before she resumed making dinner. Well, she'd managed to keep her desire for him buried for five years. She could rebury it if necessary. But it sure would be a whole lot easier if he'd quit sending mixed signals.

* * *

"This sauce is delightful, Pennington."

"It's out of a bottle."

"Oh. Well, I like the way you served it. And the salad, too."

"Cut it out, O'Shaughnessy. This dinner is a tribute to the culinary skills of several major corporations, and you know it."

"Touchy, aren't we?"

Liz's head snapped up and a dozen nasty comebacks sprang to mind. Unfortunately, his expression took the wind from her sails. Gray eyes regarded her with understanding that showed no flicker of amusement, and Liz deflated.

She sighed. "I just don't feel like talking, okay?"

"Okay," he agreed amiably. "I'll talk and you just say 'Mmm hmm' from time to time."

"O'Shaughnessy—"

"Have you ever been tobogganing, Pennington? Or sledding down a steep hill on fresh snow?"

"Well, sure..." So much for not talking.

Tim dumped another dollop of tomato sauce on his pasta. "Sometimes," he said in the same friendly tone, "you're sledding down a steep hill with the wind stinging your face, and every nerve ending is alive with the excitement and thrill of the plunge. It's just a ride, just a short, fantastic ride." He glanced at her to be sure she was listening.

"And then," he continued, "you hit this unexpected snow drift. It's all fresh powder and it flies up in your face and blinds you. Suddenly you don't know where you're going and you don't know what lies ahead."

He looked down at his plate. "Suddenly it's a little less thrilling and a lot more frightening. So you roll off the sled. That doesn't mean you won't climb to the top of that hill and slide down all over again. But before you do, you want to think a little more about what you're doing. You want to try to be sure that nobody gets seriously hurt."

Liz felt her throat tighten and she quickly looked away from Tim. Darn, the man was turning her into a watering pot! She should have guessed. In all the years she'd known Tim O'Shaughnessy, she had never once known him to willfully hurt another person. So he *was* being noble, darn him. And careful, cautious, sensible and all those other miserably adult things. And she was grateful for it. She cleared her throat. "Thanks, Tim."

He looked her straight in the eye, his expression grim. "I don't want to break anything, Liz. Or anyone. Don't thank me for that."

Before she could do more than blink at his sudden gruffness and his growly tone, the doorbell rang. Liz, thinking it had to be a neighbor, started to rise, but Tim stopped her, heading for the door himself.

"Just in case," he reminded her.

"Great. There goes my reputation."

"Pennington, your reputation was shot the minute I moved in."

"Yeah, but until they meet you, none of my neighbors will dare mention it to my face. Once they've been introduced, you're open season."

Midstride, Tim paused and looked back at her. His face reflected genuine concern. "Is this a problem, Liz? Honestly, I never considered..."

Liz barely managed to contain her smile. "Quit being nice, O'Shaughnessy. I may be borderline Victorian, but I'm not medieval."

The last person Tim expected to find on the other side of Liz's front door was Donna's eldest son, James. Other than that UFO thing he'd heard about at the office the other day, he hadn't imagined Liz and James had any kind of relationship away from the office.

The young man seemed equally surprised to see Tim. "Oh, uh...hi, Tim. Is Liz here?"

"Sure. Come on in, James. You two got something going I don't know about?"

James flushed to the roots of his hair. He started stammering and Tim took pity on him.

"Just teasing. Come on. Liz is in the kitchen."

Tim was ashamed to admit it, but he felt a twinge of jealousy at the warm way Liz welcomed James. There was nothing but simple pleasure in her smile, and he wondered why she had never smiled at him that way, as if she was just plain glad to see him.

Well, when had he ever given her cause to be? There was no reason... Suddenly arrested, Tim stared at her, blessed with a vision of the way she used to smile at him when they had first started planning their business venture, and back during their first year or so of operation.

Damn! Had he been so tough to get along with all this time

that he had killed her liking for him? When had she become so impatient with him? So *sisterly?* Probably not too long after he had started treating her like one, he concluded glumly.

And then James fully snared Tim's attention with what he was saying.

"I was offered a job on campus today," James told Liz, "so I guess you'll need to find another janitor."

Liz was attending James with a warmth and interest that Tim was suddenly piercingly jealous of. Shocked at himself, he kept quiet, even though the subject involved him, too.

"Is it that dorm-assistant job you wanted?" Liz asked James.

"No." The boy glanced nervously at Tim. "It's in the food service, but it's a lot more hours, especially on weekends when I have the time. I can't pass it up, Liz."

"Of course not. When do you start?"

"Monday."

The boy obviously wanted to be on his way, and Tim held his peace while Liz walked James to the door. She was so nice to James, so gentle and warm, that Tim felt another pang of jealousy, a feeling that was far more terrifying to him than any amount of sexual desire. Jealousy, for him at least, required a degree of possessiveness and emotional involvement that he never wanted to feel again. Ever.

A few minutes later, Liz wandered back into the kitchen. "Great," she said, "now we need a part-time janitor. I suppose they grow on trees."

Tim spoke rustily. "We'll find another student. Maybe a high school kid. In fact, I wouldn't be surprised if Donna's other boy might be interested. He's in high school, isn't he?"

Liz nodded. "He's a junior."

"Well, he'll probably—" He broke off as the doorbell rang again. "Grand Central Station," he muttered, heading toward the front of the house. "This time it *has* to be one of your neighbors."

It was the FBI.

Her first thought was that they'd caught the person who had trashed the office, a thought she voiced as she led the way to the living room.

"I'm afraid not, Ms. Pennington," Agent Carter said. "Actually we just need to ask you and Mr. O'Shaughnessy a couple more questions.''

"I can't imagine that there's any question you haven't already asked," Liz said tartly.

"Well," Carter said pleasantly enough, "there were a couple of avenues we neglected to explore, since you and Mr. O'Shaughnessy denied any association with fringe elements.''

"'Fringe elements'?" In astonishment, Liz looked at Tim, who looked back at her with the same doubtful expression.

"In your case, Ms. Pennington," Carter continued, "we need to explore your association with SCUFO. Your secretary's son is a member, isn't he?"

"Well, yes—"

"And you gave a talk to the organization just last month, didn't you?"

"Well, yes, but—"

"Just how closely associated with the organization are you?"

"Not very—"

Carter pointed at her bookshelves. "You have quite a collection of UFO books, don't you?"

"Yes, but—"

"Wait just a minute, Carter," Tim said, interrupting the agent as ruthlessly as the agent had interrupted Liz. "I don't like the way you're talking to her. *She's* not a suspect!"

A warm feeling for Tim flooded Liz, banishing all the irritation she had ever harbored toward him. Darn, it had been a lifetime since anybody had stood up for her. Still, she was perfectly capable of fighting her own battles. She opened her mouth to say so, but Carter's attention was focused on Tim.

"Well, we could talk about *your* friends among the fringes, Mr. O'Shaughnessy." Tim's intervention had plainly annoyed him.

"My friends? Now wait one—"

"For example, there are the deranged people you counsel at that storefront veterans' center—"

This time it was Special Agent Woodrow who interrupted Carter. "That's enough, Bill."

"The people I work with at the center aren't deranged," Tim said between clenched teeth.

"Of course not," Woodrow said. "I'm a vet myself, Mr. O'Shaughnessy. Agent Carter's choice of word was unfortunate."

"Unfortunate! It was an insult! And it shows just how closed his mind is!"

Liz had seen Tim wound up before, but never in all the five years she'd known him had she seen him genuinely furious. He was furious right now, and there was something in the way he clenched his fists, in the way his eyes glittered, that was truly frightening. She got the definite impression that Tim O'Shaughnessy on the rampage would be an absolutely awesome sight. Unfortunately, the individuals he was preparing to rage against were Federal agents. Surely that would be good for a decade or so at San Quentin.

The agents were aware of the threat, too, and both of them were making subtle movements that were at once defensive and placating. Seeing the volatility of the situation, Liz did the only thing she could to protect Tim—she stepped between him and the agents. As soon as she moved, the atmosphere lightened remarkably. Both agents relaxed visibly.

"I'm not going to hit him, Liz," Tim said gruffly. "The temptation is there, but I can resist it."

"I'm sure you can," she answered. "I'm not worried about what *you* might do." And she wasn't. But as long as the two agents felt threatened by the combination of Tim's obvious size and strength, and his anger, there was a danger that *they* might precipitate the trouble.

"Look," said Woodrow, "why don't we backtrack a little and get to the meat of the matter. Carter here will keep his mouth shut."

"Fair enough." Tim forced himself to sit down in an armchair and cross his legs. Damn, even after all these years, that kind of attitude got his dander up faster than anything. He often wondered if vets from Korea and the Second World War had to put up with this kind of crap. Had people thought they were crazed killers, too?

"I understand how you might find this offensive," Woodrow said frankly, "but you have to acknowledge that some groups are more attractive to unbalanced persons than other kinds of groups. SCUFO would be more likely to appeal to a schizophrenic than the Parent-Teacher Association, for example. And like it or not,

Mr. O'Shaughnessy, some veterans *are* mentally ill, just as there are mentally ill persons among the population as a whole. It was unfortunate that Carter made it sound as if everyone associated with these groups has a mental problem. That isn't what brought us here tonight. We're concerned about the attraction factor. That's all.''

Tim nodded. He was still annoyed, and he wished he could argue otherwise, but he knew Woodrow was right. Some groups were more attractive to weirdos than others. Plain and simple. "But that still doesn't explain what you want from us. If either of us had noticed someone we believed capable of the destruction of our office, we would have told you, Woodrow. You can't possibly think we would have forgotten to mention something like that.''

"Of course not.'' The agent managed a thin smile. "I don't think the vandal is obviously unbalanced. If he were, neither you nor we would be having a hard time figuring out who he is. No, Mr. O'Shaughnessy, I think our perpetrator is a good deal more cunning than that. Superficially he probably seems very normal.''

Woodrow shifted his attention to Liz. He probably, she thought, found O'Shaughnessy's glowering difficult to endure. *She* certainly would have.

"We really just want you to think about these people, and other slight acquaintances,'' Woodrow continued. "There may be some small thing, some eccentricity or other that, if you think about it, could be the tip-off we need. Just be more alert.''

"I take it,'' Tim said after a moment, "that you don't think it's Chuck.''

"Chuck?''

"The NPS man.''

"We're still checking him out. The thing you have to remember is that the perpetrator could be anybody you know. Anybody at all.''

Tim used that opening to tell the agents about Chuck's giving Liz the article on computer terminals, and then to keep his promise to Liz. He told Woodrow about the cameras and alarms he had installed at the office, and explained that he hoped their apparent return to work there would draw the gravity man out again. Woodrow admitted that he had been thinking of proposing just such a scheme, and seemed pleased with what Tim and Liz had done.

Tim ushered the agents to the door and returned to find Liz still perched on the arm of the chair. He paused in the doorway, and for several moments neither of them spoke. They studied one another as if trying to gauge each other's reactions to this latest development.

Finally Liz broke the silence, her voice soft. "You never mentioned that you counsel at the veterans' center."

"Until a couple of days ago, you never mentioned that you see UFOs," he retorted.

"I don't *see* UFOs, O'Shaughnessy. I saw *one* UFO."

He shrugged a shoulder, aware that he was feeling petty and childish, probably because he was so damn sick of carrying Vietnam around like a mark of Cain. Why should Liz care that he counseled at the center unless she shared Carter's feelings? Maybe Liz, too, thought *veteran* was a dirty word. Maybe she thought the guys he worked with were all crazed killers. Maybe she was just another one of those people who judged without understanding.

"You sure got one hell of a library for somebody who just happened to see one UFO," he heard himself say with a bitter edge. "And you even give talks on it, for crying out loud."

"I gave *a* talk, O'Shaughnessy. One brief little anecdotal speech as a favor to a friend."

She wasn't angry, and somehow that was scaring him. Damn it, she was looking at him as if she were hurt, wounded. Or so very, very saddened.

"And the books?" he heard himself ask, cursing the devil that drove him. He didn't really care about the books, and Liz could see a UFO every day of her life if she wanted to. He wouldn't care, so long as she wouldn't look so *sad!*

"You know me, Tim," she answered quietly. "I like everything to be neat and orderly. I read all those books because I was *sure* there had to be an explanation for what I saw. I was convinced I could find it if I just kept looking." She gave a slight shrug. "I was wrong, and eventually I gave up.

"As for SCUFO, well, they're a neat bunch of kids, and they're looking for answers, too. I suppose some of them could be crazy, but most of them are just curious and having a good time."

For several minutes, he just stood there, fingers thrust into the front pockets of his snug jeans. He stared at the floor, tracing the sculptured pattern of the rug with his eyes.

"Tim, I'm sorry," Liz said finally. "I honestly didn't mean to make it sound like an accusation when I asked about your work at the center. It wasn't an accusation. Actually, I was just surprised and impressed. I wasn't aware you did volunteer work."

Slowly he lifted his head. "Why do you look so damn sad?"

"Because I *am*." She looked away, swallowing hard. "I feel as if everything's falling apart. I've always been a trusting person, and suddenly it isn't safe to trust anymore. I *hate* it, I hate the whole idea, and yet the person who destroyed our business is probably someone I know."

She turned her sad hazel eyes on him. "I also hate the fact that you ever had to go to Vietnam, and I hate the fact that all these years later you still feel defensive about it."

That rattled him a little because, stupid as it suddenly seemed, he hadn't realized that he felt defensive about being a vet. He shifted uneasily, contemplating this unexpected view of himself, and he didn't like it at all. He guessed he wasn't as well adjusted as he'd always thought he was. Well, that was something to think about another time. Right now, Liz's eyes were bright with unshed tears, and he had to do something about that.

"You can trust *me*, Liz," he said gruffly.

She gave him a wobbly smile. "I know that, Tim. I've *always* known that."

There was nothing else for it. For that he *had* to hug her, and he scooped her up from her perch as easily as if she were dandelion down.

"Pennington," he said gruffly, "that is one of the nicest things anyone has ever said to me."

She squeaked. "You're going to drop me!"

"No way!" he growled, trying to remember why it was he'd been keeping his distance from her. Oh, yes, because he was living under her roof. He was trying to avoid putting her in an untenable position.

"Tim," she begged, "please put me down before one of us gets hurt!"

He set her gently, carefully, on her feet only because he was no longer sure he could hold her without ravishing her. The need he felt for this woman seemed to grow with each breath he took, and that was the *other* reason he was keeping his distance. He wasn't masochistic enough to make the situation any harder on himself than it was already. Damn, he wished they would get to the bottom of this so he could move back into his own place. Trying to be a gentleman was apt to take ten years off his life.

"Liz?"

She was standing there as if uncertain whether to back away or move closer. "Hmm?" The floor appeared to fascinate her.

"There's a great science-fiction movie on in twenty minutes. One of the really old ones from the days when nuclear testing was mutating ants into monsters and the scientist wore a suit and drove a wood-paneled station wagon."

"A classic."

"Exactly. What say we make popcorn and watch it?"

Liz awoke during the night in a state of heart-slamming terror. Her room was as dark as pitch and as silent as a tomb. Certain that something had alarmed her in her sleep, she lay stiffly for several minutes, straining to hear or see anything. She was terrified that someone was in the room with her.

And finally, hearing nothing but the thunder of her own heartbeat, she forced herself to sit up and switch on the light. Empty. Her room was empty—except for Mephisto, who regarded her solemnly from his perch atop the dresser.

The cat, she thought as relief flooded her. The cat must have bumped something. Her mind accepted the explanation readily, but her body, full of adrenaline and ready for fight or flight, wasn't so cooperative. Sleep vanished and restlessness took its place.

This business was really getting to her, she thought, as she turned off the light and lay back down. Most of the time she managed to deceive herself into feeling irritated by the inconveniences and being angry at the unknown vandal. Right now, however, she admitted she was scared. Scared? She was petrified! Bravado had been carrying her through, but at two in the morning bravado just wasn't enough. At two in the morning, a person felt very small, very alone and very frightened. At two in the morning, the mind insisted on thinking about all the things you'd managed to suppress all day long.

Like the moment of anger that was reflected in the destruction of the Millennium Software offices. Like the note that had threatened her and Tim if they didn't stop disturbing this poor sick person's gravity.

Mephisto yowled suddenly, a sound so unlike the usually silent cat that Liz found herself once again sitting upright with a galloping heart. This time she turned the light on immediately and looked around. The cat was no longer on the dresser but was sitting by the bedroom door. Green eyes stared unblinkingly at Liz.

"That does it," Liz said irritably. "You're going out. Now!"

At that precise moment, her bedroom door slammed open, and sent a howling cat streaking across the room. A yip of fright escaped Liz in the instant before she recognized the familiar, massive figure of Tim O'Shaughnessy.

He wore nothing but black briefs. Incredibly skimpy, magnificently tight, scandalously low bikini briefs. He might as well have been nude.

Chapter 8

"Are you okay?" Tim roared.

Liz choked, her gaze paralyzed, locked to a portion of the male anatomy with which she was totally unfamiliar, a portion that was lovingly delineated by those shockingly thin, tight briefs.

"Liz? My God, Liz, what's wrong?"

She was strangling. She could feel a tidal wave of color rush upward through her cheeks, and she just simply couldn't breathe. She had had no idea...

"Liz?"

"Tim..." She managed to croak his name, feeling she really ought to tell him to put something decent on, but before she could force another word past her constricted throat, he charged across the room and sat beside her on the bed. Taking her none too gently by the shoulders, he shook her.

"Are you choking?" he demanded.

She was, but she feared for her ribs if he attempted the Heimlich maneuver, which wouldn't help anyhow because she was strangling on her own embarrassment, so she shook her head.

"Tim," she gasped. "Tim, cover yourself!"

"Huh?" He looked down at his lap and realized what her problem was. About the only thing she couldn't tell through those briefs was his precise coloring. Worse, he was becoming a little aroused because of her nearness. He hadn't realized....

And then, to Liz's everlasting delight, Tim O'Shaughnessy blushed beet red to the roots of his hair. Reaching out, he snagged a corner of her blanket from the foot of the bed and tugged it over his midsection.

"Sorry," he mumbled. "I heard this awful yowl and I thought something was wrong."

She'd gathered that. Some wicked, previously unsuspected demon in her was also beginning to enjoy herself. She would once have bet her life that Tim *couldn't* blush. "It was the cat."

He turned even redder. "Will you recover?"

"From the cat's howling or from the sight of your... your...underwear?" Even though her embarrassment was fading, there was no way she could bring herself to actually say—to actually refer to—*that*.

That was when Tim smiled, a distinctly masculine, distinctly unholy smile. "Why, Liz, haven't you ever seen a man in his underwear before?"

For the second time, violent color rushed into her face. She nonetheless managed to maintain a pose of indifference. She would *not* give the man the satisfaction of knowing just how much he affected her. "No, I haven't, but it's hardly a shock. Your exercise shorts don't leave much to the imagination, either." There, that sounded very adult and controlled.

He wiggled his brows at her. "So you've been imagining me?"

That was too much. Most definitely too much. She dived for the covers, pulling them up over her head. Every last shred of her composure was shot, and all she could see behind her closed eyelids was a vision of O'Shaughnessy as he had appeared in her doorway minutes before—and how he had looked just before he covered himself. She wasn't so naive that she hadn't recognized the signs of his early arousal. How had she reached the age of thirty without realizing that the male body was so beautiful? So *sexy?* Oh, my word, what must he look like when he was *fully* aroused?

She groaned. "Go away!" She wasn't ready for this. She would *never* be ready for this.

Her voice emerged muffled from beneath the blankets, and for just a split second, Tim hesitated. But the devil was in him now, he realized. Unexpected heat had slipped past his guard. It made every nerve ending in his body sizzle like water on a hot grill to think of the way she had looked at him. To think she had never looked at anyone that way before.

The next thing Liz knew, one very large, very warm, very hard male body was under the blankets with her, and pressed snugly and hotly to her back from shoulders to calves. The cotton flannel of her nightgown, heretofore adequately warm and modestly thick, was suddenly no barrier and certainly no protection.

"Tim!" She ought to hit him, holler at him, shriek at him to go. She ought to scramble out of the bed and escape....

And suddenly every frantic thought in her head was silenced, and the tension in her limbs turned to a warm heaviness. One of Tim's hands slipped under her to cup her breast, and the other slid boldly between her legs to cradle her femininity through the flannel.

"Tim, no..." The words escaped her on the last little bit of air left in her lungs, a thin, almost inaudible plea. Everything in the world faded away except the hand on her breast and the hand on her womanhood. Who was she kidding? She wanted this. The small voice in her head, the last vestige of sanity, was a liar. The rest of her knew better.

"Tim," said that liar, "I don't think..."

"Shh. Don't think. You need this, Liz. Just let me give it to you." He kissed the nape of her neck and gently squeezed everything he had his hands on. "It'll be good, Liz, so good. I swear I'll make it good for you."

His husky whisper sent shivers racing up and down her spine and his kneading, stroking fingers caused her legs to go numb. From somewhere she found strength for one last protest. "Tim, no..."

"Shh." She was more nervous than reluctant; he could feel it. He could feel it in the minute movements of her body as she pressed against his hands and tried to ease herself. To hell with being a gentleman. He knew what she needed and he knew what he needed and it was what they *both* wanted, regardless of what they told themselves and each other.

A shudder of pleasure took him, a shudder so intense that it shook all the breath from him in a quick, ragged sigh. Damn, it felt so good, so satisfying, so electrifying to feel her pressed to him, to have her fill his arms.

"Just rest easy, Liz," he murmured. "You don't have to do anything at all." He felt a shiver roll through her as he began to rub her in a provocative rhythm. "Just feel."

Just feel. As if she was capable of doing anything else! She had never imagined that a pair of hands were capable of doing so much! The first shimmering ripples of desire far exceeded anything she had felt before. She ought to be embarrassed. She ought to protest this intimate invasion. She ought to be horrified that Tim was touching her in this familiar fashion without her express permission. Heck, she ought to be just plain horrified.

Instead she was lost. A heavy warmth weighted her limbs. Lightning streaked from the nipple he tugged so gently through the flannel, streaked in sparkling zigzags of fire to her core. And there, with exquisitely knowing fingers, he stroked a swelling nub, again through gently abrasive cotton. An earthquake rocketed outward from her epicenter in widening waves of pleasure.

Move? There was only one way she was capable of moving, and that was into his hands. Harder. Faster. Deeper.

He felt her come apart in his arms. She shattered like the fine crystal he knew her to be. She trembled and whimpered and thrust herself against his pleasure-giving hands. And then—and then a low, aching groan escaped her.

"That's the way," he whispered encouragingly. "Let it happen."

In shuddering waves it passed through her and she subsided against him, heavy and warm with repletion. Heavy and warm with the miracle of being a woman.

And that was when he remembered he didn't have a condom.

"Don't move, Liz. Ah, darlin', *don't move!*"

Since she really wasn't capable of moving, it was easy enough to comply with Tim's gruff request. She had only tried to move because he had given her so much, that she wanted to give a little of it back. It didn't seem right to be selfish with such a gift.

But for the moment she was content to enjoy her afterglow and to savor the wonder of what had just passed. The miracle of what had just happened. *This* was what she'd been resisting for half a lifetime?

Tim had changed his hold on her so that her head rested on his outflung arm, and his other arm was wrapped snugly around her waist. She could sense tension in him, but despite it he held her gently. Caringly. Her throat tightened. He might be as tactless as a bull in a china shop, but he was unfailingly gentle. Amazingly gentle.

"Go to sleep, Liz," he said now. Gently.

"But…" She ought to blush, but the past minutes seemed to have stolen the ability from her. "What about you?"

"Don't worry about it." Now he sounded gruff.

She might be inexperienced, but she wasn't ignorant. "Tim, that's not fair!"

"No, but it's wise." He was relieved to find he could chuckle about it. It was a rueful, grumbling chuckle, but it indicated that he was beginning to see the humor in his current misery. Yep, he'd made up his mind to be a gentleman, and all his nobility had gotten him into Liz's bed in the wee hours of the morning and there wasn't a condom to be had for miles.

"But…"

"Liz, I don't have any way to protect you."

"Oh."

He was relieved that she subsided then. If she wiggled against him much more, he'd lose the last of his sanity. He could tell she was thinking hard, and he was almost afraid of what might come next. There was a limit to what a mortal man could be asked to endure, after all. A limit. And he was getting perilously close to it.

She spoke, sounding suspiciously breathless. "I could… I've heard there are…other ways."

He sighed. Actually it was nearer to a groan. Damn, she was generous and sweet, but he couldn't allow it. No way. "Not this time, Liz," he managed to say. "Not your very first time. Now close your eyes and go to sleep. Just as soon as I can move, I'm going back to my own bed."

She didn't want him to leave. At the moment, she couldn't think of anything she would like more than to sleep the rest of the night in Tim O'Shaughnessy's arms. It was surprisingly comfortable and comforting to be held this way. But for Tim it would be cruel and unusual punishment, so she resigned herself to letting him go.

A few minutes later, he eased away from her. Nearly asleep, Liz nonetheless felt him go. The bed felt terribly empty afterward.

Things were not good in the morning. Tim knew it the instant he set eyes on Liz.

He had been congratulating himself on his superhuman will-power, not because he was conceited, but because he needed to throw some kind of sop to his agonized libido. Sop notwithstanding, he felt like a bear with a sore paw.

That was quite bad enough, but one look at Liz was enough to make it worse. It was obvious to him that she couldn't decide which kind of ogre he was. Every time he opened his mouth to speak, she tensed as if she expected some kind of lewd or suggestive remark to slap her between the eyes. When he was silent, she gave him wounded, embarrassed looks as if he had humiliated her beyond bearing. As if he had done something to her.

That *really* made him mad.

One of his patron saints must have been watching over him, however, because he kept his mouth shut despite a natural inclination to take the bull by the horns. Putting himself into Liz's shoes was no easy task, because he hadn't been a virgin since the age of sixteen, and inexperience hadn't lasted much longer. Half-way through his bowl of wheat germ, though, understanding began to dawn.

Liz, he reminded himself, was about as innocent as a cloistered nun. Last night they had gotten down a little, though certainly not very dirty, and she was naturally embarrassed by the intimacy and her subsequent uninhibited enjoyment. Worse, he had ignored her protests. He knew she hadn't really meant them, and in her heart she knew it, too, but this morning it was easy for her to believe nothing would have happened if he had just listened to her. He had been listening, all right—to her body, not her voice. He should have made sure she said yes out loud, and next time, damn it, he would make sure she did.

Of course, she was thinking these things only so she could blame him for her embarrassment. And it *was* his fault that she was embarrassed, he admitted glumly. He had exposed her vulnerability and had witnessed her loss of control, and yet had refused to expose himself to her in the same way. He had failed to remember that if you were going to turn another human being into a whimpering, writhing mass of needs, you'd better turn into one yourself. Otherwise it was embarrassing. Humiliating. It could even be considered manipulative.

So much for nobility, he thought grimly. It had gotten him nothing but grief. So what now? He had a feeling that any reference to last night was going to earn him a blistering diatribe and some third-degree burn marks. Last night would have to be handled, though. In the dark. When there was plenty of time to woo her, and when he had the kind of protection that would allow him to prove his point.

Hell's bells, how could he have been so dumb?

Liz wondered how she could have been so dumb. Tim had seen how turned on she was by him, and he'd *indulged* her, she thought. *You need this, Liz. Just let me give it to you.* Hadn't he said that? Yep. Those words were branded on her brain. And he hadn't even wanted her enough to let her...let her...never mind.

Oh, Lord, it was humiliating!

Some part of her mind noted that she was ignoring a few things—like Tim's plea for her to hold still—but her self-confidence was at an especially low ebb this morning. She had never been in bed with a man before, and when she finally had gotten there, the man hadn't let her make love to him. "Protection" didn't matter. He hadn't wanted her enough to let her do...other things.

"When's the next SCUFO meeting?" Tim asked abruptly.

Startled by a topic so far from her own miserable train of thought, Liz needed a moment to collect herself. "Uh...Monday night, I think. They meet the last Monday of the month. Why?"

"I think I ought to go with you."

"I wasn't planning to go at all!"

Her fuse was sure short this morning, he thought. Not that it was ever very long. Raising his hands, he motioned for time-out.

"Let me rephrase that, Pennington. I think *we* ought to go to the next SCUFO meeting. Together."

She regarded him distrustfully. "Why?"

"Because, much as it grieves me to admit it, that idiot agent is right. And maybe if we're both on the lookout we'll pick up on something."

Liz was in the mood for a good fight, but even in her irritable

state she couldn't take exception to that. "Okay," she said
shortly. "We'll go."

"Great."

"But only on one condition."

Tim tensed. "What condition?" The condition that he get out
of her house? That he never speak to her again? That...

"On the condition that you don't say anything offensive about
UFOs to these kids."

Relief nearly knocked him silly. Then he got mad. Again. Liz
Pennington was a maddening woman. The fact that he was so
damn attracted to her must mean that he was insane. "What the
hell makes you think I would? And what the hell gives you any
right to tell me how to behave?"

She was definitely dumb, she decided. Obtuse. Stupid. Not only
had she succumbed to this lout's attentions last night, but she had
actually been considering apologizing for her shrewishness this
morning.

"I know you, O'Shaughnessy! You say what you think and
damn the consequences. Tact isn't one of your native talents!"

"Maybe not, but I *do* know when to keep my mouth shut!"
His glare would have wilted a dragon. It didn't seem to faze Liz.

She drummed her fingers on the tabletop. "You won't mean
to be offensive," she said, "but you'll see the hole in somebody's
argument, and you'll jump right into it with both feet."

He ground his teeth. "I didn't say anything to you about your
UFO, did I?"

"No, but I could tell what you were thinking."

He surged upward from the table like an inevitable force of
nature, Liz thought. Like a tidal wave or a hurricane—there was
no restraining him. He stomped toward the door.

"Where are you going?" she asked. How dare he turn tail in
the middle of an argument!

"Out," he said succinctly. "I am going to try to make up my
mind whether I should go to the drugstore to buy condoms or go
to the hardware store to buy rat poison. Either choice will probably have the same dismal effect on my future."

He paused, hand on the door, to glower back at her. "While
I'm out, you might consider that you *don't* know what I'm thinking. Not about *you*, not about your damned UFO. Not about *anything*, Pennington!"

"Tim!"

But he was already gone, and moments later she heard his truck peel out of the driveway with an uncharacteristic grinding of gears.

How *dare* he mention condoms and rat poison in the same breath!

It was the first time he'd left her completely alone since the break-in. It wasn't that he'd been crowding her—for a big, noisy, annoying man, Tim could be surprisingly inconspicuous—but she hadn't been truly alone in days. Alone, which had once been comfortable and relaxing, was suddenly very uncomfortable. The house, her home for nearly five years, no longer seemed so bright, cheerful and welcoming. Now it seemed merely...empty.

Darn it, was she actually missing the big lummox?

All right, she was in a rotten mood this morning. She was in a rotten mood *every* morning, but this morning was worse than usual. Mainly because she didn't know how to act after last night. Etiquette books didn't cover this kind of thing, especially when you weren't sure of exactly what had happened or why. She had come down the stairs on the defensive this morning and had proceeded to pick a fight with Tim.

Condoms or rat poison. In the same breath!

And it was, truthfully, her fault, not his.

So what now, Liz? she asked herself unhappily. You're confused and a little frightened, which is probably natural, considering that was the first time you...the first time that anyone had ever...well, it was the *first time* for any of that. It was scary, overwhelming and embarrassing. She had done it, but it still embarrassed her to even *think* about it.

That didn't give her the right to treat Tim the way she had. He was right. She had no business setting conditions on his conduct, never mind the implied criticism in the condition. She knew better anyhow. However maddening, aggravating and tactless Tim O'Shaughnessy might be, he nevertheless had a heart of gold. She knew that.

So he hadn't been taking advantage of her last night. He had simply been trying to give her pleasure. And he had denied himself out of consideration for her inexperience and out of a desire to protect her.

She *knew* that. She knew it deep inside in places that had never been touched before. She knew it in her heart. Why did that scare her?

And why, whenever she felt frightened, did she turn nasty? Heavens, she had sent the man out of here muttering about poison! Somehow she had to apologize without appearing to invite a repetition of last night. Not that it hadn't been fantastic. But she just wasn't sure she wanted to take that step with Tim.

Oh hell, of course she wanted to take that step with Tim. *Wanting* wasn't the problem. The problem was that she wasn't sure if that step would be wise.

A sound outside the door snagged her attention and she turned her head to see Tim stepping into the kitchen with a rather sheepish expression on his face.

"I forgot my wallet," he said.

"Oh." She couldn't help it. An errant giggle escaped her. "No poison?"

He scowled. "No condoms, either."

Color suffused her face, a pretty pink, he thought.

"Maybe that's just as well," she said quietly.

"Try standing in *my* shoes," he groused. "Damn it, Liz, what are you so all-fired scared of? You can't possibly think I would ever hurt you."

"Not physically," she agreed, feeling all funny and warm inside because he had understood that she was afraid. He was a surprisingly understanding man. "And not intentionally. You're a nice, kind, generous-hearted man, Tim. But we've got to be able to work together for the rest of our lives."

He pulled out a chair and straddled it. "Fact is, Lizzie, I can't work with you the way things are."

Her stomach sank like stone. "Tim..."

"Shh." His expression was rueful. "I haven't written two lines of code since the night we went out for seafood. All I can think about is trying out the entire *Kama Sutra*. With you. That's what it's come to."

Her cheeks turned rosy, and all the air left her lungs. *The* entire *Kama Sutra*? At last she found energy to drag in some air, and on a gasp said, "What...what should we do?"

He leaned forward and caught her chin in his hand, holding her gently, but nonetheless making her look at him. "We go with the flow, Lizzie. I'm buying that protection. You just leave everything up to me."

"But..."

He shook his head. "Eventually, I'll ask you. Eventually, I'll get carried away and make another pass at you. And you say either yes or no. It's that simple, Liz. And that final."

That simple? That final? That was the problem. Why was he doing this to her? Why couldn't he just sweep her up in his arms and...

Chicken, Liz. You are chicken. And for heaven's sake, if you want the man to make the decision for you, then you really want to say yes, and you ought to have the guts to admit it.

And he really wasn't asking for very much. An unequivocal yes or no was a reasonable request. He wasn't asking her to seduce him, he wasn't asking her to perform a striptease at high noon or indulge in some exotic form of foreplay. He had just simply asked her to tell him straight-out: did she or did she not want him to make love to her?

He definitely had a right to know that.

And she didn't have the nerve to answer.

Although it was Saturday, she and O'Shaughnessy spent the day sitting at right angles to one another. Facing their monitors in Liz's basement, Tim having brought his old system over, they clacked industriously at their keyboards and studiously avoided locking gazes. Liz wasn't accomplishing anything at all, despite her pretense, and she suspected Tim wasn't doing much better. What was he thinking? Was he as uptight about her answer as she was?

Tim was uptight.

Whatever had possessed him to deliver an ultimatum to Liz? She must think he had lost his marbles. She was a *virgin,* for crying out loud! She had a right to be gently wooed and seduced, to be swept away on passion and romance until culmination was inevitable and welcome.

He ought to tell her to forget it, that he hadn't meant it, that he was sorry.... He sighed. He ought to, but he wouldn't. He was entitled to know where she stood, and she was a thirty-year-old woman who ought to be able to tell him that much. If she wanted him, he had a right to know. If she couldn't bring herself to tell him that much...well, maybe he ought to look elsewhere. There was a time for damning the torpedoes, and this wasn't it. He would *not* spend the rest of his life wondering if he had seduced an unwilling virgin. No way.

It had been a stressful week, Tim thought, and here it was Saturday night, and he and Liz had worked all day in her basement, missing a perfectly glorious Indian summer day. There ought to be a law against it.

The clock in Liz's kitchen reminded him that seven o'clock was fast approaching and that it was his turn to cook dinner. Liz had vanished upstairs to take her bath. She always took a bath at the end of the workday, he was discovering.

Closing his eyes, he could see her quite plainly in his mind's eye, her auburn hair caught up carelessly on the top of her head, her eyes closed as she languished in a heated, scented pool of water. He knew it was scented because it wafted from her and the bathroom both when she emerged. Something like lilac, only softer, more elusive.

His loins clenched and his heart slipped into double time. She'd be up there for at least half an hour, the devil in him purred. It would only take him ten minutes to run down to Hannibal's Drugs and buy what he needed. A whole box. A dozen. If he ever got into Liz's bed again, she was going to know she had been loved. Desired. Wanted. And he suspected that his forty years weren't going to slow him up much. Not with Liz.

He muttered a word that could have been a prayer or an oath and tried to concentrate on cooking dinner. The next thing he knew, he was in the cab of his truck, driving toward the drugstore.

How, he asked himself, could he keep this up? It was driving him crazy, this conflict between his most basic needs and his highest principles. He didn't think he had ever felt so messed up and tangled up in his feelings except about Nam. Then, too, there had been a conflict between his basic need to survive and his principles. He was still fighting that battle. Was he going to spend the rest of his life battling himself about Liz?

He pulled up right before the drugstore, and for a moment he actually thought he was going to back up and go home without getting what he'd come for. As long as he didn't have them, there would be one last thing to stop him. One last scruple he couldn't sacrifice.

But then, coiling into his mind like a cooling breeze on a steamy summer day was a question: who was he to make decisions for Liz? Why was he agonizing over his principles when the decision, in the end, should be hers? Surely it was for Liz to decide when and how to abandon her virginity?

He bought the condoms. A whole box. The most expensive kind. His hands were shaking when he drove back to Liz's house.

Sunk up to her neck in faintly scented warm water, Liz tried to relax. Ordinarily a long soak in the tub was the best way to unwind at the end of a day, and she needed desperately to unwind. She'd spent the whole day under the most incredible tension because of Tim.

It was because of Tim that she wasn't unwinding. Last night he had taken a few strands of her deepest fantasies and had tugged them into reality. He had showed her a glimpse of heaven, and the glimpse had far exceeded her wildest, most insane, most romantic imaginings.

With her eyes closed, she remembered the feel of his large hand kneading her breast, and remembered how aching pleasure had spread out from that touch in widening waves. Her thighs clenched, capturing only silky water between them as she remembered the deep, intimate stroke of his fingers. And all that through cotton flannel!

Memory alone was arousing her. Her breath grew shallow, her flesh tingled and a deep pulsing drew all her attention inward.

She wished...she wished Tim would climb those stairs right now. She wished he would walk through that door and kneel beside the tub. She wished that her eyes would open and see him there, see him reaching out to touch her breasts, her thighs. That he would take a washcloth, silence her instinctive, breathless protest with a kiss, a deep hot, throbbing kiss. That he would soap that washcloth and lave her gently, starting at her chin and working slowly—oh, so slowly—downward. She would stare into his gray eyes until she couldn't keep her eyes open any longer.

And then he would draw her up and out of the tub. He'd dry her, gently. Sensuously. And then—

Liz sat abruptly upright, her heart hammering. What was she

doing daydreaming when the man was right downstairs? When he had made it plain that he wanted her and that all she had to do was say yes?

Oh, God!

She wanted to, there was no denying it. She wanted to, yet she was terrified to. How could she explain the crazy flip-flopping her feelings were doing? How could she want and fear the very same thing? She was incapable of making the decision because her emotions pulled her both ways with equal strength. What she wanted, what she really wanted, was to have the decision taken out of her hands.

If he would just make one more pass, she would probably turn into putty for him. But again, it was a matter of asking without asking. She wanted to provoke him into seducing her, but didn't know how. She wanted it just to happen!

That understanding brought her out of the tub. While she watched the water spiral down the drain, she dried herself briskly, trying to ignore how exquisitely sensitive her skin seemed to be.

Maybe if she wore something provocative to dinner. Maybe if she didn't wear a bra, and wore a thin, silky blouse unbuttoned right down to her cleavage. Maybe if she wore...

Damn! She didn't own one silky, slinky, sexy piece of clothing. Not one. For too many years she had been trying to play down her female attributes. Even her one cocktail dress buttoned to the chin and had long sleeves. How could she turn T-shirts and jeans into sexy garments? How could she vamp in a sweat suit? Even assuming she knew how to vamp or had the courage to try.

Kneeling, she scoured the tub and rinsed it thoroughly, leaving it clean for Tim. He was a dear in some ways, she thought as she scoured. He might leave the toilet seat up and squeeze the toothpaste from the top, but he always scrubbed the tub after he used it. And wiped down everything else, except his shaving mug, judging from the continued cleanliness of her bathroom.

Rising, she smiled to herself and tried to battle the waves of desire that kept wanting to bury her in their warm, seductive heat. He'd try again. He had said so. Maybe by then she would know her own mind. Because suddenly it didn't seem so darn vital to remain uninvolved or to protect against possible pregnancy. In fact, except for Tim's resolve, she probably would have gotten herself pregnant last night.

And the really shocking thing that caused the corners of her mouth to pull up and her breath to catch, was that she suddenly realized she wouldn't have minded at all if she had gotten pregnant. In fact, the very notion filled her with a kind of delightful exhilaration. It would be nice to have Tim's child, and for once she didn't try to talk sense to herself.

Maybe...maybe it wasn't being a single parent that mattered most. Maybe what really mattered was who the father was. Because standing beside her bathtub clad in nothing but her own skin, Liz Pennington realized that all other considerations aside, she would love to have Tim's child. She would love to have that part of him, even if she could never have anything more.

So maybe she had something in her closet that would pass for sexy. Maybe there was something she could do or wear or say.

Grabbing one of Tim's bright orange towels, because they were so much bigger than her own, she wrapped it around herself, ignoring the pink jogging suit she had hung on the back of the bathroom door. There had to be something sexier than that in her closet.

Wrapped in nothing but the bath towel, she stepped out of the bathroom, planning to run to her bedroom. Tim, she believed, was downstairs in the kitchen cooking dinner.

Instead, he was standing halfway up the staircase, one foot hovering above the next stair, a small box in his right hand.

Tim looked up and time stood still. His breath caught in his throat, and his heart began a heavy, languorous beating, a primitive, pagan mating rhythm. She froze, like a startled doe caught in headlights, and stared back, towel clutched to her breasts.

He would never in his wildest imaginings have envisioned just how sleek she was. Full breasts hidden beneath oversize shirts had created a chunky look that, even while he had guessed it was exaggerated, even after he had held her and knew her slenderness, hadn't prepared him for her sheer grace and slimness. He had known her legs were long and slender—not even loose jeans could entirely hide that—but he hadn't imagined the grace of her thigh and calf, the satin sheen of her skin.

His mouth went dry as his gaze skimmed over her and then he raised his eyes to hers. She watched him almost warily from beneath the tumbling topknot of her long hair but there was more than wariness there, and it was that which made him climb a step. And then another.

She clutched the towel tighter and swallowed visibly, but she didn't run, or even draw back. He took yet another step and her lips parted.

"Liz?" His voice was a low, intimate growl. The question was implied.

Her tongue darted out to moisten her lips. "Tim?" She barely croaked his name, a question.

He stopped, one stair below the top. He had already told her she would have to say yes or no, and he was going to stick to that if it killed him. But heaven help him, he didn't have the strength to ask the question. He could give her the chance to escape, but he couldn't bring himself to spell it out. He was past that. The sight of the yearning in her hazel eyes had pushed him way past. They both knew she wanted him. But they both needed to hear her say it.

"Liz?"

She hesitated, understanding the import of this moment. Fantasy lay behind her, and reality waited ahead. It was up to her to determine *which* reality would emerge.

Licking her lips again, she stepped hesitantly toward him. It was a small, small step, a shy step, barely six inches. Made with a small, very feminine, delicate foot, Tim thought, looking down at it. Everything about Liz was small, feminine and delicate, he realized suddenly. Never had he been so aware of his own size and strength, of the ease with which he could harm something so delicate without even trying. For an instant, he worried that he might not know his own strength, that with a careless grasp he might crush.

Slowly he raised his gaze once again to hers. She ought to be afraid of him, he thought suddenly. He was older, bigger, rougher. He was no gentleman. He offered her nothing that she couldn't find elsewhere in a prettier package. She shouldn't...

But she did. She took another tentative step forward, offering him a trust that made him ache. How could she trust him so? How could she, in all her innocence, step toward him and offer him such a priceless, precious gift? She should demand assurances, require promises, swear him to gentleness and care. She deserved so much more! She should...

But she didn't. She took yet another step and suddenly let go of the towel.

Helplessly, his eyes followed the downward slide of orange terry cloth and soaked in every newly bared inch of smooth skin. Full breasts, tips tilted and crowned in delicate pink. Slender waist, so slender he knew he could certainly span it with his hands. Flat, smooth tummy, a gentle hollow between the swelling curves of her hips. Dusky shadow at the juncture of her thighs, soft-looking dark curls, thick and tempting. Long, long legs that he wanted, needed to feel wrapped around him.

Perfection. Every blessed, delicate inch of her was perfection.

She stepped forward another half step and he looked straight into her eyes.

"Yes," she whispered. "Yes."

Chapter 9

Still a step way from her, Tim knew that, once he took that last one, nothing would ever be the same again. He'd bedded his share of women in his life—though not nearly as many as Liz probably imagined—but never before had he felt this sense of significance in the moment of decision. His entire future was about to be affected.

He climbed that last step, anyway. The moment of decision had been over the instant Liz dropped that towel. Even if he hadn't wanted her until he shook with it, he couldn't have walked away after that. Dropping that towel had made her so completely and utterly vulnerable that his throat ached with emotions he couldn't begin to name. In those moments, he could have scarred her for life, but she had trusted him not to. Damn, were his eyes actually stinging?

She was trembling and frightened and determined. He could see all that in her eyes in the instant before he sheltered her nakedness with his body. Wrapping his powerful arms around her, he hugged her close and let go of an endless, ragged breath. She was here, tucked against him, and nothing had ever felt so good or so right or so satisfying. He pressed her cheek to his chest, against his rapidly pounding heart.

"You're sure about this?" he said huskily, because suddenly nothing he wanted mattered an ice cube in hell against what was right and best for Liz.

She nodded; he felt the movement against him. He felt, too, that she had, for the moment, reached the limits of what she could say or do. Her courage had been all used up. Now it was up to him.

He still held the box of condoms in his hand, and as he hugged Liz, he saw it and smiled inwardly. It was because of them that he had been coming up the stairs at precisely that time, intending to tuck them safely away in his bedroom just in case. It was because of them that this had happened.

Still smiling, he leaned back a little and thrust the box into one of Liz's hands, where it rested against his cotton-covered chest. "Hold this," he said huskily.

Her eyes fluttered open not six inches from the box, and he watched as the flood tide of red rushed into her cheeks. She didn't pull away, though, or run. No, she closed her fingers around the box and held it. It was all the remaining assurance he needed.

Bending, he slipped his arm beneath her knees and lifted her high against his heart. At once she hid her face shyly against his shoulder. Tenderness swamped him and he bowed his head to brush a gentle, reassuring kiss against her temple.

"Ah, Lizzie," he said softly as he carried her toward her room. "My darlin' girl."

Liz hated to be called a girl, but when Tim did it, it didn't feel at all derogatory. The words *darlin' girl*, spoken as Tim spoke them, with such husky warmth, made her feel cherished and incredibly special. More so, they made her feel things she had never dared allow herself to feel before—she felt small, soft, protected. For just this little while, it felt so good to give herself into Tim's care. For just this little while, she needn't be strong and self-sufficient.

She had drawn the curtains earlier against the deepening autumn night, and only the small reading lamp on the night table illuminated the room. Tim kicked the door shut behind them, closing out everything else, sealing them into a cocoon.

Gently, oh so gently, he laid her upon her bed. Softly, so very softly, he tugged the comforter over her.

"Tim?" Her heart skipped several beats as she thought he was going to leave her. Why else had he covered her?

"Shh..." He sat beside her and looked down at her, a funny, soft sort of half smile on his firm mouth. "Shh..." he whispered again, and touched a single fingertip to her lips. But not to silence her. No. He stroked her lower lip lightly, awakening tender flesh to newly erotic sensation. "There's no rush," he murmured. "None at all. Just all the time in the world to savor...and learn...and discover...." Bending, he touched his lips to hers, a delicate, questing touch.

She hadn't expected this. She had expected something rougher, faster, hotter, blunter. Something more like Tim. She hadn't expected him to make her feel like a precious, fragile blossom.

Something inside her, a protective wall so old that she had long since forgotten building it, cracked and crumbled. In that instant, a fleeting instant before his tongue touched hers and drove such things from her mind, she felt all the years of hurt and loneliness, and realized just how badly, how desperately, she had needed to be treasured.

Tim's tongue found hers in a rough, warm caress that sent heat cascading along her nerves. Tilting her head instinctively, she opened wider, begging for deeper caresses. He growled deep in his throat and eased closer, nearly shouting his pleasure when her arms stole around his shoulders. She tasted so sweet, and her hesitant passion aroused him as nothing in his life ever had.

"Touch me, Lizzie," he whispered against her mouth, her cheek, her ear. "Touch me."

The roughly whispered command caused her insides to clench, and she opened slumberous eyes. "Where?" she asked huskily.

"Anywhere. Everywhere." He caught her earlobe gently between his teeth, and felt an almost savage delight when she shivered.

"Too many clothes," she complained thickly, and pulled at his shirt. "Tim..."

It nearly killed him to pull back, but swiftly he did so, yanking his shirt up over his head, and tossing it aside. Slow down, he warned himself. Slow down. The first time only happens once.

But as soon as he leaned over her, before he could even resume kissing her sweet, addicting mouth, she plunged her right hand into the thick gingery hair on his chest and combed it with delicate strokes that inflamed him without satisfying him.

"God, Lizzie!" The words nearly burst from him. "Harder, darlin', harder. I won't break."

For a terrifying instant, her hand froze, and he thought he had scared her. He could have groaned from frustration and disappointment, and from anger at himself for hurrying her. Damn it, she was innocent beyond belief, and there was no way she could understand what *he* needed when she didn't yet understand what *she* needed.

But then she robbed him of breath. "Like this?" Grabbing a handful of that silky pelt, she tugged, and when he groaned softly, she smiled. That smile held so much satisfaction that a breathless laugh escaped him.

"Yeah," he said. "That's the general idea. And the more turned on I get, the rougher I like everything."

His frankness was a turn-on for her unlike anything she had ever dreamed. Every single cell in her body clamped with pleasure. But what she wanted more than nearly everything, she realized with something like wonder, was for him to enjoy every minute of this. Her own throbbings and achings and tinglings hardly seemed significant. What she wanted, what she needed, was to give him the most memorable lovemaking of his life.

And she didn't even know where to begin.

He saw that flicker of doubt in her eyes, and he was instantly concerned. "Lizzie," he said gently, capturing her face between his hands, "did I shock you?"

"No. Oh, no." She barely whispered the words, and met his gaze bravely. "It's just that I feel so...that I don't know what to do to please you."

"Ah, darlin'," he said huskily, "don't worry about that. Not now. Just being able to love you is all the pleasure I need, and later...there's always later for learning other things."

Bending, he kissed her with gentle reassurance, and then he stood. While she watched with wide, disbelieving eyes, he reached for the snap of his jeans.

"You told me my shorts left little to the imagination," he reminded her, tugging the jeans down over his hips, leaving another sinfully brief pair of briefs, navy blue this time, as his only concession to her maidenly nerves.

Quickly she looked up at him, too embarrassed to stare, and found a glint in his gray eyes. The fact that he was teasing her now, here at this impossibly intimate moment, reassured her as nothing else could have.

"They left *enough* to my imagination," she admitted in a wispy voice. Her heart hammered in her chest as he returned to her, lying full-length beside her.

He gave her a grin and then waggled his eyebrows as he pried the box from her clutching fingers. "If you need to hang on to something, hang on to me," he suggested. He turned and dropped the box onto the night table, then returned to her.

That was when she began to believe this was really happening. The teasing glint was gone from his eyes, replaced by something hotter, something more intimate. Something determined.

"Are you sure you want to do this?" she asked suddenly, her voice cracking on a couple of words.

"Am I sure I want to do what?" he asked, his hot gray eyes skimming her delicate features. Was he sure? That didn't even enter into it. Not anymore. He was past being sure about anything, and past caring whether he was.

"Well..." Her voice cracked again, but she made herself meet his eyes purposefully. This was right for her, but she had to be sure it was just as right for him. After all, just this morning he had been talking about rat poison. "There are so many...other women who would be thrilled to...to do this with you."

"Are there?" The glimmer of humor eased some of the intense heat of his gaze.

"Of course there are," she said, regaining some of her tartness. It was a brief show of spirit, and didn't last much longer than the sound of her words. "Tim...oh, Tim, what if I disappoint you? I don't know how—"

He silenced her with a kiss. It was a kiss that offered no quarter, that boldly informed her she was about to be claimed, and that suggested she might be wise to shut up and let him do...exactly what he was doing.

When he lifted his head to smile down at her, she was breathless and her eyes were glazed. She looked stunned.

"I don't care about what other women want," he said gruffly. "I only care about what *you* want, Lizzie. Do you want me?"

She blinked and tried to gather one or two of the thoughts that seemed to have melted into molasses. Somehow, she understood that there was a word that needed saying. "Yes. Yes. Yes..."

He had cocooned her nakedness in blankets, but now he entered the cocoon himself, sliding under the covers with her, tangling his long, powerful, hairy legs with hers. The rough texture of his legs was erotic, as erotic as the contrasting satiny smoothness of the skin of his back, where her hands seemed to have wandered of their own accord. She could feel every single one of those highly honed muscles flex as he shifted and stroked her back and thigh.

"It's going to feel even better, Lizzie," he promised as she sighed with sheer pleasure. "Except for one little hurt I won't be able to avoid...." God, he *hoped* it would be a little hurt. He didn't exactly have a broad experience with virgins. Tranh, whom he had loved as much as life, had been raped by a VC years before he'd met her. With her he had needed to overcome a different kind of pain. He hadn't needed to inflict any.

Liz touched his lips with her fingertips. "I know about that," she said huskily. "I know." She didn't want him to worry about that. *That* was the least of her own worries, taking a decided back seat to whether or not she would please him. Every insecurity she had was now waking viciously and yapping at the heels of her wavering self-confidence. Surely it took a lot of gall to ask this experienced, attractive man to teach her the ways of love?

"You're beautiful, Lizzie," he said gruffly, tugging the pins from her hair. "I mean it, and believe me, I don't say that very often." When he had tossed the last pin away, he combed his fingers through the long, shiny locks. "Your hair has been driving me crazy. I've been having all kinds of X-rated visions of it trailing over my skin while you touch me in ways you've probably never even imagined."

She figured her imagination was probably a little wilder than Tim gave her credit for, but that didn't keep her from blushing at the idea that he might be fantasizing about those very things himself. "Actually," she heard herself confess throatily, "actually, I've been having a few, uh, visions of my own."

"Yeah?" His expression was delighted as he smiled right into her eyes. "Tell me?"

It was a coaxing plea, but she wasn't ready for that yet. Somehow, lying here against his nakedness didn't make her feel nearly as exposed as telling him her fantasies would. "I can't." Her whisper was nearly inaudible. "I'm sorry."

Never in a million years would she have believed that gruff, bluff, hearty Tim O'Shaughnessy could look so gentle and tender as he did just then. Her throat ached in response to that look, and she drew a shaky sigh when he gathered her even closer, pressing her breasts to his furry chest.

"The only thing," he said, "absolutely the *only* thing you have to do from here on out is tell me if I do anything at all that you don't like."

Not that he gave her much opportunity to speak, Liz thought hazily a short time later. His mouth kept hers too busy for speech as his hands painted liquid heat over every inch of her skin. Those hands were subtly rough from calluses and hard work, a roughness she found intoxicating. And they kept urging her closer and closer with gentle little touches until she found herself twined around him like ivy.

And wide open to seeking fingers that slipped between her legs and found soft, moist, incredibly sensitive flesh. A single touch shot lightning along her nerve endings, and drew a deep, deep groan from her depths.

"Sweet Lizzie." He sighed raggedly.

The world tilted wildly for a moment and then she realized that he had lifted her over him, that now she straddled him. Before she could fully realize just how exposed he had made her to his mouth and hands, his mouth and hands were on her, driving every other thought from her mind. She shivered. Gently, so gently, he laved her swollen nipple with his tongue, just long enough to make her want more, and then he drew her into his mouth and sucked. A gasp escaped her as sensation zigzagged through her. Then his hand found her dewy core once more, and made wickedly exciting movements there, caressing at first lightly, then harder as she moaned and leaned into his touch.

"Ah, Lizzie!" He nearly groaned her name, his own passions being fueled by her response to his caresses. The woman was incendiary, her every reaction to him a seduction of his senses. His blood was pounding, his body tensing as wave after wave of heat washed through him. If he had ever wanted a woman this badly, he couldn't remember it.

Until the day he died, he would remember what happened then. Suddenly Liz reared up and sat back on her heels, on his thighs. And then, with gentle, hesitant hands, she touched him through his briefs.

His groan sounded as if it had been ripped from the very root of his soul. Encouraged, she touched him more boldly, and then gripped the top of his briefs, tugging downward.

He caught her hands, stilling her, and smiled lazily at her from gray eyes. He looked, she thought in a flash of whimsy, like a sunning, contented lion. "I don't want you to faint from shock, Lizzie," he said huskily.

"Are you that big?"

His jaw dropped, just a little, and then a choked laugh escaped him. "I was thinking more in terms of virginal nerves."

"Oh." She tugged at his briefs. "I think I'm past that," she told him seriously, hearing the throatiness of her own voice, feeling the solid, slamming beat of her heart, knowing that she wanted every shimmering moment of this experience. Shyness had ceased to have meaning, replaced by driving needs more basic than modesty, older than humanity. The mating urge ruled her now.

"Tim?"

"Hmm?" He was watching her with an odd sort of smile on his face, his hammering need for fulfillment momentarily forgotten in the wonder of Liz Pennington. Had he really, ever, believed her to be just another fellow software wizard? Had he ever been so blind? She was a wizard of more than one kind, he found himself thinking as he compliantly lifted his hips and let her strip his briefs away.

He half expected her to flinch or pale or look doubtful. Instead, she studied him intently, as if judging a work of art, and then she looked up and met his gaze. "You're beautiful," she said simply.

His chest tightened and he held out his arms, wanting to feel her on him, every inch of her touching as many inches of him as she could reach. She settled on him, her thighs lying on either side of his, her face resting on his chest right over his breastbone.

"I bet," she said softly, "I know where you wanted my hair to trail over you."

A soft laugh escaped him. "I'll bet you do." He ran his palms over her soft, silky skin from shoulder to fanny, savoring the unexpected affection of the moment. "God, you're a wonder, Lizzie," he said warmly.

"I wish you wouldn't call me that," she said, raising her head so she could look down at him.

"Lizzie? What's wrong with that?"

"Lizzie Borden."

"Oh." The laugh caught him between one breath and the next, shaking him from head to foot with such violence that she hung on to him so she wouldn't fall off.

"I don't see what's so funny," she complained, even though the corners of her own mouth were trying to twitch upward, and the urge to laugh was rising from the pit of her stomach.

"Lizzie Borden. Damn it, Liz," he said, chuckling, "I never once thought of Lizzie Borden in connection with you. Attila the Hun, maybe, but never an ax murderer!"

She scowled down at him. "Attila the Hun?" She tried to sound outraged, but didn't quite make it. Instead, her own laughter escaped, pealing gaily through the room. "Uncle," she cried. "Call me Lizzie. I'm sorry I complained."

And then, between that breath and the next, their eyes met and caught, and they remembered where they were. How they were. Laughter died. Breath shortened. Nerve endings sparked.

Tim's hands rose from her small, sweet bottom to clasp her cheeks gently and urge her mouth toward his. "I always wanted to be able to laugh while I was making love," he murmured. "I'd begun to think it was impossible."

His words plucked something deep inside her, struck a warm, golden chord. She'd never imagined laughing and making love at the same time. She had never dreamed that something so new and strange could feel so right and easy. With a sigh, she gave Tim her mouth to plunder however he chose.

He caught her lower lip between his and nibbled gently on it before soothing it with a sweep of his tongue. God, he was nearly out of his mind with wanting her, but beyond his desire for her, there were other feelings shimmering in the wings, every bit as strong, and they made him want to draw out each caress, each sensation, until he had spun them into silken threads of magic for her.

Needs long denied took flame and the gentle foray of his tongue into her mouth took on the driving rhythm of a primitive drumbeat. She made soft sounds deep in her throat, and twisted against him, seeking to answer hungers she barely understood. Here, she needed a stroking caress. There, she needed a hard pressure. And just over there... She couldn't feel him close enough, hard enough, alive enough to satisfy her. She needed to be crushed by him, invaded by him, taken by him.

As if he understood, he rolled them over and tucked her beneath him, settling his great weight between her thighs, feeling the warm humidity of her womanhood close to his aching, throbbing erection. Close, but no closer. Not yet. Propped on elbows above her, he used his lips and tongue to drive her higher and higher.

As a man, he loved women in all their shapes and sizes and colorings. He loved their softness, their curves, their mysterious bodies. He was a breast man from way back, as well as a leg man and a tush man—an everything-about-them man. And right now he was determined to show Liz why. Her breasts were exquisite, and he told her so as he drove her crazy by licking, sucking and nipping at them. He showed her that they were exquisite instruments of pleasure for the both of them, and not until she was moaning and rolling her hips wildly beneath him did he give her a moment to catch her breath. Sliding up over her a little more, he waited for her breathing to settle before he kissed her again.

Her stunned eyes fluttered open, dark with new knowledge of what it meant to be a woman, and a new understanding of erogenous zones. And from somewhere came the fascinating notion that if she liked it that much, he might like it every bit as much. Lifting her head and twisting her neck, she found one small, pointed nipple in the gingery fur that covered him. With all the delicacy of a grooming cat, she licked him.

The jolt shot through him like an electric current and he jerked sharply against her, nearly convulsing in reaction.

She smiled up at him with so much satisfaction that he would have laughed under other circumstances. "You like that, too." It wasn't a question.

He was long past talking. Instead he shifted, offering himself to her again, holding her head to him with one massive hand so that her neck was spared. Liz was good at taking hints. She took this one with a great deal of pleasure.

The zap shot straight from his nipple to his groin and he froze, going completely and totally rigid with unparalleled pleasure. Never before…never before. He was poised at her portal and he suddenly realized through a throbbing sea of desire that if he didn't get that protection now, he was going to miss the opportunity altogether. Soon he wouldn't give a damn about anything but climbing the peak.

With a groan, he rolled away from her and reached with a trembling hand for the box on the bedside table. Rolling onto her side, Liz watched him with hazy, slumberous eyes.

In her imaginings, she had been unable to deal with this part. She had always thought it would have to be an interruption, a disturbance, an unwelcome intrusion into a fantasy of feeling.

It was not. She watched Tim open the plastic packet, watched him touch himself to roll on the prophylactic, and she felt a spasm of desire so strong that she reached out and touched him, helping him to protect her.

A stunned gasp escaped him as her fingers closed around him. He watched her touch him, unable to believe that she would do that for him, that she would turn a necessity into a seductive act.

Something inside Liz melted like a chain reaction in a nuclear furnace. She needed. Past thought, past reason, past awareness, she needed this man, and when he moved over her at last, she was so open and receptive that she knew, absolutely knew, he was going to sink into her until they were one from head to toe, until there was no him, no her, just them.

Tim wasn't half so confident or so certain. Awareness battered back his hunger and he wondered whether it would be easier for her if he took her swiftly or slowly. But what if hurrying would tear her more? God, what was he doing?

He did it anyway. Slowly. Giving her plenty of time to adjust to his invasion. Sweat poured down his forehead, dropping onto the pillow beside her as he held himself back, held himself in and watched her face for any indication that she hurt too much. The absolutely overwhelming need to bury himself in her was all that kept him going in the face of his concern for her. That, and an awareness that women *did* survive this.

Her eyes opened and met his suddenly. He was at the barrier; he felt the slight resistance. She felt it, too, and waited with wide-eyed awareness of the coming transformation.

"Lizzie?" Her name was little more than a gasp.

"Yes." Unequivocal, perfectly audible.

Aw, hell, he thought, and did it.

He gave a moan that nearly drowned her soft cry as he buried himself all the way in her hot, wet depths. Ah, it felt like home after a lifetime of wandering! Lowering his head, he kissed her, held her, waited for some indication that she was no longer hurting. Relief swamped him when her arms closed around him, and he shivered when her warm breath caressed his ear.

"Tim?" she breathed.

"Hmm?"

"Isn't there more?"

For an instant, he didn't move a muscle. Then slowly he raised his head and looked down into her hazy, misty hazel eyes. There was, he thought, a definite gleam there. Sort of a wicked, devilish, teasing light. Desire clamped him instantaneously in its vise.

"Like this, you mean?" he growled and moved himself in and out, just a little, very slowly, alert for any sign of discomfort.

She bit her lower lip and nodded. "Sort of like that. And if I do this...."

She did *this* with the instinctive skill of a courtesan, rocking her hips up against him, causing a friction that drove the last coherent thought from his brain.

He took her. Purely, simply, fantastically, he took her.

And she loved every single second of it.

They stayed sealed in their cocoon the rest of the evening, the mood unbroken even when Tim called out for pizza and went downstairs to meet the delivery man. Sinfully, they ate their meal in bed like a couple of kids, Tim wearing only his briefs, and Liz wearing his oversize T-shirt.

Afterward, replete on the pizza and soft drinks, they lay back together on plump pillows. Liz curled up against Tim's side, her head on his shoulder, his arm around her. Gently she combed her fingers through the wonderfully soft hair on his chest. It was a marvelous thing, she thought, to lie with a man—to lie with Tim. That thought almost drew a sigh from her because she knew he would weary of her eventually, and eventually they would be just business partners again. She wondered if she would be able to carry it off. And then she pushed the thought firmly aside, refusing to let her fears ruin this miraculous time with Tim.

Idly she picked up the religious medallion he was wearing around his neck and studied the small oval that hung from a thin, steel chain. "Saint Christopher? I thought he wasn't a saint anymore."

"They say he never even existed." Tim's voice was deep, lazy, warm with repletion. "My mother gave me the medal just before I shipped out to Nam. You'll never convince her that Christopher's no saint. Me, either, I guess."

That was an unexpected glimpse of a side of Tim she had never even suspected existed. "But you were hurt."

"Nothing that hasn't mended."

She found herself wondering if that was true. Something about the short way he had answered her questions about Vietnam suggested that there was still some tender scar tissue, of the emotional kind. In fact, with each passing day, she was coming to believe more and more that hearty, bluff, uninhibited Tim O'Shaughnessy was all smoke and mirrors, that the man she had once believed hadn't a sensitive bone in his body was full of them and busily trying to hide them, too.

Carefully, she dropped the medal onto his chest, watching it nestle once again into his hair. Then her fingertips began to wander gently, lightly, touching old scars and sensitive nerve endings. Her throat tightened uncomfortably as she thought about all the painful things he had survived. And there was probably a lot more to it than he had told her or would ever tell her.

"Ahh, Lizzie darlin'." He sighed, and tightened the powerful arm he had snugly wrapped around her small, soft shoulders. "You make a man think he can almost defy gravity."

"You feel like you're flying?" There was a small, breathless catch in her voice as she recognized his growing arousal in the small changes in his voice and body. Again! He wanted her again! Pleasure and delight poured through her.

"I feel like I'm falling," he said huskily. "Free-falling. Like the first time I stepped out of a plane. Only this time there's no parachute."

She tilted her head up so she could see his face, and found he had closed his eyes. His fingertips had begun to stroke her arm gently, and his breathing was growing shallow. "Scary," she said.

"Like when I fell in love with Tranh," he said with sudden gruffness. "Free-falling without a parachute."

And then had come the crash of her death, Liz thought with a sudden jolt in her stomach. Free-falling without a parachute. No wonder he swore he wasn't a forever man anymore. No wonder.

He felt the tension in her, and it pierced his haze of comfortable pleasure enough to make him aware that he had somehow disturbed her with what he had said. Turning onto his side, he pulled Liz to him, throwing his leg over hers and capturing one of her breasts in his large, warm palm.

"That's awful, Tim," she said, her breath shattering as passion rose in a swelling tide. "Scary. You don't want..."

"For a little while," he whispered roughly, "for a little while, we can defy gravity, Lizzie darlin'. For a little while, we can fly."

For a little while. That's all he was offering, but her last clear thought was that she was going to take it. Every single minute he offered her, she was going to accept and cherish and treasure.

Liz woke to a miserable autumn day. Despite the drawn curtains, she could hear the driving rain and the gusting wind. Ordinarily such weather would have made her groan in misery, but this morning it didn't matter. Pressed up against her back was all the sunshine and warmth she could have asked for, and his fingers were dancing wickedly along her arm.

"About time, sleepyhead," he growled teasingly. He reached across her and switched on the bedside lamp.

Smiling even before her eyelids reached half-mast, she wiggled onto her back. Tim raised himself on his elbow and smiled down at her. She'd never seen him smile quite that way before, she thought hazily. Sort of...tender. Sort of...happy. Sort of...delighted.

He lowered his head and his mouth nuzzled hers in gentle welcome. Oh, yes, she thought, Tim O'Shaughnessy knew how to kiss. In no time at all, he had her nerves humming like the strings on a fiddle.

And then the lout threw back the covers. Instantly she blushed from the top of her head to the tips of her toes. "Tim!" Her hand scrabbled for the covers but failed to find them.

"Damn, you sure look good in pink," he said mischievously,

suppressed laughter evident in his voice. "Your pink jogging suit is great, but not half as fantastic as the birthday suit."

"O'Shaughnessy!" she wailed, but when she tried to roll away, he caught her.

So very gently he caught her, and so very tenderly he pulled her to him and covered her nakedness with his own. No one had ever touched her with such gentle caring as he did right now. It made her throat ache.

"We've got to do something about your shyness," he told her huskily. "You're beautiful, Liz. Voluptuous. Built like a Valkyrie. Do you know what the Valkyries were, Liz? Forget the stuff you've seen in comedies about Wagnerian operas. Valkyries were Odin's handmaidens. And they were the ones who chose the warriors for Valhalla. Think about it, Liz. Imagine a Valkyrie that a warrior would follow to his death."

"Tim..." She was overwhelmed and embarrassed all at once. He was so lavish!

"You're beautiful, Liz. Beautiful enough to cavort naked in the daylight like a wood nymph. Hell, Liz, you're *stacked*."

The last declaration startled a choked laugh out of her, but her heart was aching, and her soul was yearning, and somehow she wriggled herself even closer to Tim, pressing her face into his strong shoulder, tangling her legs with his, curling up into a soft warmth.

"How about we take a shower?" he asked huskily.

"A shower?" she repeated on a squeak. Something like lava settled heavily in her center.

"You like that idea?" he asked huskily, brushing his lips against the top of her head. "Yeah, a shower. With lots of slippery soap. I'd lather you all over...."

"Tim..." That was a sigh, pure and simple. "We'd never fit in that tub."

"Five dollars says we will."

And that was how she came to be standing under the spray a few minutes later, so absorbed in Tim that she forgot to be embarrassed by her own nudity. There wasn't a whole lot of room to move around, and she got most of the spray while Tim got most of the cold air, and she was sure this was dangerous to life and limb, but who cared? Tim O'Shaughnessy was built like Michelangelo's *David*, and he gave her leave to explore him freely.

In broad daylight. With her hands. With her eyes. With her whole body.

And he liked it. Oh, yes, he loved it. She could tell and he let her know without any prevarication. She loved making him gasp. She thrilled when she made him shudder, and trembled herself when he trembled. Eventually, though, he gave an unsteady laugh and took her hands from him, telling her frankly that he was going to collapse if she did just one more thing.

"It's your turn now," he said, and took the bar of soap from her suddenly limp hand.

If he missed a square inch of her, it had to be the soles of her feet, and he took care of that later when she no longer needed to stand on them. The strength of her legs abandoned her, and he had to help her from the tub. He toweled her dry, leaving her to wonder dazedly why she had never dreamed that a towel could be a tool of such wicked pleasure. And why she had never noticed what a great color orange was.

Naughtily, she pranced down the hall stark naked with a grinning Tim right on her heels. Together they fell onto her bed and the world whirled out of focus on a cyclone of pleasure that carried them up, up and away. And this time they toppled over the top together.

A long, long time later, Liz opened one eye and looked directly into the warm gray of Tim's gaze. "Where are we?" she asked.

"Damned if I know," was his satisfied answer. "And damned if I care."

Finally though, other hungers needed appeasement. Liz retrieved her pink jogging suit from the bathroom and pulled it on. She then headed downstairs, promising Tim the best pancakes in the state.

Just as she reached the foot of the stairs, the doorbell rang. She went to answer it, expecting a neighbor who needed a couple of eggs or some other ingredient for Sunday-morning breakfast.

She flung the door wide. And screamed.

It was the biker.

Chapter 10

"Tim!" she shrieked. "It's the biker!"

In steel-studded black leather. Life-size and in Technicolor. And looking every bit as unnerved by this encounter as she was. His hands flew up in a placating gesture, and he backed swiftly away from the door.

"Tim!"

There was a crash from upstairs and a resounding roar. "I'm coming, Liz!"

The sound of Tim's shout had a curious effect on the biker. He stopped backing up and instead propped his shoulder against the porch stanchion. His expression faded from horror to enjoyment.

Liz opened her mouth and drew another deep breath, when it suddenly struck her that this was not the behavior one would expect from a menace to society. Quite the contrary. Snapping her mouth shut, she peered more closely at the biker. Gray eyes twinkled at her. There was something familiar....

"Where is he?" Tim came charging down the stairs, barefoot, clad only in unsnapped jeans.

Liz stepped back from the door. "I guess he's harmless," she said drily. "Otherwise I'd already be dead."

Tim peered past her. "Pat? Pat, what the hell...?"

"You said you didn't know any bikers!" Liz exclaimed, suddenly irritated. "You mean I've been worrying all week about a friend of yours?"

"I don't know any bikers," Tim said, a grin creasing his face. "Liz, meet my brother Pat."

Entering her foyer was the most disreputable-looking individual she had ever seen. He was dressed from head to foot in steel-studded black leather. His dark hair reached his shoulders and he wore a beard that needed trimming. His left arm was in a sling and splint, his motorcycle boots—complete with chains—were scuffed and filthy. Liz blinked and stared.

"Your...brother?" She couldn't imagine Tim being related to anyone so obviously...unsavory.

"Yeah. Come on into the kitchen, Pat. We're getting ready to make breakfast."

She wanted to sink. She wanted to die. She wanted to crawl away into the darkest, deepest hole. *His brother.* Here she was dressed in nothing but her pink jogging suit. Not even a bra or a pair of panties. And Tim wore nothing at all except that scandalously undone pair of jeans.

Surely there was a hole somewhere she could fall into? A dark closet?

"Liz, c'mon," Tim said as he passed her, taking her arm and drawing her along. "Pat's a cop, you know."

"A cop?" That startled her out of her mortification. "A cop?"

"Undercover," Tim explained as he dragged her with him into the kitchen. "Sit, Liz. I'll make the pancakes."

She sat. Her legs wouldn't have supported her much longer anyway, and her mind was busy trying to decide on a mode of escape. Of all people to find them like this. The only worse person would have been her mother.

"You sure caused enough uproar around here last week," Tim told Pat. "Our business was broken into the same night you ran into Liz in the parking lot. Even the FBI is looking for you. Where'd you vanish to?"

"I just drove up from the city for the evening. I had a red-eye flight to Dallas to catch, so I couldn't wait. Anyhow, four days at home with Ma fussing every minute was all I could handle."

"What happened to your arm?" Tim asked as he turned on the stove and tested the griddle's heat with a couple of drops of water.

"A narrow miss with some drug dealers," Pat answered.

Liz dared a look at him and found him regarding her with sympathy. He didn't look much like Tim, she thought, except for the eyes. They had the same nice eyes. Pat, though tall like Tim, was rangy in his build, not at all bearlike, and his coloring was dark.

"So, are you on leave?" Tim asked.

"Actually, I'm in hiding."

Liz felt her jaw go slack. This couldn't really be happening.

"From whom?" Tim asked, flipping a couple of flapjacks onto a plate and setting it before his brother.

"Everybody." Pat took a mouthful of pancake and suddenly looked blissful. "These are fantastic."

"What 'everybody'?" Tim asked.

"My cover's so deep, even the cops are looking for me," Pat said. "I got shot and my control told me to clear out for a few weeks, so here I am. Bad timing, I guess." He looked at Liz significantly. "Guess I'll mosey on down to Atlanta and visit Brendan."

"Why? You're welcome to stay here," Tim said.

Liz glared at him. This was *her* house, darn it. Didn't he have the common decency to ask her first?

"I don't think so, Tim," Pat said. "This isn't your house."

"Liz doesn't mind, do you, Liz?"

She wanted to kill him, but what could she say? She'd get him for this later. "Of course I don't mind."

"See?" Tim grinned. "Besides, you're just the guy we need, Pat. You wouldn't believe what's been happening around here."

"Dad told me," Pat said. "That's half the reason I came instead of going to ground somewhere else. Dad said you were too damn casual about what happened, and then you up and decided to move in with your business partner—he figures you felt she needed protecting, and if she needs protecting..." Pat shrugged. "He also figured, since I'm free for a couple of weeks, that I could check things out."

Tim looked at Liz. "Dad thinks I'm helpless because I'm not a cop."

Liz had other things on her mind. Chest heaving with indignation, she stared daggers at him. "You told your *father* you were moving in with me?"

"Well, he had to know where he could get in touch with me, Liz," he said reasonably. "You know how parents get when they can't find you."

"I am going to kill you, O'Shaughnessy," she said, spacing her words and biting each one out like a bullet. "I. Am. Going. To. Kill. You." Head high, she stormed out of the kitchen.

In typical male fashion, Tim didn't follow her immediately. No, he let her stew for a while, gave her plenty of time to devise all kinds of tortures for him, and then gave her enough time to start feeling like a fool. Like a rude fool. And just as she was feeling embarrassed by her own conduct, he knocked quietly on her bedroom door.

"Liz?"

"Go away, O'Shaughnessy."

"I can't do that."

"Sure you can. Just turn around and walk away!"

"I really can't do that," he replied, and walked into her bedroom. He took it as a positive sign that she hadn't locked the door. She wanted to be soothed and calmed, and she was willing to consider an apology. He figured he owed her a couple of them.

She stood at the window, presenting him with a rigid back. She hugged herself tightly; it was a defensive, protective posture he recognized at gut level. The sight made him ache. This was no lady on the attack. She felt frightened. Scared. Unsure. Alone. Damn, he couldn't stand the thought of Liz feeling alone. Not after all they'd been through together. Whatever might happen between them, he would have thought that by now she would know she could always depend on him. That he would always be here for her.

He closed the door behind him and crossed the room until he stood right behind her. He could feel her warmth over the small distance, an invisible radiance. "I'm sorry," he said quietly.

She didn't answer.

"I've been on my own for a long time, Liz. It's been nearly twenty years since I answered to anyone except at work. If I've got any excuse for acting like a barbarian, that's it. I'm used to deciding things on my own and going ahead without consulting anyone. Guess I can't do that anymore.''

She hunched a shoulder. He couldn't tell for sure if it was a dismissal or an encouragement, so he decided to interpret it as the latter.

''I've been bulling my way with you all along, Liz,'' he continued quietly. ''I'm sorry. I've pushed and prodded and ridden roughshod....''

''You read Regency romances?''

Startled, he stared at the back of her head. ''What's that got to do with anything?''

She turned and showed him a forlorn face. Her arms remained protectively wrapped around her, though, so he knew he wasn't over the dangerous ground yet. ''That's the only place anyone rides roughshod over anything these days. Yes, you *did*, Tim. This is *my* house. It was *my* right to offer the invitation. You just take over, and I'm running out of patience with it.''

''You do a pretty good job of standing up to me,'' he reminded her.

''Yes, I do, but I don't want to have to do it all the time, Tim. Don't you see? It's exhausting and frustrating and maddening.''

''I know.'' And he did. ''You'd ride roughshod over anyone but me, Liz. And you damn well know it.''

Color stained her cheeks. She hated to admit he was right. She was used to having her own way, too. ''Why do you read Regency romances?''

''I read some of everything. I'm a compulsive reader. Quit trying to change the subject. We need to iron this out. I can't stand to see you like this.''

''Like what?''

''Like this.'' He took her wrists in a gentle grip and opened her arms, pulling her up against him. ''Looking like you're all alone and friendless. Like you've got nobody to take care of you but you. You're not alone, Liz. Whatever happens, however mad you get at me, I'll be here. No matter how hard we fight, I'm on your side. I promise.''

Everything inside her just crumbled into mush at that declaration. She found herself huddled against him, wrapped snugly in his strength. She found hot tears running down her cheeks.

Tim felt them fall on his chest, and they seemed to sting. For an instant he felt a male's natural panic at a woman's tears, but the moment passed. "It's okay, Liz," he assured her, and hauled her even closer. He rubbed her back gently. "We can always work things out somehow. Always."

She managed a nod, and sniffled back her tears. "Sorry," she said.

"For what? There's nothing you need to feel sorry for. I'm the one who should be apologizing."

"I was rude before," she said.

"Hell, so was I. Pat's used to it. He's my brother, isn't he? Besides, he knows I was out of line."

She twisted her head, trying to see him. "He can stay here. I *would* have invited him."

He smiled gently down at her. "I know you would have, darlin'."

"Your brother must think I'm pretty weird," she said hesitantly.

"No. He knows you've been dealing with me. Pat's an okay guy, Liz. Honestly. He's recuperating from a pretty bad wound, but he'll be a lot of help with this gravity man thing. I'm sure he'll have all kinds of useful ideas for us." He gave a rueful laugh. "He'd *better* be useful. He's just deprived me and the FBI of our favorite suspect."

"Is your other brother a cop, too?"

"Brendan? Sort of. He's a postal inspector."

"That gets pretty hairy these days, I hear. So how come you stayed out of law enforcement, Tim?"

He dropped a kiss on her forehead, and then another on the tip of her nose. "I had my fill of guns a long time ago. More than my fill." He saw the questions in her eyes, but shook his head. "Another time, Liz. It's too early in the morning for soul baring. Now why don't *I* make *you* some pancakes?"

Tim took Pat over to his place later in the morning to get a rollaway bed for Pat to use. Liz had persuaded Pat that he really was welcome to stay at her house, but he insisted he would do so only if he slept in the basement family room, where he would intrude less on her privacy. Thinking of the sounds that must have emanated from her bedroom last night, Liz blushed and made only a token protest.

For a little while it was a relief to have the house to herself again, and she puttered around dusting and straightening and polishing. She even gave some consideration to thinning out her plants so Tim would feel more comfortable, but she hesitated, partly because she couldn't bring herself to just discard them, and partly because she wasn't sure just how much Tim really objected to them. He made a big deal out of it, but he seemed more amused by her greenery than threatened. Maybe he would discuss that with her when he finally got around to the promised soul baring. In the meantime, the plants would just stay.

The rain and wind let up, so she opened windows to let in fresh air. She was standing at the screen door, looking out into her backyard, when she noticed a white business-size envelope tacked to the porch rail. Probably some kind of advertising, she told herself, ignoring the fact that advertising would have been tacked to her front door, not her back porch.

The minute she held the envelope and looked at her name and address, she knew it was not advertising. It had clearly been typed on some kind of manual typewriter, not on a computer printer as most commercial mailings were, and showed both typos and broken letters.

Disturbed, Liz stared at it, and actually considered throwing it away. Some cowardly instinct suggested that the contents of that envelope couldn't hurt her or frighten her if she didn't know what they were. Worrying her lower lip between her teeth, she stepped back into the kitchen and reached for a butter knife to use as a letter opener.

Inside the envelope was a single, folded piece of watermarked onionskin paper, and on it, in faded ink, was a brief, senseless typed message.

> If you don't stop disturbing my gravity,
> I am going to get the devil to beam
> resonances into your mind

The proverbial goose walked across her grave then. The chill ran up and down her spine and made her scalp prickle. Without an instant's hesitation, she picked up the phone and dialed Tim's apartment. Cowardly or not, she didn't want to be alone.

"O'Shaughnessy," he answered.

"Tim? Tim, I just got a letter from the gravity person." Quickly, hating the faint tremor in her voice, she read it to him.

"Hell's bells," he swore. "Liz, stay put. I've got Laurel and Hardy here right now. I'm sure they'll send someone over to get the letter. I'll be back just as soon as they let me go."

"Let you go? Tim, what's going on? What happened?"

"It looks like the gravity man was here last night, Liz. My place is trashed."

Agent Carter came personally to collect the letter, in the company of another agent Liz hadn't met before. She was glad to see Carter, though just how glad she only realized when she saw him. She didn't know what she would have done if a total stranger had come to her door. Suddenly she didn't feel as if she could trust anyone.

"I suppose you touched it," Carter said as he looked down at where it lay on her kitchen table.

"I'm afraid so," Liz said, wondering why she felt stupid. She had had to open it, after all. Stupid would be using tweezers to perform an ordinary task.

"Much? Did you handle it a lot?"

"Well, I don't think so. I pulled it out, unfolded it and held it with one hand while I looked at it. After I called Tim I set it down. I haven't touched it since."

The other agent, Wallace, handled the letter with tweezers. Liz watched his dark hands with fascination as he gingerly slid the paper into an evidence bag along with the envelope. This was the kind of stuff you only saw on TV and here it was happening in her own kitchen. She decided that it was more enjoyable on TV.

"Did this letter ring any bells with you, Ms. Pennington?" Carter wanted to know. "Did anything strike you as familiar about it?"

Liz shook her head. "When I saw the envelope, I got a little uneasy. I knew it wasn't ordinary, because of the typed address, but I sure didn't expect anything like this."

"So you noticed only that nothing about it was familiar."

"I noticed that nothing about it was *right*. That's all. With computers, you don't see much of that kind of thing." She looked from Carter to Wallace. "How bad was Tim's place trashed? Was it like the office?"

"Yeah." Wallace clipped the word. "It's a mess."

She looked back at Carter. "Do you think this person might attack us physically? Is he dangerous that way?"

"I don't know," Carter admitted. "I'm going to turn all this stuff over to our psychiatric experts and our profilers and see what they come up with. If it looks as if you're in personal danger, we'll let you know, Ms. Pennington. At the moment, we just can't say." With that, the agents left.

Great, Liz thought. Alone again, she found herself remembering how she had felt back in high school when for a time it had seemed as if her house were haunted. To this day she told herself she didn't believe in such things, but she remembered how scared she had gotten in the dead of night when she heard strange sounds. She felt a little like that now, as if every sound were threatening. As if unseen eyes were watching.

Paranoid or not, she closed all the windows and doors, and drew all the curtains against the gray day.

What did that guy mean by "I am going to get the devil to beam resonances into your mind"? Was that a threat? Was it meant to be a threat? Lord, it was all the creepier for being so obviously irrational.

A knock sounded at the kitchen door. Before she could even tense, she heard Tim calling her name. Running, she hurried to let him in.

He caught her right up off her feet, hugging her tightly. "Are you okay, Liz? Really?" Before she could answer, he kissed her soundly on the lips, a kiss so loaded with affection that she felt her darn throat tighten up again.

"I'm fine," she said breathlessly. "Really. Oh, Tim, what do we do now?"

He set her down carefully and slung his arm over her shoulders, guiding her to the table. "Have a cup of coffee and talk about it. Pat stayed at the apartment with the criminologists to see if anything turns up that might give us a lead. And you and I are going to have a long talk about taking a long vacation. Maybe to Alaska. Or Hawaii."

Liz sat and watched Tim start the coffee maker. "We can't take a vacation with all of this going on, Tim."

He sighed. "No, I know we can't. But it sure sounds good." He leaned against the counter, folded his arms and crossed his feet at the ankles. If he'd thought that she would listen, he would have put her on the next flight to anywhere, far away. Hell, he could send her to his parents in Dallas. Dad would make sure she stayed out of trouble. But she wouldn't listen. Trying to get that girl on a plane would require hog-tying and gags. A straitjacket. Damn.

All that fire, he found himself thinking. Beneath that practical, no-nonsense, bristly facade, the girl was sheer fire. A tempest. Impossible to control. Wasn't that what drew him to her in the first place? She might provoke him to murder, but she would never bore him. Never had, never would.

That was when he realized just how much he'd grown and changed in the years since his marriage. Tranh had been the perfect Oriental wife. Obedient, quiet, a reflection of her man's every wish. Nonthreatening. A lovely, loving young girl who might have, given another fate, turned into a lovely, loving woman. But she never would have tested his mettle. And she never would have reflected his strength the way Liz Pennington did. When he looked at Liz, he could see how he had grown. He could see that he was strong, confident and firmly centered in himself. A weak man would never survive Liz. The thought made him grin.

"What's so funny, O'Shaughnessy?"

"Are you still going to be calling me O'Shaughnessy when we're ninety?"

"I have no intention of being anywhere near you when we're ninety," she said tartly.

"You'll be there all right, Pennington. We're shackled, remember? Remember what that lawyer said about partnerships? Harder to dissolve than marriage? Do you remember that?"

His grin was downright evil, she thought. "I remember. It doesn't matter, O'Shaughnessy. There'll be no business once we retire."

He waggled his brows. "What if I refuse to retire?"

Liz sighed. "Quit evading the real issues, Tim. We're never going to reach retirement if this gravity person decides he needs to kill us."

"A liberated female to the bitter end," he remarked. "Gravity person. Personally, I think it's a gravity *man*. Men are likelier to be violent than women. Statistical fact."

Liz simply stared at him. She refused to dignify his attitude with a response.

"Okay," he said finally. "No fooling around. I'll be as sober and serious as a judge, I swear. Not that that'll get us anywhere. We don't have a damn thing to go on, in case you haven't noticed. We need a clue that makes some sense. Gravity doesn't make any sense. Do you know anyone who spouts on about gravity?"

She shook her head.

"Me, either. Zilch. Tomorrow night we've got the SCUFO meeting. Maybe we'll pick up on something there."

"I doubt it. They all seemed like pretty normal kids to me."

O'Shaughnessy grinned wickedly. "That's because you've seen a UFO."

Just how was she supposed to take that remark? Liz was still wondering the next evening when she and Tim climbed into his truck and set out for the SCUFO meeting. The nature of the gathering being what it was, they both wore freshly pressed jeans. Tim wore a white Western shirt. Liz wore a fuzzy blue mohair sweater. Tim figured the only thing that could make that sweater any more perfect was if it was pink. He said so.

"It figures you'd like pink," Liz said.

"Why? Why does it figure?"

"Because it's such a feminine color."

"Oh." He decided not to take that one on. He charted a slightly different course. "Actually, darlin', I don't like pink per se. I like it on *you*. It does nice things to your coloring." That sweater also did nice things to her general appearance. It lovingly hugged her anatomy in ways that were causing confusion in his ordinarily clear head. He was beginning to think that it had been very wise and very canny of her all these years to come to work wearing shapeless, baggy T-shirts and other such unflattering things. Otherwise he'd have been on his knees begging for mercy years ago.

"Thank you," she said finally. She wasn't used to compliments, and she realized she'd been unnecessarily difficult about this one. Did she really mind that Tim liked her in pink? Or that he obviously liked this sweater? Of course she didn't, so why was she giving him a hard time?

"Thank you"? Liz had settled for a mere ordinary thank-you?

That silenced him for a moment, as he wondered if she were feeling well. Probably nervous about tonight, he decided.

"Pat's coming to the meeting, too," he told her. "Act like you don't know who he is."

"Why is Pat coming?" She twisted on the seat and tried to read his expression in the light from the dashboard.

"He figured he'd act a little crazy and see if he couldn't get someone to discuss gravity with him. No big deal. Even Carter didn't object to the idea of Pat trying to sound people out tonight."

Figuring that if Carter thought it was okay, there was no need for her to worry about it, Liz raised only a single objection. "I can't imagine that any of these kids will want to talk to him if he comes wearing that getup he was in this morning."

"Looked pretty raunchy, didn't he?" Tim sounded admiring. "What he does is tough. He's worked for a number of different police departments around the country, and he always does deep cover. The kind where he can't even carry identification. Not even the cops know he's a cop."

Liz shook her head. She thought Pat sounded crazy, but figured Tim wouldn't care for that opinion. "I suppose Brendan behaves more normally? Postal inspectors don't go undercover, do they?"

Tim shrugged. "I really don't know. Brendan doesn't. He's been on a few big drug busts, that kind of thing, but he doesn't live on the edge like Pat does."

"You have an interesting family," Liz said. "It must have been nice growing up with brothers and a sister."

Tim flashed her a smile. "Not always. It wasn't the neighborhood bully who gave me my first bloody nose. And there was never enough hot water."

Small things that sounded more like fond memories, Liz thought. "Tonight's the night that guy what's-his-name is giving his talk on UFO abductions," she said, suddenly remembering. Lord, this was one evening she'd just like to skip. She might wonder about what she had seen all those years ago, but abduction by aliens was in another class altogether.

"Yeah. Wilfred White. I'd almost forgotten about him. Pennington, this promises to be a fascinating evening."

She wished she shared his optimism.

* * *

The meeting was packed. Tim evidently wasn't the only non-club member who recognized the name Wilfred White. Liz looked around in amazement at the rapidly filling gymnasium. In one sweep she recognized the Flints, a police officer and his wife who lived in her neighborhood, Bill Carstairs, who ran the hardware store in the shopping center near her house, and Carrie McMahon, a columnist from the local paper.

"We're not going to be able to learn a thing tonight," she said to Tim. "We might as well have gone to the movies."

He was scanning the crowd, too, but instead of nodding agreement, he smiled. "This is fascinating, Liz. I never thought so many sober, respectable pillars of the community could be interested in UFO abductions. Look, there's Slim Hazeltine from the city council."

"That's not surprising. Slim in the weirdest person.... I never understood how he got elected."

"People figured that nobody owned him. Look, Liz, there's Eli Stoner from Stone Technologies. Do you suppose he got that NASA contract?"

Before Liz could reply, Tim was urging her toward Eli Stoner. For every giant corporation involved in software development, there were three or four small firms founded by hackers, and Stone Technologies was one of the more successful ones. Eli Stoner was a little strange, a leftover hippie from the sixties, but he could be a lot of fun to talk to.

But how were they ever going to pick the gravity man out of this crowd? Liz wondered. It was hopeless. Even if they stood face-to-face with him he probably wouldn't stand out in the middle of all these other eccentrics, like Bill Campbell who made the evening news last year by sitting on the roof of his house and playing his bagpipe at three in the morning. The memory of *that* made the corners of her mouth want to tug upward.

She managed to keep a straight face, though, even when Tim tugged her past a young man in green makeup who had pointed ears.

"Isn't this something, Liz?" Tim whispered to her as they closed in on Eli. "Every weirdo in the county is out tonight."

And plenty of ordinary people were here, too, Liz thought as she continued to scan the crowd. The strange ones were easy to pick out, but they made a definite minority.

"Hey, Eli," Tim said warmly, giving the man a high-five. "How's business?"

"Pretty good, man," Eli answered, smiling at Tim and winking at Liz. "I got that NASA contract, the one for the firmware for the Shuttle Improvements. I was planning to call you about subcontracting with you. I thought you and Liz might want to work on some of it."

"You know we would," Tim answered. However, he was a scrupulously honest man, so he added, "We had a little trouble, though. Did you hear? Our office was vandalized. Suppliers are estimating a month before they can get us back up to speed with Tempest equipment, so if this stuff is going to be classified—"

Eli shook his head. "None of it's classified. Did they catch the vandals?"

While Tim answered, Liz looked past Eli and saw Pat O'Shaughnessy. At least she thought it was Pat O'Shaughnessy. He was wearing a long black cape and a black brimmed hat with a big red feather in it, and he was smoking a huge cigar. Waving the cigar airily, he talked earnestly to a couple beside him. They both looked as if they ardently wished they could escape.

"I'll give you a call tomorrow about setting up a meeting," Eli was saying. "Gotta go. The old lady's shooting daggers at me. Later, man." He sauntered off.

Tim stared after him, smiling. "It kills me, Liz. It just kills me. That guy was getting gassed in Washington for protesting the war while I was over there up to my neck in swamps and bullets. If I'd met him back then I'd have probably socked him in the jaw. And he would have offered me a joint."

"And now you're both chief executive officers of software firms."

He looked down at her, the bemused smile still on his face. "Yeah. Ain't it something?"

She guessed it was. "I saw Pat."

"Chains and leather?"

"Opera cape and feathers."

Tim threw back his head and laughed. "Come on, Liz, let's find a seat and get crazy. Damn, I love this!"

Much to Liz's vast relief, Tim didn't really want to get crazy. He sat quietly beside her throughout White's talk, only occasionally betraying himself with a snort or a muttered word.

White himself turned out to be a less flamboyant speaker than she had expected. He wasn't at all wild in his presentation, and offered his claims in a voice of calm reason that was very persuasive. Liz almost felt as if she were sitting in one of the many lectures she had attended in her college days—except that this one was a far sight less credible. No matter how persuasive White might be, she couldn't accept the idea of UFO abductions.

And part of her problem with that was that she had seen a UFO. It hadn't abducted her.

Glancing sideways at Tim, she found him apparently absorbed in White's talk. When was he going to ask her about her UFO? she wondered. She was sure he would eventually. She knew him. He was intrinsically incapable of leaving anything alone. The amazing thing was that he hadn't yet asked her about it.

He was far more interesting to her than White's statistics on how many people claimed to have been abducted. It wasn't often that Tim simply held still. He was an active, involved, on-the-go kind of person. It felt like a luxury—like a fur coat in the cold, or a hot shower on aching muscles—just to be able to sit here and fill her eyes with him.

He was such a large, strong-looking man. Awareness of his size gave her a funny, clenching feeling inside, and to heck with liberation. She loved how safe she felt with him. She wouldn't hesitate to walk down the darkest street in town with this man beside her. And she'd cut out her tongue before she would admit it to him. She could just imagine the satisfied sparkle that would come to his eyes if he heard that. Oh, yes, he would *love* to hear her admit that.

Slowly he turned his head and looked straight into her eyes. He had known she was staring at him, she realized. She could see the satisfaction in those gray eyes, and color began to rise in her cheeks. But there was more than satisfaction in his look. There was warmth. Heat. Hunger. She recognized that look now, and responded to it with an inward heat of her own. The air in the room was suddenly thick and hard to breathe.

Slowly, slowly enough not to startle her or draw attention, he reached out and caught her hand. With a gentle squeeze, he drew it onto his lap, holding it against the top of his thigh. Her cheeks flaming hotly, Liz quickly faced front and tried to focus on Wilfred White. She was aware of nothing, though, but Tim's thigh beneath her palm. If she moved a scant inch...

She listened to White, but she never heard a word he said. Reality had somehow narrowed to the palm of her hand and the heat beneath it. The solid, muscled flesh beneath it. The man attached to that flesh. The man who was her business partner. The whole time she was sinking into the delights of being a woman, some corner of her mind kept pointing out that she was going to regret this. Oh, yes. But she would do that another day. In fact, Scarlett O'Hara could have taken lessons from Liz Pennington just then.

At the end of his forty-five-minute talk, White opened the floor for questions. Liz had to hand it to him—the man was patient in the face of some outright hostility. One woman accused him of blasphemy. Others came flat out and told him he was suffering from schizophrenic delusions. That made Tim sit up a little straighter, and his grip on Liz's hand tightened. Most questioners, however, seemed excited and intrigued by White's claims.

Suddenly Tim let go of her hand and stood. As big as he was, he was acknowledged almost immediately by White.

"There are a couple of things I don't really understand, Mr. White," Tim said.

Liz braced herself and stared at her knees, sure Tim was about to say something horribly mortifying, or something horribly inflammatory. Instead, she was shocked by his pleasant, rational query.

"If I understand what you've been saying," Tim began, "you believe these UFOs are selecting individuals for a kind of lifelong study."

"That seems to be the logical conclusion one can draw," White agreed. "There can't be any other reason why the aliens would return for the same people again and again."

"Agreed," Tim answered pleasantly. "But that doesn't rationally fit in with the rest of your claims. For my part, I can understand a scientific desire to study a new species. To that point, I find these aliens quite comprehensible. What I *can't* find any logical or scientific support for are your claims of genetic experiments. At least I presume that's what you believe is behind these crossbred infants you claim to have seen in alien nurseries.''

Oh, boy, Liz thought, and stared at her knees, hoping she was invisible.

"I don't see why you find this hard to understand," White said. "Clearly the aliens are studying our genetic compatibility."

"If so," Tim retorted, "then their motives resemble some of the concentration-camp activities of the Third Reich. Some Nazi scientists tried to crossbreed humans and apes, and this smacks of the same kind of thing. Genetic studies can be pursued without…"

The rest of his statement was drowned in a cacophony of upraised voices. In the midst of the sudden confusion, Liz grabbed Tim's hand and tugged him back down into his chair. People were arguing vociferously over his accusation, and Liz had to shout at him to be heard.

"Why did you say that?"

He shrugged and leaned toward her ear. "Because half the people in this room are thinking that these supposed aliens are saviors of some kind. Sometimes you have to point out things to people, Liz. Most of us are too damn accepting and not half as critical as we ought to be."

"I *knew* you were going to say something offensive," Liz said. "I knew it."

"So what?" he demanded. "The truth often hurts, and it's just too damn bad."

At that moment, Donna's son James crouched in the aisle beside them. "Good going. Mr. O'Shaughnessy," he said. "I couldn't believe that nobody saw anything wrong with what White says is happening. It's weird. It's almost as if you say 'experiment,' and everybody gets all cooperative."

"People are intimidated by science," Tim said, giving Liz a "see…?" kind of look, as if to say not everyone was dense.

By this time, the room had begun to quiet. Then the really unusual types started coming out of the woodwork. One man wanted to know if the aliens had made any predictions about earth's future. Another asked if it was true that the aliens had sex with their abductees. At that, Liz sank lower in her chair. She had forgotten how bold people could be, even in public forums. Until this moment, she hadn't realized just how sheltered her partnership with Tim had kept her.

Another man, an individual garbed head to foot in white, stood up and announced that he, too, was an abductee. Utter mayhem broke out when he announced that the aliens would be returning on October 31, at midnight, and that they would land on Davis Hill, an unpopulated, wooded hill in the middle of the Bleaker farm.

Several minutes passed before order was restored. Leaning over, Tim whispered in Liz's ear, "We absolutely can't miss *that*, Liz."

"Are you crazy? You can't possibly think I'm going out to Davis Hill in the middle of the night to wait for a UFO!"

"Why not? Damn it, where's your sense of adventure? Every loony in the county will be there!"

"Every loony in the county is *here*," she reminded him. "And I don't hear a one of them talking about gravity!"

"What about gravity?" asked a loud, unhappily familiar voice in the restored quiet of the gymnasium.

Liz, nearly groaning, turned her head to see Pat O'Shaughnessy, red feather bobbing, cape swirling, standing in the middle of the cavernous room.

"What about gravity?" White asked pleasantly. "I don't follow your question, sir."

"I mean what about gravity?" Pat said irritably. "What are these damn aliens doing to our gravity?"

A movement to the right caught Liz's eye and she turned her head to look. That was when she groaned, and a moment later Tim groaned, too.

Laurel and Hardy, otherwise known as Special Agents Woodrow and Carter, were closing in on Pat.

"Damn it," Tim said. "I've got to stop them, Liz. They'll give away the game."

"You said Pat told them he was going to—"

But Tim was already gone, charging up the makeshift aisle to intercept the agents. Liz winced when he caught them by the arms and by force of sheer brute strength marched them toward the back door. Liz could see that he was talking to them, talking fast and furiously. She didn't think it would help. Oh, well. It had been a great partnership, she thought as she watched them walk out of the gym.

Was a life sentence to Leavenworth sufficient cause to dissolve it?

Nobody else in the gymnasium seemed to have noticed anything. Grateful for that much, Liz hurried after O'Shaughnessy, thinking that perhaps her presence would keep Carter from shooting him. Carter hated Tim, probably because Tim wasn't intimidated by him. She had seen it in the man's expression, which wasn't quite professional whenever he looked at O'Shaughnessy. Something snagged at the pocket of her jacket, but she ignored it, feeling a couple of stitches pop as she tugged free.

Outside, the night had turned bitingly cold, and she drew her light jacket around her. The parking lot was fairly well lit, and it took her only an instant to spy the three arguing men. They were keeping their voices down, but from the way two of them were gesturing, she could tell tempers were running high. At least nobody had pulled a gun yet.

"He's doing it on purpose!" she heard Tim say as she approached. "I'm telling you, he's trying to draw the gravity man out. Damn it, Carter, my brother's a cop!"

"Being a cop doesn't make a man immune to insanity," Carter growled back. "What he said in there was *crazy*. Exactly the kind of crazy we're looking for. Don't you think it's funny the guy would show up in the middle of all this stuff?"

"What's funny about it? He's my brother. He shows up in my life anytime he feels like it! He was in the damn hospital when the vandalism started!"

"Can he prove it?"

Woodrow interrupted. "Dumb question, Carter. It's easy enough to find out. Look, O'Shaughnessy, brother or not, he's out of his jurisdiction. I want him to stay out of this."

"He's not acting as a cop, Woodrow. He's acting as my brother. He's trying to help Liz and me. This gravity man is ruining us!"

Silence greeted that statement. Neither agent could argue with that.

"Look," Tim said more reasonably, "Liz and I can't take much more of this. We can't get any of our work done, and now he's trashed my home. So what do we do? Much longer and we'll be in default on our contracts. Much longer and Millennium Software is going to be a very cold, very dead pipe dream.''

"We understand that, O'Shaughnessy," Woodrow said quietly. "Believe me, we've got every possible person working on this, including the local police. We want this guy as badly as you do."

"Do you?" Tim sounded doubtful. Liz could understand why. She couldn't believe the FBI cared as deeply as she and Tim about their business.

"We do," Woodrow said. "This guy broke into classified containers. We still aren't a hundred percent certain he didn't take anything. Of course we want him." He turned and looked at Liz for the first time. "Keep him and his brother out of the way, Ms. Pennington. Let the bureau do its job. It may not happen as fast as you'd like, but we always get our man."

Tim stared after him and Carter as they returned to the gym. "I thought that was the Mounties," he muttered.

"What?" Liz queried.

"You know. The Mounties always get their man."

"Oh."

He turned suddenly and wrapped his arms around her, hugging her tightly. "Sorry, Liz. I guess I worried you."

"A little," she admitted on a shaky laugh. "I can't help thinking it's unsafe to give a hard time to law officers."

"This is still America, darlin'."

"Some cops shoot first and ask questions later. A lot of good the ACLU can do you if you're dead."

"You know, you've got to do something about this paranoia you feel around cops. You're talking to a man whose family belongs to that crowd."

"Carter's not a member of your family," she reminded him drily, "and it's Carter I'm worried about."

Chapter 11

"**I**'m sorry." Tim pulled the truck into the driveway and switched off the ignition.

Liz turned to look at him, but at that moment he turned off the headlights and they were plunged into utter darkness. "For what?"

"Dragging you to that meeting. It was a waste of time, wasn't it?" It wasn't a question.

"I thought you were enjoying yourself."

"I was."

Liz thought she saw the gleam of his teeth as he smiled, but then he slid across the seat until their thighs touched. He might as well have set a match to her nerves. All of a sudden she was aware of only Tim, of his size, his strength and his maleness.

"I *am*," he said, amending his statement. "I *am* enjoying myself." Bending his head, he found her earlobe with his teeth and sighed when a shudder ripped through her. "Ah, Lizzie, Lizzie, darlin' girl…"

Suddenly, she admitted to herself that she didn't mind him calling her Lizzie. Turning her head, she met his mouth with hers and gave herself up to Tim's miraculous, sexy, earth-shaking kiss.

"Let's go inside," he said, a few moments later. "Will you make me some of your fantastic hot chocolate?"

"Hot chocolate?" Her quivering insides thought that sounded awful. "Sure."

On unsteady knees, she climbed out of the truck and entered the house. Somewhere between climbing out of the truck and entering the kitchen, Tim decided he didn't want hot chocolate after all. Instead, he pulled Liz into his arms and kissed her again, rubbing himself against her in blatant demonstration of his wishes.

"Am I shocking you?" he asked, and rocked himself against her one more time, slowly. Deeply. With a smothered groan.

"Do you want to shock me?" she asked on a mere breath, surely the last breath left in the universe.

"Do you want me to shock you?" There was a stifled laugh in his voice, one that sounded more like a laughing moan.

"Yes," she gasped. "Shock me."

He glanced quickly around and saw that the kitchen curtains were already tightly drawn. "How about here on the kitchen table?" Gray eyes sparkling, he waited for her reaction.

"Table?" She repeated the word blankly, and then, even as her cheeks turned crimson, she started to smile. "What's the matter, O'Shaughnessy? Too weak to make it up the stairs?"

Too soon for shenanigans, he decided and anyway, he just now remembered that his brother might show up at any minute. But he liked the way Liz had teased him back. That was a damn good sign, that she felt comfortable enough to tease about this.

"You asked for it," he said with mock reluctance, and scooped her up, swinging her over his shoulder like a sack of grain.

Liz shrieked. "Tim, put me down! You'll drop me! I'll be crippled for life!"

"No way, Lizzie. That would ruin my plans for the rest of the evening." He patted her bottom affectionately.

"Oh, my God," she groaned as he climbed the stairs and the floor fell farther and farther away. "Tim, I'm going to kill you!"

"Promises, promises. All threat and no action. I'll make it up to you, Liz. I'm going to lick you all over like an ice-cream cone. How's that sound?"

That silenced her. Completely.

The bedside lamp was on so they could see one another as they cuddled together in the afterglow of lovemaking. Tim O'Shaughnessy was a born toucher. He touched her constantly, in little ways and big ways. Liz's life had been barren of such affection before, and she was acutely aware of even his briefest gesture.

He would make a great father, she thought. He would touch and cuddle and hug his kids, and tease them and play with them and just generally be a big, warm, loving part of their lives. And why was she thinking about such things? This relationship would come to an end eventually because they'd get sick to death of being together twenty-four hours a day. To sustain the partnership, they would have to break this off. She was sure of that.

Besides, Tim had made it clear he wasn't going to love ever again. Nowhere did she see any evidence that he was wrong about that. All these years since Tranh, he had had only casual relationships. How else had he arrived unattached at this place in time? So...

She sighed and snuggled closer. She didn't want any complications, either. She liked Tim too much to risk losing him to the bitterness of a failed relationship. Gradually, little by little, they would back away when this gravity business was settled. They'd return to their separate existences.

Right.

And in the meantime, she was going to savor each and every second of the magic he brought into her life, and ignore the fact that she'd given him every last little piece of her heart. She was his now, body and soul, and she could never let him know that. Never.

"Liz?"

"Hmm?"

"I really think we ought to go out to Davis Hill on Halloween. It's just the kind of thing that might appeal to the gravity man."

"It might," she admitted. "But just because he thinks our computers are destroying his gravity, that doesn't mean he's even remotely interested in aliens."

"I know." It was his turn to sigh. "But Lizzie, what else do we have to go on? The biker turned out to be my brother, and I figure by now the FBI would know if there was anything weird about the NPS guy. What else is there?"

"Not a thing." She kissed his shoulder and thought what a

miraculous thing it was to be held like this. What an absolutely wonderful thing it was to be free to touch him whenever she wanted. What an incredibly, amazingly fantastic thing it was that he appeared to feel exactly the same way about touching her and being held by her. Her fingers strayed upward over his chest, and found the scar from the bayonet. "God, Tim, it scares me to even think about how close—"

"Shh." He silenced her with a squeeze and a kiss. "Life is full of close calls. What if I'd never noticed you at the trade show? What if you'd slipped out of the convention center before I caught up with you?"

She found that idea surprisingly scary, too.

"Of course," he said a moment later, "you may wish I'd never set eyes on you if we don't run this gravity man to ground."

"Don't you dare even *think* such a thing," she said sharply. She pushed herself up on her elbow so she could glare down at him. Tim tried very hard not to look at her exposed breast, knowing it would infuriate her if he got distracted.

"Damn it, O'Shaughnessy," she said with uncharacteristic profanity, "we're *partners.* We shared equally in everything from the start—the risks, the finances, the failures and the successes. We share equally in this, and I don't want you acting like it's somehow your responsibility alone! I'll never, ever, regret going into business with you, even if we go broke."

He felt the corners of his mouth pulling upward even though his insides were aching over her words. "Really?"

"Really." She flopped back down huffily. "Men!"

"What's wrong with men?" he asked, propping himself on an elbow over her.

"You must think I haven't got a brain in my head, or the wit to use it if I did!"

He was genuinely startled by that indictment. "What the hell makes you say that?"

"You act like I only went into business with you because you forced me somehow. As if I'm not capable of making my own decisions!"

"I never said that. Damn it, Liz, what's eating you? I was just feeling as if...as if..."

"As if I would never have gotten into this mess if you hadn't forced me. Don't be an idiot."

He frowned down at her in silence for a long moment. "Are you trying to pick a fight?"

She bit her lip and then all the fight just drained out of her. She *had* been trying to pick a fight, she realized. They'd gotten too close, somehow, and she was trying to back away. Wise, maybe, but unfair nonetheless. "Sorry," she said.

He let it go. He knew how prickly Liz was, how irrational she could get over some things. He was also aware that because they were two different people he wouldn't always understand what she was feeling or thinking. What appeared irrational to him unquestionably made excellent sense to her.

Leaning over her, he sprinkled kisses here and there. "I'm worried," he admitted between kisses. "We can go on for a while like this, but if we don't start delivering some kind of progress on our contracts, we're going to be in trouble."

She sighed and turned a little, unconsciously, wanting his mouth to graze her nipple. Crazily, impossibly, she wanted him again already, but she didn't want to embarrass him by asking. Innocent but not ignorant, she was perfectly aware that men needed some recovery time.

"I called some of our customers today," he told her, his voice thickening a little. "They were pretty nice about it, but I don't know how long they'll—" He broke off and lifted his head so he could look at her. Hoarsely, he asked her, "Did you like it when I licked you?"

Heat flashed through her at supersonic speeds. Her affirmative sounded more like a moan.

"I never got to finish," he muttered, recalling how she had just about shattered before he reached her navel. He still had the nail marks on his arms from where she had grabbed him and pulled him up over her.

"Do you still want me to shock you, Lizzie?" he asked huskily, running a tentative hand down to the juncture of her thighs. Once there, he insinuated gentle, knowledgeable fingers into her moist, swelling folds. "I want to kiss you right here, Lizzie," he whispered, closing his eyes and giving himself up to his own blooming heat.

"Tim..." His name was a catch in her quick breath. She was lost, utterly lost, in the sensations he unleashed. Her legs parted helplessly, her hips raised beseechingly.

"I want to taste you," he murmured, sliding lower. "I'm going to taste you. Say no now, Lizzie...."

She was past saying no to anything at all.

The instant she awoke in the morning, Liz's cheeks began burning with a furious blush. Tim hadn't shocked her half as much as she had shocked herself. And even in her state of utter embarrassment she was already thinking of ways she would like to...shock herself some more.

A shaky sigh escaped her and she squeezed her eyes shut as she realized that Tim O'Shaughnessy had turned her into an utter wanton. It was...wonderful!

A quick glance from the corner of her eye told her that he still slept deeply. Poor man. He'd exerted himself strenuously last night. She managed to swallow a wicked giggle before it disturbed him, and she eased carefully from the bed.

Mephisto was impatient to get out the back door, and he darted around her ankles as she descended the stairs in her robe and scuffs. "Darn it, cat," she grumbled. "One of these days you're going to make me break my neck."

Frost coated the world. Everything in her backyard glistened in fairy-tale white, and Liz paused a moment with her hand on the doorknob to enjoy the view through the window. Evidently the unusually warm autumn had decided to turn normally cold at last. Pulling the neck of her robe closed over her throat, she opened the door for the cat and watched the plume of her breath turn white in the chill. A pearly pink glow came from the eastern sky to meld with the last blue shadows of fading night.

Gorgeous, she thought, and used her foot to gently nudge the suddenly reluctant cat out the door. That was when she realized that someone was huddled on her back porch. She drew in a deep breath, a cry of fright building at the back of her throat, but then she saw the red feather.

"Pat?"

He had evidently dozed off as he leaned against the porch pillar. At the sound of his name, he sat bolt upright and looked at her. "Oh," he said, and relaxed visibly.

"What are you doing out here?" she asked. "You haven't been out here all night, have you?"

"Naw. I spent the night with Laurel and Hardy, and when I got back here an hour ago, the door was locked."

"I'm sorry. I never thought to give you a key!"

"That's okay. Is Tim up?"

"Not yet." Something about the sight of Tim's scruffy brother brought out unsuspected maternal instincts in Liz. She decided he needed a good breakfast. "Come in and warm up."

Rising with evident stiffness, he brushed himself off and followed her inside. "I'm getting too old for this crap, but don't tell Tim I admitted it. I hate it when he says I told you so."

"Me, too," she admitted with a laugh. "Pull up a chair. Coffee will be ready in just a couple minutes."

Pat dropped his cape over the back of a chair and hooked the feathered fedora on the doorknob. "I had quite a talk with those two FBI agents last night. They were pretty ticked off at Tim and me."

"I thought they might be." As soon as she had the coffeepot dripping, she turned her attention to making home fries. "I don't like the way Carter looks at Tim."

"*Woodrow* doesn't like the way Carter looks at Tim," Pat said. "There's something not quite right about that guy. Anyway, don't worry about it. I managed to convince them I can be useful."

"Why should you be?" Color flooded her cheeks and she paused in dicing onion to look at him. "I didn't mean that the way it sounded."

He gave her a smile so very like Tim's that she could hardly believe it. "Don't worry about it. O'Shaughnessys aren't used to tact."

"I've noticed." She gave a small laugh. "I just meant, you're recuperating from a serious wound. You ought to be getting your rest, not sitting around on cold porches at dawn."

His smile widened. "I knew that would arouse your sympathy. I figured you might offer me breakfast."

She had to laugh. He was a charming rogue, though not quite as charming as his brother. "How do you like home fries?"

"'Like' hardly begins to cover it."

Tim made his appearance just as Liz finished frying the bacon. His greeting was grumpy. "I was going to cook breakfast."

Liz caught sight of Pat's twitching lip as she turned around, so she was at least partially prepared for the sight of Tim. He wore skin-tight, navy blue jogging pants and nothing else. His tawny hair stood up wildly on his head, and a day's growth of beard made gingery fuzz on his cheeks and chin.

"Sit down," she said as she passed her gaze over him. Even disheveled and cranky he was pinup material. "I'll get you some coffee."

"I'll get it," he growled. "Even-steven, remember? You're not supposed to be cooking this morning."

"So what? Yesterday was my day, and *you* cooked. What the devil is eating you, O'Shaughnessy?" She was beginning to get annoyed. No woman wanted to be talked to this way after a night of lovemaking. Certainly not after a night of lovemaking in which the word *inhibition* had virtually ceased to have meaning.

He glowered at her. "I woke up alone."

Her cheeks flamed and her ears burned. How could he? How could he say something so devastatingly intimate in front of Pat? But Pat appeared undisturbed and possibly deaf, training his full attention on yesterday's newspaper. Liz, unable to think of any reasonable response to this outrageousness, turned her back abruptly on Tim and slammed the frying pan back down on the burner. "How do you like your eggs, Pat?" she asked.

"Runny, sunny-side up. Thanks."

Tim looked from Liz's rigid back to Pat's averted face. All right, he was acting like an idiot. But when he'd awakened and found Liz gone, he'd panicked. He'd feared that last night had shocked her and that she would be furious with him this morning. Finding her calmly cooking breakfast rather than plotting his painful demise, he had felt foolish for panicking. And, feeling foolish, he had acted foolishly.

But what the hell. He'd been behaving like a four-star idiot since the instant he noticed that his business partner was a gorgeous, voluptuous, sexy young woman. Or maybe he had been an idiot all along and now he was just coming to his senses.

Regardless, he owed the lady an apology. Releasing a sigh, he crossed the kitchen and slipped his arms around her waist from behind. He thought she relaxed just a little at his touch. At least she didn't go stomping off in a fury.

"I'm sorry, Liz." He seemed to be saying that all the time lately.

"For what?"

That was a loaded question, considering they weren't alone, so he settled on the one thing that wouldn't embarrass her. "For grumping at you."

"Forget it, O'Shaughnessy."

"I've sunk to the level of *O'Shaughnessy* again?"

"You've always been *O'Shaughnessy*. I'm not so sure it was very bright of me to let you become anything else."

Tim winced. "Ouch."

"You like your eggs over easy, right?"

He watched the businesslike way she cracked those eggs against the edge of the frying pan, and decided that she really wanted to crack his head. The trouble of it was, he didn't think he could blame her. He was the one who had rocked their comfortable boat enough that they were in constant danger of capsizing what had been a perfectly good partnership. The gravity man was only part of the problem here, and even after they got him out of their hair they were going to have to deal with the mess they—*he*—had made.

Tim settled down at the table, catching a sympathetic look from his brother as he did so. He returned a glare, thinking that Pat couldn't possibly begin to comprehend what was going on here.

For that matter, he wasn't sure he comprehended it himself. He'd known he would be risking their partnership. He'd known that Liz was a virgin. He'd known that she was a forever lady. He'd known that. All of it. Now he had to deal with what he'd done to her and himself.

He had wanted her. He had wanted her so badly that he had lost common sense and charged ahead like a cavalry brigade gone out of control. Hell, he still wanted her so badly that he was hardly capable of caring that he'd turned everything into a huge mess for them. The bottom line was that he had wanted her so much that *not* pursuing her would have eventually caused him to rupture the relationship. Denial and fulfillment had exactly the same ending in this situation. Amazing. Terrifying. Hilarious, too, or it would be once it stopped hurting.

So what now, O'Shaughnessy?

He looked at Liz, watched her as she placed a platter of eggs, bacon and home fries in front of Pat, and then one in front of him. He watched her settle into her own seat with one strip of bacon, a spoonful of potatoes and no egg, and watched her pour herself a mug of coffee from the carafe.

He got this funny feeling when he looked at her, and it wasn't all sex. He'd never felt quite this way before—sort of sad, sort of happy, sort of empty and sort of full. And all he wanted right now was for Liz Pennington to smile. Genuinely smile. Happily smile. She had the world's sunniest, most beautiful smile. It filled her hazel eyes with light and pinkened her cheeks. It warmed him right to his toes.

At the moment his toes were feeling pretty cold, and it looked as if it might be a while before Liz Pennington felt like smiling.

"Great breakfast, Liz," Tim said. He had a strong feeling she hadn't gone to all this trouble for his brother, and from the way she was picking at her plate, she hadn't cooked for herself, either. Well, if you put that together with last night...

Struck, he stared at her, and then started grinning. "Hey, Pat?"

"Yeah?"

"Can you get lost for a while?"

"Only if I can take my breakfast with me."

Liz looked from one to the other. "What's going on? Why should Pat get lost? Tim?"

Thank God, it was back to *Tim* again. "Never mind. It'll wait until my dumb brother here finishes stuffing his face."

Pat swallowed. "Dumb, nothing. When a lady cooks a meal like this, only an idiot passes it up. I am not an idiot."

"Neither am I," Tim remarked. "So why don't you get to the point?"

Pat glanced at Liz.

Tim shook his head. "Liz and I are partners, Pat. As the lady reminded me last night, we share everything, and that includes the trouble. What gives?"

Pat took a swig of coffee before he answered. "The gravity man was at the meeting last night."

Liz stiffened. In a single fell swoop, uneasiness returned, blighting the fragile beauty of the morning.

"Are you sure?" Tim demanded of his brother. "How *can* you be sure? What happened?"

"It was right after the meeting let out. I went to the men's room and while I was in the stall, somebody stuck his head into the rest room and hissed that it wasn't the aliens who were disturbing the gravity, that it was the computers. By the time I managed to get out of the stall, he was long gone and there was nobody in the corridor outside to ask if they'd seen him.''

Shivering suddenly, Liz rubbed her upper arms. "Creepy."

Pat looked at her and nodded. "I've been a cop for a long time, and I know creeps. This one is distinctly weird. Weird enough that he wanted me to know who was really disturbing the gravity. This guy is totally out of touch with reality, Timmy. Completely nutso. If I were you guys, I'd keep my back covered."

Tim stiffened. "You think he's dangerous? Even the FBI won't commit on that.''

"Those guys have got bosses and they have to be careful what they say. They're not allowed to say anything the bureau doesn't want to show up in the newspaper. I don't have any such problems at the moment, and I'm telling you, I think this guy is crazy, and he might be crazy enough to hurt somebody. I can't say that for sure, but, hey, why chance it?''

Needing to do something, anything, Liz started a fresh pot of coffee and stared out the window over the sink. The frost was already melting from the backyard wherever the rising sun had reached. The maples had lost all but a few of their red leaves, the oaks were barren except for a couple of patches of yellow. Autumn was almost over.

"Did you tell Woodrow about the guy?" Tim asked his brother.

"Called him first thing when I got to a pay phone. I spent half the night getting the third degree. I hope you appreciate what you've gotten me into here, boyo.''

"Hey, I didn't ask you to help out. You volunteered for this all on your own.''

They sounded exactly like brothers, Liz thought, turning around to look at them. They looked like brothers, too, despite their differences in coloring and bulk.

"So what do we do now?" she asked. She was, for once in her life, flat-out of ideas and opinions. In fact, if she had her druthers, she'd climb under a quilt with Tim in some dark hidey-hole and stay there until this mess blew over. But she didn't have her druthers. When had she ever?

Tim looked at her, and the light just about went out of his day. There was no smile there, no look of a woman who had been well loved. There was simply a gray kind of fearfulness, a kind of acceptance of inevitable loss. Once or twice before, she had given him the feeling that she expected all good things to go away. That was what she was feeling right now, he would have bet on it.

Instinct brought him to his feet and to her. He slung his arm around her shoulders and tucked her up against his side.

"What now?" he said. "I'll tell you. We'll keep working in the basement here, and pretending that we're working at the office. Maybe we can draw the bastard out again. We may have to turn this place into a fortress for a while, but if so, we will. Whatever it takes, Liz, we're not going to knuckle under. We'll make it somehow."

She had turned her face up and watched him throughout this speech, and now she nodded. There was something brave in her expression, in the steadiness of her green eyes as they met his, he thought. He could see the courage in her, courage he suspected she was unaware of. Life was dealing out punches, and she faced them. That simple. That priceless. That admirable.

He squeezed her and then looked at his brother. "You agree?"

"I guess so," Pat said. "But I won't be much good at drawing this guy out if he discovers we're related."

Tim shrugged. "Small loss. Liz and I and our computers are all it takes to draw him out. We're the bait. I'd just feel a hell of a lot better knowing you're around to protect Liz, too."

Pat evidently agreed. The understanding was that the house was never to be left unoccupied, and Liz was never to be here alone. Liz didn't like it, but a look from Tim silenced her. Even-steven or not, she didn't know a thing about self-defense or guns or anything else they might have to rely on. Pat carried a pistol. Tim, she recalled, had that deadly-looking hunting knife, and had appeared to know what to do with it.

Well, he was a former Green Beret.

At that thought, Liz looked up from the dishes she was washing and across to the other side of the kitchen where Tim was on the phone with Donna explaining the latest developments. She kept getting this jarring sensation with Tim, this sudden, sharp awareness that he was not the man he appeared to be on the surface. In fact, it seemed that the Tim O'Shaughnessy she had known for so long was a front designed to keep people at a safe distance.

He was a bold, brave man, she thought. He didn't seem to fear anything, even looking like a fool, which was something most people feared at least as much as they feared death. She was willing to bet he didn't fear death, either. And he was quick with his tenderness and concern. Quick to care and protect. Quick but secretive. He sheltered himself behind silence. He hid the real Tim O'Shaughnessy from the world.

He refused to be vulnerable.

As he hung up the phone, Tim caught her staring. He parted his lips as if to speak, and then closed them again, studying her as thoughtfully as she studied him. He was measuring her, she thought. In some subtle way he was taking her measure. And then he reached some kind of decision.

"It looks like it's going to be a nice day, Lizzie. Maybe we'll take the afternoon off."

She opened her mouth to protest instinctively, but the words never emerged. They wouldn't really be working at the office anyway. What difference did it make if they skipped out?

The afternoon turned into one of those incredible autumn days that always made Liz feel glad to be alive. The air was chilly, chilly enough that she was grateful for her bulky knit sweater and jacket, but the sun was still warm, so strong as to make her skin tingle. The light had that pale, almost buttery color she associated with no other time of year, and just-fallen leaves rustled on the ground everywhere, adding bursts of scarlet and yellow to the world.

Tim gave Donna the afternoon off, and he and Liz stood in the office parking lot and watched her drive away.

"Let's get out of here," he said.

He drove them away from town and into the country, pulling over at a hiking trail. "Are you game?" he asked her.

The trail wound back through the autumn Catskills, and an hour later they emerged onto a rocky promontory, with a view of the old, tree-covered mountains and valleys. There they leaned back against lichen-covered rocks to take a breather and enjoy the view.

The wind had a bit more bite on the exposed cliff, so Liz was grateful when Tim moved to one side to provide a windbreak for her. She was even more grateful when, a little later, he drew her into his arms. It felt so nice to be held this way, to feel the solidity of his chest beneath her ear, to feel the strength of his arm around her back, while sharing the beauty of the afternoon.

"The Catskills always seem magic to me," he remarked. "Did I ever tell you that I lived around here when I was a kid?"

"Is that why you were so agreeable when I said I thought it would be nice to start our business in this area?"

"Yep. I always liked it here. Dad was a cop in Kingston, but we lived in Saugerties. Nice little town. Anyway, I guess I soaked up Rip Van Winkle and the Legend of Sleepy Hollow with my cornflakes. Here I am all these years later and these mountains still seem magic. The whole Hudson valley seems magic."

"When did your family move to Dallas? And why?"

"Dallas offered Dad a bigger paycheck. At least that's the story he tells. Mostly I think we moved because my mother's relatives were a pain in the neck. I guess Dallas seemed far enough away to be safe."

"Was it?"

"For a while, anyway." He touched her hair gently, stroking it lightly. "Then they discovered the airplane. Mom's family is loud and boisterous, very close and very critical. I'm grateful I was out of school before they discovered they could afford to fly. Frankly, they drive me crazy." He shifted a little, settling her more comfortably.

"Did you go into the army right out of high school?" Her heart speeded up as she spoke, and she wondered if he would talk about that period or if he would back away from it as he usually did. A long moment passed in scary silence.

"Yeah," he said finally. "My best buddy and I both signed up together on one of those delayed-enlistment programs. Basically, back then, that meant they'd let you graduate before they grabbed you. Man, we thought we were such hot stuff." A quiet, rueful laugh rumbled briefly in his chest. "Not only did we volunteer, but we volunteered for the Special Forces. Made it, too. Then we were *really* hot stuff. I have to hand it to the army. They sure know how to brainwash an eighteen-year-old into thinking he's an indestructible fighting machine. Only we weren't indestructible."

Feeling a tension in him, Liz moved even closer and stroked

his chest with the palm of her hand. "No," she said softly. "You weren't indestructible."

"Hal—my buddy—lasted a week. Do you know that the guys who've been out for a while in the field don't even talk to the new grunts? And do you know why? Because they know most of us are going to die in the first firefight."

The arm around her shoulders had become like a steel band, holding her with such strength that it just barely missed hurting. But his other hand, touching her hair, remained gentle, tender.

"Hal died?" she dared to ask.

"Yeah. Blown to smithereens. I wasn't so damn cocky after that."

She didn't know what to say. What could anyone say to that? She hugged him.

"Then I met Tranh," he said after a bit. "My unit was stationed really far forward. Really...isolated. The closest we came to other Americans was when the reconnaissance planes or bombers flew overhead. She risked her neck by associating with me. It was common for the VC to come during the dead of night and wipe out anyone they considered a collaborator. I guess we were both dumb. It just happened, and somehow we both survived it."

"You weren't dumb," Liz said softly. "Sometimes you have to take a risk."

"Yeah." He lifted her hand from his chest and looked at her fingers. Long, slender, graceful fingers. Why hadn't he noticed that before? She had beautiful hands. Then he carried her hand to his mouth and kissed each delicate finger. "I still remember the first time I jumped out of an airplane."

"That must have been scary."

His eyes opened suddenly, and he smiled. "I didn't believe the parachute would open."

"No?"

"No. But it did. Sometimes, though, you just have to believe that you can defy gravity," he murmured in the instant before he took her mouth in a breath-stealing, mind-stunning kiss of savagery.

He had always been so gentle with her before. He had coaxed and led, soothed and cajoled. This time he met her as an equal and demanded that she meet him the same way, at a primitive, earthy level. At a hungry, ferocious level. At a place she had never dared trespass before.

For an instant she felt frightened, and then something wild and untamed rose in her, a ferocious, unfettered yearning for something uncivilized. Something basic. Something so primitive and utterly honest that society had no words for it.

She wanted to be claimed, conquered, possessed. She wanted things no liberated woman in her right mind would admit to, and the realization penetrated the rising heat in her pounding blood.

Tim felt the change in her, felt the uncertainty in her. He let go reluctantly, tucked her face into his shoulder and waited for sanity to return. She was precious, this woman. Too precious to frighten.

She was still resisting this relationship, he realized. In her mind, this was a temporary thing, a passing madness that would vanish like smoke. She was living in the constant expectation that tomorrow, or the next day, everything would return to normal. And normal meant the way things were before the gravity man. Before Tim O'Shaughnessy had set his male sights on her.

Well, it was a nice notion, but he knew better. Nothing was ever going to be the same again for either of them. From the instant he had realized that he wanted Liz, there had been no going back. That's what frightened her. Hell, it frightened *him*.

They needed to look forward now, not back, but he didn't see how he could manage to convince her of that when he didn't know what the shape of the future would be. Or even what it *should* be. If they didn't manage to run the gravity man to ground pretty quickly, they were going to be out of business. The sensible thing to do in that case would be to look for a job. No problem. Programmers—*good* programmers—were always in demand. Liz would find a job straight off, and probably have to move halfway across the country.

That's what she *should* do. He certainly wouldn't ask her to stick around and make all the sacrifices that would have to be made if they were to try to resuscitate Millennium Software. No, he would definitely urge her to seek a good position elsewhere.

He wouldn't look for one himself, however. If there was one thing Tim O'Shaughnessy knew for absolute certain, it was that he didn't fit in in corporate America. In fact, there weren't many places that he did fit. He fit at Millennium Software, but that was because he fit with Liz.

But it wouldn't be long before Liz would leave. Oh, she wouldn't want to. She was a loyal partner, and her first instinct would be to stick it out.

But he wouldn't let her. She deserved a lot more than that would bring her.

In fact, when he started thinking about what Liz deserved, he started feeling uncomfortable about himself. It had been many years since he had envisioned himself in the role of a provider. Not since Tranh's death. Like the vast majority of men, he thought in such terms only when some woman made him.

Liz made him think of such things, he realized with a sense of shock. Here she was, treating this like some kind of life crisis that would pass off, something that would soon be forgotten, yet she had him thinking about the kind of provider he was—or rather wasn't.

Good Lord. That was creepy.

Liz stirred and sighed. "Tim? I'm getting cold. Can we go back now?"

Going back was out of the question. That was the problem with reality. People, like time and events moved in only one direction, and there was never any opportunity to reconsider and redo.

But then, did he really want to?

The brisk walk back to the truck warmed Liz up and took the chill from her fingers and toes, not that she noticed. While he had held her, Tim had gone away somewhere. He had stroked her and caressed her, but the gestures had possessed an absent quality that disturbed her. Inevitably she wondered if it had been the mention of his wife that took him so far away.

Well, so what if it was? He'd warned her about that. And things between them would have to get back to normal pretty quickly anyway, if they were to survive into the future as business partners.

Smothering a sigh, she turned her head and watched the autumn countryside flash by. It was wimpy of her, but she had to admit that she had been pretty content with her life before Tim made a pass at her and the gravity man decided to pick on them. She had liked her work, she had enjoyed her friends and if she had occasionally felt something was missing—well, no one on earth had a *perfect* life.

Now everything was upside down, nothing was the same and she had the insane feeling that Tim—if he were of a mind to—could be the cement that filled all the cracks and chinks of her life.

But he didn't want to. She realized that men weren't comfortable with emotional expression, but Tim didn't even admit to anything beyond the easy, comfortable feelings. He could be her buddy and her lover, but he wouldn't trust her with his softer feelings or his vulnerabilities. She saw that every time she got him to talk about the past. He spoke of his life in terms of events and facts, not in terms of feelings and experiences. As long as he kept that distance, they would never be any more than buddies.

Turning her head, she looked at Tim and felt the soul-deep ache she always felt when she looked at him. His craggy Irish face, his shaggy ginger hair, his huge hands and powerful shoulders—just the sight of him made her feel warm and goopy.

Five years ago, he had burst into her life wearing a business suit and joggers. She had recognized him instantly even though she had never met him before. It was a purely emotional recognition that utterly defied logic. It was that strange connection that had carried her out to the all-night diner with a man she didn't know well. The world was a dangerous place for a woman alone, but Tim O'Shaughnessy made her forget her common sense. Against all reason, he made her feel safe.

It had been an instantaneous meeting of minds, one that, despite all their quarreling, hadn't diminished in all this time. Truth to tell, they enjoyed their squabbles. It was a form of play and relaxation that suited them. As for the rest of it—a long, long time ago, Liz had realized that Tim saw her as a colleague and nothing more. Once that had become clear, she had buried her attraction to him and satisfied herself with friendship. She had some pride, after all.

Looking at him now, however, she had no trouble connecting with her feelings at that first long-ago meeting. Tim had had an immediate, overwhelmingly male impact. Never in her entire life had anyone else made her so aware of her own femininity or his maleness. It had been like a sudden overload, with a door opening unexpectedly in her mind. Meeting Tim O'Shaughnessy for the first time, Liz Pennington had suddenly known that she was a sensuous woman. That she had the capacity to desire, to hunger, to want. To *need.*

How was she ever going to endure going back to business as usual?

Chapter 12

Pat played a mean game of poker. Liz hated any kind of card game and declined to join him and Tim at the kitchen table two nights later. Instead, she wandered into the living room and settled onto the sofa, with soft music on the stereo and Mephisto on her lap. The cat was getting to be a pain, probably because he was used to her undivided attention, and lately he hadn't gotten any at all. Now, he curled up and kneaded her with his paws. The prickle of his claws was not welcome.

"Down, cat," she ordered sternly, and urged him toward the floor. He decided to argue and, after a short tussle, Liz grabbed him by the scruff of his neck and marched him to the back door.

The honeymoon was over, she found herself thinking sourly as she put Mephisto out. Not only for the cat, but for her and Tim, as well. For a woman who was used to living alone, finding herself sharing her home with two men felt a little like trying to live in Grand Central Station. Everything felt so *public* now. Not that Tim was doing anything that couldn't be done in public. Not that Pat was making any kind of pest of himself. On the contrary, he was trying so hard to be inconspicuous that she was constantly on edge for fear of making him feel any more out of place.

It had been cute tonight, though, when Tim took his turn cooking dinner and Pat had attempted to help. Where Tim treated cooking as an advanced science requiring both skill and talent, Pat was clearly of the fast food and frozen dinner school. Before long, the two brothers had sounded like six-year-olds who couldn't agree on the rules of the game, let alone who was going to be the cowboy and who was going to be the Indian. When the volume had gotten too high, Liz had retreated to the basement and the computers they had installed in one brightly lit corner.

In the past few days, life had begun, finally, to resettle into a routine. Each morning, they went to the office and did whatever work they could manage on the outmoded equipment, trying to keep up an appearance of business as usual. At the end of each business day, they took copies of their work home and after dinner descended to Liz's basement, where the equipment was now updated enough to perform all but their classified work. For the moment, they were holding their ground, and the added hours seemed like a small sacrifice.

And that morning, accompanied by Tim, Liz had gone to the bank with all of the archived software disks she had been keeping in her basement. They were now locked in a safe-deposit box, where they probably should have been all along.

Sighing, Liz closed the door behind Mephisto and turned back to the kitchen. Pat was a lot better at poker than he was at cooking, and right now Tim was looking seriously disgruntled.

"I think I'll do a load of wash," Liz said into the charged atmosphere. "You guys got anything you want to toss in?"

Two male heads swiveled, and two pairs of gray eyes pinned her.

"You're kidding, right?" Tim said after a moment. "You don't really want to wash our dirty socks."

"Well, of course I don't *want* to," she answered tartly. "But since I'm going to do laundry anyway, it just seems civilized to offer to toss yours in with mine. Okay?" The *okay* was belligerent enough to pass for a challenge.

Pat, who had discarded his outrageous gear for surprisingly ordinary jeans and sweatshirts, suddenly looked like a male who was lying low. The playing cards held him in thrall. Tim, however, had never been able to pass up a challenge from Liz.

"I know you, Liz. Demons will be ice skating in hell before you offer to do a man's wash. What's eating you?"

"A better question is what's eating *you,* O'Shaughnessy. I made a perfectly courteous, civilized offer that has nothing to do with *men,* or demons skating in hell. My mother raised me to be *polite.*"

"Polite doesn't extend to doing the laundry of a pack of unwanted houseguests."

"Fine. Forget I asked!"

As she stomped out of the kitchen, she heard Pat say, "Damn it, Timmy, what the hell's got into you? That's no way to handle a woman."

Tim's response held a quiver that might have been suppressed laughter. "Don't let her hear you use the word *handle.* Nobody *handles* Liz."

Damn straight, Liz thought as she yanked her jacket out of the closet. And she knew what was eating both her and Tim: he had started sleeping in the guest room again. She knew why he was doing it. At least she thought she did. He had panicked. All his moral scruples and all his principles had reared their ugly heads, and Tim O'Shaughnessy had remembered that he wasn't a forever kind of guy. Men did this kind of thing, she knew. They tended to think with their hormones until their hormones settled, and then they remembered they weren't forever types. *No* man was a forever type.

The really lowering thing, though, was that she was prepared to accept that, and had spent the past couple of days trying to figure out how to let him know. It was humiliating to realize that she'd accept the crumbs eagerly because they were better than nothing. Lord! She squeezed her eyes shut against the ache of yearning and the pang of self-disgust.

"You're not going out by yourself, Liz."

Tim's flat declaration brought her spinning around to find that he had followed her into the hall.

"Out? No, of course not. Why?"

He glanced down at the jacket she held.

"Oh. No, I'm just going to wash this." She started searching the pockets for forgotten tissues and cash register receipts. "I always mean to wash this in the spring before I put it away for the summer, and I always wind up washing it in the fall after I've worn it an embarrassing time or two."

"Would you like to go for a walk?" He stepped closer, close

enough that she could just barely detect his faint, masculine smell, mixed with the scent of the soap they now shared. On him it smelled good. Her heart tripped and then accelerated.

"A walk?" she repeated on a suddenly splintered breath. Until that moment she hadn't realized just how badly she had needed to know that he still wanted to be alone with her. To be with her. The past couple of days had been a frightening slip into the past when they had been business partners only.

"Yeah." He stepped closer, a man edging tentatively toward his goal, braced for almost certain eruption. He knew perfectly well he had been keeping an exaggerated distance the past couple of days. It was becoming increasingly difficult to remember why he was doing that. He'd felt as if he had been crowding Liz, that he had rushed her into intimacy too rapidly, that they needed a little time and distance to be sure....

Of what? Sure of *what?* That he was nearly crazy from wanting her? That he didn't give a damn about tomorrow if only he could have her today? That it mattered whether she smiled or frowned and that he was sick of being lonely?

Damn it! Her skin looked like magnolia petals, a crazily romantic thought for a man who had never had such a thought in his life, and who hadn't seen magnolias since the days of his army training.

"You terrify me." The words escaped him as if propelled by force.

Liz's eyelids fluttered a little before she raised her gaze to his. His gray eyes smoldered, but there was a hint, just a hint, of vulnerability in the set of his mouth. She remembered what that mouth was capable of, and color stole slowly into her cheeks.

"You terrify me, too," she admitted on a mere breath.

He closed his eyes a moment, and then snapped them open, snagging hers with a heated gaze. Slowly, very slowly, he lifted a large hand and touched her cheek with a single fingertip. It was a tentative touch, a gentle touch, a touch that made her feel fragile and priceless.

"How about that walk?" His voice was a husky promise.

"Okay."

"I'll tell Pat."

As he turned away, her trembling hand closed on a scrap of paper in the jacket pocket, and she noticed that a couple of the stitches were pulled at one edge of the pocket. Dimly, she remembered snagging it at the SCUFO meeting. She would deal with it later, she thought as Tim reemerged from the kitchen. Slipping on the jacket, she forgot all about stitches.

Tim pulled his own jacket out of the closet, and with eyes that were hungry for him, she watched him tug it on. She wanted to fill herself with him, with his every movement, with the sheer size and maleness of him. With the way light played on his gingery hair and the planes of his cheeks. With the way his eyes darkened when they fell on her. With every blasted little thing.

He held out his hand and she slipped hers into it, watching the way his grip swallowed her smaller hand. So big, she thought, and was struck anew by how he dwarfed her.

"Liz?" There was a question in his voice, in the way he looked at her, and she blushed, realizing that she had been gawking like a star-struck kid. "Shall we go?" he asked.

"Yeah. Sure."

They strolled down the darkened street, Tim measuring his pace to hers, and for a while were silent. A gusting wind whipped leaves around their feet, and wisps of silvery cloud chased across the full moon.

"I love this time of year," Tim remarked. "There's always magic to autumn, to the shortening days and the cooling weather. And I always get so I think I can't wait for the first snowflake. Snow means Christmas, and I've always loved Christmas."

Liz hadn't looked forward to Christmas in years. Christmas meant all her friends were busy with family, and Tim always shut down the business for the week so that Donna could visit her sister in Syracuse and he could fly home to Dallas. Christmas, for her, meant a week of empty boredom. And every year she hoped that next year would be different, that she would somehow magically find the person with whom she would spend the rest of her Christmases.

It looked as if this year was going to be even worse than usual. This year she would probably spend the entire week missing Tim while he was in Dallas. So much for hopes of magic.

"What's wrong?" Tim asked. He had heard her sigh.

"Nothing." Not at the moment, anyway. He was with her, holding her hand, his entire attention focused on her. Funny how good that felt.

"Liz, I swear we'll get through this." It was a rash promise, but it was a promise he needed to make. Somehow, some way, he would make sure she was all right. Even if it meant giving her a job recommendation that would carry her away from him. He would do anything, regardless of what it cost him, simply because he couldn't stand the thought of her hurting.

She turned her face up and smiled at him, a sweet, warm smile that made his heart ache. "I know we'll be okay, Tim. Whatever happens. It's weird, but through all of this, I've just never doubted that somehow everything will come out all right in the end." She squeezed his hand. "I guess it's because we're facing this together. If I had only myself to depend on, I'd probably be a whole lot more scared."

Oh my God, he thought, as the gift of her trust resounded through him. Oh my God. He was stunned by her faith in him. He was humbled. And it made his heart swell. Turning, he gathered her to him and hugged her tight right there in the middle of the darkened sidewalk. A car passed behind him, and honked. Tim lifted his head to smile down at the pale blur of Liz's face.

"Some folks ain't got no couth," he said lightly.

She gave a small laugh. "Us? Or the guy in the car?"

"I vote for him." Slinging his arm around her shoulders, he started them walking again.

"Okay," he said a half a block later. "We'll stick it out. It might get kind of hairy, but the main thing I've been worried about is your safety, and I honestly think that, between us, Pat and I can protect you."

Liz rubbed her cheek against him. "You could protect me a whole lot better if you weren't sleeping on the far side of the house."

He missed a step and his arm tightened around her shoulders. Five or ten seconds passed before he could find his voice. "I'm not sure that would qualify as protection, darlin'."

"Whatever gave you that crazy idea?"

He drew a deep, not quite steady breath. "I don't know. I kind of had this feeling that I'd pushed you into this relationship. I seem to remember being pretty, uh, forceful about a few things."

She was suddenly, incredibly touched. Just a couple of days ago she had been thinking that Tim shared nothing of his vulnerabilities, that he kept himself hidden, yet here he was letting her know that he was indeed vulnerable. Maybe she was just in too much of a rush. Maybe she ought to let things move at their own pace. Maybe she ought to let *Tim* move at his own pace.

"You didn't rush me," she assured him quietly. Shyly, not really certain why she felt that way, she lifted her arm and snuggled it around his waist beneath his unzipped jacket.

He squeezed her shoulders. The wind gusted again, and a whirlwind of leaves danced across the sidewalk and into the street.

"I love this weather," Liz remarked. "The wind always makes me feel...free, I guess. Excited. It excites me somehow."

He liked the sound of that. Offhand, he could think of a dozen or so ways to add to her excitement, but not outdoors, even if it was dark. He sought safer avenues of conversation. "What do you think of Pat?"

"He's neat."

He chuckled. "That wasn't your first impression."

She smiled. "I wish I'd had a brother. That's something I'll always feel I missed."

The wistfulness of her tone prodded him to a realization. "You never talk about your family."

"I don't have much of one. My father left when I was quite young and my mother was an only child. She remarried when I was in college, but I don't have much in common with her husband's family. She comes to visit me for a few days every so often, but she's busy and..." Liz shrugged. She'd never had to try to explain before, and it made her uneasy.

"You mean she doesn't have time for you," Tim said flatly. He heard it all in the uncertainty of her tone.

"She's busy," Liz said defensively, and tried to shrug his arm away. She felt accused somehow, and she didn't like it. "She has three children now—"

"Yeah, and I'll bet the hubby doesn't like having you around because you're a reminder that he's not the first. I've known plenty of guys like that. Never understood them, though."

"Will you quit this cheap psychoanalyzing?"

"Why?" He stopped walking suddenly and took her by the shoulders, turning her to face him. "How old was your mom when she had you?"

Confused, her emotions in a miserable turmoil, she stared up at him. A nearby street lamp highlighted half his face, baring his strange intensity. "Fourteen," she said.

"Your mother was *fourteen?*" That was even worse than he had imagined. "You poor kid!"

Liz's chin thrust forward. "She was good to me. She worked hard, very hard, and she took care of me. I never went hungry or cold, Tim. So what's the point?"

"The point is, your father was a kid, too, wasn't he?"

"Well, yes, he was just a little older than she was.... Tim, what's going on? What difference does any of this make now?"

"It helps me understand you a little, that's all." Bending, he kissed her forehead, brushed a kiss on each cheek, and then gave her lips a gentle one.

They resumed walking, but questions swirled through Liz's brain, not the least of which was: exactly *what* did he understand? Finally, unable to stand wondering what he was thinking, she came flat out and asked.

He shrugged and tugged her closer to his side. His arm felt like a bulwark against the world. Its weight, its strength, made her feel sheltered. God, it was absolutely going to kill her when he decided to move on. Her throat tightened at the thought.

"I guess," he said after a moment, then hesitated anew. "Liz, swear you won't get mad, at least until you hear me out."

She leaned her head against him. "I promise." She was beginning to think there wasn't a thing she was capable of refusing this man.

"Well, I've been kind of confused. I mean, well, a man doesn't expect— Aw, hell, Liz, I can't talk about this. You'll never understand. You'll think I'm saying something I don't mean."

"Try me."

He remained silent, but she could feel the tension through his arm. She had a pretty good idea what he was driving at, and since he'd brought the subject up once before, when they were a heck of a lot less intimately acquainted, she was surprised that he was stalling now. "What's wrong, Tim?"

"Simple," he said on a short, mirthless laugh. "I suddenly realized I give a great big damn. I'm ashamed of myself."

"For what?" Darn it, the man was driving her to distraction with all these hints and evasions.

"For the way I've treated you. Hell, Liz, I've been treating

you like some kind of—'' he gritted his teeth and spit it out
''—like some kind of conquest.''

She tilted her head and looked up at his chin. The glow from
somebody's porch light illuminated the knotted muscle in his jaw.

''Is that how you've been seeing me?''

He sighed, and let go of the tension. ''No. Not since I first
asked you to go out with me. But I haven't been treating you
much better.''

''Oh, I don't know about that,'' she said. ''You haven't made
me feel that way. And you've always been a damn-the-torpedoes
kind of guy.''

''True.''

''And you've been wondering, but afraid to ask, what the devil
makes a woman hang on to her virginity until the age of thirty,
right?''

Uh-oh. ''Well—''

''And now you've come up with some bullheaded notion that
I was scared off of sex somehow in childhood, possibly because
my mother was so extremely young when she had me, or because
my father abandoned me, right?''

''Well, it had—''

She cut him off and yanked away from him, furious at his
simple analysis of reasons that were far more complex. Furious
because all of her reasons hadn't amounted to a hill of beans when
it came down to actually wanting a man. Wanting Tim. ''Let me
tell you something, O'Shaughnessy. I was a virgin because I
wanted to be. Because I never wanted any man but y—'' She
tried to bite off the word, but he heard it anyway. She saw it in
his eyes, in the sudden parting of his lips. Horrified, she turned
and started to run. She didn't care where she was going, only that
she not have to face his reaction to what was surely the most
humiliating, embarrassing admission of her entire thirty years. If
he wanted to gloat, he was going to have to do it without her for
an audience.

His legs were a lot longer. He could have caught her in just a
few strides, but instinct told him she would be a lot easier to
manage once she had run off her emotions. Instead, he followed
her a half-dozen paces behind, keeping watch over her all the
while.

"I'm going to get you eventually," he said, puffing, a block later. "You're going to pay for that."

"Get lost, O'Shaughnessy."

"Like hell. What in the hell kind of thing is that to tell a man, anyway?"

"Shut up!"

"No way, darlin'. You asked for this."

"I didn't ask for anything!" A stitch grabbed her side and she nearly groaned.

"Are you tiring yet, sweetheart? Do you have any idea what it does to a man to hear something like that? How long, Liz? Since we met at the trade show? I thought you'd kill me if I made a pass at you. Why do you think I behaved all these years? Honey, I ain't no saint!"

"I don't believe you." The words escaped her on a dying gasp. Her legs and her lungs burned fiercely, but she didn't want to give up. Not yet.

"No reason you should," he admitted. Damn, he hadn't realized she was in such great shape. She must spend as much time jogging as he spent lifting weights. "Liz, I swear, I buried those, uh, feelings because you were so obviously uninterested. It seemed stupid, anyway, to risk the business partnership over something like that."

"So what happened, O'Shaughnessy?" she demanded breathlessly. Pooped, her legs turning to lead, she halted and bent over, drawing in huge lungfuls of air while resting her hands on her spread knees.

"I don't know," he admitted. Standing beside her, he threw back his head and let the night cool him down. "It felt like a dam suddenly broke, like all of it just came to a head. Call me crazy."

"You *are* crazy," she gasped. "Insane. You can't possibly expect me to believe you."

"Why not?" He glared at her. "Damn it, Liz, you don't really think I followed you all over that convention center for hours simply because I recognized a fellow hacker."

"Why not? That's what you've been telling me for years."

"I lied. Hell, you had so many No Trespassing signs all over you that only a moron would have missed them. What made you put up all those signs? Because, believe me, if they hadn't been there I'd have made a pass at you *years* ago."

She straightened and returned his glare. "I never wanted to be wanted only for my body. That's easy. That's common. I was sick of that before I was sixteen!"

"I guess I can see why," he admitted.

The door of the house behind them suddenly opened, and yellow light poured out onto them.

"Everything okay out here?" asked a man in suspenders.

"Yeah," Tim answered. "Sorry we bothered you."

The man ignored him and looked pointedly at Liz. "Are you okay?"

"Yes, everything's fine," Liz said, mortification heating her cheeks as she recognized Don Flint. "Sorry. We argue all the time. It doesn't mean anything."

After a moment, Flint nodded and went back into his house.

"Liz—" Tim wanted to apologize, but she cut him off.

"Just shut up," she hissed. "That was Don Flint."

"So?"

"He's a cop. Darn it, Tim, this is humiliating."

"That's why I was going to apologize."

She swiveled her head and peered up at him. "You were?"

"I was. I'm sorry. I'm never going to be a silk purse, Liz. I'm just going to be me, come hell or high water. I'm not tactful, and I'll probably make you mad in public again, but I'm sorry for it. I realize I don't have the kind of polish you—"

"Wait a minute." Remembering herself, she grabbed his hand and started dragging him back down the street toward her house. "Not here, Tim. I'll get mad again. And you leave me out of this. I've never told you what I want, and you've never asked, so don't you go making any assumptions."

"You sound just like my mother," he grumbled, but beneath the grumble there was a definite hint of amusement. She hadn't given up on him yet. Now he just had to convince her that he was good for something besides embarrassing her, yelling at her and making love to her. He couldn't imagine what those other things might be, but he'd work on it. Just because he wasn't a forever kind of guy didn't mean he wanted this relationship to be a short one. No, he kind of liked the way things were right now, so he'd better think of some reasons for Liz to want to keep them this way. In the meantime, making love to her was *all* he wanted to do. World War III could start right now and he wouldn't be deterred. He was going to love this lady until she begged for mercy. Oh, yeah!

That intention survived all of thirty seconds after they stepped into the house. As she pulled off her jacket, Liz remembered that she wanted to wash it, and needed to mend those torn stitches. Automatically she shoved her hand into the pocket to empty it, and came up with the scrap of paper. It was not, however, a forgotten receipt.

As she smoothed it out, she croaked Tim's name. He turned at once from the closet where he was hanging up his jacket, and became immediately concerned. Not once in all the years that he'd known her had he ever seen Liz turn as white as chalk.

"What is it?" In a single long step he was beside her. "Lizzie, what is it?"

Mutely, with a badly trembling hand, she held the scrap out to him.

He scanned it quickly and swore. "Where'd you find this?"

"In my jacket pocket."

He heard the fright in her voice, saw it when he lifted his eyes from the paper to her face. "In your pocket?" It hit him like a hammer blow. The creep had been close enough to put something in her pocket. That close. My God.

If you don't stop disturbing the gravity, I will have to kill you. Please don't make me kill you.

She was sure she would never feel warm again. Sitting in the familiar brightness of her kitchen, she wondered why everything looked so normal when nothing would ever again be the same. And the chill, the chill she felt went bone deep, yet it had nothing to do with the room's temperature. Tim stood at the stove, stirring hot chocolate according to her directions, while Pat tipped back in a chair and talked in jargon on the phone to Special Agent Woodrow. Pat was suddenly all cop. Tim was suddenly all angry, protective male.

"Here, darlin'." Tim set a steaming mug of thick hot chocolate before her on the table, and she wrapped her hands around it, seeking warmth.

Pat hung up the phone and muttered an obscenity. "I don't think either of those guys is playing with a full deck," he told them. "Woodrow says their psychiatric expert still feels the guy is harmless. The theory is that if he were likely to harm either one of you, he would have started with that, not with smashing the equipment."

Tim shook his head. "That note sounds like the gravity man is being pushed by something or someone. Like someone is forcing him to do this."

"Exactly. That worries me. Thanks." Straddling a chair, Pat took a mug of cocoa from Tim. "Liz, you studied abnormal psych, right?"

Liz managed a nod.

"If I remember correctly, a schizophrenic's voices can actually make him do things. Or make him feel as if he's being forced."

She nodded. "I read about one case where the woman burned herself all over with cigarettes because her voices said she needed to be punished."

Tim swore. "Great. Wonderful. So maybe the gravity man is being told he has to kill us. Will he do it?"

"He might," Pat said, and glanced at Liz for confirmation. "It doesn't mean he'll get away with it, or that he'll even make an effective attempt. I mean, this guy's unhinged enough that he might try to kill you with a ray gun. Who knows?"

Hours later—at least it seemed to be hours later—Liz stood at the window in her bedroom and stared down at the darkened street. Never had the threat loomed as large and as real as it did tonight.

Tim had kept her pretty well distracted through most of this, she thought. He'd kept her fighting mad or weak with desire nearly every blasted minute. Nothing was distracting her right now, though. Right now she was cold and scared and feeling very much alone.

She felt as if she were being *stalked*. That note had been typed before the SCUFO meeting. That meant the gravity man had intended to give it to her. Had come expecting to find her there. Had come hunting her for the purpose of giving her a chilling warning. He had found her that easily, and had gotten close to her that easily. Which meant that he could kill her or Tim that easily.

The bedroom door behind her opened with a click and she

whirled around in time to see Tim briefly silhouetted against the hall light. Then the door closed again and he became only a dim blur in the weak blue light of the moon. He halted a few inches in front of her and cupped her face gently between his two large hands. Just as gently, he turned her head up to him.

"Are you okay?" he asked softly.

"Yes."

The word emerged on a mere breath, a breath so tightly held that he knew she was lying. With a heavy sigh, he released her face and wrapped his arms snugly around her. He needed to hold her like this, he realized. Feeling her pressed to him this way, feeling her filling his arms, feeling the warm whisper of her breath on his chest, feeling what made her a reality—these things satisfied an almost physical hunger in him, and the satisfaction spread through him in warm, gently lapping waves of contentment.

Only this was no time to be feeling content. Aching for her, he rocked her gently back and forth. A long time ago, he had learned that the very things you most wanted to spare your loved ones were the very things you couldn't protect them against. Tranh, for example. He had managed to snatch his wife from the jaws of a deadly war, from all the horrors and deprivations that made up her daily life, but what had she gotten? Death, alone in the silence of a strange country where she couldn't even call for help.

Well, that was in the past, and he'd finally forgiven himself for it. Liz was in the here and now, and there didn't seem to be a thing he could do for her. In her terse insistence that she had never gone cold or hungry, Tim had heard what she hadn't said. It wasn't enough for a child to be fed and kept warm. A child needed to feel safe and protected, to feel secure. He would have bet his last dime that Liz had never felt that way. It made it all the more remarkable that she had taken the risks of going into business with him. She was one gutsy lady.

And he would have given his right arm and both legs if only he could make her feel safe now. Damn it, hadn't he sworn he would never get himself into a situation like this again? Hell, he hadn't let a woman get any closer than arm's length in all these years, yet here was Liz, already curled right up in a certain warm and tender spot inside his chest. What if she didn't want to be there?

He felt her arms close around his waist, and felt her hug him just as snugly as he hugged her. Damn, but that felt good!

Well, he thought, standing here and worrying about things sure wasn't going to fix anything. Bending, he startled a laugh out of her by sweeping her up into his arms and carrying her toward the bed.

"Bet you didn't guess I had it in me," he said gruffly.

"Actually," she replied as he let her feet slide to the floor beside the bed, "I've watched you pump enough iron to know you had it in you." She caught her breath as his hands found the hem of her sweater and started lifting it.

"Tomorrow's Halloween," he said as his fingers trailed upward against the satiny skin of her back. His hands performed double duty, lifting her sweater and exciting them both. "Maybe we'll get all this settled tomorrow."

"And horses will fly." She tried to sound dry, but her sweater vanished over her head at that moment, and her voice quivered. "Tim...Tim, let's not talk about that...."

"Okay." His lips were suddenly busy anyway, trailing along the soft curve of her shoulder toward forbidden places. She smelled so sweet, so fresh. And that hair, that glorious fall of hair. He tunneled his fingers into it, combed through it and draped it around her like a veil before he reached for the hooks of her bra.

"You have the most beautiful, wonderful hair," he breathed huskily in her ear as his hands cupped the delicious fullness of her breasts. Against his palms he felt her nipples harden swiftly. He was hardening, too, and just as swiftly. Who would have thought a couple of days without her touch would feel like a hundred?

Peeling her jeans down her soft, smooth legs was another delight, and one he wanted to savor fully. He wanted to go slowly, to draw out each and every precious moment, because he had the oddest feeling that no matter how long, how well, how carefully he loved this woman, he would always want more.

Liz was impatient, however, flaming beneath his caresses, twisting and turning and tugging until she succeeded in tumbling them both onto the bed. The laugh that escaped her held a definitely triumphant sound, and made him laugh, as well. Finesse was lost as they tore at one another's clothes, and Liz yielded a huge, deep, satisfied sigh when, at long last, she was pressed full length to Tim's nakedness.

He felt so good everywhere, and her hands roamed restlessly, soaking up every nuance of smooth, warm flesh, of varying textures of hair and skin. There was nothing soft about him, not anywhere, and she reveled in the hard strength of his body, just as he reveled in her satin softness. It was their differences that made being together so good, she thought in hazy pleasure, just as their differences of opinion made their relationship so stimulating.

He had brought her far in a very short space of time, but now she blazed her own trails, seeking every possible way to bring him gratification. She explored him from head to toe, mapping him in her memory, noting every catch of his breath or flinch of muscle.

And finally, when he could endure no more, he lifted her over him as effortlessly as if she were a breath of warm air.

"Take me," he said in a voice so hoarse, so gritty that the mere sound of it sent fresh rivers of need pouring through her. "Now."

Much later, lying curled against the warmth of his side as he slept, she remembered the sound of that hoarse command and knew that as long as she lived she would cherish the memory of it. It made her feel warm and needed in ways she had never dreamed were possible, and she stored it up against the empty days that were bound to come. She knew better than to hope that Tim wouldn't tire of her. He had tired of every other woman he had dated during the years she had known him. Yes, he would tire of her and she had better be prepared to handle it in an adult manner.

But in the meantime, she would store up all these precious memories. And she would never forget that, once, Tim O'Shaughnessy had wanted her so much that his voice had become gravel and his hands had trembled. To be wanted like that, just once in a lifetime, was more than anyone had a right to expect.

Chapter 13

Tim's muttering and mumbling woke Liz in the early hours of the morning. Her first instinct was to shake him gently and wake him, but even through the foggy wisps of her own sleep she quickly realized that he was having no ordinary dream. Concerned, she sat up and switched on the bedside lamp. The instant the light cascaded over him, Tim sat bolt upright and roared a string of enraged curses.

And just as suddenly, he woke up. A huge shudder passed through him, and then all the tension seeped from his back and shoulders. He swore softly.

"Are you all right?" Liz dared to ask.

A long moment passed before he answered. "Yeah," he said roughly. "I'm fine. Sorry I woke you."

"It must have been some nightmare," she offered tentatively, and reached out to touch his shoulder.

He flinched at her touch, revealing his state of tension as no words could have. Liz quickly withdrew her hand and lay back on the bed. "Do you want me to leave the light on?"

Again there was a perceptible pause before he answered. "No. Go ahead and turn it off."

After the room was again plunged into darkness, several

minutes passed before he sighed and lay back beside her. Another few minutes crept by; then he turned over to cuddle her against him.

"Sorry I woke you," he said again.

"It's okay." Gently she cupped his cheek with her hand.

He turned his head a little so he could kiss her palm. So soft. So smooth. He could smell himself on her skin, mingled with her own delicate fragrance, and it brought him fully into the present moment as nothing else could have.

He spoke, his voice little more than a murmur. "I haven't had one of those in a long time."

"Nightmare?"

"Sort of." He slipped his fingers into the silky strands of her hair and cradled the back of her head, bringing her face closer to his shoulder, making it possible to feel the warmth of her breath.

"What was it about?"

He shook his head; she could feel the movement against her cheek. "You don't want to know. And I really don't like to talk about it." He gave her a quick squeeze. "Did I frighten you?"

"I didn't have time to be scared. You were sure swearing a blue streak, though."

Ordinarily when he had these nightmares, he found it necessary to get out of bed, to pace around, turn on the lights, do any number of things to remind himself of his present place in space and time. Over the years the dreams had become fewer, but scarcity didn't make then any easier to shake. They were so vivid, so real, that when he blinked awake he could still smell the acrid odor of gunpowder and the musty scent of heavy vegetation, could still smell the fear, the blood and the burning flesh. It took a while to shake out of that.

But Liz's presence had brought him out of it more quickly, more easily. Her voice had been like an anchor in the dark. He guessed he owed her something for that. An explanation of some kind.

"I get these nightmares sometimes," he said into the dark over her head. He could feel her attention, an almost tangible thing in the air. She wiggled just a little closer, letting him know with her body that she was there for him. He stroked her hair, her shoulder, the graceful line of her back, and thought about how nice, how infinitely precious, it was to be close like this with another human being.

"Do you get them often?" she asked.

"Once, maybe twice, a year. I used to get them a lot. Some shrink at the VA hospital said it was a normal reaction to the war, and that it'd quit eventually. Eventually has been a lot longer coming than I thought it would be."

Her hand stroked the line of his jaw, his neck, his shoulder. It was a soothing, comforting touch, the kind of touch he hadn't received from anyone in a very long time. The kind of touch he had refused to accept from anyone, he admitted suddenly. He recalled the occasions he had turned away from even his mother's concern and desire to comfort him. Sort of like a wounded animal, he thought, trying to hide away in its den.

He didn't want her to say anything. To this day, defensive and bitter though it might be, he felt only another vet had the right to say anything about what had happened, about what was still happening. Only another vet had the understanding to commiserate or sympathize.

What he needed—what he suddenly, astonishingly realized that he had needed all along—was simple, unquestioning, uncritical acceptance of where he had been, of what he had done, of the man he had become.

And that was what Liz was giving him right now. She touched him with hands that said she cared and held him close in a way that would have been impossible if she didn't accept him just as he was. She scattered soft, tender kisses along his jaw and across his chest, kisses no one could possibly bestow without caring. They were kisses that said she ached for him even if she couldn't understand, kisses that said she would take away all his pain if only she could.

The recognition was like a thunderbolt in his brain, waking him from a sleep he hadn't known was muffling his emotions. It was an acutely discomfiting experience.

Liz felt him stiffen and she guessed that his dream was still troubling him. She waited, hoping he would talk about it, but he remained silent. He continued to hold her, as if her presence comforted him, but she nonetheless felt the distance he set between them like a wall. In some subtle way, he had withdrawn from her, and even in the intimacy of her bed, it seemed he had never been further away.

Morning seeped into the bedroom through the cracks around the edges of the curtains. With wide-open eyes, Liz watched fingers of light slip around corners, beckoning the world to wake to the new day. It was the last day of October. Halloween. Tonight Tim wanted to go stand in the cold atop David Hill and wait for aliens in the hope that the gravity man would show up and tip his hand. Unreal. This whole damn mess was unreal.

Unreal included the man lying behind her in her bed. In the silent room, she could hear the faint whisper of his deep, steady breathing, and in the small gap between their bodies she could feel his heat. *Unreal.* Too bad the pain wouldn't be just as unreal, just as difficult to believe, when he decided enough was enough.

Because, fool that she was, she wasn't going to be the one to call a halt to this relationship. So far she had managed to avoid letting him know the depth of her emotional involvement with him; this way, at the very least, she would still have her pride, but Lord, Lord, the pain was going to be *real.* She'd had a taste of it last night in his arms, in those terrible, stark moments of his emotional withdrawl from her.

She'd wanted him for so very long, had buried her feelings for him for so very long, and yet now here they were, all on the surface like exposed nerve endings. Delicate, sensitive, easily wounded.

It was easy, too easy, to recall the exact moment she'd fallen in love with him. Five years ago, sitting on a cracked vinyl bench in a sleazy all-night diner in Denver. Listening, looking into his intense, bright gray eyes as he painted his vision of the future with enthusiasm. Watching as his hands described wide arcs of excitement, nodding as he scribbled on paper napkins, smiling as he invented Millennium Software right before her eyes. Loving the way he drew her into his future as if she were already a part of it. Loving the way they were never, not for so much as a minute, strangers to one another.

Loving the way they had stepped from the diner at dawn into a pearly mist that reflected the neon glow of its sign, the way Tim had looked down at her, a smile crinkling the corners of his eyes and said, "Well, Pennington, do you think we should do it?"

We. What an infinitely precious word. Tim had made them one as easily as that, snatching Liz Pennington's heart right along with her mind, her future, her dreams, her hopes and her goals.

And for the past five years she had squabbled and fought with him simply because it was the only available outlet for her intense, tangled feelings. It was a diffuser, a *de*fuser. As long as she was quarreling with O'Shaughnessy, she could ignore all the warm, melting feelings she felt for Tim. But quarreling didn't work anymore. Quarreling had suddenly become a prelude to other things, hotter things, more dangerous things. How was she ever going to handle it when they were just partners again? How could they ever recover that easiness, that trust, that blessed lack of awareness?

"Mmm...you're all tensed up."

That husky whisper in her ear tensed her even more as Tim closed in on her, pressing himself to her back, slipping one arm beneath her and one over her. She was suddenly wrapped in him, surrounded by him. Sheltered by him. He was so big, so warm, so hard, so smooth, so...sexy.

"Are you worrying, Lizzie?"

"A little," she admitted. Her voice was still husky from sleep. When his huge hand swallowed her breast and his fingers began toying with a susceptible nipple, speech became nearly impossible.

"Damn it, Lizzie," he growled. "You feel so out-of-sight good to me. All soft and warm and silky. I won't let anything happen to you, you know. You don't need to be afraid, darlin'. I swear I'll take care of you."

That was too much to bear. She wrenched out of his arms and sat up, glaring down at him. The sheet fell to her waist, but she ignored it.

"Darn it, O'Shaughnessy, I swear you make me madder than anybody I've ever known!"

"What the hell did I do?" He lay on his back and looked up at her, his expression somewhere between exasperation and frustration.

"I don't want anybody to take care of me! That's for babies! I don't need anyone to 'take care of' me!"

He was frowning at her, but he was also thinking as fast as he ever had. He wasn't sure how he had managed to light her fuse, but he had the feeling it had more to do with what she had been thinking about before he woke than anything he had said since. All right, so his choice of words had been unfortunate, but they didn't justify this kind of response.

Lifting a hand, she shoved a handful of hair back from her face and continued to glare down at him. He scowled back, but he sure didn't look intimidated, she thought. But then, she wondered with a sudden sense of her own absurdity, how could she possibly intimidate anyone while she was practically shoving the large globes of her naked breasts into his face? She'd never intimidated Tim O'Shaughnessy anyway. It was one of the many rare qualities about him that attracted her.

"Sorry," she said.

Sorry? Liz was apologizing? On her own? Without prompting? That was when he saw the twitch at one corner of her mouth, and from there he looked into her hazel eyes to find a misty spark of dawning humor. Well, her rage wasn't quite believable when she was sitting there looking like centerfold of the month. But still, they had to get something straight.

"I didn't mean what I said the way you evidently took it, Liz."

She nodded slowly. "I'm just as capable of looking after myself as the next person, male or female."

"I know that. It's just that you bring out all my protective instincts." He hesitated and then confessed. "Not to be taken wrong, or anything, but I don't ordinarily feel protective. I guess I don't know how to handle the feeling."

"Try burying it." It was a stupid, useless thing to say, but it was the only thing she *could* say. Not to be taken wrong? What did that mean? And what did it matter? The only thing left was to carry this off without sacrificing her pride along the way. So that when the day came, as it inevitably would, she'd be able to walk into her office and say good morning to Tim O'Shaughnessy without wanting to flee in embarrassment.

He watched the play of emotions over her face, a flitting, swiftly changing landscape, and wished he could read her mind. Something was tearing at her. Something was causing her dread and fear and the foretaste of pain. He could think of only one possible cause: the gravity man.

Reaching out, he drew her down to him, pressing her close to his chest. "They'll get him, Liz. Sooner or later, he'll make a mistake and they'll get him. Things'll get back to normal. Really."

But she didn't want things to get back to normal. Not anymore. The pain would kill her.

Nothing ever went according to plan, Tim thought sourly, and certainly not whenever Uncle Sam was involved. By dinnertime that evening, Tim was wishing some Russian spy would blow Laurel and Hardy off the face of the earth.

The FBI planned to be present on Davis Hill at midnight. That was bad enough. But the sheriff also wanted to be there, because it was within his jurisdiction. If some crowd was gathering on private property, then he and six or seven of his deputies were going to be there to protect that property, especially when its owner was an influential man in the county. For some reason, it never occurred to anyone that the deputies could just as well entirely prevent the trespassing, rather than simply acting as crowd control.

"The truth is," Woodrow explained to Tim over a cup of coffee, "I suspect the property owner believes in UFOs. He'd rather have a crowd to witness events than be left without any witnesses at all."

"Great. So the place is going to be crawling with lawmen, probably tripping over each other. If that doesn't scare the gravity man away, then he's definitely scareproof."

"You're forgetting something, Timmy," Pat added. "This gravity guy is crazy. His voices are making him do something he clearly doesn't want to do, judging by his note at any rate. He's apparently a lot more frightened of his voices, of having his gravity disturbed, than he is of the cops. If he were worried about being caught by the police, he wouldn't be doing this."

"You could say that about most criminals," Tim said drily. "Allow me to remind you that if this guy weren't scared of being caught, he wouldn't be hiding behind anonymous notes."

"Good point," Liz said.

"Look," said Woodrow. "We're hoping he'll turn up tonight because he's obviously into this UFO thing or he wouldn't have been at the SCUFO meeting Monday night, right?"

"Right." Tim spoke with exaggerated patience. He knew all this already. It was the whole damn reason he was going to this crazy thing tonight. Couldn't they understand that he was worried they would scare the guy off?

"So we figure he'll show up looking for aliens. And we hope that he'll see you and Ms. Pennington and get upset enough about his gravity to give himself away. Obviously we're not going to be out there acting like heavies. None of us are. And a couple of deputies who are there to perform crowd control duties aren't going to worry him because their presence is expected. He won't know they've also been advised to keep a lookout for him."

Tim lifted a shaggy eyebrow. "So you and Carter are going to put on jeans and jackets and go out there looking like ordinary slobs, huh?"

"You got it."

"This I have to see." He couldn't imagine either Woodrow or Carter passing for anything approaching ordinary slobs.

Liz sent Tim a warning look and wished he wouldn't insist on irritating the agents.

"So," Tim asked sarcastically, "what are the city police doing about this?" It was out of the city's jurisdiction, so he certainly didn't expect the answer he got.

"Oh, they're sending a couple of officers to participate," Woodrow answered easily. "The case started in their jurisdiction, after all."

"Cripes," Tim said later to Liz. "Do you believe this? The only thing we'll lack is the National Guard. Or how about an IRS agent or two? Maybe they could get the gravity man for income-tax evasion."

"Don't be ridiculous, Tim."

"Why not? That's what got Al Capone."

Liz sent him a sidelong look. "Right. But in order to find out if he's guilty of tax evasion, they have to know who he is."

"I know that." He caught the tremor at the corner of her mouth and suddenly grinned. "I'm grousing too much, huh?"

"Yup."

"Well, I can't help thinking that this is going to turn into a Keystone Kops adventure."

Liz's tone was dry. "That was to be expected."

"Why?"

"Have you forgotten what we're doing? We're going out to Davis Hill in the middle of the night on a cold Halloween to wait for the arrival of an alien spacecraft in the hopes that we'll find a man who believes he needs to smash our computers and maybe kill us because we're disturbing his gravity. Does that sound *normal* to you? Surely you aren't trying to pretend that anything about tonight isn't preposterous?"

His expression grew grave. "Lizzie darlin', the danger isn't preposterous, whatever the circumstances."

"I know." Closing her eyes briefly, she envisioned the destruction of their office, the sheer, terrifying viciousness of it. "I'm glad the place will be crawling with cops, Tim. We'd be foolish to try to handle this alone."

"I wish I could keep you out of it entirely." But he frankly didn't know how. He couldn't leave her alone, wouldn't let her out of his sight, and the cops would only insist she come along anyway to act as bait. When all was said and done, with all the cops who were going to be on Davis Hill tonight, it would probably be the safest place in the entire county—unless, of course, somebody fired a gun. He swore under his breath.

"Relax, Tim," Pat drawled from the other side of the room. "Save up your energy for later tonight when it'll be useful."

"Easy for you to say," Tim shot back. "For you this is just another job. It's a little more than that for me."

"Well, if you won't get your mind off this," Pat said threateningly, "I'll get it off for you. Maybe I'll tell your lady what we used to call you in the neighborhood."

Liz's ears pricked up. "Was it that bad?"

Tim felt his earlobes heat. "Watch your step, Paddy. I outweigh you by thirty pounds and my arm isn't in a sling." Weird, he thought. He was barely forty years old, and he could still feel annoyed—naw, embarrassed was a better description—well, actually *hurt* probably came closer to the truth. Okay, he could still feel hurt and embarrassed and annoyed that he had been picked on for being such a gangly, uncoordinated toothpick. It was as absurd as hell that the petty cruelties of childhood could still evoke a reaction. It was so absurd, in fact, that he took the bull by the horns and told Liz himself. "They used to call me Tiny Tim," he said shortly.

That was when an incredible thing happened. He expected Liz to give one of those small laughs people give when they think they're supposed to be amused, but really don't see what the joke is. He expected her not to understand why it mattered at all, or maybe, at best, to dismiss the nickname as a ridiculous cliché.

Instead, something in her face grew breathtakingly soft, softer than he'd ever seen his hot-tempered partner look, and that included during lovemaking. Her green eyes turned almost luminous, a description he'd often read and thought to be unpardonably romantic, and all she said, in a voice as soft as sunlight was, "Oh, Tim."

That was the truly incredible thing. Liz understood. More than that, she cared. It was such a stupid little thing that it shamed him to admit it had ever bothered him to begin with, yet her understanding of it was as important as anything that had ever happened in his life. From his own mother the best he'd ever gotten on this one was, "Ignore it and they'll get bored and stop it, Timmy." Somehow, "Oh, Tim" did what no advice had managed to do.

Unnerved by the force of his emotional reaction to her response, he turned gruff. "No big deal," he said.

"Right," drawled Pat with brotherly disregard for his sibling's feelings. "That's why you had to remind me that you have thirty pounds and an arm on me."

Tim glared at him. "I *still* have thirty pounds and an arm on you, Paddy."

"Okay, okay." His gray eyes, so like Tim's, twinkled with unholy pleasure, but he held his peace.

At eleven, just as Tim and Liz were getting ready to leave, Woodrow called.

"The crowd is already gathering," he told Tim. "When are you guys leaving?"

"Right now. Pat went on ahead. He may already be up there."

"He is. One of the sheriff's deputies called in his description. Why couldn't he just wear jeans like everyone else?"

"My brother, Woodrow, has *never* been like everyone else. And I wouldn't knock him, if I were you. He's been a great help to the bureau in a couple of cases."

"I know," Woodrow said. "Believe me, I did a background

on him. It's the only reason I'm letting him get involved like this."

"Right," Tim growled as he hung up the phone. "As if you could stop him, you jerk."

"Tim?" Liz was waiting patiently by the door. "What's wrong?"

"Nothing the complete and total disappearance of agents Woodrow and Carter from my life won't cure."

"This sounds like more than a little leftover hostility toward Hoover." She locked the door behind them, and then let him help her into the cab of his truck. He'd fallen into the habit of doing that, and somehow she had come to like it. She knew for a fact that it wasn't something he did automatically, so it made her feel special and cherished.

"I guess it is," he admitted as he swung up into the cab beside her. "My dad was an ordinary cop, you know. The kind who walked the beat back when cops actually walked a beat, and the kind who rode around in a patrol car when that got to be the thing. Anyway, like most cops, he wasn't too fond of the FBI. I guess I soaked it up with my Pablum. But I can see it with Woodrow and Carter, the attitude these Feds have. They think they're better than the rest of us."

"Well, I guess I can see why they might feel that way. A sense of elitism is often used to mold men into a cohesive group, and to motivate them to greater efforts."

Tim finished backing the truck out of the driveway, but before he started them down the street, he flashed her a smile. "You're really something, Pennington."

Pennington. Ridiculously, her stomach sank. He was already placing a distance between them, she thought. This was it. After tonight, if they caught the gravity man, things really would go back to normal. Completely normal. He in his apartment, she in her house, and only the business between them.

Last night, and then again earlier this evening, she'd felt as if she had somehow made him uneasy, as if she'd somehow gotten too close. That had to be the reason why he was distancing himself now. Things had gotten too intense. While Tim O'Shaughnessy would never be a silk purse, he had the innate instincts of an honorable man. Before they'd even become involved he had warned her that he was not a forever kind of guy.

And he had told her that he would never love again. Not in so many words, of course, but the message had been as clear as crystal when he'd spoken of loving Tranh with wholehearted devotion as being something only a young man could do.

An affair, a brief and fleeting thing, a treasure trove of memories to take out and dust off on some future lonely evening. A wondrous, warm span of time to twinkle brightly in her past like a Christmas ornament. That's what this had been and would be. All that mattered now was easing through the next weeks with her pride intact and in a way that wouldn't damage their business partnership.

Because, she admitted with bitter honesty, she would die if Tim left her life completely. Even if they were never again to be lovers, she would need his friendship. He was so much a part of her after five years, that the gulf his absence would create would tear her apart. So there it was. Love of the worst kind. The kind of love that deprived you of even the strength to walk away. Good going, Liz.

Davis Hill rose sharply upward at the edge of a cornfield that had been planted on the very edge of a river. Tilled fields in this rocky countryside were flat patches scattered among the hills and mountains. The county road passed right by the edge of the mowed field, and cars had already commandeered both shoulders for quite a distance. Tim managed to squeeze the truck in between a Toyota and a Suburban at an angle that put one front wheel in the ditch and left his tailgate perilously near the edge of the road.

Frozen ground crackled and popped beneath their feet as they crossed the cornrows toward the hill. Liz nearly tripped over the upthrusting stump of a cornstalk, but Tim caught her elbow and steadied her.

"How many people do you suppose are here?" she wondered aloud, catching sight of other shadowy figures moving through the night toward the hill.

"From the number of cars I'd guess a hundred, maybe a few more."

"I'm surprised," she said quietly. "I honestly didn't think so many people believed in this kind of thing."

"I read somewhere once that a majority of Americans think UFOs are a phenomenon that deserves serious study." He glanced around, taking in the shadows of people all heading the same way.

"It looks like some kind of horror movie, doesn't it, Pennington? *Night of the Living Dead* or something like that. All the zombies heading toward some central location where a human sacrifice—"

"Cut it out, Tim! This is bad enough without making it even creepier."

He broke stride and peered down at her. The moon was in its last quarter and rapidly moving clouds kept darkening the night even further, but Tim managed to read her expression. "You're really nervous about this, aren't you?"

"Yes!" She jutted out her chin and stared up at him. "Sometimes I think I'm the only person on the face of the earth who understands the seriousness of what's been going on around here! Darn it, Tim, doesn't it make you feel just a little bit uneasy, knowing that somebody is thinking about killing you?"

"Well, of course." He averted his face a moment, and then looked down at her. "I guess I'm just more used to it than you are, Lizzie. I learned a long time ago not to think about someone trying to kill me, because there isn't a damn thing you can do until somebody actually tries it."

Vietnam. Suddenly it was very much there, and very much a real, living, breathing part of this man that she loved. He had been places and seen things and done things she couldn't begin to imagine. Didn't want to imagine. Things that had scarred him and hurt him and yet had given him a special kind of gentleness and compassion.

"I'll take care of you, Liz," he said for the second time in twenty-four hours, but this time she didn't object. This time the words wrapped her in warmth. Wherever this man had been, whatever he was capable of doing, he would do it only to protect and defend. She ached for him. Oh God, how she ached for him! If she had a million years and all the words in the dictionary at her command, she would never, ever, be able to fully express just how much he meant to her. Just how much she admired him and loved him. Just how wonderful he was.

Reaching out, she touched her palm to his cheek. "I know you will," she said. Rising on tiptoe, she pulled his head down and brushed her lips against his. Then, squaring her shoulders, she resumed her march toward Davis Hill.

The climb was steep, though not too rough, and they were both breathing pretty heavily by the time they reached the top of the hill. A large crowd had gathered, some carrying lanterns, others flashlights, and from every direction they caught snatches of excited conversation. The main subject seemed to be what kind of alien display would occur this evening, not whether there would even be one. A gathering of true believers, Liz thought as she and Tim halted on a slightly elevated part of the hill. That, and the combined effect of the thrill seekers' portable lights, allowed them to see nearly the entire crowd. The sheriff's deputies made a highly visible, reassuring presence. Woodrow and Carter were nowhere to be seen, a circumstance Tim remarked on with pleasure.

"Oh, I'm sure they're here somewhere," Liz replied as she continued to scan the crowd for familiar faces. "Look. Is that *Donna?*" She couldn't imagine what their secretary would be doing at a gathering like this.

Tim squinted in the direction Liz pointed, and shook his head. "I don't see her."

"Must've been someone else."

"Probably." He turned to her suddenly and took her by the shoulders, giving her a little, emphatic shake. "Listen to me, Liz. No, don't you get on your high horse. Just listen. This is important."

Her instinctive flare of anger at being manhandled and ordered to listen to him died. In his face she saw a concern that made a mockery of the rules of etiquette. "I'm listening."

His eyes bored into hers. "Okay. There's no time to go into all kinds of survival tactics, so I'm going to give you just two rules. Hard and fast. No improvisation. Promise to follow them?"

She nodded, never taking her eyes from his. He was really worried. Genuinely, sincerely, terrifyingly worried about her. "I promise."

"If you hear a gunshot, or anything that sounds vaguely like a gunshot, you fall to the ground. Instantly. Flatten yourself out and hug Mother Earth. Got it?"

She nodded.

"And if somebody grabs you, I don't care who, unless it's me or Pat, you faint."

"Faint?" How was she supposed to do that?

"Pretend to faint. Pick your feet right off the ground and sag. Anybody trying to drag you away or hold you at gunpoint isn't going to be able to hold you up by himself. He'll have to let you fall.''

That was when Liz got scared. She thought she'd been scared before, but now she realized that what had come before was only a foretaste of fright. Standing there, looking up into Tim's beloved face while he told her these things in perfect seriousness, she discovered what it was to be truly frightened.

''Live long, et cetera.''

Liz swung around at the sound of Pat's voice, and found him staring down his nose at her. Green skin, pointed ears and a light blue velour shirt completed the costume. She cracked up.

''Not a very flattering response,'' Pat remarked, straight-faced. ''I thought I looked great. After all, what else do you wear to an alien reception?'' He looked at Tim. ''I'll be near.'' Then he moved on, continuing to give the greeting and special hand gesture so familiar to science fiction fans everywhere as he walked around.

Tim spoke in an undertone. ''Pat discovered a long time ago that the best place to hide is in plain sight. Say, you never told me about your UFO.''

Liz, who had turned her attention toward the southern sky, barely spared him a glance. ''You never seemed particularly interested.''

''But I am. What exactly did you see?''

''Lights. You were right about that. Just a pattern of lights like a lot of other people have seen.''

''Oh.'' He looked swiftly down at her and then resumed his continual survey of the crowd. ''How close were they?''

Liz shrugged a shoulder. ''I don't know. There wasn't really any way to tell.''

''What did it look like?''

She raised her arm and pointed. ''Just like that pattern of lights over there.''

Tim looked, blinked twice, and then swore softly. Just then, a voice in the crowd called out, ''Look! To the south. There they are!''

Every person on the hill turned to look. Weird, Tim thought. Out of all the weird things he had seen in life, and all the weird things he expected he had yet to see, this was one sight he had never thought to encounter.

At about thirty degrees above the southern horizon, well above the treetops, there were six very bright lights. Brighter than Venus by far, and moving steadily in a northerly direction, no doubt about it. It was impossible to tell if they were six individual lights or a single craft. If it *was* a single craft, he thought, then it was a hell of a big one. He had watched enough aircraft approach in Vietnam to have some sense of size and distance, and his senses were telling him that this thing, if only a single object, had a diameter approaching a hundred yards in all directions. Which was utterly ridiculous. So it had to be multiple craft. Still, the formation was breathtakingly tight and steady.

That was when the lights began to wink out, one by one, in a clockwise pattern that gave the definite impression of rotation. The thing was spinning.

"See?" Liz breathed beside him. "That's *exactly* what I saw two years ago." The hilltop was incredibly quiet as more than a hundred people stared in wonderment. "Explain it to me, Tim."

"I can't." It galled him. He was sure there was a logical, ordinary explanation of some kind—there usually was—but for the moment it escaped him. Something was nagging at him, though, an indefinable sense that this wasn't the first time he had seen something like this.

Around them cameras whirred and clicked as people tried to take time-lapse photos of the approaching spiral of lights.

"I wish I had *my* camera," said James, suddenly appearing by Liz's elbow.

She turned her head, and saw he was staring, rapt, at the lights. "Me, too," she said. "I really didn't think we were going to see anything."

"This is what you saw before, isn't it?"

"Exactly the same thing."

"It's fantastic. Do you think they'll land?"

"No, why should they?" If there were a *they* at all, Liz thought, returning her own attention to the lights. Whatever it was, she wasn't ready to swallow the idea of aliens actually landing.

"But think of all we could learn from them," James said in a hushed voice.

Liz had grown accustomed to that attitude since her own sighting. People were somehow inclined to equate technological achievement with moral advancement. "The thought terrifies me," she told James bluntly. "We already know more than we're equipped to handle."

James tore his eyes from the approaching lights and looked at her. "You want to stop them from landing?"

"Stop them?" What an odd choice of words. "How could I possibly stop them?"

"Look out!" shouted a horrifyingly familiar voice. "Look out! They're disturbing the gravity! They'll destroy the gravity completely!"

Liz looked and saw Pat, hardly aware that her mouth hung open. He sounded so *convincing*. That was the terrifying part. He didn't sound like he was pretending at all.

A deputy standing a few feet beyond Pat hesitated visibly. To Liz it seemed apparent that he was torn between having been told Pat was on the right side and having been told to look out for some weirdo who babbled about gravity.

"Don't be ridiculous," said another voice, one that sounded suspiciously like Agent Woodrow. "It's impossible to destroy gravity!"

"No, it isn't!" Pat spun around to face Woodrow directly. Woodrow did indeed look like a surprisingly ordinary slob in jeans and a jacket. "I'm telling you, those aliens are destroying the gravity. They've been doing it for weeks. I've felt it!"

"James, let's get out of here *now*."

Liz was astonished to hear Donna's voice, clear as a bell, punctuate the sudden silence after Pat had finished speaking. Turning, torn between watching the unfolding drama between Pat and Woodrow, and verifying that Donna was indeed here, she looked at James, and found him trying to free his arm from his mother's grip.

"God, what a bunch of weirdos," someone behind Tim muttered.

Tim caught Liz's elbow and tried to draw her back, away from everyone, but she had suddenly become glued to the ground.

"No," James told his mother, and grabbed Liz's other arm. Suddenly he raised his voice. "I told you, it's not the aliens who are disturbing the gravity. It's the computers!"

Chapter 14

"Get him!" Woodrow's cry pierced the sudden, abrupt silence on the hilltop.

Hearing it, James yanked on Liz's arm so hard that Tim was forced to release her for fear of hurting her. Liz fell back against James and felt his arm close around her throat with incredible strength.

"Lizzie," Tim roared. "Do what I told you!"

Faint, she thought. Tim wanted her to faint. But then she saw the gleam of Carter's gun barrel. It was pointing directly at her and James, and she knew if she fell to the ground, he'd shoot James. Maybe kill him. She couldn't allow that. Gasping for breath, her heart hammering wildly, she forced herself to stay upright on shaky knees.

"Lizzie!"

Her eyes strayed from Carter's gun to Tim's face, and she could scarcely believe the anguish she saw written there. She wanted to tell him, to explain, but James was squeezing her throat too tightly. All she could do was try to signal with her eyes.

"Let go of the woman, James," Carter said menacingly.

"No...no...." Sounding wild and lost, James backed up a few steps, and Liz choked as his arms tightened even more.

"James, don't hurt her," Donna's voice begged. "James, don't...."

"Let her go," said Woodrow. "If you hurt her..."

"If you hurt her," Tim said in a voice as slick and smooth as steel, "I'll kill you, James. Let her go. *Now.*"

James started babbling something about the gravity, and how it didn't matter if he died if he didn't save the gravity, but Tim didn't pay any attention to his words. Instead, his muscles tightening like bands of iron, he edged around to the side a little and waited for an opportunity. The strength of James's hold was giving Liz some trouble breathing, but she was getting enough air that it wasn't his immediate concern. No, his concern was to get her away from James uninjured.

"Proctor," said Agent Carter, "if you let the woman go, we'll let you walk away. That's a promise."

James turned instinctively toward Carter, and it was all the opening Tim needed. Leaping forward, he brought the blade of his hand down sharply on James's forearm. The youth let out a howl as pain stabbed him, and he let go of Liz.

Tim was ready. Reaching out, he grabbed Liz and swung her up into his arms. In the blink of an eye he had her safely away.

Carter and Woodrow moved in immediately, and the last thing Liz was able to see as Tim carried her swiftly away was Donna swinging her fist at Carter.

The eastern sky was just barely beginning to lighten when Tim and Liz emerged from the police station. Hoarfrost coated the world with its wintry white, and each puff of breath froze into a visible cloud.

On the third concrete step down, Liz halted and threw back her head, staring up at the still star-studded sky. "It's beautiful." She sighed.

Tim found himself crazily imagining the words freezing in the air before her, found himself recalling snatches of youthful fantasies of snow princesses and chaste love, of dashing knights and high ideals.

They were fantasies dreamt by the boy he had once been. That boy had died in a rice paddy years ago. He'd grown up, become a man. He'd put away all the things that had cost him pain, had severed himself from most everything else, cocooning himself in

the small world he had wrested from reality. Millennium Software
had been his hiding place, his kingdom, his fortress. Once a week,
he'd ventured out and battled his own dragons by battling the
dragons of other vets at the center. Otherwise he hadn't done
anything that thousands of other vets hadn't done. He might as
well have found himself an isolated mountain peak and spent his
days patrolling an imaginary perimeter with a high-powered rifle,
waiting for enemies who never came.

It's beautiful. It was amazing that after a night like this one
she could still say that. Standing there in the cold, in the autumn
of yet another year, watching Liz Pennington soak up the inef-
fable beauty of a night dying on the cusp of dawn, Tim
O'Shaughnessy suddenly understood with crystalline clarity why
it was that he had invited her into his fortress.

She sighed, unleashing another white puff, and lowered her
head. Shoving her hands deep into her jacket pockets, she started
down the steps again, and Tim followed.

"We've got to do something for them, Tim," she said in a sad
voice. "There's got to be some way we can help."

"Donna shouldn't have hit Carter."

"No, but you would think he could understand why she did it.
She was only trying to protect James. She was just being a
mother."

"Are you suggesting that cops should go around taking blows
from everybody's mother or brother or kid sister?"

Liz sighed again. "I guess not," she said presently. "When
you put it that way—"

"When I put it that way, I sound like a cop's son, don't I?"
he said gruffly. "Look, Pennington, I know a really good lawyer.
He volunteers down at the center. I'll call him a little later this
morning. He'll see that James gets some psychiatric help and will
probably be able to get Donna off with probation. But I don't
think he'll be able to get her off entirely. It's not just her hitting
Carter that's a problem here."

No, it was her having written down the safe combinations and
leaving them in her desk so that James had been able to get into
the safes and into all the classified data. It was her having knowledge of his crimes and keeping silent to protect him, thus making
herself an accomplice. Woodrow kept saying that if only Donna
had told him what was going on from the outset, he would have

seen to it that James got help, and Liz found that she believed the agent's sincerity. But Donna had kept silent and matters had been compounded with a second breaking and entering, a second vandalism, and finally a veiled death threat. There were probably a half dozen or more different things James could be charged with.

And he *was* going to be charged. Woodrow had been adamant on that score, and so had the local police. Charging James, Woodrow said, would ensure that James could be forced to get psychiatric treatment. At least everyone agreed that the young man needed help more than he needed prison. Even Carter agreed, and that surprised Liz.

Tim opened the door of the truck for her and helped her in. "It's been some adventure, Pennington."

On the edge of the seat, one foot still on the running board, she paused to look at him. *Some adventure, Pennington.* The sudden piercing pain in her heart, the sinking sensation in her stomach, gave her an inkling of the agony she was facing. Some adventure. And now he would drop her off at her house, wish her good-night and drive off to his own apartment.

Turning, she pulled her leg in so he could close the door, and all the way home she stared straight ahead in stony silence, afraid that if she opened her mouth only sobs would emerge.

Not very encouraging, Tim thought, scanning her rigid figure from the corner of his eye. No Trespassing signs stood out like spikes all over her. Why? What had he done? Did she want him gone now that she no longer needed his protection?

But that didn't seem right. He knew Liz wasn't that hard-as-nails type who would do something like that. And he was sure she didn't give herself easily or cheaply. If she did, he wouldn't have been the first man in her bed. No. So what the hell was bothering her?

He pulled into her driveway and switched off the truck's ignition. He was suddenly so pumped on adrenaline that he was breathing as heavily as a marathon runner. What if she said good-night and climbed out of the truck?

He was making no move to climb out of the truck. The realization settled on her like lead, sinking her stomach, tensing her muscles. Her heart began a rapid, painful thudding. This was it, she thought. Now he would say, "It's been fun, but now everything can go back to normal.'' Yeah, that's what he would say. And she would kill him. She would absolutely, positively kill him.

"Liz?"

"Yes?"

"We need to talk."

She didn't like the sound of that, but that was how they came to be sitting across from one another at her kitchen table with mugs of hot chocolate between them. It had to be a gene she'd inherited from her mother, she thought numbly, this inability to discuss anything, especially earth-shattering, life-shattering things, without serving a hot beverage first. That this was going to be earth-shattering was evidenced by Tim's uncharacteristic inability to blurt it all out.

"When did you get tactful?'' she demanded suddenly, looking at him with hurt, defiant green eyes.

"Tactful? What makes you think I'm trying to be tactful?'' His eyes were as hot as hers.

"The way you're glaring at that mug as if it's supposed to do the talking for you.''

His scowl deepened. "Some things aren't easy to talk about!''

"You never had that problem before."

"That's because I never had to say these things before!''

They were nearly shouting, Liz realized. That was no way to preserve this partnership past the end of their romantic relationship. She shouted back anyway. "Say it, damn it!''

"You don't swear. Look, Pennington—''

"Don't you *dare* call me Pennington after all—after all—'' Speech deserted her as pain overwhelmed her. *Pennington.* Oh, God, how could he call her Pennington?

Had he actually been comparing this virago to the snow princess of his youthful dreams? How could he have forgotten how prickly, how irritable and irritating, how—"Oh, God.'' His stomach sank like a lead ball as he saw the corners of her mouth quiver and her eyes blink rapidly. "Oh, God,'' he said again. She was going to cry. He was making her cry.

Realization unbarred some long-locked place in his soul, opened some kind of floodgate. In an instant he was around the table, damning the torpedoes, damning the consequences, damning the partnership, the business, the next forty years.... Dear God, don't let her cry because of me!

"Lizzie...darlin'...sweetheart..." Mumbling every endearment he could think of, he hauled her up into his arms, cuddled her close, rained a storm of kisses all over her face. "Ah, darlin' girl, don't cry!"

Those words elicited the first silvery teardrop. It squeezed from beneath a closed eyelid and hung on the delicate curve of her cheek like an indictment. He drew a ragged, shuddering breath and stared at it, seeing himself with a clarity that was horrifying. How could he have done this to her? He hadn't meant anyone to get hurt, and now they were both dying inside because—because—

Because he wouldn't say what needed saying. Because he was a cheap, chicken-hearted, yellow-bellied emotional coward!

"Damn it, Lizzie! I *love* you!"

She gulped a huge sob.

"Liz. Liz, didn't you hear me? I love you! But damn it, woman, if you don't answer me quick— Do you hate me? Do you want me to get lost?" He was growing more frantic with each passing second. What if he had misread her entirely? What if she *had* just wanted an affair? What if—

Slowly she opened huge wet eyes, and sniffled another sob. "Oh, Tim, Tim, I love you so much!"

Relief hit him so forcefully that he groaned and his knees nearly buckled. "Thank God. Thank God." Whispering the words in prayerful litany, he lifted her from her feet and carried her up the stairs to her room. Their room. The place where the first cotton-candy wisps of long-forgotten dreams had been reborn.

"We'll make it, Lizzie," he vowed as he laid her gently down and lay beside her. "We'll make it together. Business, partnership—the works. Kids, even. God, did I just say that? Yeah. Babies and diapers and the next forty or fifty years. No divorce, no custody battle, just you and me making it work."

"Tim—"

But he silenced her with a gentle finger laid across her lips.

"I'm getting ahead of myself here, darlin'. There's something I better get off my chest before I ask you to say yes."

A fist clenched her heart. Barely born joy dimmed. This seemed serious. "What?"

"You know those lights we saw tonight? The UFO?"

"What about them?"

He closed his eyes, afraid of her reaction. "Those were the lights of six small planes flying in tight formation."

"How can you know that? And why would they flash lights like that, so that it looked as if it was rotating—Tim! How do you know?"

He opened his eyes and looked like nothing so much as a kid caught in a deception.

"Because," he said, "I know the guys who fly the planes. They do a lot of formation flying for air shows, and sometimes, for a kick, they fly at night. It always unleashes a rash of UFO reports when they do. Anyhow, they flew tonight because Woodrow asked them to. But I swear I didn't know it was them until Woodrow told me this morning."

She stared at him, her mouth opened in astonishment. "So my UFO was just those guys?"

"Well, I don't know about what *you* saw the first time. But they've been doing this for years, Liz. It could have been them."

She nodded slowly. "It looked just the same as what I saw tonight." And then she smiled. "That's great! That's fantastic!"

"It is?"

"Sure. It's the explanation I've been trying to find for years. Fantastic!"

He drew her closer. "Then you're not mad at me?"

"No, I'm not mad." And she wasn't. At the moment she was hard-pressed to give a darn about UFOs anyhow. One could land right outside her bedroom window and she wouldn't even glance at it. "I thought you had a question to ask me."

"I do." He drew a deep breath and looked down into her beautiful green eyes as daybreak's pink light brightened the room. "Will you defy gravity with me, Lizzie? Will you marry me, and have my children and be my partner for the rest of our lives?"

Tears filled her eyes, and her throat tightened. "Yes," she whispered huskily. "Yes, yes, and yes. For the rest of our lives."

A long, long time later, Tim's husky whisper reached a drowsy Liz. "But darlin'?"

"Hmm?"

"The plants have to go."

Liz's answer was a joyous, musical laugh.

* * * * *

SPECIAL EDITION

Stories of love and life, these powerful
novels are tales that you can identify with—
romances with "something special" added
in!

Fall in love with the stories of authors such
as **Nora Roberts, Diana Palmer, Ginna Gray**
and many more of your special favorites—as
well as wonderful new voices!

Special Edition brings you
entertainment for the heart!

SSE-GEN

SILHOUETTE® *Desire®*

Do you want...

Dangerously handsome heroes

Evocative, everlasting love stories

Sizzling and tantalizing sensuality

Incredibly sexy miniseries like **MAN OF THE MONTH**

Red-hot romance

Enticing entertainment that can't be beat!

You'll find all of this, and much *more* each and
every month in **SILHOUETTE DESIRE**. Don't miss these
unforgettable love stories by some of romance's hottest
authors. Silhouette Desire—where your fantasies will
always come true....

INTIMATE MOMENTS®
Silhouette®

If you've got the time...
We've got the
INTIMATE MOMENTS

Passion. Suspense. Desire. Drama. Enter a world
that's larger than life, where men and women
overcome life's greatest odds for the ultimate prize:
love. Nonstop excitement is closer than you
think...in Silhouette Intimate Moments!

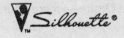

Silhouette®

SIM-GEN

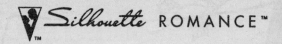

What's a single dad to do when he needs a wife by next Thursday?

Who's a confirmed bachelor to call when he finds a baby on his doorstep?

How does a plain Jane in love with her gorgeous boss get him to notice her?

From classic love stories to romantic comedies to emotional heart tuggers, **Silhouette Romance** offers six irresistible novels every month by some of your favorite authors! Such as…beloved bestsellers **Diana Palmer**, **Annette Broadrick**, **Suzanne Carey**, **Elizabeth August** and **Marie Ferrarella**, to name just a few—and some sure to become favorites!

Fabulous Fathers…Bundles of Joy…Miniseries… Months of blushing brides and convenient weddings… Holiday celebrations… You'll find all this and much more in **Silhouette Romance**—always emotional, always enjoyable, always about love!

WAYS TO *UNEXPECTEDLY* MEET MR. RIGHT:

♡ *Go out with the sexy-sounding stranger your daughter secretly set you up with through a personal ad.*

♡ *RSVP yes to a wedding invitation—soon it might be your turn to say "I do!"*

♡ *Receive a marriage proposal by mail— from a man you've never met....*

These are just a few of the unexpected ways that written communication leads to love in Silhouette Yours Truly.

Each month, look for two fast-paced, fun and flirtatious Yours Truly novels (with entertaining treats and sneak previews in the back pages) by some of your favorite authors—and some who are sure to become favorites.

YOURS TRULY™:
Love—when you least expect it!

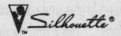